THE GUNPOWDER GIRL

A compelling saga of love, loss and self-discovery

TANIA CROSSE

Originally published as
Cherrybrook Rose and *A Bouquet of Thorns*

JOFFE BOOKS

Revised edition 2020
Joffe Books, London
www.joffebooks.com

First published in Great Britain as *Cherrybrook Rose* 2008
and *A Bouquet of Thorns* 2008

Join our mailing list and become one of 1,000s of readers enjoying free Kindle crime thriller, detective, mystery, and romance books and new releases. Receive your first bargain book this month!

We love to hear from our readers! Please email any feedback you have to: feedback@joffebooks.com

ISBN 978-1-78931-497-7

AUTHOR'S NOTE

George Frean was the real-life proprietor of the Cherrybrook Gunpowder Mills. Research showed him to be a just and kindly gentleman and he is portrayed as thus in this novel.

The ruins of the gunpowder mills stand on private land and can only be viewed from the public footpath. Anyone who trespasses does so entirely at their own risk.

All details regarding conditions at Dartmoor Prison at the time of this novel are believed to be correct, but this is a fictional story and should not be considered a statement of fact.

ACKNOWLEDGEMENTS

First of all, a massive thank you to Joffe Books for re-releasing this abridged version of two earlier titles from my Devonshire series (previously published as prequel and sequel *Cherrybrook Rose* and *A Bouquet of Thorns*). Also, my deepest gratitude, as ever, goes to my good friend Paul Rendell, Dartmoor guide and historian and editor of the *Dartmoor News*, who is always so willing to share his extensive knowledge of the moor with me. Particular thanks go to Dartmoor Prison historian Trevor James, for all his support and time providing precise historical detail. I must also thank our long-standing friend Colin Skeen, barrister and magistrate, for his research into the history of the legal system on my behalf. Others who contributed information were the late Tavistock historian Gerry Woodcock, the late retired physician Dr Marshall Barr, and the British Army Museum.

If I have made any errors, they are mine and not theirs.

CHAPTER ONE

It was *her*, wasn't it?

Ned Cornish felt his heart buck in his chest, and he drew back round the corner of the building in the main street of Dartmoor's Princetown. He waited for his heart to settle back into its normal place, all the while savouring that mixture of excitement and bitterness that swirled on his tongue each time he saw her. But he couldn't resist slinking back to spy on her, unobserved as he leaned against the side wall of the building.

A pall of dust had been lifted from the parched surface of Prison Road by the clattering hooves of the charging horse. But then the billowing cloud came to a whirlwind stop outside the Albert Inn right in front of Ned, loose stones scattering in every direction as the rider brought the stampeding animal to a violent halt. One long, shapely leg was swung over the hairy neck, two well-shod feet landed lightly on the ground, and taking the reins behind the foaming mouth, the rider led its mount, meek as a lamb now, towards Ned, grinning from ear to ear as she greeted him.

Ned gave a lopsided smile in return as he stepped forward. Rose Maddiford was a one, and no mistake. It wasn't every father who'd let his daughter gallop all over the moor on a crazy nag. But then it was well known that Henry Maddiford, manager of the gunpowder mills three miles away at Cherrybrook, doted on his only child and had apparently done so ever since his dear wife had died giving birth to her. But Ned was glad he indulged her so readily. She rode *astride*. And beneath the full riding skirt, her legs were tightly clad in breeches as if she were a young man. Ned almost drooled as he glimpsed them quite clearly as she dismounted — as if he hadn't seen them often enough before! But that was the effect Rose always had on him.

And it was something to relieve his humdrum life. Boring, desolate place, Princetown, slap bang in the middle of the moor. Ned's knowledge — or interest — in history was meagre to say the least. But he knew that some idiot, Sir Thomas someone or other, had once attempted to drain the local bogs to grow crops and establish a farming community. Well, Ned could have told him it wouldn't work. But now, three quarters of a century later, convicts from the gaol down the road were forced to clear huge boulders from the prison fields and dig drainage ditches, often up to their waists in vile, brackish water, under the eye of armed Civil Guards.

They'd been at it, apparently, for the twenty-five years since the old prisoner-of-war depot had been re-opened as a convict gaol, and it worked well enough for cattle to graze, at least. But even if Princetown had become a thriving settlement with roughly a hundred warders and their families living there, it was mortal exposed, always windy and often swathed in damning mist even in July or August. Fourteen hundred feet above sea-level, it was exposed to lacerating cold and deep snowdrifts in winter and miserable, rainy summers. No wonder any son of a warder would be off to better climes to make his own way in the world just as soon as he was old enough — that was if his entire family hadn't had so much of the place that they'd already upped sticks and moved away somewhere more hospitable.

Ned sometimes wondered why he didn't move on himself, rather than working as a stable boy at the Albert Inn. But there were two problems. One was that stable work was all he'd ever known and he could well go from the frying pan into the fire. The other was Rose Maddiford. Whenever she swept into Princetown and needed to leave that confounded animal in his care for a few hours, he blessed the morning his father had deposited him at the stableyard to do his first day's work at the age of nine, for his family needed his wages to survive.

That was years ago, and now he was a strong, bulky youth with a wicked sense of humour and an eye for the girls. His secluded room above the stables behind the inn had seen more than one maiden willingly deflowered. Rose Maddiford was not amongst them, and never would be. And Ned worshipped the ground she stepped on.

She came towards him now, her cheeks flushed with the exhilaration of galloping across the moor, her ebony curls rippling wildly down her back in a shining cascade from beneath the apology of a hat that sat, somewhat askew, on the top of her beautiful head. Her slanting, violet blue eyes danced, and beneath the jacket of her riding habit, her straining breasts heaved up and down above her slender, pliable waist.

Ned watched them. And his smile broadened.

'Good afternoon, Ned,' Rose greeted him. 'How are you today?'

Ned's heart beat faster. 'All the better for seeing you,' he answered truthfully, contemplating her willowy figure. Her slight frame made her appear taller than she was, and her halo of unruly hair gave her at least another inch.

Her full red lips broke into a short laugh. 'Flattery will get you nowhere with me!' she chided playfully.

Ned sniffed. She was certainly right there! No one had ever got so much as a harmless kiss out of Rose Maddiford. It was as if she was unaware of her tantalising charms. She was devoted to one man alone, and that was her father!

'You off to visit young Molly?' Ned asked, his chest giving a little jerk of jealousy.

'*Miss* Molly to you!' Rose grinned. 'But, yes, I am. So you will look after Gospel for me, won't you? There'll be sixpence in it for you, as usual.'

Ned grunted his displeasure. If it weren't for Rose, he wouldn't have gone near the animal for two guineas, let alone sixpence! Bad-tempered creature it was, at least it was the minute Rose was out of its sight. Black as the devil, and that would have been a better name for it, Devil, Ned thought! As for calling it Gospel, well!

When he'd questioned Rose on her strange choice, he couldn't quite fathom her explanation. It was something to do with the monster's dark coat, and the religious chants that the African slaves in the American cotton fields apparently sang to ease their aching spirits. Well, Ned didn't know anything about *that*. He didn't even know where America and Africa were. A long way off, he knew that. But then to Ned, so was anywhere beyond Plymouth which he visited possibly once a year. Back along, there'd been American as well as French prisoners of war held in what was now the convict gaol. So America couldn't be *that* far away, Ned reasoned. Americans spoke English, so America must be nearer than France where they gabbled on in some incomprehensible language — or at least, Ned imagined they did. But, to be honest, he wasn't really bothered where other countries might be. It hardly made any difference to *his* life, did it? He could write his own name when he put his mind to it, and that was enough for him.

Except when it came to Rose. Then, and only then, did his ignorance trouble him. Apparently she *devoured* books. And Ned knew she read the *Tavistock Gazette* each week from cover to cover. Not only did it report local news, but national and international events as well, events Rose evidently discussed at length with her father. It was no wonder she was way out of Ned's league. *And* out of the league of virtually every young male in the vicinity, although plenty of them wouldn't have minded getting their hands on her virginal figure!

'You can put that nag of yourn in the end box,' he ordered with a disgruntled snort. 'And take its tack off yoursel, if you wants to. *I'll* not go near the brute.'

Rose raised a teasing eyebrow as Gospel nuzzled against her shoulder. 'You're not afeared, are you, Ned?'

Ned flushed. But he wasn't going to let Rose's clever tongue get the better of him, so he threw back his head with a throaty laugh. 'No. But the marks 'aven't quite faded from the last time 'er bit me, and I doesn't want a matching set just yet.'

It was Rose's turn to look abashed. 'I'm really sorry about that,' she said with feeling. 'Of course I'll see to him myself. I'm just grateful to have somewhere safe I can leave him.' And so saying, she clicked her tongue and led the infamous beast into the stable Ned had indicated, emerging a few minutes later with the heavy saddle which the youth was pleased to take from her, delighted at the opportunity to show her some gallantry. He lowered his eyes to the gleaming leather with a lecherous smirk. An *astride* saddle, of course. But that was Rose Maddiford for you, wasn't it? And his heart sighed as he watched her stride out of the yard.

* * *

Rose hurried down Prison Road with a spring in her step. The prospect of spending a few hours with her good friend, Molly Cartwright, filled her with happiness. Though she left the centre of Princetown behind, there was still a general bustle of activity in the warm, early autumn sunshine. Just beyond the encircling wall of the barracks which was her destination, work was continuing apace on the new accommodation block for the prison warders and their families. Molly's mother was praying they would be allocated one of its thirty flats, each of which was to boast two tiny bedrooms, a small living room and a working scullery. And who could blame her, when two adults — three if you counted Molly who was nineteen — and five younger children had been squeezed into just two rooms in the decaying barracks for years!

Rose paused for a moment to contemplate the progress on the new building. There was some way to go before it would be finished, despite the convicts that swarmed over the growing edifice like ants in their drab uniforms with the distinctive arrows. And they *worked* like ants, too, at least they did if they didn't want to feel a warder's truncheon across their back.

The term 'hard labour' was somewhat of an understate-ment, Rose always thought. Inhuman it was sometimes, in her opinion, non-stop, physical toil. Some worked on the prison itself, doubling or trebling in size the original pris-oner-of-war blocks; others at clearing the extensive prison lands. If not that, then digging mountains of peat for the new adjacent gasworks which supplied light for the prison itself and all prison property within the village; or slaving on the public roads or in the prison quarry a hundred yards or so further down towards Rundlestone. Still, if you didn't like it, you shouldn't have come, was the old prison saying. Hardened criminals, most of them, violent, incorrigible vil-lains. Though some were merely habitual thieves or forg-ers, but sentenced to a minimum of five years to qualify for Dartmoor's infamous gaol. But what if, Rose's questioning mind considered, you really were wrongfully convicted . . .

She flicked her head as if tossing out the unwelcome thought, and marched up the side road and through the gate-way of the barracks compound. A woman was lugging a bas-ket overflowing with laundry to the wash-house in the centre of the compound which served the hundred or more families who were crowded into the eleven barracks. Children too young to attend the new prison officers' school — built and maintained, it went without saying, by convict labour — played safely outside in the sunshine, including little Philip Cartwright. The wife of one of the twenty-four Civil Guards who were all housed in number six barracks, was leaning against a wall, her stomach jutting with her first child, as she chatted to a neighbour. Rose hailed everyone as she passed, and then bounded up the steps to the Cartwrights' humble dwelling in number seven barracks.

The door was ajar, and she called out as she crossed the threshold. The small room was a jumble of garments and linen, for Molly and her mother were tackling the weekly mountain of ironing. The air was heavy with warmth and moisture, a strange mix of the freshness of ironing and the acrid smell of the peat fire that smouldered in the small grate where the two spare irons were reheating whilst Mrs Cartwright used the third.

'Oh, Rose! How lovely to see you!'

Molly's cheeks were flushed with the heat and she pushed back a wayward wisp of ginger hair that had escaped from beneath the plain white muslin cap on her head. Her small but well-shaped mouth broke into a grin, and above it, her eyes, a distinct feline green, danced with delight.

'Well,' Rose replied with a tilt of her head, 'I'd not seen you for a week and I wanted to make certain you were behaving yourself.'

A faint smile lifted Mrs Cartwright's workworn face at their irrepressible visitor, but with eight mouths to feed and the apparel of eight bodies to launder, she had no time to stop and chat. But Rose always brought a breath of fresh air into their lives, and was always welcome. Besides, she was a lady, and perhaps one day some practical advantage might come of their association and lift Molly from the stultifying future she faced at present.

Molly's lips, however, twisted into a mock grimace. 'Behave myself!' she groaned. 'And what chance d'you imagine I'd have to do ort else?'

'Well, I don't know! Perhaps one of the new Civil Guards?' Rose teased. 'There's one particularly attractive fellow . . . Why don't we walk down to the quarry and see if he's on duty there?'

'Oh, Rose, you'm a real devil!' Molly chuckled. 'But I cas'n. Look at this pile of ironing! The girls'll be home from school directly, and we must get it finished by then.'

'Let me help, then.' And throwing her riding gloves onto the bed Molly shared with the elder two of her three younger sisters, Rose unfastened the jacket of her riding habit, tossed it on top of the gloves and rolled up the sleeves of her shirt.

'Now, what can I do? Or would it be more use to you if I start preparing the meal?'

Mrs Cartwright shook her head. Heart as big as the ocean had Rose. And it wasn't an empty gesture. The girl knew how to cook, sew and iron, and would work as hard as any of them. And so it was that by the time the three younger siblings arrived back from school, the laundry was stowed away on the airing rack, Rose had rescued little Philip from the compound and cleaned him up, and a pile of bread and dripping was waiting on the table next to a heap of vegetables prepared by Rose's hand ready for the cooking pot for supper. While Rose supervised the tea, Mrs Cartwright sat with her feet up, sipping the hot brew from a chipped enamel mug. So that by five o'clock, the two young women were able to set out, arm in arm, down the road towards Rundlestone.

Work on the new accommodation block would soon be stopping for the night, and Molly paused to glance ruefully at its progress. 'I do hope as we gets one of they flats!' she sighed deeply. ''Tis so cramped in the barracks and we're all getting so big.'

Rose's heart tore. It was hard to know quite what to say. She felt so sorry for the Cartwright family, but she didn't want to offend. 'What about your brother, Brian? Could he not be moving out soon? He *is* sixteen.'

Molly cocked an eyebrow. 'Too old to be sleeping on the floor in the same room as mesel and Annie and Emma, you mean? I'll not disagree with you, there. Though he's usually so tired arter his work, he sleeps like a log. But it looks as though Annie's got a live-in position down in Yelverton so she'll be finishing school, so at least 'twill be one less squeezed into the bed. It shoulda been me really, being the eldest girl, going into service. But I've always been needed at home, and it sort of stayed that way.'

'And I'm so glad it did!' Rose beamed at her.

They had inadvertently stopped to look at the growing walls of the building, and as if of one mind, continued on their walk. It might not do to stop too long. The sight of two pretty young women had already attracted the silent attention of more than one prisoner, and that could cause trouble. And so they stepped out briskly, their eyes averted, as they approached the gaol itself. But, familiar as they were with its grey, stone severity, neither could help glancing at the forbidding complex. Within the horseshoe shaped outer wall, the cell blocks radiated like the spokes of a half wheel, an ominous backdrop to the workshops, hospital and lesser buildings at the front of the compound. Over them all towered Number Five Prison, the first block to reach five-storeys. Constructed by convicts with stone from the quarry, it had only opened two years previously, and yet they knew from Molly's father that damp was already seeping into some of the three hundred unheated cells.

Rose shivered as they passed the main gate, for even her own comfortable home with its blazing fires could be cold in the depths of the long Dartmoor winter. She squared her slim shoulders. It had been a glorious autumn day; she should enjoy it whilst she could, and put such dark thoughts aside.

'Amber's still behaving like a lunatic,' she began anew. 'She's so willing to learn, but the instant she sees a rabbit or something, she forgets everything I've taught her and won't obey a single command!'

Molly's face lit up at the mention of Rose's young dog, far more of a pet in her opinion than the fearsome Gospel, of whom like most other people, she was petrified. 'But she's only a puppy, Rose! You cas'n expect her—'

'She's nearly a year old. She should be able to contain herself by now. I want to be able to take her out riding with me.'

'What! And frighten everyone even more than you does already with that monster you calls an 'orse!'

Rose blinked her eyes wide, and then the pair of them fell about laughing as they wandered on down the road. As their merriment subsided, they paused again to gaze on the sheer immensity of the landscape. And yet what they could see was merely a small patch of the three hundred and sixty or more square miles of spectacular scenery, exposed, rugged hills with impressive outcrops of granite tors, or pretty valleys and sheltered pockets of fertile farmland that made up Dartmoor. A hostile wilderness, and yet a luring sense of peace and infinity.

'Get along there, you, six four nine!'

Molly flicked her head with surprised pleasure. ''Tis Father's voice. He must've been on duty at the quarry today.'

They both turned instinctively to peer down over the stone wall on their right. Behind them, on the opposite side of the road, was the entrance to the heavily guarded quarry. But to avoid the inmates marching down a public road, a tunnel passed beneath the highway, emerging on the other side onto prison farmland and a track that entered the gaol by a side gateway in the massive wall. The day's back-breaking toil was over, and a line of weary convicts, some — the least trustworthy — chained together with heavy leg-irons, were dragging themselves back towards the comfortless buildings that would swallow them up until it began all over again the following day. The track was immediately below the two girls who watched from their vantage point, entirely unseen.

The line of men in their ugly uniforms was being marched out of the tunnel accompanied by several armed guards and even more prison warders, amongst them Molly's father. Jacob Cartwright had worked since a boy in the Dartmoor quarries, his skill and experience gaining him a respected position as the years went by. That was how Rose and Molly had originally met, when Jacob had come to Cherrybrook to order gunpowder for King Tor quarry, and for some reason had brought Molly with him. But he wasn't getting any younger, and some time ago had decided, like others of his colleagues, that being a prison warder would provide more suitable employment for a man of more mature years. The Governor had to be careful who he employed, and Jacob fitted the bill admirably. A sturdy local, experienced in directing strong-willed men, and of course his expertise in quarrying was invaluable. He was a fair and just warder, popular with the inmates, for though he would deal toughly with those who deserved it, he was one of the few who found room in his own strictly regulated role to reward good behaviour with clemency and understanding.

He hurried along now, his sharp eye ever watchful, unaware of his eldest daughter and her friend looking immediately down upon him. The girls knew not to utter a sound, for his concentration must not be distracted for one second. It filled them both with unimaginable horror, therefore, when one of the convicts behind him swiftly picked up a heavy stone that happened by some oversight to be lying by the side of the track, and went to smash it over his head.

The scream lodged in Molly's throat, while beside her, Rose's jaw hung open in appalled disbelief. But in that terrible moment, another prisoner bound forward and in a brief struggle, plied the weapon from his fellow inmate's grasp. Before Jacob Cartwright could turn round to investigate the scuffle behind him, two Civil Guards emerged from the tunnel and spying the second convict with the rock still in his raised hands, rushed forward. One of them slammed the butt of his Snider carbine into the man's stomach. He fell to the ground, dropping the stone, totally defenceless against the two guards who became intent upon kicking him into submission with their steel-capped boots.

Molly remained motionless, her knees nearly giving way, but indignation drowned Rose's senses in unleashed fury. In a trice, she flung aside her riding skirt, vaulted the stone wall and careering down the steep bank, began to pummel the back of one of the guards.

'No, you senseless fools!' she shrieked. 'It wasn't *him*! He *stopped* the other one!'

Her fists ceased their ineffectual pounding, and she stopped, eyes flashing and her dark curls whipping across her face like some wild witch.

Jacob Cartwright had by now turned round and he jabbed his head at Rose. 'Thank you, miss,' he said, deliberately without any sign of recognition, she realised. 'And you two,' he went on, addressing the two guards. 'Stop before you kill 'en, will you!'

His authoritative tone was at once obeyed, though tension crackled along the halted line. Those who were near enough to see were clearly confounded by the savage but beautiful apparition that had descended from nowhere, her chest still heaving deliciously up and down with outrage.

'Is this true?' Jacob demanded of her.

'Yes. Of course it is! *He* was the one who was about to hit you over the head with the stone!' she accused, pointing at the guilty villain who merely grinned back. '*That* poor fellow stopped him, and those idiots—'

'All right, all right!' Jacob tried to interrupt.

'We saw it all from up there! Ask any one of these men—'

'Calm down, miss,' Jacob warned in a low voice. 'Never ask a prisoner to cop another. Now!' he continued as he turned back to the guards. 'I believe what this young woman says. Six four nine's always been a troublemaker. I'd just that second had to rebuke 'en. The *other* fellow's new. Model prisoner, so far. So, all right, everyone! Show's over! Move along now!'

A general moan rumbled along the line of convicts as they began to trudge back towards the prison. It had been a rare entertainment, and that untamed, spirited wench . . .

'Yes, get up, you bastard.'

Jacob had already moved on and didn't see the final blow that one of the guards inflicted with his boot upon the prostrate form of the prisoner. But Rose did, and the soldier's shin felt the crack of her own foot. She saw him scowl at her, but she glared back, shoulders braced challengingly. With another scathing glance in her direction, the guard backed away, dragging the criminal to his feet. The convict stifled a gasp of pain, but lifted his head to look at his saviour.

The tortured expression on his face was a spike in Rose's heart. He was relatively young, fine creases only just beginning to radiate from the corners of his clear hazel eyes, so she imagined he could be no more than thirty. His cap had been knocked from his head, and she could see his hair had been clipped so closely, the scissors had grazed his scalp in places. A trickle of blood was curling down his chin from his torn lip, but the pained shadow of a smile twitched at his mouth and his gaze held hers until the other guard cuffed him about the ear and forced him to stumble onwards.

Rose watched as the rest of the work party was marched past, a strange knot in her chest. A convict. Guilty of some heinous crime. Ah, well . . . He must surely deserve to be incarcerated in Dartmoor's infamous gaol. Put to some of the most gruelling toil known to man. Rose knew that the quarry was probably the most feared and hated of prison work. No care was given to the prisoners' safety — except if Warder Cartwright was on duty. He wouldn't allow even a convicted felon to be maimed if he could help it. Others were less mindful and as well as paying no heed to other dangers in the quarry, would order convicts to pick out by hand any unexploded charges. It wouldn't be the first time a hapless villain had been blinded or had his hand blown away when the powder went off belatedly.

Rose somehow prayed that the prisoner — whoever he was, but who had possibly saved Jacob's life — never suffered such a tragedy.

She buried the dreadful thought somewhere deep in her passionate young mind, and retrieving her hat from amongst the grass at the side of the track, scrambled back up the slope to where Molly was waiting.

CHAPTER TWO

Rose held the colossal steed in check, keeping the reins short in her gloved hands and low down on either side of the gleaming black neck. She could feel the power in Gospel's clenched haunches as he danced sideways in an effort to escape her tight constraint. But Rose was not in the mood for their usual mad gallop as they left Princetown behind.

The incident by the quarry tunnel had thrown her senses into some strange confusion. Molly had been like a quivering jelly, wanting to return home at once. It had taken every ounce of Rose's ingenuity to persuade her to complete their walk. Think how your mother will worry if you tell her your father nearly had his head split open by a convict, Rose had argued. Of course, *she* had been upset, too, for she was fond of Mr Cartwright, but there was something else that had torn at her heart. The unmerited beating the prisoner had received at the hands — or more precisely, the *feet* — of the guards had sickened her, but even more than that, when the fellow had looked straight into her eyes, she had felt a curious pull on her innermost feelings. He was a convicted criminal, guilty of some appalling act to warrant incarceration in the dreaded Dartmoor gaol, and yet the vision of his anguished face was haunting her.

She glanced swiftly over her left shoulder towards the menacing silhouette of the prison buildings outlined against the sky. What would the convict be doing now, which part of the gaol he was in, locked in his cramped, damp and lonely cell for the night? But then Rose's attention was snapped back to the road as they crossed the bridge over the Blackabrook. Gospel had decided to take exception to the tumbling waters and was side-stepping restlessly. But Rose was determined to keep to a walk, her mind locked in a brown study. What was the fellow's crime, she wondered. New. A model prisoner, Mr Cartwright had said. He would have at least five years to serve then, for that was the minimum sentence for Dartmoor. Five years . . .

They gained the brow of the hill and all at once the panorama of the isolated hamlet of Two Bridges lay beneath them, the picturesque West Dart river valley bathed in the apricot evening sunlight. The breath caught in Rose's throat, the beauty of the dell with its old arched bridge once again intoxicating her mind, though she had seen it a thousand times before. The water twinkled merrily as it rushed over the rock-strewn riverbed in its hurry to be across the moor and down to the sea, lengthening shadows playing mysteriously on the clear, deeper pools.

Gospel shook his head and snorted impatiently. He knew he was nearing home and the handful of tasty oats the stable lad would feed him. But why was his mistress holding him back? The road dropped steeply into the valley, then sharply climbed the far side, but the horse took the incline as easily as swishing away a fly with its tail. And then, as they turned onto the road towards Postbridge, the familiar surroundings finally soothed Rose's soul, and with a resolute clamping of her jaw, she gave the animal its head.

Gospel's muscles exploded like coiled springs. Rose could feel the strength of his body beneath her as he powered up the hill, stretching every sinew of his vigorous limbs. Rose gripped with her knees as she sank into the one, two, *three*, one, two, *three* rhythm of his pounding hooves, gathering speed until the glorious moment when the canter broke into a gallop and they surged forward as if of one being. She leaned out along his arched neck, her own body rippling to his flowing motion, the only guidance she gave him being to keep to the softer ground and not risk his legs on the hard-baked dirt of the road. Her hair streaked out behind her like the tail of some meteor, the wind whipping through her head and driving out all memory of the convict who, for one incomprehensible moment, had touched her heart, but who she would never see again.

On and on, until the extensive site of the gunpowder mills came into view, its sturdy buildings spread out, for safety reasons, on either side of the Cherrybrook valley. Rose sat back in the saddle, easing gently but firmly on the reins. By the time they reached the first cluster of powdermill cottages, the gelding's pace had slowed to a trot. The lengthy gallop had hardly made him sweat, and Rose herself would have been happy to continue out over the moor for another hour. But the evening was drawing in with that autumnal sting in the air despite the sunny day, and she knew better than to trust the treacherously changeable Dartmoor weather at night.

'Evening, Miss Rose!'

'Good evening, Mr Roach! How's little Sam?'

'In fine fettle now, thanks to the medicine and the broth you sent over! Mrs Roach cas'n be thanking you enough!'

'Oh, it was nothing. I'm just pleased he's better.'

Leaving the main road behind, she rode on along the powdermills trackway to what, if anything, could be called the centre of the isolated community, a large building that served as both Methodist chapel and school, another row of neat little cottages, the manager's house, a substantial coop-erage and several other outbuildings. Up to a hundred men had worked at the mills not so long ago, living in the pur-pose-built cottages including those near Higher Cherrybrook Bridge. Others resided at nearby Postbridge village, whilst some tramped in each day all the way from Chagford, Peter Tavy and even Tavistock.

There weren't quite so many employees now, and that was a worry to Rose and her father. Demand for gunpowder had fallen recently with the closure of many of the local mines, though considerable amounts continued to be supplied to the massive Dartmoor quarries, including that of the prison, and also the Cornish slate quarries. The powder was carried by horse and wagon to a number of outlying magazines or storage sites across the moor, or directly to where it was required. Further afield, it was exported via Plymouth all over the south west and as far as South Wales and Gloucestershire, since licensed gunpowder factories were few and far between.

However, eight years previously, a scientist by the name of Alfred Nobel had invented a much safer explosive called dynamite, and its usage was spreading. Nevertheless, Cherrybrook remained a hive of activity with all its skilled labourers, coopers, carpenters, the blacksmith, the wheelwright, and all the wagoners and stable staff. And Rose Maddiford, the venturesome daughter of the manager, knew and cared for every one of them and their families.

She turned Gospel onto the path at the rear of the cottages, and they clattered into the small stableyard behind the manager's house. Rose dismounted with her usual flourish as Joe Tyler hurried out of the back door, his young face split with his welcoming grin. At his heels pranced a boisterous gold-coloured dog, tail waving furiously to and fro as it bounced around its mistress's legs.

'You'm late, Rose!' Joe chided, his cornflower eyes dancing. 'Florrie's proper vexed at holding dinner back. You'd best look sharp!'

But Rose bent to fuss over the jubilant dog, her lips parted in a knowing smile. 'See to Gospel for me, would you, Joe? Wouldn't do to keep Florrie waiting now, would it?'

Joe chuckled. He knew as well as she did that Florrie's scolding would be no more than a mother hen's clucking over her wayward chicks. Joe had served Henry Maddiford, his daughter and their housekeeper for seven years now, ever since Rose had rescued him from the cruelties of his master at a livery stables in Plymouth. He had instantly become one of the family, wrapped in the Maddifords' kindness. Rose was like an older sister, although now Joe was eighteen, he sometimes looked at her in a different light. But Rose was Rose, hare-brained, open, unique in his eyes. Taking your breath away, and filling your heart with exasperated love.

Rose flounced through the back door, poking her head briefly into the kitchen. 'Oh, Florrie, that smells delicious, and I'm mortal hungry. I'll just slip upstairs to change, and then I'll be down afore you know it!' Then she raced up the stairs two at a time, Amber the dog bounding up behind her, before Florrie Bennett had time to open her mouth.

'Rose, dear!' Henry Maddiford's eyes crinkled as his daughter floated into the dining-room five minutes later. His heart lurched painfully, for with her tangle of hair partially tamed into a knot on her head while the remainder swung down her back, she was the image of his darling Alice, lost to him twenty-one years ago. Rose had changed for dinner, not into an evening dress for she did not possess such a thing, but into a simple yet sophisticated affair of burgundy velvet styled in the latest fashion. All created by her own hand, Henry sighed wistfully. Alice would have been so proud.

'Sorry I was late back.' Rose bounced forward, depositing a kiss on Henry's balding head before she sat down opposite him at the table. 'You know I went to see Molly, and well, the time just flies when I'm with her! They were doing the ironing, so I had to help so that Molly and I could walk the triangle, and we had bread and dripping for tea, and—'

'Well, I hope you've enough room left for this yere dinner, young maid! I've spent all arternoon—'

'But of course, Florrie! That looks absolutely mouth-watering! And I'm starving!'

'Well, I don't know where you put it, I'm sure,' Henry chuckled, shaking his head as he reached for his napkin.

'I only hope as 'tidn spoilt,' the older woman grumbled, trying to conceal the grin that was battling to break over her round face.

'It looks superb, Florrie! But then you *are* the best cook in the whole of Devonshire!'

Rose's exuberant smile won Florrie's heart for the millionth time. The housekeeper could never be cross with Rose for more than a minute. She'd helped raise the child from the day Alice Maddiford had died, newborn babe in her arms, and Florrie had always looked upon the headstrong girl as her own. Her already ample bosom swelled with pride, not so much at the compliment as at the winning ways of her charge who could charm the clouds from the grey Dartmoor skies.

'Of course!' she agreed, her cheeks wobbling with laughter now. 'Though I've yerd tell there's a good French chef at the Bedford Hotel nowadays.'

'And I'm sure you're every bit as accomplished as he is,' Henry told her. 'And next week you'll have another chance to prove it. Mr Frean will be paying us one of his visits, and several of the shareholders will be accompanying him, so I'd like you to put on one of your best luncheons. Some of them are coming from as far afield as London, so it'd be nice to put on a good spread and show them we provincials can produce as excellent cuisine as in the capital.'

He winked at his housekeeper as she wiped her hands on her apron. 'Well, I'd best put my thinking cap on!' she announced.

'Enjoy your own dinner first, though, or you'll faint from lack of nourishment.' Not that there was any fear of that, he thought mildly to himself.

'Yes, of course, sir.' Florrie turned to leave the room, but paused with her hand on the door handle. 'I'll do you proud, I promise.'

'Thank you, Florrie. I know I can rely on you.' The gentle smile remained on Henry's face as his faithful servant closed the door behind her, and then he turned to his daughter. 'So, you had a good afternoon, then?'

'Mmm!' Rose nodded enthusiastically as she swallowed a mouthful of food. 'Oh, this is superb! I'm certain Florrie will surprise your visitors next week!'

'Talking of which . . . ' Henry cleared his throat, and his features moved with unusual solemnity. 'I want you to be there as the *perfect* hostess, to show them that everything in the garden is rosy, if you'll excuse the pun.'

Rose's fine brow puckered. 'And isn't it?' she enquired, her eyes meeting his steadily.

Henry slowly pursed his lips, moving his gaze to stare at his wineglass whose stem he was rubbing between his forefinger and thumb. 'Not as rosy as it used to be. You know so many of the copper mines have closed in recent years, and those that are surviving on arsenic are worked on a smaller scale than before.'

Rose's frown deepened. 'But they're only a small part of our trade. What about all the quarries on the moor? And the new one at Merrivale? That's proving a good customer, isn't it?'

Henry gave an anxious grimace. 'Only so-so, as yet. And any of them could decide to change over to dynamite at any time. Sad to say, overall, our sales are down.'

'Hence the meeting.' Rose sucked in her cheeks. 'But I can't do anything about the sales. That's the agent's job.'

'But you can help to make a good impression. And . . . we may need to start making some economies ourselves.'

Rose's complexion paled as she blinked at him. 'But . . . ' she stammered, her heart suddenly beating wildly. 'I can keep Amber and Gospel?'

'Of course. But only if you give up other luxuries.'

'Oh, thank you, father!' She sprang up from her chair and threw her arms about his neck. 'I'm certain I can find lots of things to do without!'

Henry patted the back of this beloved child who had held his life together, but as he gazed out over her shoulder, he only wished the answer were so simple.

* * *

Rose dropped her sewing into her lap and rising to her feet, went to stare out of the parlour window. The weather had changed dramatically overnight. Rain had swept in from the west, smiting Dartmoor with a lashing deluge that had driven away the last vestiges of summer. The storm had battered relentlessly against the sturdy walls of the house, refusing to abate until mid-morning, and even when it did, a dampness hung in the air in fat, almost tangible droplets. Rose would have liked to saddle Gospel, though, and follow one of the familiar tracks across the moor, since she knew it would be unwise to venture off the path with the threat of a disorientating veil of mist. But much as her spirit yearned to be away, there were other matters that required her attention. She'd spent a couple of hours sat at the kitchen table opposite Florrie as they'd planned the luncheon for their guests the following week. And now she was patiently sides-to-middling a worn sheet, a long, boring process but one which allowed her to ponder what her father had said the previous evening.

Economies. Well, she was quite happy to make this one, even if it was a tedious task. Florrie had taught her to sew simple items when she was a young child, and from then on she had developed her skills in all manner of directions. She only had to study a new style in a magazine, and she could create it for herself. All that would have to stop now, though there was no reason why she shouldn't alter some existing garment. But so long as she could keep Gospel, she didn't mind. She would do without a fire in her bedroom throughout the long, dank winter. A stone bottle filled with hot water from the kitchen range and placed between the sheets would be quite sufficient. As a household, they ate well, but cheaper cuts of meat, for instance, could be just as tasty when cooked to Florrie's special recipes. There were numerous sacrifices they could make that would scarcely be noticed, and all their problems would be solved.

Yes, she decided with satisfaction, as she contemplated the progress along the track outside the house of a small wagon under whose tightly secured tarpaulin she knew would be stowed barrels of gunpowder, or ready-pressed cartridges. The horse pulling the wagon plodded steadily, the long hair or feathers on its lower legs washed and brushed by Joe. Though he helped Rose with Gospel and also did the heavy jobs about the house, his main employment was in the powdermills' stables.

The thought made Rose purse her lips. As long as they all stayed together, nothing else mattered, and she was sure they could do without the fripperies of life. She had plenty of clothes in her wardrobe, and shoes and boots for all eventualities. Her father was equally well attired. They could do without wine on the table every night, except perhaps on Sundays, and with her sewing skills, she could always repair instead of replace, as she was doing now. Her father's position as manager of the powdermills brought with it this comfortable, rent-free house which had been her home ever since she could remember, and a generous salary. So there really was nothing to worry about.

She dragged her gaze away from the wagon as it trundled on into the mist, and turned her eyes instead in the opposite direction. Sure enough, her father was walking past the cooperage next door, dead on time for his luncheon at half past twelve. Rose hurried out into the kitchen to make sure everything was on the table. It was too cold to eat in the dining-room without a fire, so they might as well start as they meant to go on. A reluctant Florrie had set the meal in the warmth and comfort of the kitchen where the range was continually alight. It seemed no hardship to Rose, and her father was a sensible man and would entirely agree with her logic.

As he came in through the kitchen door, he raised a slightly surprised eyebrow at the table which was neatly set with the remains of last night's beef cut into wafer-thin slices, various jars of homemade pickles, and bread baked by Florrie's own hand. The kettle was singing on the range, and Florrie glanced up apprehensively as she made a pot of tea, for never had she served the master a meal in her kitchen!

She needn't have worried. A slow smile pulled at Henry's mouth, instantly dispelling the tiny doubt in Rose's mind. 'What a good idea! It's nice and cosy in here, and that dampness outside gets through to the bones. I can hardly believe it after yesterday.'

'The weather had to change some time, sir,' Florrie observed. 'Now you just get a cup of this yere hot tea down you, and you'll soon warm up.'

Henry obediently sat down at the table, winking a bright blue eye at his daughter as he did so. Rose relaxed as she cut slices of the delicious smelling, mouth-watering loaf, and passed the plate to her father. They both tucked in, Florrie ensuring they had everything they needed, for though they were eating in *her* kitchen, she wouldn't dream of sitting down to her own meal until they had finished, and the master had gone back to work.

It was as Henry was pouring himself a second cup of steaming tea that they all heard it. Rose snatched in a sharp breath and held it as her eyes snapped wide. Her gaze met her father's across the table, and for a split second, his motionless face was inscrutable.

It was Florrie who broke the silence. 'Saints preserve us!' she cried hysterically.

But Rose and Henry weren't listening. They were already on their feet, and Henry had shot out of the door, in his desperate haste, knocking the freshly poured tea all over Florrie's snowy white tablecloth. If he noticed, he didn't pay any heed, and neither did Rose as she sped out of the house after him. Horror shuddered through her body, leaving her heart thumping in her chest. She ran behind her father, for though he was turned fifty, he was fast on his feet.

'Oh, God, this is all we need,' she heard him hiss between his teeth as he halted abruptly at the point along the track where numerous stone buildings opened up before them. Stopping beside him, Rose gazed across the gentle valley where the Cherrybrook played peacefully along its rocky, gravel bed. They were both staring instinctively towards the three incorporating mills high on the opposite slope, spaced well apart for safety reasons. Incorporating, or finely blending the three separate ingredients of the gunpowder, was the most dangerous process and the obvious site for an explosion, but as father and daughter narrowed their eyes at the massive stones that formed the solid walls of the mills, they could neither of them make out any signs of mishap.

''Tis the corning 'ouse, sir!' someone called, and then agitated men, emerging from every door, began running towards the corning and dusting house on the nearside of the river. It was uncanny with so many feet making no sound in the muffling echo of the mist, but of course every man changed his hobnailed boots for leather-soled shoes on arrival at the powdermills each morning, as the slightest spark of metal on stone could cause an explosion. Neither Henry nor Rose could go a step further until they had done the same. Rose plunged after her father into his office to kick her feet into their special footwear, before racing down the track to the next in a line of buildings strung out above the west bank of the river.

Henry came to a halt, raising his hands so that every man stood still. Rose fixed her eyes on him, her pulse thudding. At close quarters, she could see his face working painfully, but he was in charge, their leader. Everyone looked to him for instructions, and he must not let his heart, which ached to get inside and rescue anyone injured, rule his head.

'No one must go in! Not yet!' he ordered. 'Fred?' he questioned, raising an eyebrow at his foreman, a giant of a man who stood, arms akimbo, the leather apron he, like every other worker, wore, making him look larger than ever.

'I doesn't know what's 'appened, Mr Maddiford, sir,' the fellow answered, 'but no one goes in till we knows 'tis safe. It don't appear too serious. The roof be still on.'

Henry sucked in his cheeks as his eyes travelled keenly over the exterior of the corning house. Beside him, Rose's pleated brow throbbed. Nobody had, as yet, staggered out, though a pall of grey-brown smoke with its distinctive smell had billowed through the glassless windows and was hanging in the saturated air in a choking smog. Was someone lying unconscious inside? Rose's heart beat savagely, every second an hour as they waited . . .

Edward James stumbled from behind the sturdy structure, half supporting himself on the stone walls, dazed and visibly shaking. In an instant, his colleagues surrounded him, keeping him upright as he struggled to reach his respected boss.

'I only went outside fer set the rollers in motion,' he stammered, his face white and anguished with his need to explain. 'There were a lump o' cake stuck to the bottom. 'Twere too big fer get out wi' the wooden shovel so I poured a pail o' water over it, an' turned the rollers on fer crush it like we always does, an' the next thing . . . ' He shook his head, his eyes wild with shock as he gazed fearfully over his shoulder at the doorway. Though the initial acrid cloud still clung to the mist in long threads, no more smoke had drifted from the interior of the building.

'Was anyone inside?' Henry demanded, his eyebrows fiercely dipped.

'N-no,' Edward James stuttered, his teeth starting to chatter. 'We'd just stopped fer eat our croust. Young John'd just . . .'

'Ais, I's all right,' the youth called from somewhere in the crowd.

The taut lines on Henry's face slackened, and Rose felt herself sag with relief. She heard her father muttering something under his breath, and then he turned to his foreman. 'Reckon it's safe enough now, Fred?'

The big chap nodded, and as they both stepped cautiously towards the doorway, Rose went to follow, but Henry put a restrictive hand on her arm. 'Not you, Rose. It's too dangerous.'

Rose swallowed hard as she stared at him, her eyes deep, glistening orbs of alarm. 'And . . . what about you, father?' she croaked.

'It's my job,' he reminded her. 'Now you look to Eddie James. Poor fellow's in shock.'

Rose bit down hard on her lip. If anything happened to her father . . . Accidents weren't a common occurrence at the gunpowder mills. There were strict government rules which must be rigidly obeyed in order to retain the licence, but it was still a dangerous business. And any incident, even relatively minor, was a sharp reminder of the need for constant vigilance.

Rose forced herself to turn her attentions to Edward James, sitting him down and ordering someone to fetch him some water. But at every moment, her eye was trained on the doorway to the corning house, her own pulse trembling until her father reappeared, his face set grimly.

'Right, men, you can start clearing up the mess now,' he instructed. 'And for God's sake, be careful. You carpenters'll have to work day and night to repair the machinery. And in the meantime, I need you in my office, Eddie James. I'll have to give Mr Frean a full written report.'

He strode away up the track without even glancing at his daughter, a measure reflecting, she knew well, his worry over the situation. A common practice, one which should have been safe, had resulted in an explosion, albeit a small one, and nobody was to blame. But Henry was responsible, both for the factory and his men, and sometimes he bent beneath the strain. Rose's heart jerked as her eyes followed him, her dearest, kind, thoughtful father of whom she was so proud.

CHAPTER THREE

Rose frowned at her reflection in the mirror and smoothed down the front of her bodice. She'd chosen the most modest of her special outfits, a soft grey affair in finely woven wool. Florrie had helped to twist her hair into a complicated chignon down the back of her head, and she'd fixed a small lace cap onto the crown of her glossy curls.

She looked the perfect hostess for the occasion. She must do her level best for her father who'd been worried enough over the shareholders' inspection *before* the explosion. He and his men had been working flat out to repair the machinery damaged in the blast, and have production back on full level by today. Nevertheless, Henry would have been hard pressed to explain the mishap and would no doubt have had to answer some difficult questions during the visitors' tour that morning. So when they appeared at the house for luncheon, Rose was determined to make it such an enjoyable experience that any misgivings about the gunpowder factory would be dispelled.

She took a deep breath as she hurried down the stairs to the dining-room. The fire was crackling merrily, and the table that Florrie had polished with what she called a good lot of elbow grease, gleamed with the best silver in the house.

Rose had cut the last of her namesake blooms from the sheltered patch in the front garden, and arranged them in a vase in the centre of the table. Now she stood back with a satisfied smile. The room looked tasteful and welcoming, yet not overdone, suitable for a competent manager who was paid a reasonable salary for his position, yet was not a drain on the company's resources.

'Oh, bless us, they be coming!' she heard Florrie wail from the hallway.

'Oh, Florrie, don't you fret none!' Rose swept out of the dining-room and followed Florrie back into the kitchen. 'It's all perfect, and I for one can't wait to sit down to this superb meal you've prepared. My mouth's watering at the smell of it all!'

She beamed radiantly, her eyes sparkling with confidence, and Florrie paused, hands on hips, as if drawing reassurance from her young mistress. 'Well, if anyone can sweet talk them, my dear, 'tis you! So you go out there and . . . and just be yersel!'

Rose threw a last winsome glance at her and then went to arrange herself in the parlour, the correct place for the lady of the house to receive her guests. She could hear the group of men coming up the garden path now, and a few moments later, voices in the hallway as they removed their hats and coats. She clasped her hands in her lap and straightened her back, then tipped her head with an engaging smile as the door handle turned and Henry stood back to allow his guests to enter the room.

'Rose, my dear, how pleasant to see you again!'

Rose got to her feet and dipped her knees in a polite curtsy, as George Frean, proprietor of the mills, stepped across to her and took her hands in his. The elderly man was a fair and respected employer, and had watched her grow from an affectionate child to the accomplished young woman who stood before him now.

'Gentlemen, may I introduce my daughter, Rose,' Henry said from somewhere near the door.

The gentlemen in question were crowding into the room behind Mr Frean whose broad back obscured Henry Maddiford's daughter from their view. He moved aside then, his face lit with a proudly paternal smile as if it were *his* child they were to have the honour of meeting. He was waiting for the effect she would have on the visitors, and he was not disappointed. The amazement on each face was almost comical, from the three mature investors to Mr Symonds, a young fellow on his first mission for his family's wealth. The callow youth flushed scarlet, but the only other visitor, a Mr Charles Chadwick who Rose judged to be in his late thirties, at once contained his emotion at this unexpected ethereal vision of loveliness, and came forward to bow smartly over her gloved hand.

'What a delightful surprise,' he said in his crisp London accent. 'I invested in Cherrybrook many years ago, but had I known Mr Maddiford possessed such a beautiful daughter, I should have paid a visit long before now.'

Rose's demurely lowered eyes flashed a vivid violet and she raised her chin stubbornly. 'My father does not possess me, Mr . . . er . . . ?'

'Chadwick,' he answered, quite astonished.

'Well, Mr Chadwick, radical though it may seem to you, I believe my father sees me, if not as his equal, then as a complement to his own role in life. He protects and provides for me, and I ensure he has an efficient and comfortable home to return to at the end of each day. And should you have visited in earlier years, you would have found in me a mere cheel, not deserving of any attention.'

'Cheel?' Charles Chadwick raised a bemused eyebrow.

'Devonshire,' she replied somewhat curtly, 'for child. Usually female.'

She turned on him such a sweet, angelic, *stunning* smile, in contrast to the sharp sarcasm of her words, that his heart turned over in his chest. That this graceful, sublime beauty possessed — and he was almost afraid even to *think* that word again — such intelligence and wit, was enchanting! Here he was, supposed to be questioning the finances of his investment, and instead finding himself bewitched by this spirited, quite glorious young woman.

'I did not intend to offend, Miss Maddiford.' He managed to draw the cloak of self assurance around himself again. 'Quite the opposite, in fact. Please, I beg you, forgive me.'

Her eyes bore into his, trying to gauge if his words of remorse were genuine, and then her long silken lashes swooped onto her flushed cheeks and she bent her head in an indication of a nod. She appeared calm and collected, and yet her pulse was vibrating. What an idiot! She was supposed to be soothing troubled waters, and instead she was giving one of the major shareholders the length of her tongue! In an attempt to make amends, she looked up at Charles Chadwick with a beguiling smile.

'*I* should be the one begging forgiveness, Mr Chadwick. I do have this . . . fierce independence that runs away with me at times.'

'Oh, don't apologise! I find vivacity in a lady quite splendid.'

His brown eyes danced somewhere between amusement and rapture, and Rose felt relief sigh from her tense body. 'Will you take some madeira, sir, or perhaps some dry sherry to warm you after your inspection of the works? It's quite chillsome today, though at least it's not raining. Gentlemen, which would you prefer?'

She moved away, the refined hostess once more, circulating amongst their guests with easy charm. Mr Frean, of course, she knew well. He was more like an adopted uncle, her father having no other living relatives, and so it was no difficulty to remain by his side, nodding politely when necessary, and waiting to recharge any glass that was in danger of becoming empty. She did her best to ignore it, but she felt many a furtive glance in her direction, and most frequent of them all, was Mr Charles Chadwick.

The knock on the door was hardly heard above the business discussions and when Florrie entered the parlour, she glanced about nervously but Rose saw her agitation and came forward with a dazzling grin.

'Ah, Mrs Bennett!' She winked cheekily at the housekeeper, knowing that with her back to the room, no one else could see her face. 'I take it luncheon is served?'

'It is indeed, miss.'

'Thank you, Mrs Bennett. Now then, gentlemen, would you care to come through?'

Rose gestured graciously towards the open doorway, and with the usual cacophony of 'After you' and 'No, after you', she led the procession into the dining-room. Henry, naturally, occupied the head of the table with Mr Frean on his right, while Rose sat at the far end facing her father along the length of the table in order to attend to the gentlemen at that end. To her utter dismay, Charles Chadwick seemed riveted to her side, and he it was who drew out the chair for her and then seated himself next to her.

'Thank you,' she smiled becomingly, though she could feel herself bubbling with animosity. Surely he could see that his attentions were not welcomed? He was supposed to be there to discuss business, not make advances towards the manager's daughter! *And* he was old enough to be her father — at least, in Rose's eyes he was. He really ought to know better!

'Well, Henry.' George Frean spoke between spooning Florrie's mushroom and celery soup into his mouth. 'You seem to have recovered quickly from the minor incident last week.'

'Thanks to the hard work of the men,' Henry replied guardedly. 'Their loyalty is very much due to the fact that we treat them with respect. Gunpowder manufacture requires skilled labour, skills acquired over years, so we do our best to avoid changes.'

'The repairs were not too costly, then?' one of the investors demanded over his rotund stomach.

'As you've seen, our machinery is made of wood to avoid explosions, and timber is not the most expensive commodity.

31

The carpenters' skills and dedication had the corning mill up and running again in a few days. They know their jobs depend on it. As for the practice that seems to have caused the incident, we are investigating.'

'You are following all the government directives?' young Mr Symonds put in, clearly to impress upon Miss Maddiford that he was not as wet behind the ears as he looked, for as he threw her a purposeful glance, his cheeks suffused with crimson.

'Without question,' Henry assured him. 'I have the papers from the last inspection in my office if you should care to peruse them after luncheon. All the regulations are strictly abided by.'

'But it is still a dangerous and risky business,' Charles Chadwick considered, and then, turning to Rose with a half-patronising, half-challenging smirk, he added, 'would you not agree, Miss Maddiford?'

Inside her breast, resentment fumed with livid force, but Rose's face was a picture of composure. The last thing she wanted was for the wealthy Mr Chadwick to withdraw his considerable investment in the mills.

'Indeed, I do not, Mr Chadwick,' she told him, her steady eyes meeting his. 'There's been no serious accident here since 1858, before my father took over as manager. Whereas serious injuries and not infrequently deaths occur regularly in the quarries and especially the mines hereabouts. Everything possible is done to reduce the risks to a minimum. As I'm sure you'll have seen on your visit, all machinery is wooden, including shovels. The men wear leather-soled shoes and leather aprons. The buildings are set well apart, especially those that require chimneys. The floors of the incorporating mills, for that is the most dangerous process, are covered in tanned hides, and the interior walls rendered to facilitate cleaning. And in the unlikely event of an explosion, the walls are so thick and the roofs are made of flimsy wood and tarpaulins, so that the force of any blast is funnelled upwards, blowing off the roof rather than damaging the machinery or anyone inside. So I would say that overall, it's actually quite safe.'

Her mouth closed in a compressed line as she realised seven pairs of eyes were trained upon her. If only her heart would stop bouncing in her chest. She felt that Charles Chadwick had deliberately driven her into a corner from which she must fight to escape. Was he playing with her, as a cat plays with a trapped mouse? It certainly felt like it, and now embarrassment flamed in her cheeks at her animated response that had drawn everyone's attention.

It was George Frean who rescued her. 'My dear Rose,' he chuckled, 'you speak so eloquently, I fear I will soon be out of a job! But everything our young hostess says, gentlemen, is quite true. And as for competition from dynamite, well, such change is often resisted. As you have seen from the books, trade is still lucrative and promises to be so for some time, even if not quite at the same peak as in earlier years.'

'I fear you are being a little optimistic,' one of the older investors frowned. 'I shall give it some thought on my return to London, but I may want to suggest some changes.'

'May I ask if you could give me an indication of what they might be?' Henry enquired cautiously.

Rose released a slow, calming breath as a lively discussion developed around the table. She rested her hands in her lap, bowing her head as etiquette demanded of a hostess in a man's world. But as she did so, her eye caught Charles Chadwick as he flashed her a sympathetic, *approving* smile before he joined in the debate. Rose's face was an impassive mask, but she listened intently to every word exchanged. The conversation gradually drifted away from business, assisted by the arrival of Florrie's fish course of local salmon followed by a magnificent crown roast of lamb. By the time the sumptuous Charlotte Russe dessert arrived, the conversation had divided into several private dialogues, and Rose was vehemently wishing she could escape the present company, saddle Gospel and head out across the lonely moor to freedom.

'Tell me, Miss Maddiford, when you are not extolling the virtues of the powdermills, what do you find to occupy your time in this isolated location? Perhaps you are an expert in . . . What is it ladies like to excel in? Needle-point, or perhaps some other virtue such as painting? Or music?'

Rose's heart sank like a stone as Charles Chadwick's voice dragged her spirit back from its reverie. But his expression was soft and inviting, warm flecks in his mahogany eyes and the corners of his mouth lifting pleasantly. Perhaps she was being a little hard on him, and it was her duty to entertain her guests and instil in them feelings of goodwill by the end of their visit.

'I have to admit to being quite skilled with a needle,' she said with a genuine shyness that brought a peachy glow to her flawless complexion. 'Though I put it to practical use rather than such things as tapestry. And then I have Gospel.'

'Gospel?' Charles gave an intrigued frown.

'My horse,' she replied flatly, but couldn't prevent the brilliant light that shone from her eyes at the thought of the beloved animal.

'So, you *ride*, do you, Miss Maddiford?' Charles asked, his heart almost tripping over itself in his enchantment. 'Or perhaps you mean you drive a gig?'

'Oh, no,' she answered with a spark of indignation. 'I mean, I can drive a gig, yes. Though it's a dog-cart we have. But that's no good out on the moor. Gospel and I, we like to go for miles . . . ' She stopped abruptly, her mouth clamped shut, as she realised she'd let her tongue — and her passion — run away with her. Hardly the done thing for the lady of the house!

But Charles Chadwick was lost in some strange emotion that was beyond his usual comprehension. Had she been studying his face, Rose would have seen it tighten in some odd spasm, and he had to clear his throat before he could speak again.

'Splendid! Then tomorrow I shall hire a horse and you can take me out and show me . . . well, wherever you would like on this beautiful moor of yours! We're all staying at the

Duchy Hotel in Princetown. We were to return to London tomorrow, but *I* shall stay on. I have thought what a wild and spectacular place Dartmoor appears to be, and I'm sure, Miss Maddiford, you will prove a most knowledgeable guide.'

Did he see her flinch, the flints of ice in her eyes? Who did he think he was? But she had answered her own question before she'd finished asking it. He was a major investor in the powdermills and it was her duty to humour him!

'Why, Mr Chadwick,' she almost croaked, her voice dry. 'I fear I cannot accept such an invitation. It would be unseemly—'

'Oh, I shall of course seek your father's permission,' he assured her with an enthusiastic smile as he glanced towards Henry who was deep in conversation with Mr Frean and their older guests. 'I'm sure he will feel able to rely on my integrity as a gentleman.'

Charles watched as her lovely mouth tightened, her chin set stubbornly. She was magnificent, the most beautiful creature he'd ever clapped eyes on, yet driven with such captivating spirit. His normal indifference to women had been wiped out in one fell swoop, and for the first time in his life, his heart was enslaved.

Charles Chadwick was deeply, hopelessly, irrevocably in love . . .

* * *

'Rose, will you please sit down!'

For once, Henry raised his voice to his daughter as she angrily paced the parlour carpet, kicking at the full hem of her skirt each time she spun round. She halted then and glared at him, her lips in a petulant knot, before she swung into the chair opposite Henry's and sat bolt upright, her head erect and obstinate as she stared sightlessly out of the window.

Henry sighed weightily, his shoulders slumped, as he lifted his weary eyes to her face. 'I do appreciate how you feel, but—'

'How could you, father!' she rounded on him. 'How could you give your consent to me riding out with a complete stranger!'

'A stranger to us, perhaps, but not to Mr Frean.' Henry pulled in his chin, knowing that was not the true reason for her objection. 'I didn't give my permission until I'd spoken to Mr Frean who assured me Mr Chadwick is of a sound reputation. You don't think I'd allow you to go unless I knew you'd be quite safe, do you?'

Rose's mouth twisted, and then she lowered her eyes in submission. 'I suppose not,' she muttered under her breath. 'But—'

'Listen to me, Rose.' Henry leant forward and placed his hand over hers. 'This has nothing to do with the powdermills. This is to do with *you* and *your* future.' His voice was low, ragged with emotion. 'I'm . . . Not to beat about the bush, I'm not getting any younger, and one never knows what lies around the corner. If there were to come a day when I couldn't work any more, well . . . To be honest, I've made little provision for my own future, let alone yours.'

Rose raised her eyes to his familiar, beloved face, tears trembling on her lashes. 'Father, don't say such things,' she scarcely managed to whisper.

But Henry put up his hand. 'I'm sorry, Rose, but they *must* be said. I want to see you settled.'

The flame immediately reignited in her breast. 'Settled, perhaps. But not with that . . . that pompous, arrogant . . .'

She broke off, at a loss to describe the contempt she held for Mr Charles Chadwick, but Henry was not to be deterred. 'Well, perhaps not to Mr Chadwick,' he conceded gently, 'but think on it, Rose. Trapped out here in the middle of this wilderness—'

'But I love the moor—'

'I know you do. But what opportunity do you have to meet suitable, eligible bachelors? A beautiful, vivacious, intelligent girl like you should have the pick of society, and—'

'I don't want the pick of society! If I wanted anyone, which I don't, I love the people we live amongst, people like Joe—'

'No, Rose, that wouldn't work,' Henry stated flatly. 'I *know* you. Better than you know yourself. Joe's a grand lad, but you need someone more . . . intellectual, let's say. And you're twenty-one. Most girls of your age would be long married by now.'

'And Mr Chadwick must be at least forty, and I don't *want* to be married to anyone! I just want to stay here with you, father!'

The tears were brimming over her lower eyelids now, and Henry came to put his arms around her. 'My dear child, you'll never know what happiness you've always brought to me,' he murmured into her hair. 'But time must move on, and if you love me as much as you say, then you will listen to me in this. All I ask is that you at least try to get to know Mr Chadwick a little better. He's neither pompous nor arrogant as you said. He's simply accomplished and confident from the society into which he was born. The poor fellow is clearly quite bewildered by what he feels for you. As for being forty, well, I should believe he's somewhat younger than that. I should have preferred someone more of your own age, I admit, but it means he can provide *security* for you. And . . . he's not exactly *ugly*, now, is he?'

Henry pulled back and lifted her chin to him. Her eyes met his, not seeing his face, but that of Charles Chadwick. His eyes were brown, flecked with amber strands that made them gleam brightly. Wide set and not unkind, she supposed, and his shapely mouth was apt to turn upwards at the corners. The colour of his hair was chestnut with no sign of grey, and he was tall and trim of figure. No, she had to admit, he was not unattractive, and perhaps she had been more than hasty in her judgement of him.

She focused on Henry's hopeful face again, and slowly nodded. 'All right,' she reluctantly agreed. 'I'll ride out with him tomorrow. And then after that, we'll see.'

'Well, neither on us can say fairer than that.' Henry's face moved into an expression of soft compassion. 'I wouldn't want you to miss out on such an opportunity without giving it your full consideration. But by the same token, I wouldn't allow you to enter into a loveless marriage just for the sake of money.'

'Well, then,' Rose replied, her eyes shining with crystal brilliance once more, 'we'll just have to see how Mr Charles Chadwick shapes up. Won't we?'

CHAPTER FOUR

A sharp wind had driven away the grey, overnight rain to leave a clear, pale blue sky. Globules of water twinkled on the wild grasses, the bog cotton and the cobwebs that were slung across them. Rose had secretly hoped the lashing deluge would continue all morning and deter the cosseted Londoner from their expedition, but she supposed it would only have delayed the evil moment. And if she were honest, she was curious as to how Charles Chadwick would stand up to the gruelling terrain she had planned for him. Whether or not he was a good horseman, she didn't know. But she was about to find out!

The damp weather of the past week had softened the ground, so Rose allowed Gospel to canter leisurely up and down the hills between the powdermills and Princetown. Mr Chadwick had wanted to call for *her*, but she'd insisted that was pointless as she wanted to show him a part of Dartmoor that lay to the south. The truth of it, though, was that she wanted time to collect her thoughts.

She'd never before considered the question of marriage. She'd brooded all night on what her father had said, tossing sleeplessly until she'd spent an hour with her forehead pressed against the cool surface of the windowpane as the rain beat furiously on the other side of the glass. All she wanted was to continue the pleasant life she led now, but though she fought against it like a demon, she knew that Henry was right. Perhaps Charles Chadwick would prove more acceptable today, and if it was going to make her father happy, she should at least give the fellow a chance.

As she came into Princetown, she slowed Gospel to a trot. She could feel, with surprise, butterflies fluttering in her stomach. But Charles Chadwick was only a man like any other, so why should she be feeling like this?

There he was now, outside the Duchy Hotel's stone-pillared portico. He was seated upon a large chestnut horse that Rose imagined he must have hired from the hotel's stable. He tipped his head in greeting as Rose brought Gospel to a halt just a few feet away.

'Good morning, Mr Chadwick.' She turned her vivid smile on the businessman, hoping she could throw him off his guard. By the way his brown eyes stretched, she sensed she had succeeded. But then, as expected, he appeared to gather his composure and raised his bowler hat from his well-brushed hair.

'Good morning, Miss Maddiford,' he replied, grinning now with what seemed relaxed amusement. 'I see you ride *astride*. Most . . . unusual for a young lady.'

Rose's chin tilted obstinately. '*You* try riding Gospel side-saddle. On second thoughts, don't try riding him at all. He'll only throw you. The only other person he'll tolerate on his back is Joe, our stable-lad.'

Charles eyes sparkled nonetheless. 'I meant no criticism, your riding astride. It simply . . . took me by surprise. But then, you are a very surprising person altogether.'

'And is that supposed to be a compliment?' she bristled haughtily.

'Of course!' Charles gave a short laugh, his face bright and expectant. 'So, where are you taking me on this fine morning? I can't believe how lovely it is after that rainstorm overnight.'

'Typical Dartmoor weather,' Rose shrugged. 'It can change in minutes. One of its charms, and why one must always take care. A mist so thick you can hardly see the ground can come up that quickly.'

'I can imagine.' The chestnut had fallen into step beside Gospel as Rose turned him to retrace their way a few yards before taking a lane on the right which led almost immediately onto the moor. 'So, where *are* we going?'

'Well, I thought I'd educate you in our local history. That is, if you're interested?' she added a little acidly.

'Why, I should be fascinated!' Charles turned to her with a warm, genuine smile. It made him look attractive, Rose thought, then abruptly averted her gaze as heat flooded her cheeks.

'The gaol was originally a prisoner of war depot,' she went on briskly. 'During the wars against Napoleon Bonaparte. It was the idea of Sir Thomas Tyrwhitt. He were a wealthy gentleman towards the end of the last century. Friend of the Prince of Wales. He built himself a country house called Tor Royal. You'll see it through the trees in a minute,' she explained, waving her arm vaguely ahead of them, 'where the road bends. Just a farm now, like any other. But he had great ideas about reclaiming the open moorland and creating an agricultural community. Didn't work, of course, so they built the prison instead. There *are* parts of Dartmoor that are quite fertile, but up here, it's almost impossible. The prison farmlands, now parts of *that* are under cultivation, but of course, they've got all the free labour of the convicts to clear and drain the ground. Work them like donkeys, they do. Inhuman oft times.'

'Good heavens, do I detect some sympathy for the felons?' Charles asked, surprise echoing in his voice.

'Oh, yes.' Rose glanced across at him with an adamant jerk of her head. 'Well, sometimes, certainly. Of course, some of them deserve it, I agree. Those guilty of violent crimes, say. And I agree with the next man that crime of any sort merits punishment. But here, sometimes, it's downright cruel the way they're treated. For those guilty of lesser crimes, anyway.'

'And do you never fear being attacked by an escaped convict, a young woman like yourself?'

'What, when I'm out on Gospel? Goodness, no! It'd go badly with anyone who tried to accost me *then*! Besides, it's not often any prisoner gets away. They shoot them if they try running off, you see.'

'Well, I'm not quite sure I agree with your sentiments, but I'm pleased to be assured of your safety. Gospel is certainly a formidable animal! Oh, is that, what did you call it, something or other Royal?'

'Tor Royal? Yes, that's right. Fairly modest for the man who founded Princetown. He built a tramway, too, from here down to Plymouth to serve the quarries on the moor as well. Only horsedrawn, mind. The war prison closed after hostilities ended, of course. The tramway didn't flourish again until the prison re-opened for convicts. That was in 1850. Transportation were coming to an end, and they needed something to take its place. Sir Thomas never knew, though. He died long afore. But enough of the history lesson. We're heading out to the Whiteworks tin mine now. So, what do you think of the open moor?'

Charles rose up in the saddle to obtain a better view, and scanned the horizon appreciatively. 'It's certainly breathtaking. So vast and wild, yet so beautiful.'

Despite herself, Rose felt a translucent aura glowing on her face at his enthusiasm. 'Yes. It's its endlessness, its . . . its enormity, I suppose. It makes you feel part of the earth, and yet part of the sky at the same time. As if you, too, can go on for ever. Comforting, yet so exciting. Do you not agree, Mr Chadwick?'

'I do indeed! But perhaps you might address me as Charles, at least when we're alone together?'

Resentment immediately prickled down Rose's spine. 'And how often do you believe that might be, Mr Chadwick?' she asked icily. 'I am merely obeying my father and showing a visitor some of the delights of Dartmoor! We're not actually going to the tin mine, by the way, but over to that stone cross over there,' she said, neatly changing the subject. 'There's lots of them on the moor, we're not sure exactly why. Possibly medieval waymarkers. And then I'll show you something even more mysterious.'

And with that, she squeezed her heels into Gospel's flanks and gave the animal his head. Gospel needed no more encouragement and catapulted into a headlong gallop, flying over the uneven ground with ease. The ancient cross disappeared past them in a blur, and then up and away they raced, skimming over the thick tussocks of tall coarse grass that peppered that part of the moor and forced Gospel to arch his neck as he lifted his fine legs to clear them. The sharp air against Rose's cheeks cooled her indignation, so that by the time they finally gained the vantage point she was aiming for and they skidded to a stop, her spirit had been calmed.

She turned in the saddle to glance back at her companion. The chestnut mare was having difficulty picking her way over the rough terrain she was unaccustomed to, but Charles appeared quite comfortable and kept his seat perfectly. Rose's mouth twisted. Why didn't he fall off? That would have wiped the smugness from his face! Irritated, she turned her attention to the rugged vista before her while she waited for him to catch up, Gospel pawing impatiently at the ground.

'Bloody lunatic,' her sharp hearing caught Charles's muttering as he approached, and somehow it brought a satisfied smirk to her face. 'You really should take more care, Miss Maddiford!' he admonished, raising his voice as he drew level with her.

'Oh, Gospel's quite used to it. He'll slow down if he's unsure.'

Charles opened his mouth as if to argue with her, but then his eyes focused on something strange in the distance and his brow puckered with curiosity. 'What on earth is that?' he asked instead.

'That's what I was going to show you. An ancient stone row. There's lots on the moor, but this is my favourite.'

'How fascinating!' Charles's eyes shone with genuine interest, and Rose tipped her head in approval as she urged Gospel forward at a walk. 'And how unexpected. I had no idea there were such things on Dartmoor. I know of Stonehenge on the Salisbury Plain, but I thought it was unique.'

'You live and learn, Mr Chadwick. Not that these stones are anything like the size of those at Stonehenge. I've never been there, of course, but I have read about them.'

'You read quite a lot, then, Miss Maddiford?'

'Oh, yes. Especially about other places.'

'You'd like to travel, then?'

'Oh, no, Mr Chadwick. Dartmoor is quite sufficient for me.'

'You wouldn't care to visit me in London? Yourself and your father, of course,' Charles added hastily. 'You would be most welcome as my guests, and I could show you all the sights. We could go riding on Rotten Row!'

'Rotten Row? What's that?'

'It's a fashionable bridleway in Hyde Park,' Charles explained. 'You'd have to ride at a more moderate pace, though. If you cavorted about at your normal velocity, you'd upset all the ladies who parade up and down on pretty little ponies a baby couldn't fall from!'

He chuckled at the picture it evidently evoked in his mind, and Rose couldn't help but smile. Perhaps he wasn't so obnoxious after all. 'You ride quite well yourself, Mr Chadwick,' she admitted.

'Perhaps,' he snorted wryly. 'But I've never seen anyone of the fairer sex ride like you do.'

Rose lowered her eyes. She knew she was a superb horse-woman, yet she found it an embarrassment to receive such a compliment from Charles Chadwick's lips. For once in her life, she felt unsure of herself, and it unsettled her.

They rode on in silence, breathing in the fragrant freshness of the damp grass and peaty earth beneath their horses' hooves, until they reached the curious line of standing stones set in the ground. Rose eased on Gospel's reins and the animal came to a halt, standing quite still as if he, too, had become swamped by the uncanny atmosphere. Rose's eyes smouldered a smoky amethyst as she contemplated the scene before her, its familiar power holding her in its hypnotising spell.

'Oh, Mr Chadwick, no!' she called as she was shaken from her trance by the horse and rider moving slowly forward. 'You must dismount. To show respect.'

Charles stopped at once, and glancing back over his shoulder, landed lightly on the ground as Rose came towards him, leading Gospel by the reins. 'The stone circle at the other end is an ancient burial site, or so we believe. For village chiefs. Or maybe priests.'

'And the stone row?' Charles replied in a low voice.

'We don't know. Perhaps graves of ordinary people, or marking the way to the sacred site.'

'Well, it's certainly impressive. It must be, what, nearly a quarter of a mile long at a guess.'

'There are some over a mile and a half, but they're much further away.'

'Good heavens.'

She looked at him askew as they ambled along the row of stones. He clearly appreciated the mystic grandeur of the place which elevated him considerably in her esteem. Her keen eyes scanned the horizon, the moor seemingly endless and stretching to infinity. It was easy to understand why it had been chosen as a ceremonial site.

'They must have been some sort of pagans. Druids, perhaps?' Charles mused softly.

'Possibly. But I don't suppose we'll ever know for certain.'

They walked on, easier now in each other's company, stopping a while by the stone circle before remounting. Somehow there seemed little to say, and Rose set Gospel at a canter, leaving the ancient monument behind them and gradually heading downhill until they crossed over a small bridge and climbed the valley on the far side. Charles followed passively, not pausing until they reached the gushing, evidently manmade waterway that blocked their path.

'Dock Leat,' Rose answered his enquiring expression before he had a chance to speak. 'There's lots of leats on the moor. Brilliant engineering, using the contours of the land to maintain the correct flow. You must have seen those at the powdermills yesterday. This one's for drinking water and such at Devonport, mind. Take care crossing. The mare mightn't be used to it.'

Rose led the way over some huge flat stones that were set across the leat to form a bridge, and Charles followed, the mare treading gingerly on the unfamiliar surface.

'Race you to the top!' Rose yelled unexpectedly as they reached the far side. 'Up there!' she nodded, waving at what to Charles seemed like an impossibly steep crag.

And she was off, laughing into the wind as Gospel charged forward along a narrow grassy pathway through the rock-strewn landscape. Charles shook his head. There was no way he could catch up with her. But it didn't seem to matter.

He'd never been one for women's company. The ladies of London society with whom he was acquainted held no pleasure for him. He'd maintained a mistress once in his youth. She'd been a virgin, as had he, and though he'd kept her purely for his carnal satisfaction, he'd held a certain fondness for her. But knowing he'd never marry her, when she'd fallen pregnant, she'd sought help in a London back street and had died as a result. Since then, Charles Chadwick had turned his back on the female race. Until now. His mind had been intoxicated, his heart quickened and enflamed. There was no one in the world like Rose Maddiford, and he would have her as his bride to honour and to worship.

Having dismounted near the bottom, she was now standing on the summit of the rocky tor, silhouetted against the skyline, her arms lifted and spread towards the heavens. Charles's heart was in his mouth as she appeared to be on the very edge of the sheer drop. Abandoning the mare next to Gospel, he scrambled up the granite outcrop in a frenzy of anxiety. But to his relief, when he reached her, he realised Rose was in fact well back from the dangerous edge.

She was waiting patiently for him, a rapturous smile firing her face and tendrils of wild, curling hair escaping from beneath her hat. Charles knew then that he loved her with a power beyond his comprehension. He *must* have her.

'There! Have you ever seen a view like that?' she demanded, gesticulating with a wide sweep of her arm.

Charles breathed in deeply. It was as if the world lay spread out at their feet, a gentler part of the moor with the river valley and tiny villages below them, and far in the distance, a shining ribbon of water.

'That's the River Tamar,' Rose informed him. 'On a clear day like this you can see all the way down to Plymouth, and the sea all the way along. And if you turn around, you can see right over the north of the moor! Looks like mountains from here. An amazing view in all three hundred and sixty degrees, wouldn't you agree? In fact, when I'm up here,' she said, suddenly solemn, 'I feel as if I'm up in heaven. Looking down on the most beautiful landscape God ever invented. I feel so at peace, I'd have no regrets if I dropped dead just now, *here*, at the most wonderful place on earth.'

'Well, I sincerely hope you don't,' Charles murmured, 'drop dead, I mean, when I've only just met you.'

Rose blinked at him, her cheeks blushing a deep burgundy as she cleared her throat. 'This is Sharpitor,' she snapped hotly. 'That steep ridge in front of us is Leather Tor. And over there, that's Peek Hill, but the view's the same. And it's more than two miles to Princetown on the road, so I think we'd better be heading back. The mare looks tired out.'

'Not surprising, chasing after you!'

Rose's eyes flashed a midnight blue, and with a disdainful flick of her head, she scurried back down over the rocks. Leaping into the saddle, she turned Gospel homeward. Charles sighed as he remounted. Damn it! It was meant to be a joke, and instead she had taken offence. He could see that if he wanted Rose as his wife, he would have to learn to treat her quick temper with kid gloves.

* * *

'Good day, Rose!'

A grin of relief split Rose's taut face as they trotted back into Princetown. The ride home had been tense. Charles Chadwick was a stranger, an outsider who had invaded her private world and somehow tricked her into disclosing some of her innermost thoughts. She would never forgive him!

'Molly!' she responded with a brightness that was meant to slice at Charles's arrogance.

Molly screwed her head to look enquiringly up at Rose's companion. 'Been for a ride, have we?'

'Oh, this is Mr Chadwick,' Rose replied, flapping a casual hand in his direction. 'An investor in the powdermills on a short visit, and I were just showing him part of the moor.' And when Molly continued to gaze at Charles with her sweetest smile, Rose went on irritably, 'Mr Chadwick, this is my dear friend, Miss Cartwright. Her father's a prison warder.'

A stiff smile tightened Charles's lips as he raised his hat. 'Miss Cartwright,' he managed to grate with affected pleasure. 'You will forgive us, but I was just about to accompany Miss Maddiford to her home.'

'Oh, I'm quite capable of seeing myself home, thank you, Mr Chadwick. Besides, Molly . . . Miss Cartwright and I haven't seen each other this week, and I should like to converse with her. In private, if you please,' she added frostily as she swung her leg over Gospel's neck and alighted on the ground.

Charles merely bowed his head. 'Then I shall wish you both good day. But I should be obliged if your father and yourself would honour me with your company at dinner tonight at my hotel. I shall send a carriage for you both at, shall we say, seven thirty?'

And before Rose had the chance to force a word from her gaping mouth, he turned the chestnut mare and disappeared at a brisk trot towards the said hotel.

Rose's cheeks puffed out with indignation and she stamped her foot as Molly giggled beside her.

'Oh, Rose, you do look quite funny!'

'I don't know why *you're* laughing! That bumptious, impudent prig didn't like the idea of my having friends among the . . .'

She broke off, her lips twisted with shame, but Molly only shook her head. 'The working classes? I don't mind you saying it, for 'tis true. We'm hardworking, honest folk, and proud of it. And I bet *he* works, only in a different way. And he looks as if he's took a shine to you, Rose!' she teased merrily.

'Well, he can take his shine somewhere else, the insufferable, boorish—'

'Handsome, polite, well-heeled gentleman!' Molly finished for her. 'You should be flattered, Rose! I wish someone like that would show an interest in *me*,' she ended ruefully.

Rose bit her lip. Yes. To Molly, someone like Charles Chadwick would be manna from heaven. But no one of his ilk would ever look at her, pretty though she was, for anything more than a swift dalliance. Perhaps Rose should be grateful, for even she was somewhat below Mr Chadwick's league. Maybe she should give him another chance, after all.

CHAPTER FIVE

'Rose?' Henry prompted over breakfast.

Rose was staring blankly at the cup of tea she'd been stirring for the past five minutes. Her father's voice startled her and she threw up her head with a jerk. 'Sorry, father?'

'We were talking about Mr Chadwick. You must give the poor man an answer of *some* sort. You've kept him waiting long enough.'

The groan in Rose's heart deepened. Charles had returned to London after extending his visit to nearly a fortnight, almost every minute of which he had spent at Rose's side. But it seemed he couldn't concentrate on his affairs in the capital, and after a couple of weeks, had been back again, wooing her with flowers and other gifts, and trips to the seaside, culminating in his asking Henry for her hand the night before business matters required his urgent return home. It was now mid November, dreary, wet and miserable up on the moor, and despite numerous letters from Charles, Rose still had not given him an answer.

Her eyes met Henry's across the table. 'I don't know,' she moaned pitifully. 'I've been over and over it in my mind, but I just don't know.'

'Have you discussed it with Molly, for instance?'

'Molly? She thinks just because he's handsome and has money, I should jump at the chance!'

'But . . . ' Henry faltered, 'you're not Molly.'

'No,' Rose said stonily.

'Then you must tell *me* exactly how you feel. The whole honest truth, mind.'

He smiled encouragingly, and the frozen knot inside Rose's chest melted a little. 'I know you'd like to see me settled and secure,' she began tentatively, and watched as Henry steepled his fingers and rested them against his lips. 'But if I married Mr Chadwick, I'd have to live in London, so far away from you, and I couldn't bear that.'

'Not necessarily. I'm sure Mr Chadwick could afford to keep at least a modest house down here, and I should want proof of his financial security before I gave my consent anyway. But . . . there is far more to consider than that,' he said with an enigmatic lift of his eyebrows.

Rose licked her lips. There was something solid inside her, and try as she may, she couldn't uncurl its iron fingers. 'Mr Chadwick is . . . polite. A gentleman. Very attentive.' She hesitated. Lowered her eyes. '*Too* attentive. I feel I'm being coerced into a relationship, though in the most charming way. At least . . . ' She bowed her head, not wanting to offend her father's feelings for the man he considered a suitable prospective spouse. 'At least, *he* thinks he's being charming. *I* just find him . . . I'm sure he'd make an excellent husband, but I . . . simply couldn't love him.'

Her mouth compressed into a harsh line and she swallowed before lifting her eyes to her father again. For several seconds, Henry sat motionless, then slowly he nodded his head. 'And . . . do you know what love is?'

Rose blinked hard and her pulse began to beat faster. 'No. Not for another man. I've never felt what that is. But . . . I know what my love for you is, father. It's warm. And trusting. And . . . ' Her eyes suddenly sparked with a piercing sapphire light. 'I know what my love for Gospel is! He lifts something deep inside me, as if we share the same spirit.

Surely if you really love someone, you must feel something like that?' And then her face closed down, as if someone had drawn the shutters over a window. 'But I *don't* feel like that about Mr Chadwick.'

Henry contemplated her a moment longer, her impassioned speech pricking at his heart. 'Then there's no more to be said. I'll write to Mr Chadwick this evening and inform him of your refusal.'

'Oh, thank you, father!'

Rose's shoulders slumped with relief. She sprang to Henry's chair and bent to wrap her arms around his beloved neck. He patted her shoulder, cheek pressed against hers, and his eyes closed as he endeavoured to shut out his distress. For how could he break it to her that, without Charles Chadwick's money, Gospel would have to be sold.

* * *

Rose padded up and down her bedroom, unconsciously chewing on the nail of her little finger. She should feel relieved, but she didn't. She very definitely did not want to marry Mr Chadwick, but was it a wise decision? And was her father being his usual understanding self, or was he really deeply disappointed, despite his words?

She rubbed her hand hard over her forehead. If she didn't stop her restless tramping, she would wear a hole in the carpet, or so Florrie would have said. The shadow of a smile flickered on her pursed lips. Dear Florrie. At least she would always be there. And Joe, and Gospel and Amber, who at this moment was stretched out on the floor, nose on her paws but with her eyes dolefully following her mistress's movements.

Gospel. If anything could soothe Rose's spirit, it would be a crazed gallop across the moor. Perhaps over to Princetown to see Molly. Or to some lonely place, such as the twisted, stunted oaks of ancient Wistman's Wood. Somewhere she had *not* taken Charles Chadwick!

She pulled off her skirt and petticoats and wriggled into her riding-breeches before donning the jacket and full skirt of her riding habit over the top. A small hat secured with a long pin, a scarf wound around her neck, gloves ready in her pocket, and her boots would be waiting by the back door after she had put her head round the kitchen door to tell Florrie where she was going.

Dankness stung her nostrils as she strode across the yard, Amber bouncing excitedly about her heels. Joe had turned Gospel into the field behind the buildings early in the morning, so that the animal could kick up his heels and expend some of his boundless energy. Rose went in search of his bridle before leaping over the gate in her customary unladylike fashion, while Amber wormed her way beneath the bottommost bar.

Gospel whinnied with pleasure when he heard Rose call, before thundering across the wet grass and snorting great wreaths of hot breath as he came to a slithering halt before her. He nuzzled into her shoulder bringing a smile to her face as she stroked his strong, sleek neck. When she'd first bought him, he'd been the devil's own job to catch. But now he knew it usually meant a wild, exhilarating dash on the open moor with his gentle mistress on his back, and he was as eager for the adventure as she was.

She slid the bridle over his head, slipping the bit into his mouth, and fastening the chin strap, led him towards the yard to remove his blanket and saddle him before they streaked off in whatever direction she decided upon.

Her fingers froze on the buckle of the girth strap.

Her sharp ears had caught that hiatus of unearthly silence that precedes the boom of an explosion by a split second, and then the thunderous crash that shattered her eardrums, reverberating through the valley before slowly rolling away on an ever fainter rumble. For several moments, not a muscle in Rose's body moved. Only her heart beat steadily while her brain absorbed what she did not want to believe. But she *had* heard it. As her pulse accelerated, pumping frenzied life into her limbs, she gave a hoarse cry, and abandoning Gospel, she ran.

She fled along the footpath to her father's office. Flung open the door, praying she'd see Henry pulling on his leather-soled shoes. He wasn't there. From years of habit, she changed her own footwear in an instant, and was flying down the hill, her heart hammering in her chest, the breath dry and rasping in her lungs.

She stopped dead. Unlike the minor mishap a few months past, it was immediately apparent where the explosion had occurred. Away on the opposite hillside, number one incorporating mill was engulfed in an opaque curtain of black smoke . . .

Rose was transfixed, her mind wrapped in horrified curiosity. She wanted to run, but the leaden weight of her legs imprisoned her. And then she joined in the macabre, hushed convergence of leather-muted feet, speeding along the river bank, past the various processing houses, across the bridge over the Cherrybrook and up the track on the far side. Those workers who could safely shut down their machinery, had spilled out from their posts and were milling breathlessly on the hillside, calling in restless agitation as they awaited instructions, or numbed into silence by the picture of destruction before them. The shroud of smoke was reluctantly drifting into the mist, revealing what little remained of the charred and broken roof timbers and the flapping remnants of the tarpaulin that until a few minutes before had covered them. Splintered shards of the massive wooden machinery had been blown through the roof and window apertures in the blast, and lay scattered about the grass together with tatters of the heavy tanned hides that lined the floor of the mill.

Rose's heart caught in her throat. She turned her head in disbelief, yet her eyes still clung to the scene of devastation. She tore her gaze away, searching for her father among the crowd and expecting at any moment to hear his reassuring, authoritative voice as he calmly took control of the appalling situation.

It started as a tiny kernel deep in her breast, slowly unfurling until its fingers spread like strangling tentacles through her being, crushing her last vestige of hope.

'Have you seen my father?' her lips quavered as her eyes blindly quizzed every shaking head that swung before her. 'Have you seen my father?!?' she screamed now, frantically running from face to face, tripping, blundering over the rough grass, the sea of anxious expressions foaming into one blurred, surging wave. As she turned to join her gaze to theirs as they stared at the smouldering building, she knew.

'NO!!' A savage wail echoed from her heaving lungs as she dashed forward, howling dementedly, only to be restrained in the iron circle of Fred Ashman's arms. He struggled to hold fast to her writhing, flailing body until the agony emptied out of her and she suddenly went as limp and lifeless as a rag doll.

* * *

The world gathered itself around her, cruel and tormenting. She wanted to slip back into the peace of unconsciousness, to snuggle beneath the safe and comforting blanket that had smothered her mind, but she knew even in her semi-comatose state that she had to face the hostile cold of reality.

She forced open her eyes open. She was in the kitchen, slumped in Florrie's chair by the range. Florrie herself was seated at the table, her head bowed over an untouched mug of tea, her eyes red and swollen, and the usually merry lines on her face set into a grim, appalling mask.

It was the sight of her that made Rose remember.

She sat bolt upright in the chair, her heart taking a huge leap and knocking against her ribcage. The last thing she remembered . . .

'Father!' she shrieked in her head, but her lips only mouthed the word, her eyes bright pinpoints of terror.

Florrie looked up, her plump cheeks wobbling. 'Upstairs, my lamb,' she murmured, her voice the croak of an old, old woman.

Rose's head swam as she sprang from the chair and raced up the stairs two at a time, her feet, still in their leather-soled shoes, making no sound. The cold brass of the doorknob was a shock in her hand. Was she ready? To see what was in the room? Her father, his arms crossed over his chest. Perhaps with Florrie's snowy sheet already laid over his head.

She trembled. Her hand hardly able to open the door. Blood pumping fearfully, angrily, through her veins. How dare they — whoever *they* were, God, perhaps? — take her dearest, beloved father from her like this.

A dark-suited man stood in the room, his back to her as he sorted something on the bedside cabinet. He turned when he heard her to smile gravely over his shoulder, nodding down at the bed before continuing with what he was doing. Dr Power from Princetown. Prison surgeon, but also physician to local people who sought his help, and so known to everyone.

A bud of hope blossomed, and then shrank, in Rose's breast as she drew her gaze to the bed. Only her father's face was visible above the neatly arranged bedclothes. It was still streaked with black grime, settling in lines in the folds of his skin, though someone, probably Florrie, had evidently tried to wipe away the worst without causing him too much distress. One side of his forehead, spreading down across the temple though thankfully missing his eye, was a raw mass of black and red bubbles that stretched into his matted, bloodied hair. Other than that, he lay perfectly still, like a corpse, but for the shallow, rasping breathing of his lungs.

Rose stood. As horror washed over her in a pulsing torrent. Somehow Henry must have been aware of her presence and his eyes half opened. 'Rose,' he choked, and his taut face relaxed.

Rose dropped onto her knees, fighting against the welling tears in her eyes. 'Father,' she whispered back, forcing a wan and deeply loving smile to her quivering lips. 'Oh, father, you'll be all right now,' she told him, her voice soft and gentle as an angel.

'Yes,' he breathed, and then coughed harshly so that she could smell the smoke from him. 'And Peter?'

Rose's heart squeezed. Even as he was, he was anxious, as ever, about his men. Rose turned her questioning eyes to the doctor, ashamed that she hadn't given a thought to anyone else. Dr Power gave a solemn, almost imperceptible shake of his head, and Rose felt ice run through her veins. Peter Russell, his wife, their five children.

Her tender gaze moved back to Henry's damaged face. 'I . . . I don't know,' she said, the lie coming easily to her lips, for how could she burden him with the knowledge. It could wait. For now.

'I was . . . giving him the length of my tongue.' Henry's voice chafed in his burning throat. 'There was grit on the floor. Some must have got into the trough.'

His words had become agitated, and as Rose stretched out a calming hand, she was aware of the doctor coming up behind.

'Hush now, father,' she managed to croon. 'You must rest. Have a little sleep, and I'll be here when you wake up.'

'Your daughter's right, Mr Maddiford,' Dr Power said firmly over her shoulder. 'The morphine will make you sleep. Don't fight it.'

Henry's bloodshot eyes lifted to the doctor's face, then rested back on his beloved child before drooping closed, the tense lines in his skin slackening. Rose bent forward. The reverent kiss she placed on his cheek left an acrid taste on her lips. She got to her feet, Dr Power ushering her politely out of the door, and as she glanced back, Henry was already asleep.

'A word, if you please, Miss Maddiford.'

Rose stood for a moment, his quiet tone taking some seconds to percolate through to her numbed brain. 'Of course,' she muttered, and led the way down to the parlour, floating down the stairs as if in some strange, unreal dream.

'Please, sit down,' the doctor invited her, which seemed odd in her own home.

She obeyed, perching uneasily on the edge of the armchair. The fire was out. One of their economies. Rose shivered, crossing her arms tightly across her chest. 'He . . . will get better, won't he?' she stammered, not quite sure how she articulated the words.

Dr Power squatted down on his haunches in front of her, his forehead twitching. He was used to dealing with hardened criminals, treating the constant diarrhoea that afflicted almost each and every prisoner due to the dubious water supply, the chills and chest complaints of those forced to work up to the waist in icy water as they drained the farmland, the severe injuries caused by accidents with explosives at the prison quarry, or — the part of his job he hated — deciding if a convict was fit enough to endure some vicious corporal punishment. So how could his heart not be touched by this beautiful, distraught young woman whose grief already ravaged her lovely face.

'I'm afraid your father's condition is worse than it appears,' he began compassionately. 'He has other deep burns to the front of his body. In time, they should heal, but burns are very much prone to infection. I am also concerned that somehow in the blast, his spine has been damaged. It could well be no more than severe bruising which has compacted the nerves of the spinal column, in which case in a few months, perhaps, things may return to normal. But at the moment I'm sorry to say he feels nothing below the injury. He has already proved incontinent. And I fear I must warn you, Miss Maddiford, that if the spine is permanently damaged or even broken, then . . . your father will never walk again.'

His voice had drifted about her, like a mist that would slowly lift and allow the sun to shine through and the world would be bright and happy again. But it wouldn't. The cloud was there to stay. For ever.

She lifted her head, tears spangling in her eyes. 'Thank you, Doctor, for your honesty,' she managed to tear the words from her throat.

'I really am very sorry. I will do everything in my power to keep him comfortable, and God willing, he will make some recovery. Now, I do apologise, but I must return to my official duties. But I will be back again later. You know where I am if you need me in the meantime. I'll see myself out. And . . . well, Miss Maddiford . . .'

He squeezed her shoulder as he passed, for really they both knew there were no words. Rose listened to his footsteps in the hall, the front door closing softly. Silence then. Just the clock ticking steadily on the mantelpiece.

Just an hour or so ago, she'd been deliberating the wisdom of her refusal of Charles Chadwick's proposal. That seemed so unimportant now. So unimportant and of no significance whatsoever.

She buried her head in her hands and wept till her aching soul could weep no more . . .

CHAPTER SIX

Rose stood, staring blindly at the empty fireplace in the parlour. Outside, the moor lay frozen beneath a searingly cold blanket of February snow, and Rose drew the shawl more tightly about her narrow shoulders, exhaustion clouding her brain. Between them, she and Florrie had nursed her father, day and night, for three months. There was no time for long, carefree gallops on Gospel's back, or cosy chats with Molly by the Cartwrights' hearthside. What flesh had once adorned Rose's slender figure had fallen from her bones, and the skin was taut across her cheeks.

She scarcely turned her head at the knock on the door.

'Come in,' she answered, her voice dull and lifeless.

Dr Power entered the room and he gave a weighty sigh. 'No change, I'm afraid, Miss Maddiford.' He hesitated, the sight of the forlorn young woman tearing at his soul, but it must be said. 'I fear we must face up to the situation. Barring any unforeseen recovery, which I very much doubt, I believe your father will remain paralysed.'

Rose nodded her head. Yes. She didn't need the physician to tell her. The swelling on Henry's spine had long since subsided, but for weeks now he had still neither moved nor felt any sensation below the mid-point of his back, the only progress he had made being his regaining control of his bodily functions. His lungs remained weakened by smoke inhalation, and scar tissue twisted the side of his forehead, but his upper body remained strong. He could feed and wash himself, and move himself about in the bed, even issuing directives and to some extent taking up his responsibilities once more as manager of the powdermills. But never again would he stride amongst his men and the various buildings of the factory they worked in.

'Thank you, Dr Power,' Rose murmured wearily. 'I know you've done all you can. It's much appreciated.'

The doctor drew in an awkward breath as he reached into the breast pocket of his coat. 'I only wish,' he said gravely, 'that the outcome had been a better one. And that I didn't have to present you with my bill. I have kept it as low as possible.'

The memory of a smile strained at Rose's mouth as she took the envelope from his hand. 'Mr Frean has kindly said he'll pay for my father's treatment.'

'Ah,' Dr Power nodded, for there was nothing more to say on the matter. 'And to be honest, there is little reason for me to visit again. You and Mrs Bennett are making an excellent job of caring for your father. Just keep exercising his legs several times a day to keep the blood flowing and reduce the strain on his heart. Of course, if you've any concerns, do send for me at once.'

'Yes, I will. Thank you, doctor.'

'Any time, Miss Maddiford. I'll see myself out.'

Rose was alone again, her gaze resting unseeing on the envelope in her hand. So, that was it. Her dearest, hardworking, active father cut down and crippled for life. She squared her shoulders, her forehead swooping into a determined frown. There was nothing more the good doctor could do. But *she* wouldn't give in! The fight began to creep back into her veins. If her father's condition was never to improve, then there must be ways by which his existence could be returned to as near to normality as was humanly possible. A tiny seed of hope had been planted at the back of her mind. She would leave it there to germinate, to be pondered upon so that the right decisions could be made.

Just now, there were other matters she needed to attend to. They were running low on coal, and the pantry was nearly empty. Time for a trip into Princetown. She would take the dog-cart, of course, and Polly, the gentle cob that pulled it. And even that put another burgeoning idea into her head.

* * *

'I'm afraid I can't serve you, Miss Maddiford,' the shop-keeper in Princetown's general store announced.

Rose's neck stiffened and she blinked in astonishment. Had she heard right? 'I'm sorry?' she questioned, her brow puckering into a frown.

'I were proper sorry to hear about your father's accident, but I'm afraid I can't serve you,' the woman repeated, 'not until your account be settled. The cheque you gave me from your father has been returned by the bank.'

'What?'

'Here. See for yourself.' The woman flicked through the till, and passed the cheque, with its ugly red bank stamp, into Rose's trembling hand.

A wave of disbelief washed from Rose's throat down to her stomach as she gazed down at it. The writing, her father's signature, danced before her eyes. She couldn't believe . . .

'Thank you,' she mumbled incoherently, shame burning in her cheeks as she made for the door. Outside, the biting cold stung into her body like a million piercing arrows, tears of humiliation turning to frost on her eyelashes. Surely this must be a mistake? It must be! Some new clerk at the bank. Yes, that must be it.

What should she do now? Well, there were two other grocers in the village. Her father didn't have accounts with them, but she had some coins in her purse, not many, but enough to buy some tea, flour and yeast, and a couple of pounds of potatoes. They could manage on that for a few days. Until the matter was resolved. With a joint from the butchers, as she had settled that account with a cheque from her father on the same day as . . . Oh, good God! Would it be the same there?

She left Polly tethered to the rail with the horse-blanket thrown over her back, since she couldn't leave the animal standing still without protection in these temperatures. Rose's feet crunched in the snow as she made her way to the other shops, the butchers first, her hand quivering as she opened the door and a horrible sinking feeling in her stomach.

Mr Roebuck looked up with his usual kindly smile. 'Ah, Miss Rose, how be your father?'

His sympathetic tone restored her confidence. Oh, yes, definitely a mistake. 'No better, I'm afraid. But thank you for asking. Now, I'd like a hand and spring of pork, if you please,' she asked. It was an awkwardly shaped joint and therefore cheaper, but there was usually plenty of meat to be found on it.

Mr Roebuck cleared his throat and leant confidentially towards her. 'I'm sorry, Miss Rose,' he said in a low voice, 'but the bank wouldn't accept your father's cheque. Puts me in a difficult position, you sees. I can maybies let you have a couple of strips of belly. And a pound of tripe for that dog o' yourn, but only if you pays me now. In cash. I cas'n let you have ort more than that till your account be settled.'

Rose gazed at him, and she was sure her heart missed a beat. This couldn't be happening!

She forced her most winning smile to her lips. 'Oh, Mr Roebuck, I do apologise. I believe there's been some error at the bank. I'll have to go into Tavistock to sort it out. And I'm afraid I have little money with me, so I won't buy anything today. But I'll be back in a day or two.'

'As you wish, Miss Rose. I really am proper sorry.'

'Don't worry about it,' she beamed cheerfully in an effort to disguise the tremor in her voice. 'I understand.'

'My regards to your father,' the poor man called as she left the shop.

She stood outside on the frozen ground, unaware of the gnawing cold that pinched at her toes and turned her flushed cheeks to ice. She breathed in deeply through flared nostrils, and the pain of the glacial air in her lungs seemed to bring her to her senses. Flour and potatoes were all she could think of. She had enough in her purse for those. At least they wouldn't starve. But even those were useless without coal for the range to cook them on.

Rose closed her eyes, forcing herself to think back. Henry hadn't given her a cheque for the coal-merchants, had he? So perhaps they hadn't sent a bill yet. But it had been three months since the explosion. She took all the post up to her father unopened. He dealt with it, then gave her back any papers to put away in his bureau in the dining-room, which she did without looking at them, for they were her father's. But what if . . . ?

She strode determinedly into Mr Richards's establishment. They only had enough coal to last a week in these arctic temperatures, two if they were blessed with a sudden thaw and were careful in their consumption. But they already were, the kitchen range and the grate in Henry's bedroom being the only fires that were lit, both she and Florrie shivering in their beds at night. It was warmer in Joe's room over the stables, she often thought ruefully.

The groceries first, for the shop served a dual purpose. With the food items stowed in her basket, she stepped up to the kiosk that served as the coal-merchants' office, and tapped nervously on the window. Mr Richards glanced up at her over his horn-rimmed spectacles.

'Yes?' he asked gruffly, for he wasn't known for his friendliness.

'Please could you deliver us some coal, Mr Richards?'

Rose watched through the small square of glass as he thumbed through a ledger and finally opened it at a particular page that seemed to warrant his scrutiny. He sniffed, wriggling his nose, before turning his small eyes on her. 'Your last bill's not been paid yet,' he growled.

Rose's heart sank to her boots. 'Are you sure you've sent one?' she replied with feigned innocence. 'I've not seen one.'

He scowled and flicked through another smaller book. 'Definitely. But you can have this carbon copy.' And tearing out the page, he slid it through the narrow gap beneath the window.

Rose folded it between shaking fingers and pushed it into her purse, trying hard not to look at the feint blue figures at the bottom of the thin paper. 'I'm so sorry, Mr Richards. It must have been overlooked. Everything's been upside down since my father's accident. I'll see to it forthwith,' she smiled in what she hoped was an assured manner. 'Now, when can you deliver?'

'Hmm,' the man grunted as he pinched his moustache between his forefinger and thumb. 'You can have a couple of sacks the day after tomorrow. But 'tis all until that bill's paid.'

'Of course. I understand. Thank you.'

Her feet somehow took her outside and along the slippery ground to where Polly was waiting patiently. Rose pulled the blanket from the mare's back and climbing up into the driving-seat, turned the cart for home. Once they were out on the Two Bridges road, she braced herself to take the folded sheet of flimsy paper from her purse . . .

* * *

'Your father's asleep now, Rose dear,' Florrie announced as she puffed into the kitchen late that evening. 'I'll just make myself a cup of tea, and then I'll be off to bed myself. Will you have one, my dear?'

Rose glanced up from folding the last of Henry's night-shirts that she'd just been ironing. Ever since returning from Princetown, she'd endeavoured to hide her preoccupation. Florrie had been surprised at the lack of meat and other provisions in the shopping basket, but Rose had blamed the bitter weather for the delay in the delivery of supplies to the shops, and the older woman had accepted the lie unquestioningly. Rose had felt guilty at the deceit, but she had far more serious matters to ponder at the moment.

'Yes, please, Florrie,' she answered gratefully. 'I'm that weary.'

'And you'm not yersel today, neither,' the housekeeper commented shrewdly. 'Be summat amiss?'

Rose disguised the colour that flooded her cheeks with a heartfelt sigh. 'It's just Dr Power. He confirmed today what you and I have thought for some time. That father's never going to get any better.'

Florrie handed Rose a mug of tea, and then sat down heavily herself with her own drink. 'Ah, well,' she muttered thoughtfully. 'I suppose us should be thankful for small mercies. We still has 'en, which be more than can be said for poor Elisa Russell of her husband.'

Rose nodded solemnly. Florrie was right. But that wasn't all that was on her mind just now. They drank their tea in silence, easy in each other's company even though not another word was exchanged. Florrie finally bade her goodnight and a distracted smile flickered over Rose's face. She listened for the footfall on the stairs and then in the room above, and eventually all fell quiet.

Rose opened the firebox door, then sat back to contemplate the dying embers that glowed an ever fainter orange among the grey ashes. The day had been a hard one, first the conversation with the doctor, and then her visit to Princetown. And it wasn't over yet.

Surely there had been some sort of mistake? The cheques could both be the result of an error at the bank, but the unpaid bill at the coal-merchants' seemed too much of a coincidence. It was dated over a week before Henry's accident, so he must have received it before that fateful day, though it was possible that in his present condition it had totally slipped his mind. But the enormous delivery they'd had at the beginning of the winter was a considerable sum.

Did it really remain unpaid? If so, Mr Richards's attitude was hardly surprising, and he was being quite charitable in letting them have any more at all.

Rose got to her feet, and taking up the oil lamp, quietly let herself into the dining-room and opened her father's bureau, her fingers trembling as she reached for the growing stack of correspondence she had placed there at Henry's request. She felt like a thief in the night. But this was her responsibility now, and she had to know the truth.

One by one, she unfolded the papers. The scant private correspondence she put to one side. The rest . . . Each one made her heart thud harder and she had to sit down abruptly as the strength emptied out of her in a flood of horror. Bills unpaid, final demands. Not just the two returned cheques she knew of, both of which covered several months of purchases, but the wine-merchants' in Tavistock, the shoe-makers', Henry's tailor, animal feed — for Gospel, of course — and the fine new saddle and the necklace Henry had bought for her for her twenty-first birthday last June.

She couldn't believe it. She knew they lived well, but she'd always assumed they could afford to! Henry would always smile benevolently at her delight, but the appreciative kisses she bestowed on him were because she *loved* him, not because of what he gave her. How *could* he? How could he possibly get his own finances in such a state when he was such an excellent businessman, as Mr Frean had said on so many occasions?

Tears of panic and utter despair pricked at her eyes as she shook her head in disbelief. In her fingers quivered an irate letter from the bank together with a copy of Henry's vastly overdrawn account. She hardly dared open the last document. She was feeling physically sick and really didn't think she could take another shock. But it wasn't another demand, just a letter from Charles Chadwick.

The relief was so overwhelming that she began to read it without considering that she should never go through anyone's private mail. The letter had been written shortly before Christmas, commiserating Henry on his terrible accident which Charles had learnt of from Mr Frean, and saying that he fully understood how Rose's decision would have been put on hold for the time being. Though his heart yearned to be with her again, he would stay away until such times as Henry summoned him. That he felt he loved her more with each day they were apart, and he longed for her to do him the honour of accepting his proposal and allowing him to provide generously for her for the rest of her days.

Ha!! A bitter laugh crowed in her aching gullet until it dissolved into racking sobs of misery. So upright, so correct! He'd hardly want her *now* if he knew the truth; that she was the daughter of a debtor; of a man whose crime, not so many years ago, could have seen him in prison. Oh, no! Not that she returned Mr Chadwick's feelings of affection in any way, and she had only entertained the idea of any relationship between them for her father's sake. But *now* . . . !

No. It was time to face facts. To face the stark reality of the hostile world that lay outside the four walls of the solid house. And indeed within it, for three months ago, Henry had been a strong, vigorous man who'd made her believe that life was bountiful, and the only problem she had to confront was whether or not to marry a man who was both considerate and rich, but whom she did not love.

Now everything was changed, her comfortable existence swept away from beneath her feet. And she had no idea which way to turn.

* * *

'Why didn't you tell me, father?'

Her voice was compassionate, afraid, hardly more than a whisper fluttering in her throat. She was sitting by Henry's bedside, holding his hand and stroking the skin which had always been brown from exposure to the elements, but was now pale after three months' confinement indoors. Henry turned his misted eyes to his beloved daughter, his heart stung by the agony on her face.

'I was going to,' he said quietly, a frown of shame dragging on the ugly scarring on his forehead. 'But then *this* happened, and I really couldn't bear to. It'd put so much strain on you. You had enough to worry about. How could I possibly make it so much worse for you by telling you the truth? To break it to you that we'd have to sell Gospel, and that was just to start? You love that horse, and because of me, you'd have to sell him.'

Rose drew back with a jerk. Sell Gospel! The thought had never crossed her mind! Of all the solutions that had tumbled in her brain, selling Gospel was never amongst them. He was part of the family, like Florrie and Joe. And who would buy him anyway? He was a fine animal and worth a great deal if he'd had a temperament to match, but his bad temper would be immediately apparent to any stranger. It would a harsh bit and the whip for him, or the knacker's yard. Shock settled in the pit of Rose's stomach with all the other horrors that were seething there. It was just another nail in the coffin.

'But *why*, father?' she moaned with a forlorn shake of her head. 'Why were you always giving me so many things if we couldn't afford them? I didn't *need* them. I'd have loved you just as much without.'

Henry's faded blue eyes glistened. 'Yes, I know that, child. But I wanted you to have everything. Everything that I hadn't been able to give your mother. We were young, just starting out in life with just enough money to keep a roof over our heads and to employ Florrie. She was only meant to be temporary, to help your mother for a while when you were born. When Alice died,' his voice quavered, 'I thought I'd lost everything. That my life was over. And then I began to realise that I still had her. In you. You're so like her, you know. So I vowed that I would dedicate my life to making you happy. To making up for the fact that you never had a mother. And in doing so, I believed I was doing it for Alice, too.' He paused, and the devoted smile slid from his wan face. 'But it all went wrong. I never meant it to end like this.

You've been a wonderful daughter to me, Rosie. No man could ever wish for more. And now I've got to break your heart. And I'm so, *so* sorry.'

Rose had listened, her head bowed, and now she raised her eyes to him, deep pools of anguish. The torment in her throat was choking her, her soul torn by her love for this dear man who had been her life, and who had been cruelly reduced to a helpless cripple. She threw her arms around him, her tears dripping onto his greying hair as she rocked him back and forth.

'It'll be all right, father, I promise you,' she spluttered. 'I don't know *how* yet. But I'll work something out. Just see if I don't!' And even as she spoke, her voice began to tremble, not with dejection, but with outright determination.

CHAPTER SEVEN

'Did you find father a little better today, Mr Frean?' Rose smiled optimistically as the elderly gentleman entered the kitchen a few weeks later.

She was certainly feeling more cheerful herself, as in that time she had set her plan of campaign in motion. She had returned the saddle which, lavishly polished over the months she'd used it, showed no sign of wear, and the saddler had kindly cancelled the debt entirely. The jeweller had taken back the necklace, though Rose had been angered to see it displayed in the window shortly afterwards at the full price, and no end of hard argument had persuaded him to come down on what he considered she still owed him the for 'loan' of the jewellery. The wine merchant agreed to take back what remained of Henry's store of bottles at its full value, though Rose would still owe him a reasonable sum.

There was nothing else that could be returned, but Rose had visited the bank manager, explaining about Henry's accident and breaking down in wrenching sobs that had melted the poor fellow's heart. For Rose's part, it hadn't been difficult, for though she'd planned on play-acting, when it came to it, the appalling discovery of the dire straits of her father's financial affairs had once more grasped her by the throat, and the tears had come naturally. She'd explained all the measures she'd put in place, the manager suggesting she might also pay a visit to the pawnbrokers. In the end he'd agreed to allow her six months, interest free, to pay off her father's debts.

It wasn't going to be easy. She deposited at the pawnbrokers everything she possibly could, down to their silver cutlery and even all but one of her fine dresses and their accessories, knowing she would never see them again. They ate frugally, and no meat would grace their table until all their debts were paid off. Most painfully, she'd told Florrie that if she wanted to stay on with them, she would no longer receive any salary. Her cheeks wobbling dejectedly, the loyal housekeeper had declared she would never leave them. She only wished that instead of sending her wages over the years to her widowed sister and her five children, she had kept the money so that she could have helped Rose now. Joe had been told he'd have to pay for his keep out of his salary from the powdermills, but he was happy enough, knowing he'd been on the receiving end of Henry's generosity since a child.

Gospel, for the time being at least, could stay, his speed being useful in conveying Rose quickly on the numerous errands she'd run in order to gain grace with their creditors. Besides, she told herself, it would take time to find a buyer for him, and time was a commodity of which she had very little at the moment. The oil lamps were replaced with cheap candles, and those only lit when they could hardly see where they were going. In the evenings, Rose and Florrie would sit, straining their eyes, by the glow from the open firebox, and Henry, warmed instead by hot-water bottles filled with water heated on the range — which by necessity was alight all day — no longer had a cheering fire in his room. Rose had lit one for him this morning only because she knew Mr Frean was coming, and she didn't want him to suspect their drastically impecunious state.

'Won't you sit down and take a cup of tea?' she invited him. 'It's so good of you to come all this way just to see father.'

'I don't come *just* to see him, you know, Rose,' Mr Frean said solemnly, drawing in his chin. 'I need to keep more of an eye on the place now that your father is . . . incapacitated. And,' his mouth twitched awkwardly, 'that's what I need to talk to you about. So, yes, please. I should like to take some tea, and perhaps we can have a little discussion.'

Rose winced as she spooned some fresh tea into the pot, for they'd got into the habit now of reusing the leaves until they barely coloured the hot water before they were discarded. She watched Mr Frean from the corner of her eye as she prepared the beverage, her heart sinking as she observed the sombre expression on his face.

'So, how can I help you?' she asked, passing him a cup of tea and sitting down opposite him.

George Frean raised a ponderous eyebrow. 'We need to discuss the future, Rose,' he said gravely.

'Oh, it's all taken care of. We're going to turn the parlour into a bedroom,' she told him, hoping he thought she sounded bubbling with enthusiasm. 'Some of the men are going to do it on Sunday, and carry father down. It'll be so good for him to be out of the bedroom after all this time. And the dining-room will become his office. We're going to bring everything up from his *old* office so that he can run the business from here,' she concluded with a satisfied smile.

Mr Frean sat back awkwardly in his chair. 'The manager of the powdermills needs to be on site, you know that, Rose.'

She felt her stomach contract as she nodded with fading confidence. 'Yes, I know, so I'm going to order an invalid carriage,' she announced, though she didn't add that she had no idea how she was going to pay for it. 'And if Polly — that's the mare that pulls the dog-cart — is too big, we'll sell her and buy a smaller horse that can pull either. So father will be able to get over the entire site, wherever he's needed.'

She stopped as Mr Frean lifted his hand in a gesture of reluctance. 'I'm sorry, Rose. I have no doubt that you would make any measures you took work admirably. But I'm afraid it just wouldn't be enough.'

Rose blinked at him, a slick of cold, clammy sweat oozing down her back. 'B-but . . . ' she stammered.

'I really am sorry,' the older man sighed, the lines on his face deepening. 'I know you well enough, Rose. I'm sure you'd make everything work superbly. But you'd be relying too much on the other men. While they were running back and forth here, they wouldn't be doing their own jobs. It is your father's responsibility to inspect the site *personally* all the time, and with the best will in the world, he couldn't do so from an invalid carriage. He'd need a couple of men to lift him in and out of the thing all the time, and that would cost the company time and money it really can't afford. And I know we have an agent as well, but you know as well as I do that your father often has to visit the mines and quarries himself, and that would be impossible.'

Rose had listened, her heart thudding hard. 'I'm sure father could manage,' she protested in desperation. 'I could help him. I could—'

'Rose.' He reached out and squeezed her arm. 'No matter what answers you come up with, they'll never provide a proper solution. But even if they could, I'm afraid I find . . . ' His face twisted with embarrassment and his eyes searched into hers. 'I don't quite know how to put this, but . . . Since his accident, Henry seems a different man. He's made some wrong decisions with regard to the business. Left other matters unresolved. I-I really haven't come to this conclusion lightly but I'm going to have to ask your father to leave my employment.'

Rose lowered her eyes. Stunned. Leave Cherrybrook? She couldn't believe it. Couldn't *comprehend* the notion of leaving what had been her home for as long as she could remember. She'd seen the anguished expression on Mr Frean's face as he spoke, anticipated what he was going to say, and yet his words were too awful to contemplate. Her senses reeled away from her, and she only managed to hold onto them by some tenuous thread.

Mr Frean coughed gently, his heart breaking for this vibrant child he almost looked upon as his own. 'I can offer a month's notice,' he managed to speak through the enormous lump that had suddenly swelled in his gullet. 'But I've had to stop your father's wages with immediate effect. However, I will be giving you a hundred pounds. Not company money but out of my own pocket. As a token of my esteem for your father and his hard work and loyalty over the years.'

Rose could see the concern in his eyes. Mr Frean was a good man. She appreciated his integrity — and his generosity in the circumstances. A hundred pounds. It might sound a handsome sum, but she'd already worked out it would take more than that to clear their debts, and that was without any rent to find, let alone paying for Gospel's keep.

She slowly stirred the contents of her cup for a second time. She must find it within herself to remain dignified. Not to allow George Frean to guess at their dire financial straits, even though she didn't know which way to turn.

'Thank you,' she answered, though her voice was small. 'That's most kind of you. I'll start looking for somewhere else to live straight away.'

'Unfortunately, I believe you have no relations who might take you in,' he said gravely. 'Is there really no one?'

'No, there isn't.' Rose straightened her shoulders. 'But I'm sure we'll manage. You've been most kind. But . . . have you told father?' she asked in dismay.

Mr Frean looked at her askew. 'I'm afraid I didn't have the courage. And I thought perhaps it would be better coming from you.'

Rose paused. Gave an almost imperceptible nod of her head. 'I'm sure you're right.'

'Well, I must be off.' He rose to his feet, clearly relieved the difficult interview was over. 'But, I really am so sorry, Rose. I'll miss you both. But perhaps we can keep in touch.'

'Yes. And I do understand it's not your fault.'

'Thank you.' He sniffed slightly as he wriggled into his overcoat. 'I'll see myself out.'

And he was gone, leaving Rose alone in the kitchen. She rested her elbows on the table and dropped her head into her hands. She realised with mild surprise that she was quite calm, not even shaking now. Numbed by shock, she supposed. She must make plans, decide on the most advantageous way to use the money which her pride would have refused under other circumstances. But first — and God alone knew how — she must break the bitter news to her father.

* * *

'So, how much did you say the rent would be?' she demanded as her eyes swept over the lowly cottage which clearly needed a thorough clean!

The young clerk to the duke's estate office fingered his hat nervously. He really didn't know how to deal with this *lady* who'd come enquiring into Tavistock's humble Westbridge cottages which had been built for the town's workforce twenty-five years ago. They were of sturdy stone construction, and stood in neat rows beside the fast-flowing River Tavy. Each dwelling had two downstairs rooms and three small bedrooms. Outside was a garden with an earth-privy, a pigsty and a shared standpipe. Quite a palace for its working class tenants, many of them miners, quarrymen or foundry-workers, even though ten people sometimes lived in one crowded cottage. Respectable enough citizens, most of them, mind. But this young *lady* — for she dressed as one, spoke like one despite her local accent, and certainly *behaved* like one — what on earth was she doing seeking accommodation in a workman's cottage? The lad was quite flummoxed, and she was so lovely, he was almost falling over his own feet. When she turned her dazzling eyes on him, his heart quite definitely stopped.

'Er, one shilling and sixpence a week, this one, miss,' he babbled. 'Payable two week in advance.'

'Ah,' the beautiful girl replied phlegmatically. 'It is a little damp.'

'Oh, 'twill be fine with the range going,' he suggested, trying to be helpful. Then it dawned on him that she was probably looking on someone else's behalf. A respected servant who was retiring, perhaps. Yes, that must be it. 'There's a nice little garden,' he went on. 'Big enough to grow some flowers and vegetables . . . for whoever . . .'

'Yes. I saw. It could all be made quite presentable. I'll call into the office in a day or two to let you know my decision.'

'I wouldn't leave it that long if I was you. 'Tis the only one up for rent, and they'm usually snapped up that quick.'

'I'm sure as you can hold onto it for me.' She smiled winsomely, casting her spell more tightly about him. 'Now, would you happen to know anywhere I can keep a horse? Not a livery stable, but a field, for he's a spirited animal and needs to be able to run free. With somewhere I can bring him in at night when it's cold.'

The clerk gulped in astonishment. First this cottage, and now a horse! He'd never before met anyone like this captivating young woman. He was convinced he'd remember her for the rest of his days!

* * *

Rose's head was spinning with calculations as Gospel romped up the soaring hill onto the moor. One shilling and sixpence a week for the cottage and, unbelievably in her opinion, two and threepence for a field and a stable just outside the town. Food and fuel on top of that, candles and the occasional extra expense such as shoe repairs or medicines. Having paid off every single creditor with Mr Frean's generous gift, including the overdraft at the bank, scarcely thirty pounds remained. There was still an invalid chair to purchase, not the pony-drawn carriage she had originally planned, but a cheaper bath-chair that could be pushed on the more even surface of Tavistock's streets. The solution to the problem was, of course, quite simple. She would acquire a position, and the three of them — for Florrie was both indispensable and an integral member of the family — could live quite comfortably in the little cottage.

Feeling rather satisfied and even a little excited at the prospect of a new life, she gave Gospel his head and they streaked along the road across the moor. She would miss living in the centre of Dartmoor where it was at its bleakest yet most breathtaking. But by keeping Gospel, within minutes she'd be off and enjoying its vastness, as she was now. She could still visit her friends, the workers and their families at the powdermills, and, of course, Molly.

Her dear friend as yet knew nothing of her present circumstances. It was early March. The recent snow had melted, and though the moor wasn't cloaked in mist, it was a miserable yet mild afternoon. Rose couldn't stay long, but she had time to visit Molly and still be home before darkness closed in.

She passed the recently opened quarry at Merrivale. The business was experiencing some teething problems, but was nevertheless a welcome addition to the powdermills' customer list. Rose's mouth thinned to a fine line. It really didn't matter any more, did it? She gritted her teeth against the tears that threatened to choke her. Her world had come tumbling down, but she would *not* be beaten, and she flicked her head as she turned Gospel off the road at Rundlestone and headed towards Princetown. As they crossed over the tunnel that led beneath the road from the prison lands to the dreaded quarry, the memory flashed through her brain of the ugly incident she'd become embroiled in there at the end of the previous summer. It all seemed so long ago, so insignificant when she considered the fateful events that had overtaken her life since.

She deposited Gospel with Ned Cornish, who gave a churlish sneer when she pressed a penny into his greedy palm rather than the usual silver sixpence. It was months since last he had clapped eyes on her graceful figure that caused the crotch of his trousers to strain, though he had of course heard of her father's misfortune. The explosion at the powdermills had been the talk of Princetown for weeks. He watched Rose hurry down the road in the direction of the prison. If only matters would become *really* desperate for her, he mused malevolently, he could offer her some sort of solace, for his bed was always warm . . .

She found Molly, her mother and little Phillip proudly sitting by the glowing fire in the sitting-room of their home in the new warders' block, one of the first families to move in since the building wasn't entirely finished yet. A mug of weak, black tea was at once thrust into Rose's hands. She'd always hated the drink served like that, but now she hardly noticed, since she, too, had become accustomed to re-using tea leaves over again and doing without milk and sugar. The liquid was hot and wet, and she was thankful for that.

'How's your poor father?' Mrs Cartwright asked with genuine sympathy.

'He's quite well in himself, thank you,' Rose lied, as ever since she'd broken the news to Henry that they would have to leave Cherrybrook, he had . . . *shrivelled* was the best way to describe it. 'But,' she hesitated, girding up the courage to sound quite cheerful, 'he's decided to retire from his work.' Her eyes caught Molly's quizzical gaze, and she knew at once that her friend could see straight through the deception. 'I've found a nice little cottage in Tavistock for us to live in. With Florrie, of course. It'll be good for father to be in a town with lots of things going on. He can go for walks alongside the canal. At least, we can push him in a bath-chair.' She glanced up, smiling broadly, and got to her feet. 'I just thought I'd let you know. I'll still be able to come and see you, mind. I've somewhere to keep Gospel, too, you see. Thank you for the tea, Mrs Cartwright. I'll . . . I'll see you soon.'

Her spirit dropped down inside her as Molly sprang to her side. 'I'll come with you, Rose,' she announced, grasping a worn coat from the peg by the door.

Rose was aware of the blood pumping through her veins as Molly followed her down the steps to the street, and she was relieved to be able to change the subject. 'You must be so happy to be in your new home at last,' she said.

'Oh, yes. With father being a Principal Warder, we were almost the first to move in.'

'I'm so pleased for you all,' Rose answered, but her words were flat and disinterested. 'And how's Annie getting on?'

But Molly glanced at her sideways as they walked up the street arm in arm. 'I knows when you'm not telling the truth, Rose.'

Rose's mouth screwed into a pout, but it was no good. They'd been friends for too long.

'It is the truth,' she muttered. 'Only . . . Please, Molly, I beg you not to tell anyone, but . . . Father never made any financial plans for his old age. He expected to go on working for years more . . .'

Her voice was ragged now with despondency, and Molly squeezed her arm tightly. 'Of course. No one expects . . . So, what you means is,' she said gently, 'you've no money.'

Rose threw up her head. 'Not quite. We do have *some* money.' Which wasn't a lie. Twenty-eight pounds eleven shillings and ninepence three farthings, to be precise. 'But if I want to keep Gospel, I'll need to find a position.'

The silence that followed cut into Rose's heart like a spear, and then Molly's incredulous face dissolved in laughter. '*You*, Rose!' she spluttered helplessly. 'A position!'

Rose's eyes snapped with offence. 'What's so funny about that? I'm not afraid of hard work, you know!'

'Oh, yes, I know that,' Molly agreed, struggling to control her giggles. 'You'm my best friend and I loves you dearly, but I cas'n see you buttoning your lip like you has to if you has a *position*!'

'I guess I'll have to learn,' Rose grimaced. 'But we *will* always be best friends, won't we? No matter what happens?'

'Of course! And I'll keep you up to date with all the local gossip. I'll even tell you what's been happening with your convict!' she teased lightly.

'My *convict*?' Rose gawped at her in bewilderment. 'What d'you mean?'

'Oh, 'twere back along, but you must remember! He saved father from being attacked, and then *you* saved *him*, cuz the guards thought as 'twere him.'

'Oh, yes, I do remember something,' Rose muttered vaguely, for as far as she was concerned, it was a nasty incident she'd rather forget.

'Well,' Molly went on, 'apparently, shortly afterwards, he were set upon by some of the inmates cuz of it. 'Tis not what you does, protect a warder. Father's in charge of him, see. Been giving him as many marks as he can towards his ticket of leave, so as he'll be released early. 'Tis cuz he's strong and works hard. Swears he's innocent, and that he can prove it. Can you imagine that, Rosie? Seems quite educated, father says. Does as he's telt, and keeps to hissel. 'Tis why he's not popular with other prisoners. Beat up quite bad, he were.'

'Poor fellow,' Rose sighed. She supposed she should feel some sympathy, but she had far more pressing concerns just now. Besides, the prisoner wouldn't be the first to claim he was innocent. Rose knew that if Molly's father had a penny for every time he'd heard such a thing, he'd be a very rich man indeed!

CHAPTER EIGHT

'We *will* be happy there, father, I *promise* you,' Rose said tenderly, her voice torn with emotion as she stroked Henry's hand. His faded eyes had misted over as he stared blindly into the empty bedroom grate, something he had spent more and more time doing since she had told him of George Frean's decision a few days ago now. It worried her more than anything, for what did he see there? The flames that once would have burned brightly against the black cast iron, or the life when he could walk and run, and keep up with men half his age?

He turned his head to her, his face radiant with some quiet serenity that belied the moisture in his eyes. 'How could I be anything but happy with you, my dearest child?' he whispered, and Rose thought she would gag on the sorrow in her throat. This was her father, always so strong, so vibrant, reduced to a feeble wreck, and it was just so *unfair*.

'I won't be there all the time,' she told him. 'I'll have to find myself a position. But Florrie will be there, so it'll be just like living here really. Better, in fact, because you'll have your bed in the nice, warm front kitchen, and you won't be lonely like you are up here.'

She must have aroused his interest, for his expression sharpened. 'A job?'

'Yes. I've been looking in the *Tavistock Gazette*. There are two positions as governess advertised, both in the town. I'm going to write to them tonight.'

Henry nodded his approval, his mouth smiling wistfully. 'Who'd have thought it? My little princess going out to work?'

'I'll go into Princetown first thing in the morning to post them. And whilst I'm there, I'll have a word with the carrier. Find out how much he'll charge to take all our furniture to the cottage.'

'Furniture?'

'Well, yes. We'll have to decide what to leave behind, mind. There won't be room for all of it at the cottage.'

'Rose, dear, the furniture isn't ours to take.'

'What?' She blinked at him, the horrible, ever more familiar coldness creeping through her blood.

'Some of it is,' Henry answered, but the expression on his face told of his shame. 'Your pretty washstand and the matching stool, but I imagine you remember me buying them for you. My bureau, the rugs in each room. The grand-father clock. But everything else came with the house. Beds, wardrobes, the furniture in the parlour and dining-room, the kitchen table . . . The linen, the cutlery and crockery, all that sort of thing is ours, mind,' he added more cheerily. 'The lamps, the pictures on the walls, the china figurines. You'll be able to make this cottage you've found look quite lovely.'

Rose slowly lowered her eyes. It was just one more nail in the coffin of their shattered lives. Henry didn't know, but the handsome pictures, the china, had already gone to the pawnbrokers, and now she had learnt they didn't own most of what they *really* needed either. The essentials. Beds, for instance. She could manage on a home-made straw palliasse on the floor, but Florrie could hardly be expected . . . And Henry himself . . . Oh, it was just one more agony to cope with! Her tense lungs collapsed in a bitter sigh. The money they had left — now three shillings less since she'd paid the rent to secure the cottage — would have to cover at least two beds and the bath-chair, and anything else that they really could not do without. She had hoped to put aside most of the small sum for a rainy day, in an interest-bearing account, perhaps, to supplement her wages. And as yet, she didn't even *have* a position!

* * *

Rose stormed down the long front garden of the prestigious villa, anger burning in her heart. The mistress of the house had done her best to humiliate her. It hardly seem to matter that Rose could instruct her proposed charges in reading, writing, reckoning, history, geography and all the other subjects she considered most important.

'But since you would be teaching my *daughters*,' the haughty woman had questioned her, 'I assume you could pass on to them some of the more genteel skills, drawing and painting, for instance?'

'Yes, ma'am, I can paint and draw,' Rose replied, though how well was another matter, she thought grimly to herself.

'And can you teach singing and music? Play the pianoforte?'

Rose knew she stiffened. 'Sadly no, ma'am.'

'And do you speak French?'

'I'm afraid French was not something—'

'Is there *nothing* you can teach my girls, then? Not even needle-point and embroidery?'

Rose jerked up her head. Had she not been so desperate, she would have given this harridan the length of her tongue! But sewing, now that was something she excelled in.

'I design and make all my own clothes. There's nothing I can't do with a needle.'

'Then I suggest you look for a position as a dressmaker or a seamstress! Good day to you, Miss Maddiford! I believe you can find your own way out.'

'Oh, yes, ma'am! I believe I am quite capable of *something*!'

Rose had spun on her heel and flounced out of the room, deliberately leaving the door, and then the front door, wide open. She stalked along Plymouth Road, the anger emptying out of her and being replaced by tears of shame and confusion. Perhaps she just wasn't suited to working. But she *had* to find a job! There must be something she could do!

By the time she reached Bedford Square, her fury had calmed. She shouldn't expect her first interview to be a success. She'd managed to arrange the second for the same day immediately after lunch, so she took herself off to a bench in the churchyard to consume the bread and cheese she'd brought with her. The March wind had sharpened, snow-dust blowing in scudding circles, the sky leaden with yellow-tinged, smoky clouds. Winter was returning, and she felt it would break her spirit in two. But she *must* find the courage to soldier on, for the war had scarcely begun!

The second household couldn't have been more different. A frail young woman was sat next to a roaring fire, her two sons, aged eight and five, playing at her feet. Rose warmed to her at once. They took tea like old friends, the older boy chatting away to Rose, whilst the younger child found his way onto her knee and she slipped easily into inventing a word-game almost without realising it, while their mother looked on with a contented smile.

'You are heaven sent, Miss Maddiford, or may we call you Miss Rose?' she beamed. 'My health is not what it should be, and I believe you would be of such help to me.'

A welcoming glow tingled down to Rose's feet. She'd done it! And the little boys were delightful, bright, happy and interested. The world suddenly seemed a friendlier place.

'My husband and I had settled on a wage of three and sixpence a week, rising to four shillings after a year's satisfactory service. I do hope that will be acceptable. Payable at the end of each quarter, but we could advance you a little to begin with, if it will be of help.'

Rose felt her soul plummet like a bird shot dead in full flight. 'Three and sixpence,' she echoed tonelessly.

'Well, perhaps we could start at three and nine. If you wouldn't mind helping Nanny with her duties. She's too old to manage on her own now, but she's been with our family for so long — she was *my* nanny, you know — so we can't possibly dismiss her. You would have to share her room, I'm afraid, but it is very warm and comfortable. Now *do* say you'll accept the offer!'

Her words were pricks of ice in Rose's heart. There was nothing she would have loved more than to join this household. But three and nine would barely cover the rent and Gospel's livery. 'I'm afraid I cannot live in,' her voice quavered. 'You see, my father recently had a terrible accident that has left him paralysed, and as a result he has lost his position and the accommodation that went with it. We are about to move to one of the Westbridge cottages. Our housekeeper will come with us to care for him, but there are certain things that she cannot manage alone, so I must return each evening. And,' she looked up, and met the woman's sympathetic gaze, but would she understand? 'I have a horse. Not just any horse that I could easily sell on. He has a certain temperament . . . I fear it would mean having him put down, and I couldn't bear that. I have somewhere to keep him, but . . .'

Her face was a mask of taut muscles, matched by the compassion of the woman who had listened to her. 'Oh, my dear, I am so sorry to learn of your plight,' she said with deep feeling. 'If only we had space, I should willingly offer your father a home also, for I'm sure he is as amicable as yourself. As for your horse, I'm afraid we have no stables, either. Oh, dear. What a pity. But,' she said gently, 'I must warn you that *any* position as governess is bound to be live-in, you know.'

Rose lowered her eyes. 'Yes, of course. I-I hadn't really thought about it properly. I'm so sorry to have wasted your time.'

'Not at all. The boys and I have enjoyed your visit. Feel free to call upon us any time.'

As she walked back down the street, tears glistened in Rose's eyes. What a fool she'd been! A governess was a servant like any other, with a servant's wage supplemented by full board. Alone in the world, the position would have been ideal, but she had responsibilities. So where would they all end up? In the workhouse? She couldn't bear the thought! They'd only take her father, of course, and possibly Florrie if she couldn't find other employment, but male and female were strictly separated and they would never see each other again.

Rose shook her head. How could she even think of it? Perhaps she could set herself up as a dressmaker. But you needed time to establish a clientele, build up a business, *premises*, none of which she had. An *assistant*, then. It was only mid afternoon, but the snow-laden sky was growing darker by the minute. She should collect Polly and the dog-cart from where she'd stabled them for the day. She hadn't ridden Gospel into town since she could hardly attend an interview dressed in her riding habit, but she regretted not having his speed to convey her quickly home. But perhaps she might just have time to make some enquiries.

She drew a blank. Apprentice to a dressmaker with lodgings but no wages, or a shop assistant at a paltry salary. Oh, why wasn't she a man! She could have earned eight to ten shillings a week *labouring*, but as a woman, you received so little reward no matter how hard you worked! Perhaps she should . . . just find out about the workhouse.

The blood seemed to drain from her head as she dragged herself up Bannawell Street to the forbidding workhouse at the top. Her hand shook so violently she could scarcely knock on the intimidating wooden gates, one of which was finally opened by an even more menacing face that eyed her with hostility.

'Please,' Rose asked in a whisper, 'how does one get into the workhouse?'

'Apply to the Board. In Bedford Square,' the voice snapped. 'They won't take a fit young woman like you. Get yersen a job. Do some work!' And the toothless mouth, whether it was man or woman, Rose could not tell, broke into a jeering cackle.

'It's not for me, but for my father,' Rose blurted. 'He's paralysed, and—'

'I told 'ee. Apply to the Board. Won't take anyone unless they'm destitute. Nort but the clothes on yer back, and I doesn't mean *they* sort of clothes,' the face sneered, jabbing a finger at Rose's good coat. 'I means *rags*. Then maybies they'll take 'en.'

The gate closed with a crash, but not before Rose caught sight of two stooped figures shuffling past, clad in the drab fustian of the workhouse uniform. So degrading. Rose stood for a full minute, her own shoulders slumped. How could she have come to this? A feeble, anguished moan escaped from her lips, laced with anger and frustration. It wasn't in her to give in, but at this moment, she was so lost in defeatism that her blood seemed to have turned into water. She shut her eyes as memories of her past, happy life tortured her soul, and it was only the touch of a snowflake on her frosted cheek that sparked her brain to retrieve its grip on reality. Snow was beginning to fall, the vicious wind slicing at Rose's slender form. They were in for a snowstorm, and she had a long journey over treacherous terrain to reach home.

* * *

'Put your feet in that, young lady!' Florrie ordered, stirring a great spoonful of mustard into the bowl of hot water that she'd placed on the floor by Rose's chair. ''Tis a miracle you found your way home in that blizzard, and it coming on dark, and all. We had visions of finding you froze dead in the morning. Your poor father's been frit witless, as if he hasn't got enough to contend with!'

'Oh, Florrie, I'm so sorry you were worried,' Rose croaked. Her throat was raw from breathing in the icy wind that had ripped across Dartmoor and was still hammering at the windows of the house. 'But I know the moor like the back of my hand.'

'That's as maybe, but 'tis almost dark. You shouldn't have been so tardy!'

'Really, Florrie, I was perfectly safe.'

Nevertheless, she lowered her cold, wet feet gratefully into the water. Perfectly safe, indeed! It'd been an absolute nightmare and she'd been petrified, but she didn't want to alarm poor Florrie any more than she already had. She'd only reached half way up Pork Hill when the snow had begun to fall thick and fast, hell bent on smothering the earth beneath.

The further up onto the moor she went, the wilder the driving wind that whipped the snow into deep drifts and lashed mercilessly into Rose's face. Flakes collected on her eyelashes, and she had to keep dashing them away as she peered into the growing gloom. The wheels of the dog-cart kept getting stuck, and Rose had to climb down from the driving-seat to dig the snow away with her hands before the mare could pull the cart forward again. In the end, it was happening so often that Rose walked the rest of the way by Polly's side, her leather gloves so sodden and her fingers so numb that she could hardly feel what she was doing as she plunged them into the snow again and again. She would've been better off on foot, she'd thought ruefully, but at least the animal was company.

It was becoming more and more difficult to follow the road. Three attempts it took her to light the hurricane lamp, the gale extinguishing the flame each time she struck a match. When she finally got it lit, she'd stumbled on, holding it in one hand whilst the other held Polly's reins, sometimes stopping to lift it high and get her bearings. Merrivale Bridge, and then the occasional familiar farm or cottage so that even if she wasn't actually on the road itself, she was headed in the right direction.

At last, way across to the right, the unmistakable sight of the tiny gas lights glowing from the massive new prison block, row upon row of small cell windows, pinpricks in the shadows. Downhill and over the river at Two Bridges and the Saracen's Head. She was in two minds whether or not to stop there for the night, for she hadn't seen a soul for what must have been an hour, and was beginning to panic. But she wasn't so far from home now, and she knew how worried they would be. Surely she could make it from there? But Polly was tiring, pulling the sliding cart, Rose clicking her tongue, encouraging the poor animal. Desperate, soaked to the skin, snow on her shoulders, in her eyes and in her mouth, tears of fear and despair turning to frost on her cheeks. Somehow, she'd struggled on, and when the lights of Cherrybrook had come into view, she'd shouted aloud with relief.

'Hmm!' Florrie snorted, wrapping Rose in layers of warm blankets as she shivered in the chair. 'Well, I hope 'twas worthwhile, and you got yoursel a *position*!' she added, as if to say it was hardly worth risking one's life for in a blizzard!

Rose's eyes darted upwards. She said nothing, but Florrie tilted her double chin, and Rose knew she'd understood.

'Oh, well, never mind. Summat will turn up. Now, you get this inside you.' And she thrust a mug of steaming tea into Rose's shaking hands. 'I'll go upstairs and get you some dry clothes. Oh, this came for you this morning after you left.'

She dropped an envelope into Rose's lap and waddled out through the door. Rose slumped back in the chair, trying to relax and stop the painful tremors that rattled her teeth in her head. Every muscle ached viciously, and beneath it all lay the bitter gall of defeat. She sipped at the hot, black tea, feeling its warmth seeping into her flesh. Oh, that was good, but . . . what *was* she to do?

She picked up the envelope with her other hand. She prayed it wasn't another bill, something else her father had bought and never paid for. Her heart was soothed when she realised it was a private letter, and then tripped over itself when she saw it was from none other than Mr Charles Chadwick. Good Lord, she hadn't even given him a thought in weeks — months even — for it had been . . . when? About Christmas he'd written last, and she'd never bothered to reply. Now her eyes moved disinterestedly along the lines of writing, scarcely taking in their meaning. And then something stirred within her and she sat up and read the words a second time.

When Florrie came back into the kitchen, she was surprised to find Rose deep in concentration over the letter in her hand. When Rose finally lifted her head, there was a strange expression on her face Florrie couldn't quite fathom.

CHAPTER NINE

'Mr Chadwick!'

Rose's eyes stretched as she answered the knock on the front door. Her surprise was followed by an unfurling kernel of apprehension and then of excitement that tingled down to her fingertips. It was less than a week since she'd staggered home in the blizzard, dragging herself miles through the deepening snow and wondering if she'd survive. The following morning had dawned crisp and clear, the sun shining down in glittering ripples on the newly fallen snow and turning the landscape into a magical wonderland.

Rose's head had filled with a clarity as sharp as the new day, and she'd re-read Charles Chadwick's letter with a fresh heart. It was concerned and caring, and full of tender love for her. Had she misjudged him, dismissed his affections simply because he didn't share all her views on life? Surely the most loving of spouses must disagree on something! And so she had taken up her pen.

She must word the letter carefully. Their impecunious state must not be immediately apparent. After all, she didn't want him to think she was marrying him for his money. Besides, it wouldn't altogether be true. She'd agonised long and hard over his original proposal. He was respectable, attentive, not unattractive, and appreciated her love of Dartmoor. Most importantly, he liked to ride. Surely the passion she'd spoken of to her father would come in time? And if she closed her eyes and imagined poor Henry wasting away in the workhouse, well, she was positive she would make Mr Chadwick a good wife!

And now here he was, standing on the doorstep at ten o'clock in the morning, his eyes brilliant with delight. 'Oh, my dearest Rose,' his voice sang out like a bird's. Stepping inside, he removed his hat and placed it on the hall-stand, then took her hands in his gloved ones. He lifted them to his lips, kissing each in turn, not in a sensuous manner, but in a boyish gesture of pure joy. It was in such contrast to the restrained conduct she'd known from him during his courtship the previous autumn that it chased away all Rose's doubts.

'Oh, my dear, I couldn't keep away for a moment!' Charles told her, his words falling over themselves. 'I received your letter the day before yesterday. And I thought, surely I could get here as quickly as a letter? So I caught the morning train from Paddington yesterday and arrived in Tavistock at six o'clock last night. But I could find no cab willing to venture so far onto the moor in the dark, so here I am now! I telegraphed ahead to the Duchy Hotel, and we dropped off my baggage there on the way. So, I trust my presence would not inconvenience you today?'

His eyebrows had drawn together in such earnest that Rose chuckled aloud. His unexpected arrival had whipped away the misery that had stagnated in the household all winter, and it had left Rose breathless. Oh, surely she had made the right decision!

'Oh, Mr Chadwick, I am *truly* delighted to see you!' she smiled, the strength of her own feelings confounding her. 'Do come in! To the kitchen, if you don't mind. Florrie — Mrs Bennett — and I have such a lot to do caring for father that we more or less live in there.'

The excuse cast but a fleeting shadow in her conscience and she led her visitor down the hallway. His expression shone with that almost foolish state of a man enraptured by love. Kitchen? Just now, he would have followed her to a hole in the ground!

'Rose, seeing as we are to be married,' he said hesitantly, 'could you not call me by my given name?'

The word 'married' made Rose's heart flip over in her chest. Charles's usual confidence seemed to have forsaken him, which she found even more endearing. He really did seem a different person from the suitor she had deliberated over for so long, and she began to curse herself for putting off her decision, for it would have saved her so much heartache.

She turned to face him, her eyes smiling their warm, lavender blue. 'Charles,' she repeated. And before her brain gave her time to consider, she raised herself on tiptoe, and Charles, so naturally, brought his mouth softly down to meet hers. The unfamiliar sensation of someone else's lips on hers rippled down to her stomach, and when they finally parted and she sank her weight back onto her heels, she gazed up at him, wide-eyed. He was smiling back at her, his eyes skittering about her face as if trying to imprint indelibly in his mind every detail of their first kiss.

'Er . . . will you have some tea?' she stuttered. 'Or coffee, if we have any. We've had heavy snow. It's almost melted now, as you see, but I haven't been able to go into Princetown to shop.' Not the real reason, of course, but a valid enough excuse.

'Thank you, tea would be fine.'

'Then won't you sit down? Charles?' she added with a merry lift of her eyebrows. 'Florrie's upstairs,' she went on as he obediently settled himself in a chair, 'seeing to father, so we can have a moment or two to ourselves.'

Charles's face at once sobered. 'Your poor father,' he stated gravely. 'I really can't imagine how he must feel.'

Rose bowed her head, biting her lip at the sudden, overwhelming desire to cry. Perhaps, after all these months of having to be so strong, the relief of having someone to turn to at last was letting the strain flow out of her. And Charles was being so kind that she was beginning to curse herself for hesitating so long.

She gulped down her tears. 'Yes, it's affected him greatly. But I'm sure it'll help him tremendously when he can get out and about again.'

'And to know that his beautiful daughter is to be married to a man who adores her!' Charles's shining eyes met hers across the table.

Rose averted her gaze. 'I haven't told him yet,' she faltered. 'I thought it was best to await your definite reply first.'

'Well, shall we go up, then? If you don't think he'll mind my presence in his bed chamber? When Mrs Bennett has finished, of course. But in the meantime . . .'

He stood up, and coming around to Rose, drew a small package from his pocket. She knew what was coming, and her heart reared away. This was the moment. There would be no going back, and she was inwardly bracing her daunted spirit.

Charles took her trembling left hand, and slid the exquisite ring onto her slender third finger. She felt the breath leave her body. Not so much at the beauty of the piece, but at what it meant.

'A diamond for my eternal love, and two sapphires to match your eyes. Though yours have a hint of violet in them no jewel could ever rival.'

He was studying her with an unsettling intensity that forced her to look away and turn her attention to the ring. 'Oh, Charles, it's beautiful. Thank you so much.'

'It is but a token of my love. And in return, I wish us to be married as soon as possible.' Rose glanced up at the change in his voice. It was somehow less passionate, efficient, and sent misgivings wavering through her breast. But he was right. There were many plans to be made.

'I stayed last night at the Bedford Hotel,' Charles went on, 'and got talking to some gentlemen. They told me of a property near Princetown called Fencott Place which is up for sale. Built by a wealthy friend of your Sir Thomas Tyrwhitt, apparently. From what these gentlemen said, I think it would suit our needs adequately. It has several bedrooms, servants' attic, and enough space for your father to have a bedroom and a dayroom on the ground floor. I imagine it will be your wish that he lives with us? Shall we go and have a look at it later on? There's some land available with it to be leased from the Duchy, so there'll be plenty of room for that monstrous horse of yours, and a stable-block. So, what do you say?'

Rose's mouth broadened into a joyous grin. Oh, it seemed the answer to her prayers!

'Oh, Charles! Are you sure?'

'Well, I knew you'd want to remain living on the moor,' he attempted to shrug, but couldn't stop his lips curving upwards. 'I would ask that you accompany me to London on occasion, but not every time I have to go. I wish that we could live there permanently, but I appreciate it wouldn't suit you, and that you'll want to be near to your father in his condition. But you will allow me to show off my lovely young wife to my colleagues in London just occasionally, I trust?'

His eyes were dancing roguishly, and the colour blushed into Rose's cheeks. 'We . . . you can afford all this?' she managed to croak before blurting out shamefully, 'I have no dowry, no money to bring into our marriage, you know.'

Charles merely shook his head. 'What you will bring into our marriage is priceless. And I'm a rich man. And I've never had a better reason to spend some of my money. I want you to have the most beautiful dress for your wedding. *Our* wedding.' He'd taken her hands again, kissing them reverently, and was clearly about to take her in his arms when Florrie pushed her way into the room, struggling with a heavy bowl of dirty water.

'Oh, Mr Chadwick, what on earth do you be doing yere?' she mumbled in surprise.

'Rose has agreed to marry me!' Charles crowed. 'Isn't that wonderful, Mrs Bennett?'

Rose felt the doubt sear into her heart at the shuttered look that came across Florrie's face.

* * *

'Charles, I should be grateful if you would allow my daughter and myself a few moments alone,' Henry said five minutes later, his voice a little dry, Rose considered. 'Mrs Bennett will make you comfortable downstairs.'

'Of course. I understand.' Charles smiled broadly across at Rose, a smile that she returned with enthusiasm. She listened as he tripped lightly down the stairs, and then she sat down on the edge of the bed, her mouth still stretched in a grin.

'Well, father?'

Henry drew in his breath. 'Rose, I'm not happy about this.'

The jubilation slid from her face. 'Father?' she frowned.

Henry pursed his lips. 'Why this sudden change of heart? It's because of our changed circumstances, isn't it? Without Mr Chadwick's money, we'll be penniless, or at best, living hand to mouth. But I won't have you marrying someone you don't love because of me. You must do what is right for *you*. You should take the position with that nice family in Tavistock if it's still available.'

Rose met his gaze for a moment, chewing on her fingernail. 'Yes, it's true,' she agreed, 'that our changed circumstances as you put it made me reconsider. And you know, father, I'm *glad*! You know how hard I found it to turn Charles down before. How I just couldn't make up my mind. Well, this has all just made me realise my true feelings. I can't tell you how happy it made me to find Charles on the doorstep just now! I really am doing the right thing, I'm sure of it!'

But Henry was looking at her from under fiercely swooped eyebrows. 'So what happened to that passion you spoke about so eloquently not so long ago? What happened to *love*?'

'Oh, I do believe I love Charles,' she assured him, vigorously nodding her head. 'Especially now I can see things in their proper perspective. I'll make him a good wife, and you can see how he is devoted to me. Fencott Place will be a wonderful home for us, just you wait and see!'

'There's more to marriage than a wonderful home,' Henry persisted, his tone more solemn than Rose had ever known. 'Friendship, trust. And have you . . . thought about children?'

His voice had become oddly husky, but Rose turned his wariness aside. 'Oh, yes! I should love to have children! And you'll be their beloved grandfather!'

Henry puffed out his cheeks with a reluctant sigh. 'Well, you're twenty-one, so I can't stop you. But I do hope you know what you're doing! I only want what's best for you, my child, you know that.'

'I know you do!' She flung her arms about his neck, hugging him tightly. 'We'll all be so happy, I'm sure we will!'

Henry patted her back, his pale eyes misted. He prayed to God she was right!

* * *

'Oh, Rosie, 'tis proper lovely!' Molly breathed, twisting this way and that on the seat of the wagon in order to take in every detail of the building that was Fencott Place. 'I've seen it many times afore from a distance, but you cas'n see it properly cuz of the wall and the trees. And 'tis so big!'

'Well, you'll see every inch of it in a minute!' Rose laughed, dangling the keys in front of her friend's nose.

She climbed down from the wagon so swiftly that her feet were on the ground before Joe Tyler had jumped down from the other side and come round to offer her his hand. She waited patiently while Joe helped Molly down from the high seat instead, then looked up, just in time to catch the blush in Molly's cheeks.

For some strange reason she couldn't herself fathom, Rose whipped about and stood with her back to them, feasting her eyes instead on the house that was to be her marital home. It was a mild spring day, a sea of daffodils against the dressed-stone walls bobbing their heads in the light breeze. Rose's heart gave a jerk as Molly appeared at her shoulder, and driving her qualms aside, she linked her arm through Molly's as they waltzed up to the double front door.

'This hallway's bigger than the whole of our flat!' Molly gasped as they stepped inside. 'Oh, Rose, you'm so lucky! Mr Chadwick must be so rich! A real gentleman! I told you you should marry 'en, didn't I? Oh, I be that pleased for you!'

She enfolded Rose in her arms, dancing her round in circles until Rose was helpless with laughter. Oh, *of course* Molly was right! The uncertain figure of Joe standing in the doorway caught her eye, and she waved playfully at him.

'Come on in, Joe! There's only us three here, so wander round wherever you please. Go and have a look at the stables if you like.'

Joe's crystal blue eyes shone with admiration. 'Thanks, Rose, I will. But first, where would you like me to put the things you've brought over?'

They spent an hour or so wandering about the house, Rose making mental notes as to what would be needed to ready it for her future life with Charles, while Molly marvelled at just about everything she saw.

'I think I'd lose myself in a place like this!' she exclaimed. 'You'll need so much to fill it!'

'Charles is sending down some furniture from his London house. And once we have some beds, father and Florrie and I can move in. Charles has told me to buy everything else I want down here, as he's so busy arranging his affairs in London so that he can have a complete fortnight down here for the wedding.'

'And when is the big day?'

'First week in June.'

'And doesn't you miss him, with him being so far away?'

Rose felt her heart jolt. She did miss Charles. But did she miss him as much as she should?

'Of course,' she said, but as much to answer herself as Molly. 'But there's so many exciting things to do in such a short time that I really don't get a chance to miss him too much. And he'll be coming down for a few days soon. Staying at the Duchy Hotel, of course.'

''Twould be bad luck otherwise!' Molly grinned.

Rose frowned, not quite understanding, and a shudder of unease shot down her spine. 'About time we were going back,' she announced, suddenly wanting to close the subject. It had been wonderful, sharing her joy in the house with her dear friend. And there was something she would ask Molly, but not yet. She wanted Molly to get used to being at Fencott Place first. Besides, she must ask Charles's approval, though she was sure he would agree.

When Rose had locked up and they went outside again, Joe was waiting patiently, sitting up on the wagon, long legs dangling casually as he enjoyed his free Sunday afternoon. After all, he had nothing better to do, and just now he was finding it increasingly pleasant to be in the company of one young lady in particular, even if they had known each other since childhood.

As the two girls came towards him, Joe hopped down from the wagon and took Molly's hand to help her climb back up. Rose glimpsed the look that passed between them as they stood so close to each other, almost as if they were about to kiss.

A spasm of pain twitched at her lips. The fondness between the couple appeared so natural. Wasn't that what Rose had once felt, that she wanted to marry someone she felt so at ease with? Someone more like Joe, for example?

And now she was to marry Charles Chadwick.

CHAPTER TEN

Rose stood, and trembled, on the threshold of Princetown Chapel, her face so pale that her skin had taken on the patina of ivory to match the glorious silk gown that clung about her slender figure. The organist deftly slipped from the subdued background medley into the rousing wedding march that resounded like thunder in Rose's head. Her heart was crashing painfully in her chest and all she wanted was to pick up the hem of the splendid dress and flee. But a multitude of awestruck eyes had turned upon her, the entire community from the powdermills and many people from Princetown filling both sides of the church.

Charles had invited a mere handful of acquaintances from London to witness his marriage to this country bumpkin. Moreover, the church had been seriously damaged by fire several years previously, and being just a chapel-at-ease, lack of funds meant that it had only been partly restored. Charles had protested that they should be married in Tavistock church instead. But Rose was adamant that her friends would find it difficult to travel so far, and Charles hadn't been able to refuse her pleas, even if he was reluctant to allow his own guests to see him married in a burnt-out shell, as he put it. But if they had questioned his sanity over his choice of bride, the instant they gazed on her ethereal beauty, they too fell under her spell. She was resplendent, and there was no man present who could honestly claim he wasn't a little envious of Charles Chadwick that day.

Rose squared her shoulders and glanced up at the bursting pride on George Frean's face. She smiled faintly, her cheeks frosted, as he walked her down the aisle. He must have sensed her nervousness, as he patted her hand as it rested in the crook of his arm. Every nerve in her body quivered, but surely every bride had cold feet at the last moment? The question tore at her brain for one final time, and was then answered as her father was wheeled forward in his spanking-new invalid chair to be at her side at the altar to give her away. He would want for nothing. Would live out his life, crippled but in luxury, and that was all Rose needed.

The thought steadied her. Henry was smiling up at her, though she could see tears welling in his eyes. Rose shot him her most confident glance, and then as her gaze fell upon the groom, the tense knot in her chest uncurled. Charles's adoring eyes were riveted on her, his face not so much smiling as stunned, as if she had taken the breath from him. He looked so handsome, his chestnut hair brushed until it shone, his figure trim in its grey morning-suit, every inch of him overflowing with obvious devotion to his radiant bride. Rose dipped her head demurely, her long lashes resting for a moment on her pearly cheeks in which a flaming crimson was starting to burn. Charles Chadwick loved her passionately, and if she didn't return his feelings with quite such intensity, there was still enough love between them to make a happy marriage.

Her voice lodged in her throat as she made her vows. Beside her, Charles's words were low and pronounced with reverence. As he placed the ring on her finger, she noted with some sort of comforting contentment that his hands, too, were shaking. They moved to the vestry where after some light banter with the vicar, Rose signed her single name for the last time.

The organ struck up once again as they walked back down the aisle arm in arm, and when they stepped outside, the bells were pealing vigorously from the smoke-blackened tower. A sea of beaming faces then, guests shaking the groom's hand, and who could not resist kissing the cheek of the heavenly bride? As they climbed into the ornate open carriage pulled by two dapple-grey horses, Rose turned to the crowd. Her violet blue eyes searched out her father, but he was lost to her in the milling throng. Instead her gaze landed upon Molly's grinning face, Joe beside her, waving his hat merrily at the bride, his other arm around the pretty girl at his side. And Rose felt the thorn prick her heart at their happiness.

The wedding breakfast was held at the marital home. A string quartet played softly in the corner of the drawing-room, and a sumptuous meal was set out in the dining-room. Rose sat at the table, glowing modestly between her husband and her father. On Henry's other side, Mrs Frean was warm elegance personified, with Mr Frean on her right. Rose was acquainted with no one else, as they were all friends of Charles's from London. All of them polite, and most of them not unfriendly, the meal passed quite pleasantly and Rose felt her uneasiness melt away. She held her own in the conversation, aware of Charles's approval beside her, and she felt proud that she had pleased him.

She only wished that Florrie and Molly and Joe had been present. She had invited them, but they'd declined, preferring to enjoy the festivities in the hired marquee in the garden. Food was laid out on three trestle tables, cider on tap from barrels at one end, and after the feast, a little band of two fiddlers and a drummer played their lively tunes. Soon the marquee was bursting with merriment. Raucous voices were raised in enjoyment as dancers cavorted up and down until cheeks were flushed in giddy delight.

The sedate meal in the house was over, and Charles stood up, offering Rose his arm. She linked her hand through the crook of his elbow, her fingers tingling with excitement. Yes, she was very happy. She began to relax as they led Charles's guests out into the grounds which had been hastily knocked into shape by the elderly part-time gardener and his boy, who along with a live-in housekeeper-cum-cook and a housemaid, Charles had instructed Rose to employ, since Florrie was now to devote her entire time to Henry. To Rose's amusement, Charles was playing lord of the manor to the workers who doffed their caps at him, for he was clearly unused to mixing with the working classes on a social basis.

'Congratulations, Miss Rose!' Noah Roach waved gaily as he went back inside the marquee, evidently taking full advantage of the free alcohol.

Rose shook her head with a chuckle, and lifted her jubilant face to her husband. 'Oh, Charles, would you mind very much if I spent a little time with all the people in the marquee? I've known them all so long . . .'

Charles's eyes softened as he gazed at her. 'How can I refuse you anything, my darling?' he breathed. 'But don't be too long.'

'Please excuse me,' she said aloud, turning to the ladies and gentlemen who accompanied them. 'I must just thank our other guests for coming.' And with a quick, affectionate kiss on Charles's cheek, the naturalness of which surprised even herself, she skipped off towards the marquee.

The distinctive odour of canvas wreathed inside her nostrils, and all at once she was hailed by the people she had lived among for so many years. A cry went up, toasting her name and wishing her well before the music started up again with a jolly reel. The merrymakers at once returned to prancing up and down to the jocund rhythms, and Rose's head spun with the jovial faces that flashed across her vision.

'Oh, Rose!' Molly's eyes were as brilliant as stars as she tugged on Rose's sleeve. 'This is such fun! And you looks wonderful!'

'And would your husband mind if I asked you to dance?'

Joe's face was split in a carefree grin, and Rose responded with a whoop of glee. In an instant, she was swirling dizzily amongst the revellers, her head thrown back with the joy of the dance. Joe whisked her all the way round the circle before the music came to a noisy halt, and she scampered breathlessly to Charles's side as he came in through the flapping canvas entrance.

'Shall we join in?' she panted playfully.

'I don't think so,' Charles smiled down at her like an indulgent father.

Rose looked up at him, her eyes still sparkling, as he led her from the marquee and she waved back over her shoulder.

'Really, Rose.' Charles bent to whisper in her ear. 'Could you not show a little more decorum? Thank goodness my visitors couldn't see you.'

Rose's eyes snapped. 'Just because I'm married to you, doesn't mean I'm going to turn my back on my friends, you know!'

Charles gave a short laugh. 'I should hope not! But do remember that acquaintances can be most useful in business, and we ought not to offend. You've had your jig, so could you possibly behave now? At least until *my* guests have departed, which won't be long. *Please*, Rose!' he begged, fingering a curling ebony tendril that had loosened from the pearl combs in her hair.

She pulled a mocking grimace. 'All right. But only if you promise to dance with me afterwards until your feet hurt!'

'I promise!' he grinned like a schoolboy. 'And woe betide any other man who tries to take you from me!'

He kept to his word, though his constrained stance was hardly suited to country dancing. By the time the last workers and their families had left for their little cottages on the moor, and the hired caterers had packed everything into the carts that had trundled away down the drive, the bride and groom were quite exhausted. Darkness was falling, the quiet of the moorland dusk a welcome relief after the hectic revelries of the day.

'I think I'll retire now,' Henry announced as they all sat out on the terrace, enjoying the evening air.

'Of course, Mr Henry.' Florrie at once jumped to attention.

'Goodnight, father!' Rose leapt to her feet and bent to hug Henry tightly. 'Hasn't it been a wonderful day?'

'It certainly has, my dearest child.' In her own exhilaration, Rose didn't notice the catch in his voice. When he drew away, he shook hands with Charles who seemed glued to her side. 'Congratulations,' Henry said stiffly. 'You will . . . take *care* of my daughter, won't you?'

'Naturally.'

Rose frowned. Was there some tension between the two men? But then Florrie clamped her arms about her, rotund cheeks wobbling as she openly wept. Rose pulled back, laughing lightly.

'Oh, Florrie, I'm so happy!' she told her, and the older woman sniffed.

'Goodnight, then, Rosie.'

'Yes, goodnight! Sleep well!' Rose watched as Florrie pushed her father up the specially built ramp into the house, and then she put her hand in Charles's. 'Shall we take a turn about the garden before we go to bed? It's such a beautiful night! And I must see Gospel! He'll think I'm neglecting him.'

'You and that horse!' Charles chuckled, dropping a kiss onto her hair. They threaded their arms about each other's waists, Rose leaning her head on Charles's shoulder as they picked their way across the silvery, moonlit grass. Gospel came trotting up in the adjacent field as soon as he smelled her familiar scent. As she stroked his soft, velvety muzzle, Charles's lips on the back of her neck sent a shiver of emotion down her spine. She finally gave Gospel one last kiss on his hairy nose, and ambled back with Charles towards the house, pausing for a moment to gaze up at the satin indigo sky, peppered with pinprick stars. The Dartmoor weather had been kind for their special day, and now offered them a still, romantic night. As Charles held her closely to him, his mouth suddenly came down on hers, not kind and caressing as it had always been before, but harsh and urgent. Rose wasn't sure she liked it, and felt herself tighten.

'Time for bed, my love,' Charles said, releasing her. 'You go up. I'll just have a cigar out here, and then I'll lock up.'

Rose nodded with a faint smile, grateful to escape the uncomfortable moment. Charles had instantly returned to his normal self, and she felt at ease again. Perhaps she had imagined his forceful ardour. After all, they had all consumed a great deal of alcohol during the day and weren't quite themselves. She went in through the drawing-room, then through the spacious hall and up the elegant stairway to the master bedroom. Her light footsteps echoed through the silent house, for there was not a sound from her father's quarters, and Florrie and the two female servants had been given leave to retire to their rooms in the attic.

In the little dressing room, Rose contemplated her reflection in the looking glass one last time before stepping out of the beautiful gown. Would she ever wear it again? So many brides could only be married in their Sunday best, or if they could afford it, a new outfit of a style that could be utilised again afterwards. But Rose's gown was so exquisite, it would only be suitable for a society ball, or some such event. Charles wanted her to go to London with him sometimes, and perhaps she would have an opportunity to use the lovely garment again then. She sighed as she placed it on a hanger. She was so lucky! Though nowhere else could possibly hold the same place in her heart as Dartmoor, she was looking forward to visiting the capital with Charles, and playing the perfect wife as a thank you for all his generosity.

She climbed between the sheets, leaving the lamp turned low so that Charles could see his way when he came up. It would be strange to have someone, a man, sleeping beside her. But that was what you did when you were married, wasn't it, share a bed? She stifled a giggle as she wondered if Charles snored!

She snuggled down and was almost asleep, images of the magical day swirling in her head, when Charles padded into the room. She was vaguely aware of his shadow passing from the bathroom to the dressing room, emerging again a few minutes later. Rose was curled on her side, but turned onto her back and stretched like a kitten as Charles came and sat on the bed next to her. She smiled languidly at him as she waited for his goodnight kiss, watching his eyes move about her face, two cinnamon-flecked orbs alight with wonderment.

'Well now, Rose,' he whispered, his voice thick. 'Take off your nightdress and let me see what I've married.'

Rose blinked at him as sickening horror lacerated her heart. Had she heard right, her confounded brain demanded. She reared away, pressing herself into the pillows as she felt the blood drain from her head.

Charles's eyes opened wide. 'Good God!' he groaned in disbelief. 'Do you *really* not know? Has no one ever told you what happens between a man and his wife?' He stared at her ashen, rigid face, and then his lips curved into a wry smile. 'Well, I suppose it'll be even more pleasurable to *show* you, my darling. Now, if you won't take off your nightdress,' he said as he saw her fists tightening about the top of the blankets, 'I'll have to do it for you. Now don't look so disapproving, Rose. This is what you get married *for*! Millions of couples all over the world will be doing it as we speak.'

Rose couldn't move. Only her heart hammered frantically in her frozen chest. Her eyes stared sightlessly, her pupils wide with fear. Her small hands were powerless as Charles dragged the bedclothes from their grasp. As his fingers deftly undid the buttons of her nightgown, a petrified whimper fluttered in her throat. She wanted to fight back, but could only lie there motionless as he took her exposed breasts, cupping their fullness and moaning her name against their milky whiteness.

It was only when he started to fumble with the hem of her nightgown, drawing it up to her waist and pushing her knees apart, that her instinct to protect herself was galvanised into action. She pummelled his shoulders, writhing beneath him like some mad woman from an asylum. But above her, Charles seemed oblivious, his expression glazed over. Suddenly, in the lamplight, she caught one stunned glimpse of the hideous thing that stuck out from between his legs. The next thing she knew, he was pushing it into that innermost part of her she had hitherto hardly known existed. The chilling shock made her hold her breath until the pain seared into her, slicing at her tender flesh, and she screamed aloud. Charles's hand clamped over her mouth, almost stopping her from breathing. She struggled desperately, her muscles straining as he forced himself into her in a grunting frenzy. And then he stopped for just one split second before his body gave one mighty shudder and he cried out her name before he fell down on top of her, panting heavily and pinning her to the bed.

'Oh, Rose, my darling,' Charles murmured hotly into her ear. 'I love you so much. You'll never know how I've yearned for this. You were wonderful, moving like that. Oh, my little Rose.'

His words came at her through a fog. He moved away, blew out the small flame in the lamp, then came back to kiss her once more before he settled himself on his side of the bed, sighing contentedly. Rose lay, rigid as stone, staring into the blackness until her eyes adjusted to the slither of moonlight that filtered through the curtains. Charles, her husband, had taken himself from her, but her insides still burned as if the red-hot poker were still being thrust into her.

For ten minutes, perhaps more, she didn't dare to move for fear it would increase the pain. Charles's steady breathing beside her at last convinced her he was asleep, and slowly, gingerly, she rolled onto her side with her back to her new husband, and drew up her knees, oblivious to the silent tears that were dripping down her cheeks.

She felt dirty. Abused. *Ashamed*. And yet she had done nothing wrong. *Charles* had done nothing wrong. It was all falling into place now. That was why her father hadn't been happy about the marriage. Why he'd spoken about love and passion, although quite why *love* should make anyone *want* to do what she had just been subjected to, was beyond her. But Charles had just done that appalling thing *because he loved her*. She couldn't blame him. But . . . if only she'd known! Why hadn't her father told her? But then, how could he have done? It wasn't the sort of thing a man could tell his daughter about, was it? Sons, perhaps, and surely it would have been a mother's role to . . .

She bit down on her thumb. For the first time in her life, she missed the mother she'd never known. Florrie had been her mother, a devoted servant, but perhaps it hadn't been her place to speak of such . . . delicate matters. Perhaps Florrie herself didn't know. There'd been no Mr Bennett. Like so many in her position, she'd assumed the title of 'Mrs' because cooks and housekeepers were expected to be either married women or widows. What a ridiculous convention.

And what a ridiculous farce life was, if everything was supposed to be so upright, and yet *that* was what went on at night between married couples. And all that jolly celebration of a wedding ceremony, just so as *that* could take place! She'd thought marriage consisted of romantic walks, friendship. What a fool she'd been. Her heart closed in a bitter fist. And her lip curled at the sudden image of the pretentious battle-axe who'd interviewed her for the post of governess, on her back with her legs . . .

Oh, dear God, what was happening to her? All those dreams she'd had, and now she was imprisoned just as surely as those convicts just a few miles across the moor. Except that they'd be released in time, whereas she was trapped for life. Till death us do part. With my body, I thee worship. Worship? It was hardly how she would put it.

Mangled thoughts tumbled in her head, firing her own wretchedness until morning light began to creep into the bedroom, and outside the moorland birds were twittering their chorus to the new day. Finally, when her soul was saturated with misery and it could take no more, her exhausted mind took refuge in sleep.

Charles's warm, moist kisses at her throat brought her from her fitful slumber. Her eyes sprang open, and there was his face, so full of love, hanging over her. He smiled, stroking a hank of her long tresses and then wrapping it around his own shoulders in a gleaming mantle.

'Oh, my lovely girl,' he muttered. 'I hope you slept well.'

He didn't wait for an answer, but was running his hand up and down her arm, and then the inside of her thigh. His fingers sought out the place his body had possessed the previous night, and the hideous memory slashed at her in all its foul clarity. She couldn't go through that again, and a spark of flashing rage whipped her tongue to a cutting sharpness.

'No, Charles! Get off me!' And she pushed hard against his shoulders.

'Oh, come, my lovely girl! This is what we got married for!'

His words were like shards of glass in her heart. She simply couldn't . . . '*Please*, Charles,' she begged him, tears of desperation glittering in her terrified eyes. 'It *hurts*!' she moaned, just praying . . .

'Only at first,' he said gently. 'You'll get used to it. Now just try and relax, and it won't hurt so much.'

A groan of resentment drowned somewhere inside her. She was beaten. It wasn't Charles's fault. She turned her head away, lying as still as a corpse as he did what he had to do to her aching body. When he entered her, the agony ripped through her again, and she rammed her fist into her mouth to stifle her screams. No one must hear. Her *father* mustn't know. He mustn't know that this diabolical thing that was being done to her was pure torture. She'd married Charles because she thought she loved him. Now she knew that she didn't. But it was too late. Charles had always been kind and generous, but now she realised she had bought security for herself and her father with her body, and there was nothing she could do about it.

Charles had finished, and he rolled onto his back with a satiated sigh before propping himself on one elbow and gazing down at her, his eyes crinkled softly at the corners. 'You're so beautiful,' he whispered, his voice quavering with passion. 'You'll come to enjoy it soon, I promise. Oh, I must be the luckiest man alive!' He jumped up in the bed, spreading his arms wide above his head in a gesture of sheer jubilation that under other circumstances would have made her laugh. 'Now, what would my beautiful wife like for breakfast? No, don't tell me! I'll make it a surprise! I'll go down and speak to Cook, and you shall have breakfast in bed. And think what you'd like to do on the first day of our married life. It's such a lovely day, how about a walk over the moor?'

He'd slipped into his dressing gown and slippers, and with a grand flourish, plucked one of the red roses from the vase on the dressing-table, placing it reverently on her chest before taking her limp hand and kissing it, first her wrist and then working his way up her arm. One final kiss on the tip of her nose, and he was gone, singing tunelessly on the top of his voice as he waltzed along the landing and down the stairs.

Rose realised she'd been holding her breath, and now she released it in a broken sigh. Charles was as ecstatic in his love as she was devastated by it. Oh, God in heaven, what had she done? She rolled dejectedly out of bed and onto her feet, for she couldn't stay there, between the sheets where it had happened, a moment longer. But as she dragged herself across the floor, the pain cut into her and she could hardly walk. She staggered into the bathroom and used the chamber pot, hoping it would bring some relief. But it only stung her bruised flesh more deeply, and when she looked down, there was blood on her thighs.

A whimper of despair uttered from her lips. This was to be her life from now on, and she must keep the agony of it to herself. Her heart was beyond tears, and all she wanted just now was to free herself from the physical suffering that bore into the very core of her. There was cold water in the jug on the washstand. Setting the matching china bowl on the floor, she crouched down over it and poured the cooling water over that intimate part of her, soothing the soreness and washing away the filth and degradation. Could she ever *feel* as she should, ever truly love a man so deeply that she could give herself willingly to him? Even take pleasure from it herself?

Now she would never know.

CHAPTER ELEVEN

'Would you like another cup, Rose?' Florrie asked, dropping the 'Miss' Charles had instructed her to use, seeing as the master was working in his study.

Rose looked up from the book she was reading. The three of them — Henry in his invalid chair, Rose and Florrie — were taking morning coffee on the terrace of Fencott Place. It was ten days since the grand celebration of Miss Rose Maddiford's marriage to Mr Charles Chadwick, ten days in which she'd realised she'd made the greatest mistake of her life — except when she studied her father who was being so well fed and cared for. It was worth the terrible ordeal she was subjected to most nights, at least it seemed so at moments like this when peace and harmony comforted her bruised heart.

Yesterday, her 'monthly' had started. She'd welcomed the few hours of painful cramps because it seemed it would provide her with several days respite from Charles's attentions. It still hurt her dreadfully, although possibly a little less than at first, but she felt so degraded afterwards, and perhaps she always would. But those minutes of vile obscenity — for thank goodness that was as long as it lasted — were locked away in a nightmare of bitter shadows during the bright sunny days in between, when Charles was everything a loving, attentive husband should be. More so, for he was clearly reluctant to leave her side for more than a minute.

He came hurriedly out onto the terrace now before Rose even had time to reply to Florrie's question. His face was set in a deep scowl that, Rose considered, robbed him of his handsome looks, and he came to stand behind her, laying his hands on her shoulders with an irritated sigh.

'I'm afraid I must go into Princetown to send a telegram,' he announced. 'The telegraph office will be open, I take it?'

'Oh, yes.' Rose deliberately patted one of his hands in a show of affection she did not feel, for at that moment, Henry had glanced across at them. But her mind was busy inventing an excuse not to accompany Charles if he invited her to do so. 'We're lucky to have one really, but that's because of the prison.'

'Having dangerous convicts on one's doorstep can have its advantages, then,' Charles muttered grimly.

'They're not all dangerous,' Rose corrected. 'Some are forgers. Or thieves. Not necessarily violent.'

'Well, my dear, I don't have time to argue about that now.' Charles cut her short. 'I must get to Princetown as soon as possible, and I'll have to wait for a reply, so I'll be some time. You could come with me if you don't mind the waiting. We could have lunch at the Duchy Hotel.'

Rose felt her heart thump as she whipped up the courage to defy her husband. 'If you don't mind, darling,' she said, lifting her vivid smile to him, 'I think I'll go out on poor Gospel. We haven't been out for a ride since before our marriage, and the poor animal will be champing at the bit. Literally,' she added with a forced grin.

'All right, sweetheart, but take care on that monster.' Pulling on his coat which he'd left on the back of one of the garden chairs, Charles strode back inside and, they assumed, away down the front driveway.

Relief swamped Rose's limbs and for a few seconds, she slumped in her chair before stretching with delight. She was free. For a few hours, she could be her old self again, carefree, reckless, and her spirit soared.

'I'd better go and change, then!' she declared brightly, and as she jumped up, Henry caught her hand.

'You are happy, then, my child?' he asked mildly.

Rose looked down on him, and her chest squeezed painfully. 'Oh, yes!' she cried, the lie burning her lips as she forced them into a broad smile. Henry must never *know*. Besides, the thought of racing hell-for-leather across the moors, alone, on Gospel's back, filled her with joy.

The gelding kicked up his heels when he saw Rose, shaking his head in eager anticipation as she slipped on his bridle. The warm weather had meant he'd remained out in the field overnight for the past few weeks, as having something of the thoroughbred in him, this was not sensible for much of the year. But even so, he was as desperate as his mistress for a long, mad, unrestrained gallop.

They paid a visit to the gunpowder mills first, avoiding the old house where the new manager was now installed. It held too many memories of a life when Rose had been truly happy. But she chatted with many of the workers, her old friends and their families. Then she and Gospel took a vast, circular route to the stone bridge and ancient clapper bridge at Postbridge and on to the swirling waters at Dartmeet before charging across the open moorland towards home, Rose's hair streaming out behind her as she crouched down over Gospel's flowing mane. As his strong legs ate up the miles, the wind rushed through Rose's head, blasting away her bitterness and anger.

Charles was waiting for her as she crossed the stable-yard with the heavy saddle, humming to herself with relaxed pleasure. She stopped, her heart immediately gripped with defiance.

'Where the hell have you been?' Charles demanded.

Rose squared her shoulders so that, unwittingly, her breasts jutted out pertly, causing the saliva to run in Charles's mouth. 'Out for a ride, like I said.'

'But you've been hours! It's half past three, for God's sake!'

'So?' she shrugged as she tried to push past him.

But he angrily caught her arm. 'So?' he repeated. 'I've been worried sick! Anything could have happened to you!'

'I've told you afore, I'm perfectly safe when I'm out on Gospel. Now, if you don't mind, this saddle's heavy.'

'Oh, of course,' Charles murmured, and shaking his head as if coming to his senses, he relieved her of the said item and followed her into the tack-room.

She hung Gospel's bridle on its hook and then strode past Charles and across to the terrace, cringing as she heard Charles's footfall behind her. The scene was almost as she'd left it earlier that morning.

Henry glanced up with an unconcerned smile. 'Did you have a good ride, my dear?'

'Wonderful, thank you, father,' she answered, flinging herself into a chair.

'You see, Charles, I told you there was nothing to worry about. You'll just have to get used to Rose dashing about on Gospel.'

'Well, I just don't think I could ever get used to having my precious wife gallivanting all over the moor on her own. And now I won't have to,' Charles beamed, his attitude changing to one of complacency. 'I've a surprise for you, my darling. Whilst I was waiting for the reply to my telegram, I took luncheon at the Duchy. Remember the chestnut mare I hired out from them last autumn? Well, they still had her, and she was such a suitable mount for me that I bought her. So now I can always accompany you on your excursions, and she'll be good company for Gospel. So, what do you think of that, my love?' he grinned triumphantly.

Rose's heart sank like a leaden weight. The long ride had refreshed her spirit, and she'd begun to think that, if she could regularly escape on Gospel's back, she might be able to tolerate Charles's nightly attentions with some degree of stoicism. But this!

'Oh,' she muttered. 'Oh . . . I don't know what to say. You've left me quite speechless.'

'And it's not often that happens!' Henry chuckled.

'And I've been thinking,' Charles went on with a satisfied smile. 'It was a pity that the dog-cart and that other horse belonged to the powdermills. I'm going to have to go to London, but when I get back, we must look for some sort of carriage and employ a carpenter to adapt it for you, Henry.'

'Oh, my dear boy, that would be so kind!'

'Yes, thank you,' Rose mumbled. It *was* good of Charles, she couldn't deny it. And she couldn't really blame him for buying the chestnut. He'd *need* a horse here, anyway. But to be with her on her liberating escapades, well, they would hardly be liberating if *he* was there! 'London, you say?' she asked, for that might at least bring her some respite.

'Yes. I'm afraid I must leave you for a few days, my dear.'

Rose had to conceal her pleasure. Couldn't make that a few weeks, could he?

'Nothing wrong, is there?' her father enquired.

'No, Henry, not at all. Just the opposite. My broker has had word of a new mine opening in South Africa that could prove a good investment. They're expecting to find gold.'

'Gold?'

'Yes. It may just be wishful thinking, which is why I need to go to London to investigate their claims before I put any money into it. I have fingers in many pies, but one of the best things I ever did was to speculate in diamonds some years ago,' Charles smiled proudly. 'I sponsored an acquaintance to go out to the diamond fields at Colesberg Kopje before it became known just how rich the area really was, and the licences were still cheap. You might have heard of it now as the Kimberley mine. As a shareholder, I've done very well out of it. So I'm quite inclined to take a risk with a speculation in gold. Nothing we can't afford to lose if it were to go wrong,' he added reassuringly. 'But I'll only go ahead if my enquiries are satisfactory. However, it does grieve me that I must leave you, my dearest.'

He took Rose's hand and brought it lovingly to his lips. Rose shuddered as the warm moistness on her skin reminded her of what went on in their bed at night, but she managed to say quite calmly, 'It won't be for too long, will it?'

His eyes softened as he gazed at her. 'I sincerely hope not. And when I return, we'll go in search of some suitable transport for Henry. The mare will be arriving tomorrow afternoon, by the way. Her name's Tansy, if you remember. Now, I'll be leaving after dinner. A cab is coming for me at eight o'clock, so I've already instructed Cook to have our meal served early. I'll stay at the Bedford Hotel in Tavistock tonight, ready to catch the train to Plymouth first thing in the morning. So I should be in London by six o'clock tomorrow evening.'

'You're certainly well organised,' Henry nodded in approval.

'Years of having to be one step ahead. And I have yet another surprise for you. I thought, with the mare coming tomorrow, and another animal needed to pull whatever conveyance we acquire, we'll need someone to look after them all. That beast of yours has been out in the field, but it'll need to come in when the summer's over, and I can hardly expect my wife to muck out not just one but three loose boxes, now, can I?' Charles laughed as he patted Rose's hand with the enthusiasm of a young boy. 'So while I was waiting for the reply from my broker, I asked around and I've taken on a stable lad. He can sleep in the loft over the tack-room. He'll be arriving with the mare tomorrow. Cornish, I think he said his name was. He can help with the heavy work in the house, too—'

'Ned!' Rose's eyes were wide with astonishment.

'Do you know him, then?'

'I've known Ned Cornish for years! Stable boy at the Albert Inn.'

'That's the chap. I thought I'd feel happier if there was a strong male about the place while I'm away. Which is why I wanted him to start at once. And I wondered if you'd like to think about furnishing the guest rooms to give you something to occupy your time?'

'Well, you've had a busy and fruitful day,' Henry observed. 'Made me feel quite weary just listening to you, and I feel I could do with a lie down before our early dinner. Would you mind, Florrie?'

Florrie, who was apt to keep her lip firmly buttoned in the master's presence, got to her feet with a devoted smile and pushed Henry up the ramp with a noisy heave. Charles went to go to her assistance, but they were already disappearing into the house, so he sat down again.

'Cornish can help Florrie with your father, too. I really feel it's too much for her.'

'What on earth do you think you're doing, employing Ned Cornish?' Rose rounded on him. 'Why didn't you tell me we were to have a groom? We could have asked Joe! He's the only person who can handle Gospel. Ned positively dislikes—'

'Joe Tyler!' Charles's brown eyes bulged from their sockets. 'After the way you were dancing with him at our wedding!'

'What?'

'Yes, I saw you! Arms around each other, laughing! Making a spectacle of yourself with that vermin!'

Rose's jaw fell open. 'But . . . Joe's like a younger brother to me!' she cried defensively. 'He's a respectable person. And besides, he and Molly—'

'I'm not a fool, Rose! And I'm glad I've taken on this Cornish fellow if you're not too keen on him. At least there won't be anything going on between you behind my back!'

Rose's mouth snapped shut at the sour taste that stung her tongue. 'How dare you! How dare you even *imagine* that I'd do anything like that! I'm married to *you*, Charles, for better or for worse, remember?'

As Charles glowered at her, his face began to twist, and before she knew it, she was encircled in his embrace.

'I'm so sorry, my sweetest, dearest love. But I've employed Cornish now, and unless he proves unsatisfactory, there'll be no reason to dismiss him. I *am* sorry, my darling. It's just that I love you so much, I just can't bear the thought of you being with another man. Please, I beg you, forgive me.'

Rose swallowed as she gazed over his shoulder into the house. She prayed to God that neither her father nor Florrie had heard their bitter exchange. 'Of course I do,' she muttered in reply. But in her heart, she wasn't at all sure that she did.

* * *

'Oh, Rose! D'you really mean to tell me you had no idea? You'm living with animals all over the moor all your life, and you didn't *know*?'

Rose rocked her bowed head from side to side. '*Animals*, yes! And that's just it! With animals, it's just instinct. Without feelings or emotion. I thought with human beings it'd be different. Animals don't kiss, so I thought . . .'

She broke off with a tearing sigh, and felt Molly squeeze her arm.

'Oh, Rose. With all they books you read, did you never read one on . . . on—'

'Oh, yes! But in flowers and butterflies,' Rose answered scornfully. 'But never in *people*. And do such books exist?'

Molly shrugged her eyebrows, and for a few minutes, the girls sat in silence, both of them staring out across the moor. On the prison farmland, parties of convicts were working hard, some of them digging drainage ditches up to the waist in what was cold water even on a perfect summer's day such as this. There'd be no dry clothing to change into on their return to the prison; indeed, they'd be lucky if their uniforms dried out overnight ready for the following day. But neither girl took any notice, each lost in her own thoughts.

'Must've been quite a shock, then, the wedding night,' Molly ventured at last. 'But . . . once you've gotten used to it . . . 'tis nice, isn't it?'

'What!' Rose's eyes opened wide as she whipped her head round to gaze at her friend. 'You don't mean . . . you and Joe—'

'Course not! We'm close, but nort's ever . . . Not like that.'

'So you don't know what it's like, then. If only Charles was as caring in *that* as he is in most other things. Other than being possessive over me which he wasn't before our marriage. But it's not your problem.' Rose suddenly jumped up as if closing the subject. 'I ought to be getting back. Ned's bringing the mare over later, so I suppose I should be there. I really don't fancy having him as our groom, but there you are. It's too late now. I'd far sooner have had Joe.'

''Twouldn't have been enough work for Joe. He likes to keep busy. Not like that sloth, Ned Cornish. No wonder he jumped at the chance, the great lummox!'

Rose couldn't help but laugh. As she waved goodbye, she felt her heart eased by her hour with Molly.

* * *

'Rose, my darling!'

'Charles!' Shock rippled through her body, his sudden appearance in the bedroom taking her completely by surprise. 'Your telegram said you wouldn't be home for another few days,' she said, praying he didn't see her flinch as his eyes dipped to the swelling of her breasts beneath her nightdress.

'Well, I just couldn't stay away from my beautiful wife a moment longer!' he declared with a suggestive smile. 'And I have been away nearly a week longer than expected. A very profitable week, I might add — at least, I believe it will prove to be in the future — but now I want to make up for it,' he crooned in an oily voice.

She shuddered, the pulse suddenly beating hard and fast at her temples. She tried to brace herself against his closeness, since she was his wife, after all, and her conversation with Molly had made her think that perhaps she was being unreasonable. But her resolution failed her.

'You must be hungry after your journey,' she suggested with a loving smile on her lips. 'I'm certain Cook will have something cold she can—'

But Charles shook his head. 'I had something to eat while I was waiting for the connecting train. I want something else just now.'

His eyes burned bright with desire as he brought his mouth down onto hers, soft and caressing. Rose closed her eyes, trying to respond to his gentleness which did not seem so repellent. But then his kiss became more demanding, more urgent, his tongue flicking into her mouth and his hands moving frenetically over her breasts and down between her thighs.

'Charles, no, please,' she gasped, as she managed to pull her head away.

But he merely moved his kisses down to her throat, forcing her tiny waist against his hardening manhood as he held her in an iron grip. 'Oh, struggle away, my precious one!' he murmured into her cleavage. 'I love it when you pretend to be a little tigress.'

He growled, baring his teeth, and then with a bawdy laugh, picked her up bodily, and padding across the carpet, dropped her onto the bed. Before she had time to scramble away, he leapt astride her, pinning her down, and catching both her small, flailing hands in one of his, held them firmly on the pillow behind her head.

'Now then,' Charles leered, his free hand ripping open the front of her nightgown. 'Let me see what I've been missing!'

Rose could have screamed. She dug her heels desperately into the mattress and pushed upwards in an effort to lever him from her, but he was too heavy. He sniggered again, taking her retaliation as play-acting as his eyes devoured her nakedness. She stared up at him, every taut muscle ready to fight, but it was futile. He was her husband, who not so long ago she'd thought she loved, and he was doing nothing wrong.

But at that moment, Rose wished that she could die.

CHAPTER TWELVE

'Rose, dear, it's your turn.'

She turned her head from gazing absently out of the drawing-room window and smiled at Henry before forcing her attention on her hand of cards. It was mid September, but chilly enough to have a welcoming blaze in the fireplace. Rain was coming down in stair rods and streaming against the window panes. It was only half past three in the afternoon, but the lamps had already been lit against the gloom.

'Oh, is that the best you can do, sweetheart?' Charles asked fondly, and clamping the smouldering cigar between his teeth, laid his winning flush on the table.

'You lucky devil, Charles!' Henry chuckled.

'And my poor Rose has lost every game! Never mind, my love. Perhaps you'll win the next one.'

'I don't think I'll play any more, if you don't mind.' She smiled wanly at her husband as she stood up. 'I think I'd rather get back to my book.'

'If you're sure, my darling.'

Rose settled herself in the window seat, wedging a cushion behind her back. But within minutes, she'd let the book she was reading slip onto her lap, and she leaned her forehead against the cold glass of the window. Her stifled spirit escaped outside and was flying across the wild moorland, the wind in her head and driving the misery from her soul. She could feel Gospel's muscles rippling beneath her, sharing the infinite freedom of the open skies and the endless miles of the savage beauty of Dartmoor. A veil of mist dimmed her eyes, and her shoulders sagged with emptiness. The chasm in her life was deepening by the day, and there was nothing she could do about it.

'I'm going for a ride.'

It was as if someone else had spoken the words, had leapt determinedly from the window seat and stood in defiant pose in the centre of the room. Three pairs of eyes were riveted on her, Florrie's plump face white and aghast.

'You'm not going out in this, Rose!' she cried, forgetting the 'Miss' she was supposed to employ in Charles's presence.

Rose, however, was already out of the door and half way across the hall to the stairs before Charles caught up with her. He was still holding his cigar in one hand, and with the other, he grasped her by the arm.

'You can't possibly go out in this weather. You'd be soaked to the skin in no time, and catch your death. If you don't want to play cards, is there anything else you'd rather do?' he asked earnestly. 'Shall I order Cook to make us a pot of tea?'

Rose blinked at him, and the absurdity of it drew a bitter laugh from her throat. She was perfectly capable of making some tea herself, of cooking the meal, blackleading the range. But since the day she'd married Charles, she hadn't been allowed to *do* anything. Charles saw to it that she lived the pampered life of a lady. But though he treated her like a princess during the day, in their bed she was no more than a human marionette to satisfy his lust.

'If I don't go out, I'll go mad!' she told him, flames of crimson burning in her cheeks. 'And if you're not man enough to brave a spot of rain, then I'll go alone, just like I always used to!'

'But you're a married woman now,' Charles hissed, glancing over his shoulder as if he were afraid they'd be overheard. 'I won't have my wife gallivanting all over the place looking like some rain-drenched witch for everyone to see.'

'Huh!' she snorted, her eyes glinting a livid indigo. 'How many of your London dignitaries am I likely to meet, tell me that?'

Charles inflated his chest. 'Rose, I forbid you to go!'

'Forbid me?'

'Yes! And it'll hardly do Gospel any good.'

Rose stared at him, her lips knotted as anger pumped through her veins. But the mention of Gospel's welfare pulled her up short. She hated to admit it, but perhaps Charles was right.

'All right. But only for Gospel's sake. But I *am* going out to the stables for a while. You won't object to *that*, I take it?'

'No, of course not.' His face slackened as he turned away, drawing deeply on the cigar as he went.

'And Charles, please don't smoke in the same room as my father. I've asked you before. You know his lungs were weakened in the accident.'

'I'll finish my cigar in the study, my dear. I've some business matters to catch up on.' So saying, he disappeared into the study, closing the door quietly behind him.

Rose sank down on the bottom stair with a weary sigh. Charles didn't want her to do anything without him, and it was driving her insane. The carefree independence Henry had always allowed her had been taken from her overnight, but if she had to obey her husband, she wasn't going to give in without a fight!

She went out through the back door, shrugging into her waterproof that hung in the small boot-room and changing into her riding-boots, as she could hardly go out to the stables in the soft kid shoes she was wearing. Fortunately she was dressed in a modest outfit with a russet skirt that wouldn't spoil. She picked up the hem as she ran across the stable-yard, dodging the puddles and bending her head so that the driving rain simply ran down the back of the waterproof hood.

Inside Gospel's loose box, it was warm and dry, the fragrance of clean straw fresh and welcoming. It had to be said that Ned Cornish cared well for the three horses in his charge, Charles having acquired, as promised, a wagonette and a pretty roan called Merlin to pull it.

Ned had proved diligent enough. After all, he'd hardly want to lose his comfortable position. The only task he was apt to skimp on was grooming Gospel, since the highly-strung animal retained the habit of sinking his teeth into anyone he disliked, Ned in particular. So Rose picked up the brush and began to stroke it down Gospel's sleek flank. The animal whinnied softly, turning his neck to nudge her shoulder. She laughed, her heart soothed as she kissed his soft muzzle and continued to groom him until his coat shone like glass.

When she'd finished, she wreathed her arms about his neck, her cheek pressed against his shoulder. She supposed she couldn't stay there all afternoon, much as she'd like to. But before she went back indoors, she slipped into the adjacent box to see Tansy, the chestnut mare.

'Happy as a lark, that one, not like that brute o' yourn.'

Rose turned round. Ned was leaning over the lower half of the stable door, supposedly oblivious to the continuing downpour and chewing on a blade of straw.

'It's not my fault Gospel doesn't like you,' she replied absently.

'And what about you, Rose? Does *you* like me?'

Rose shrugged as Ned came in out of the rain. 'That's a strange question when I've known you for years,' she frowned.

'I like *you*, Rose. Very much.' Ned's voice was suddenly very close to her ear. ''Tis why I wanted this job. To be near you. Even if it means being bitten by that nag next door. You wouldn't mind now, would you? Just one little kiss? I mean, now that you know what 'tis like to be bedded?'

Rose was so shocked, she didn't have time to come back with a scathing retort before Ned grasped the back of her head and kissed her fiercely.

'Get off me, you great lummox!'

Before Ned could dodge it, she slapped her palm across his face with a resounding wallop.

'That weren't fair, Rose!' he protested. 'I've given up a lot for you! All they maids I used to bring back to the stables at the Albert Inn. I cas'n bring no one back yere! Just one little favour?'

With a cry of indignation, Rose pushed him aside. 'How dare you, Ned Cornish!' she snarled, glowering at him with intense loathing. 'I've a good mind to tell my husband, and you'll be out on your ear!'

'Oh, yes?' Ned sneered. 'And what if I tells him that *you* were making up to *us*? He might just believe us, seeing as he seems to be the jealous type, and *you* might be the one to come off worse, like!'

Rose's head jerked backwards. Ned Cornish, towards whom she had never felt anything but indifference, was more shrewd than she'd given him credit for. He could have a point.

'I'll forgive you this time,' she conceded, swallowing down her resentment. 'But I won't forget it!'

Nor shall I! Ned thought venomously to himself.

Rose spun on her heel and stormed out of the loose box. The torrential rain at once lashed into her face, trickling down her neck. Too late, she pulled the hood of her waterproof over her head as she scurried across the stable-yard.

It was then that she saw him, a bedraggled, sodden vision of dripping grey fur, short black snout and huge doleful eyes that gazed beggingly at her as he limped through the puddles. Rose peered at him through the rain as he came and sat at her feet, his tail sweeping the wet cobbles as he whined at her beseechingly.

'Oh, you poor thing! Where on earth did you come from?' And she scooped the pathetic mongrel into her arms and carried him inside.

* * *

'You don't expect us to keep that mangy creature, do you?' Charles asked with mild amusement as he climbed into bed that night.

'I assume you mean Scraggles?' Rose replied indignantly. She was sitting up, hugging her knees beneath the blankets, and for once the nightly ritual was far from her thoughts. 'And he isn't mangy. He was cold and wet and hungry, and one of his paw pads was badly cut, but if we can't find his owners, what else can we do but keep him? Oh, *please*, Charles? He and Amber really seem to like each other.'

Charles shook his head with a chuckle. 'Well, if we really can't find who he belongs to—'

'Oh, thank you, Charles!'

For the first time since their marriage, she snuggled up beside him, her head resting on his shoulder. The disruption caused by the unexpected arrival of the endearing stray dog had thrown the entire household into turmoil. And it had started Rose thinking. Perhaps if she had other matters to distract her, she might be able to be a better wife. Would deplore Charles's physical attentions a little less. Which for once, he didn't seem in too much of a hurry to begin, his arm around her simply drawing her closely against him.

'Charles?' she began cautiously, suddenly encouraged to broach the subject that had been at the back of her mind for some time. 'Charles, I've been thinking. What would you think of the idea of my having a lady's maid?'

She said the last words quickly, before she lost the courage, but Charles merely raised his eyebrows in surprise.

'A lady's maid, eh? Hmm,' he reflected. 'That mightn't be a bad idea. Certainly when you accompany me to London — which I hope you will soon — it would be good to have someone to make sure you're correctly attired. And to keep you company when I have to attend to business matters. Accompany you to art galleries, that sort of thing. Mrs Bennett is hardly suitable, and besides, she needs to stay here to look after your father. All in all, I think it's an excellent idea,' he nodded approvingly. 'We'll put an advertisement in the *Western Morning News*, or perhaps one of the London papers would be better.'

'Oh, I don't think we need to advertise. Molly would be ideal.'

'Molly Cartwright!' Charles jerked so violently that Rose's head slipped from his shoulder. 'Don't be ridiculous!'

'But Molly would be perfect! We're such good friends and—'

'Rose, you need a trained lady's maid to see you are suitably attired, that your hair is properly done, and, especially when we go to London, that you are versed in all the ways of society etiquette. I hate to say it, but you have a great deal to learn in that direction! If you were to employ Miss Cartwright, *you* would have to be teaching *her* the little you know yourself. She'd bring us nothing but ridicule! Besides, I cannot have my wife associating so closely with some little trollop whose father is no more than a prison turnkey!'

Rose turned on him eyes that glinted steel. 'How dare you speak of Molly like that! She's bright and intelligent, and just because she comes from a working-class background, doesn't make her any worse than you or I! They're a good, honest, hardworking family, and I defy anyone to—'

'Oh, you are so beautiful when you're angry!' Charles almost laughed at her, but then his eyes hardened icily. 'But you will not have Molly Cartwright as your lady's maid!'

'I shall have Molly or no one!'

'Then no one it shall be, and there's an end to it.' Charles's mouth closed in a firm line, but an instant later, his face softened and he smiled suggestively at her, fingering a lock of her cascading curls. 'Now then, before this conversation, I believe we were enjoying an intimate moment together, so if you don't mind, I'd like to get back to where we were and begin afresh. Now, my lovely girl, have you forgotten that we need to do something before we go to sleep?'

For several seconds, Rose was convinced she'd explode with fury. Charles was mocking her. Humiliating her. And yet if she demonstrated her anger, fought him, it would be as if he'd won. As if she really was the ignorant child he was making her out to be. Inside, she was seething, but she lay down like the submissive wife, keeping perfectly still while Charles satisfied his need. But each thrust of his body seemed to drive another nail into her fading affection for him. She had tried. Had wanted to love him. But she couldn't. Just now, she hated him for what he'd said about Molly and her family. But she hadn't lost yet.

The battle was far from over.

* * *

Rose squeezed her heels into Gospel's flanks and he careered forward with a surge of bursting energy. She hadn't told anyone, least of all her husband, but had simply taken the animal's tack before anyone had realised, saddled him and ridden quietly out of the yard. Now they were flying across the moor towards Princetown. Rose was still furious with Charles. But if he thought he could dominate her like that, well, she'd jolly well make him think again!

She slowed Gospel to a trot as they came into Princetown. She'd leave him at the Albert Inn with the new stable lad there. She gave the startled boy a florin, as in her heart, it meant she was hitting back at Charles, giving away his money in a way he wouldn't approve of! Not that she intended to be long. She wanted to return, triumphant, to her husband as soon as possible to announce that she'd employed Molly whether he liked it or not!

She flicked up her head, relishing the secret snub as she continued down the street. But she didn't even have to walk as far as the new warders' block, as Molly was coming towards her, battered shopping basket on her arm. The instant she spied Rose, her pretty face broke into a delighted grin.

'Rose! What you'm doing yere so early?'

Rose grimaced in reply. 'I wanted to get out before anyone realised I was gone.'

'Oh, dear, that don't sound too good.'

Rose flashed her a warm smile. 'Oh, it's just that I couldn't wait to see you.'

'See *me*?'

'Yes. You see . . .' As they walked on up the street, Rose's pulse accelerated at the lie she was about to tell her dear friend. 'Charles and I have decided that I really need a lady's maid, and we thought, well, that it should be you.'

Her cheeks were aglow with guilt, but also with excitement at the prospect of Molly's constant companionship. But why should she feel so guilty? Damn Charles! She paid heavily every night for her father's security, so why shouldn't she have her way in this small matter that meant so much to her?

She held her breath, waiting for Molly's reaction, convinced that the unexpected surprise had left her friend speechless.

'Oh, Rose, 'tis terribly kind of you,' Molly spoke at last. 'I should love to be your maid. To live in that there grand house. Only I cas'n.'

Rose stopped dead and as she caught Molly's arm. 'Y-you can't?' she stuttered feebly. 'W-why ever not?'

'Cuz. Oh, Rose, I'm that sorry. A year ago, 'twould have been wonderful, but . . . ' The remorse on her face faded, and in its place, a suppressed joy shone in her eyes. 'Can you keep a secret?'

'Of course,' Rose gulped, her voice no more than a faint whisper.

'I *did* want you to be the first to know. I haven't even told my parents yet, so you will keep it to yourself? Until Joe's asked my father, leastways. You see, Joe and I are to be married. We'm just waiting for one of the cottages at the powdermills to become empty.'

Rose's heart contracted in strange pain at Molly's sparkling eyes, and deep inside, she felt something die. Molly and Joe to wed. She was stunned, though why, she didn't know. She should have guessed. A sensation she recognised as jealousy gripped her soul. Not jealousy that Molly was to marry *Joe*, for he was like a brother to her. But because they were to marry for *love*. A true, free love that fate had put beyond her reach for ever. And because it meant that the one thing that might make her life bearable was now out of the question. But the other part of her, the *real* Rose, was so happy for her friend, and she swallowed down the bitter gall of her own anguish.

'Oh, Molly, congratulations!' she forced the jubilation into her voice. 'And I promise I won't tell a soul!'

'Thanks, Rose! And thanks so much for asking me to be your maid. But 'twould not be worth it for just a few months. I be so sorry. 'Twould have been such fun.'

'Never mind. It's not the same as getting married.'

'Well, you should know that!' Molly chuckled jauntily.

The knife sliced into Rose's heart. 'Yes,' she murmured. 'Well, I'll leave you to do your shopping.'

'Goodbye, then, Rose.' And Molly sauntered off towards Princetown's few shops.

Rose watched her, sadness raking her throat. She shouldn't feel like this! And yet she was shaking as she fetched Gospel from the inn and set off back over the moor. The previous day's torrential rain had released the heady aroma of the long grass and peaty earth beneath Gospel's hooves, and Rose filled her lungs with its calming sweetness. She really should count her blessings. She had Gospel and Amber, and now the scruffy mongrel, Scraggles. She had a lovely house on her beloved Dartmoor, a financially secure future. Above all, she'd provided a happy home for her father who remained, she was sure, ignorant of her own wretchedness, when he'd been so close to entering the workhouse. She had a husband who was devoted to her . . . but who loved her so much he wanted to possess her body and soul, to crush the spirit from her. But she wouldn't let him win! Rose Maddiford, the carefree girl who roamed the wilds of Dartmoor on the massive black horse would never give in, though at this moment, she would as soon ride over to Vixen Tor, climb to the top and throw herself over the edge . . .

'Where have you been?' Charles's stiff tone reached her as she stole up the stairs to change out of her riding-habit.

She took a breath, then turned to face him, her shoulders squared. 'Out,' she said flatly.

'I can see that. But why creep out in such secrecy?'

'So that I could go alone, if you must know.'

'You don't go out alone without my permission.'

Rose pursed her lips dangerously. 'You might remember I told you on the day we met that no one owns me. If I choose to ride out alone, then I shall.'

'Oh, no, you don't. Your father might have allowed you such inappropriate behaviour, but I would remind you that you are now a married woman, and as such, you will do as you're told.'

'And who's going to make me?'

'I am, if I have to. But perhaps, madam, you'd take more care of yourself if you had a child to think of! So the quicker you become pregnant, the better!'

Rose stared at the cruelty that darkened his face. He grasped her arm, dragging her up the stairs, his fingers digging painfully into her flesh. She didn't resist. Her father and Florrie were probably taking breakfast and would hear any altercation on the stairway.

He flung her into the bedroom. But she wasn't afraid of him, oh, no! And she certainly wasn't going to let him think he'd won! So when he turned back from locking the door, instead of cowering from him, she was leisurely discarding her riding clothes, but didn't stop when she was down to her shirt. She threw the fine garment onto the floor, followed by her chemise so that her bare breasts bobbed tantalisingly as she spun round to face him, clad in nothing more than her drawers.

Charles's face was like thunder. 'Stop behaving like a whore,' he grated savagely.

'Well, it's what I am to you, so if the cap fits . . . ' Her eyebrows arched, but then she turned her vivid smile on him. 'Besides, I happen to agree that a child would be wonderful.'

Under different circumstances, she would have found the change in his expression quite laughable. Total astonishment clearly had dashed away his rage.

'Do you?' he quizzed her as if in disbelief.

'Yes, I do.' Although to be honest, she wasn't entirely sure.

Charles's mouth spread into a slow smile. 'Well, I'd better see if I can oblige. A son. You've no idea how I've longed for a son.'

His soft, genuine tone took Rose by surprise. She didn't know, of course, of the child his young mistress had robbed him of all those years ago. But just now, his gentler attitude had given her some hope. She'd been ignorant of what marriage meant, and had married Charles for an affection she knew now fell far short of love, and to provide a safe home for Henry. None of which was Charles's fault. And to have a child was something that might unite them.

Not that the thoughts were quite so clear in her head, just part of a jumble of emotions that churned inside her as Charles ran his finger from the well of her throat down to the gathered waist of her drawers, and then slowly untied the drawstring.

CHAPTER THIRTEEN

Rose missed Dartmoor dreadfully. London, however, was not without its attractions, Charles having taken her to visit the principal sights. She wrote everything down in a notebook to help her relate her experiences in detail to everyone at home on her return.

Charles's house in the fashionable square was a delight. In a terrace of like villas, it consisted of four storeys, on the third of which were the two main bedrooms and a bathroom — with, to Rose's astonishment, running water pouring forth from the taps. There were two staircases, a magnificent affair at the front of the house and another narrow stairway at the back for use by the servants. Stone steps from a door at the rear of the hall descended to a small, enclosed garden, and across the road at the front of the house was a private square to which only residents were entitled to hold a key.

It was Rose's refuge. The autumn leaves had turned to a glorious display of orange and russet, cinnamon and gold, and were starting fall from the trees. It was hardly Dartmoor, but it provided a haven of peace for her saddened heart when she yearned for the infinite miles of open moorland.

She didn't always find herself alone. She met other residents, mainly bored wives and daughters who, to Rose's amusement, seemed to relish her tales of the wild moor. At least Charles approved of these associations which kept her occupied while he was visiting his bank or his broker, or attending board meetings at one of the many companies in which he had substantial investments. He might have had a fit, however, had he known that Rose would converse with anyone who happened to be in the square, male or female, in her need to fill the days before she could return to her beloved Dartmoor.

She would sigh as she sat back on the bench and closed her eyes, listening to the pretty birdsong of the blackbird or the cheeky sparrow, but hearing in her head the bark of the wild cry of the moorland buzzard. She surprised the elderly gardener by chatting to him as he burned the fallen leaves on a smouldering fire. She even coaxed a neighbour's nanny into discussions on the care of infants, for though the families that had surrounded her at Cherrybrook had increased regularly, she realised that if she'd been ignorant of how the babies arrived, she had even less idea of how to care for one when her own time came.

A child. The first thing to happen was that your monthlies stopped, and you probably felt sick, especially in the morning. This much she knew from Molly. It hadn't happened to her yet. Not that it was for want of trying, she grimaced to herself. It seemed that almost every night, Charles couldn't sleep until he'd satisfied himself. Even when they returned dog-tired from a dinner-party or an evening at the theatre, Charles ruined her elation with his carnal demands. Sometimes she felt that if he were to show her some affection, cuddle her perhaps, she might experience *something*. But as it was, Charles appeared to ignore the fact that she, too, was flesh and blood, and needed reassurance and understanding rather than being treated like some inanimate object.

But a child might stop all that. For a while, at least. It might even bring them closer together again. Rose was still very fond of Charles, grateful for what he'd done for her father, but she could not love him. Whenever he left her at

Fencott Place while he returned to London, she never missed him. Rather she rejoiced in the freedom his absence allowed her, like a wild bird being released from a cage.

It went without saying that her going to London with him this time had been his idea, though she hadn't been averse to it. She had been curious to see his house and experience the hustle and bustle of the capital. But they'd been there for nearly the whole of October, and she was yearning to return home.

That afternoon, however, they were attending the opening of a small art gallery for a young painter Charles was sponsoring. It looked well for Charles, of course, and Rose couldn't help but feel some pride that her husband was offering the young man a unique opportunity. The artist depicted a whole range of diverse subjects apparently, and she couldn't wait to see them.

She wasn't disappointed. Ladies and gentlemen from Charles's social circle had crowded into the tastefully converted high-street shop, accepting fine champagne and fancy canapés. Rose had already become acquainted with most of the guests, and moved easily among them in her role as hostess, charming, friendly and looking demurely beautiful, or so Charles had told her approvingly before they'd set out from home.

On their arrival in the capital, he'd insisted that she should have a wardrobe full of fine clothes, but it seemed such a dreadful waste of money to her, especially with so many poor and starving people on the London streets. When Charles had caught her giving a shilling to a ragged urchin, he'd whisked her away before she'd attracted a crowd who would have the clothes off her back, he'd hissed angrily into her ear. The child's parent, or even the child itself, would only convert the coin into gin within the hour. If she must give his money away, she should at least donate it to some charitable institution that would make sure it was used to some good purpose! Reluctantly, Rose saw the logic of his argument and promptly made some generous donations to charities of which Charles approved. But whenever she went out alone, which wasn't often, she would secretly take with her a small basket of nutritious comestibles that she gave to the wretched beggars she would inevitably come upon in her wanderings!

It gave her the greatest pleasure that Charles was helping the young artist. He gave a short speech to polite applause, and then Rose was circulating among the guests again, encouraging them to consider purchasing a painting and to spread the word about the gallery. It wasn't until many of the visitors had departed that she was able to turn her attention fully to the canvases on the walls.

'Do you like that one, Mrs Chadwick?'

'It's beautiful,' she said dreamily, and dragged her enraptured eyes to the thin, gaunt man with the nervously drooping shoulders who had come up beside her. 'Where is it, Mr Tilling?'

'Oh, nowhere in particular. Just a combination of ideas in my imagination.'

'Then, it's no wonder I don't recognise it, though it does remind me of Dartmoor.'

'Then it's yours to keep. As a thank you to your husband for his patronage.'

'Oh, no, I couldn't possibly! You must agree a fair price with my husband. Have you sold many this afternoon?'

'Half a dozen,' he replied with enthusiasm.

'Congratulations! Show me which ones. Though I must say I should find it hard to choose, they're all so lovely and yet all so different. And yet . . . You paint *atmosphere*, Mr Tilling. This one is so dark and stormy, and yet that one over there, with the young woman and the two children in the garden, is so bright and happy, I can *feel* the lovely summer's afternoon. And this one—'

'I-I should like to paint *you*, Mrs Chadwick.' His voice was low, apprehensive, little more than a whisper. 'Not a straightforward portrait, but an atmospheric painting, as you put it. You are so . . . if you will allow me to say so . . . so alive!

And yet, I have been observing you all afternoon, and there is a sadness about you I should love to capture.'

Rose's heart seemed to flutter in her breast. 'I'm sure you're mistaken, Mr Tilling, but if there is, it's perhaps that I'm missing my home on Dartmoor. We're returning in a few weeks' time, but perhaps we could arrange something for our next visit, if my husband agrees.'

'I should be honoured.' And seeking her finely gloved hand, he brought it to his lips.

Across the room, Charles's attention was distracted as he spoke with an elderly gentleman of his acquaintance, and for just a few seconds, he lost the thread of the conversation before recovering himself with a jerk of his head. But the gentleman made no attempt to hide his smile.

'She's a lovely woman, your young wife, Charles. I'm allowed to say such things at my age. But you must accept that she will gather admirers. You're a lucky devil, you know!'

'Yes, I know.'

But the words were grated between his teeth, and he strode briskly over to where Rose and Mr Tilling were discussing another of his creations. Seeing him approach, Rose twisted her head to look at him with an open smile.

'Charles, Mr Tilling would like to paint me,' she announced. 'What do you think of that?'

Charles's face appeared to close up like a clam. 'And have every Tom, Dick and Harry gawping at you?' he hissed, taking her arm none too gently.

'Pardon? It'd be for ourselves, no one else,' she protested. 'I thought you'd be pleased.'

'Well, I'm not! And is this how you repay my generosity, by making advances towards my wife?'

'I do apologise, Mr Chadwick,' the startled artist stuttered. 'I meant no offence.'

'Oh, no, I'm sure you didn't,' Charles sneered. 'And keep your grubby little paws to yourself, or you'll be looking for another patron. Rose?'

Mr Tilling's jaw swung agape as Charles drew Rose's hand onto his arm and held it there in a grip of iron. A white, angry line formed around her compressed lips, her eyes snapping with outrage as he all but dragged her into the middle of the floor.

'Ladies and gentlemen, I must thank you all once again for coming, but my wife is feeling unwell and so we must leave you to enjoy the remainder of the afternoon without us. Do feel free to discuss any purchases with Mr Tilling.'

In an instant, Charles was whisking Rose out into the street where a cab seemed to be waiting for them. Rose was bundled inside before she had a chance to open her mouth, and Charles sat down so close to her, she was squashed into the corner as if he were trying to imprison her.

'How dare you behave like a trollop in front of my friends and colleagues!' he raged, his face a fearsome puce.

Rose's heart beat furiously, but from indignation and rather than fear. 'You were the one making a spectacle of yourself!' she retorted. 'I were simply being nice to everyone, just like you said. If you choose to read anything into it, then you've only got your own jealous little mind to blame!'

Her head rocked on her neck with the force of Charles's hand across her cheek. But she scarcely felt the stinging pain as she turned boldly back to him and allowed her eyes to travel over him with caustic disdain. 'Very gentlemanly, I'm sure,' she said acidly.

Charles's face sagged beneath her haughty gaze. 'I'm sorry, Rose, but it's just that I love you so much!'

'Well, you've a mighty queer way of showing it!'

She shifted in the seat, turning her back on him and gazing out of the window in severe silence for the entire journey home through the London streets.

* * *

She scathingly ignored Charles's proffered hand as she climbed down from the cab and swept up the steps to the front door. She gritted her teeth in fury, listening to Charles's footfall behind her as the door was opened from the inside. Dolly, the young parlourmaid, dipped her knee appropriately as Rose made a dignified dash for the stairs.

'Oh, ma'am, a telegram came for you, not five minutes since,' Dolly called after her. 'I was just wondering if I should take a cab and bring it to you at the gallery.'

Rose turned to stone. A telegram. It could only be bad news. She gripped the banister with white fingers as she descended back to the hallway. She glanced up darkly and caught Charles's eye. The remorse in his expression was now mingled with consternation, but Rose's own alarm had driven away any feelings of reproach towards him.

She took the envelope with shaking fingers and tore open the thin paper. The letters danced a jig before her wavering vision. Their meaning sank almost unheeded into her brain, and she handed the note to Charles for confirmation, praying that her eyes had deceived her.

'ROSE COME HOME STOP,' he read gravely. 'HENRY VERY ILL STOP LOVE FLORRIE STOP.'

Charles looked up. As Rose's legs gave way beneath her, he caught her as she slumped against his shoulder and then found herself pressed down into the chair that stood beside the hall table. When the hazy mist cleared from her eyes, Charles was crouched down before her, holding her hands and gazing anxiously into her face.

'Oh, Rose, my dearest, I'm so sorry. I—'

'I must go to him at once.'

She sprang to her feet, but swayed perilously and had to sit down again abruptly. Charles's forehead creased in a deep frown.

'There's no point setting out now, my love,' he told her gently. 'I can't imagine there'll be any trains going all the way to Plymouth until the morning.'

'We could go to Exeter—'

'And find some lunatic mad enough to drive for miles across the moor in the middle of the night? No, Rose. It isn't practical. Especially as . . . oh, dammit, I can't come with you.'

'What!' Rose's eyes opened wide, but Charles's face lengthened in an anguished grimace.

'If it was any other day, but tomorrow is the first board meeting of the South African mining company, and I *have* to be there. God knows if it was anything else . . . But, you get packed. Dolly will help you. In fact, Dolly can travel with you. But just pack a small valise for yourself. I'll bring everything else the next day. So you do that, and I'll take a cab to the station and book all our tickets and find out the times of the trains so that I can telegraph Florrie and have Ned meet you from Tavistock. It's the best I can do.'

Rose nodded. Whatever else Charles was, he could be relied upon to think rationally in a crisis.

'All right. But I don't need Dolly to come with me,' she added as she smiled at the maid who had turned a strange colour at the idea of travelling to what seemed to her the opposite end of the earth. 'I can manage perfectly well, and to be honest — and no offence to you, Dolly — but I think I'd rather be on my own.'

For an instant, Charles looked horrified, but he recognised the stubborn determination on his wife's face. After his momentary loss of temper in the cab which had instantly mortified him, he wasn't going to argue with her.

'As you wish,' he agreed. 'You should be safe enough in First Class. And, Rose, I really am sorry.'

His words rang with emotion, and Rose knew it wasn't only her father's illness — whatever that might be — or the board meeting he was referring to. That night, for the first time in their married life — apart from when they were apart or her monthlies prevented it — he did not force himself upon her.

CHAPTER FOURTEEN

The nine-hour train journey seemed to last an eternity. As the railway finally skirted the southern edge of Dartmoor, Rose's eyes were drawn in the direction of the distant uplands, knowing that, somewhere out there, her beloved father lay seriously ill. But what was wrong with him? Had Florrie panicked and it was really only something quite trivial?

Rose clung to that comforting thought, though her heart beat tremulously in time to the rhythmical clatter of the train. Each main station had been a busy cacophony of hissing steam, chugging engines and piercing whistle-blowing, after which the line up to Tavistock seemed almost peaceful. The grey autumn day disappeared into the gathering dusk, and the breathtaking views over the moor were lost in gloom. Rose was nearing home, yet every nerve was on edge.

It was almost dark when she alighted at Tavistock Station, and she was grateful even for Ned's company as she sat beside him on the driving-seat of the wagonette. Her father *was* very sick, Ned told Rose, though he knew no more than that. From his unusual silence, Rose knew it was true. Ned had lit the carriage-lamps but they did little to illuminate their way, and as they ascended the steep hill up onto the moor, Rose was reminded of another time, less than a year before, when she'd struggled along the very same road in a snowstorm. So much had happened since then. She'd thought she'd found the solution to their problems. But the happiness she'd expected for herself was proving as elusive as a moonbeam.

She didn't stop to remove her coat and hat, but flew straight into her father's room. Florrie had been dozing in the chair, and she didn't have time to blink the confusion from her eyes before Rose threw herself on her knees beside the bed and took Henry's hand. He appeared to be asleep, but when he heard her soft, quavering voice, his glazed eyes half opened in his grey face.

'Rose, my darling girl,' he mumbled, his words so frail she could hardly hear him. 'What a picture you are. Quite the lady. And happy. You are happy, aren't you, Rose?'

A mist dimmed the crystal violet of her eyes. 'Yes, Father,' she managed to lie through the strangling constriction in her throat.

'Then I can die in peace,' he whispered, and his eyelids drooped closed again.

Something jerked, and then settled irrevocably in Rose's chest. 'Don't say that, Father.'

But all she received in response was a serene smile.

* * *

'I believe your father has suffered a pulmonary embolism,' Dr Power said grimly.

Rose lifted her eyes from the opposite side of the drawing-room fireplace where she shivered with cold, despite the roaring blaze. 'His . . . lungs, you mean?' she asked quietly.

'Yes. A clot. You know his lungs were weakened by the smoke inhalation last year. The clot may be the result of his inactivity, or he may have had a predisposition to it anyway.'

'And . . . his chances?' Her voice sounded strange to her own ears. She hadn't slept for forty-eight hours, neither her last night in London nor the night she'd spent by Henry's bedside. She was exhausted, her mind ready to shut down and accept the inevitable.

'Not good, I'm afraid. The clot might disperse, but if it does, the fragments could well lodge elsewhere, in the heart or the brain perhaps. In the meantime, your father's in a lot of pain from the clot. I'm giving him morphine injections, and Mrs Bennett has laudanum to supplement it if necessary. But, if we can't reduce them, the drugs in themselves will be very dangerous.'

'So, what you're saying is, one way or another, my father is dying.'

The doctor released his breath through pursed lips. 'Almost certainly.'

Rose nodded, staring down at her tightly intertwined fingers. 'Your frankness is appreciated, Dr Power. And . . . how long does he have?'

'If we have to keep up with this high dose of morphine, a week, possibly less. But better to let him go without pain, don't you think? And when the time comes, he will drift asleep in peace and calm.'

'And if he does improve?' Rose asked with a spark of hope.

Dr Power gave a sympathetic shake of his head. 'I am so sorry, but in my opinion, you should prepare yourself for the worst.'

Rose felt her heart drag with sadness. 'It hasn't been much of a life for him,' she croaked, 'not since the accident.'

'You've done the best for him that anyone could. Take comfort from that. And I suggest you get some sleep. Mrs Bennett will sit with him, and there are servants to relieve her. And may I suggest you put some witch hazel on the bruise on your cheek. I won't ask how you came by it.' He raised a wistful eyebrow at her. 'I believe your husband will be arriving this evening?'

Rose felt herself flush. She hadn't given Charles a thought, let alone the tender spot beneath her eye. 'Yes,' she answered absently. 'He had a business meeting of the utmost importance yesterday, so couldn't accompany me, and I wasn't prepared to wait.'

'Of course. And he will be of great strength to you.'

'Yes,' she replied, though something inside her died.

* * *

'Rose, my darling, you must eat.'

But she turned her head from the tray with her hand over her mouth. 'Please, Charles, take it away. Just the thought of food makes me feel sick.'

'All right. But you will drink the tea. Or would you prefer something cold? Cook's lemonade, or some ginger beer? I'll ride into Princetown to buy some if there's none in the pantry.'

But Rose looked up at him with a wan smile. 'Tea will be fine, thank you. But maybe some lemonade later on. Perhaps I can rouse father enough to drink some, too.'

'Yes, my dear. Perhaps.'

He patted her shoulder, and her hand closed over his. The last few days, he'd been the man she'd believed she had married, kind, affectionate but without demanding his conjugal rights. Not that she'd been to bed since she'd returned home, a fact that worried both the doctor and Charles. Now he padded silently out of the room, sensing that she'd prefer to be alone in her vigil.

The tea was hot and sweet, soothing, and she drifted in a somnolent haze. The autumn sunlight penetrating the room in hesitant shafts gradually faded into noiseless twilight, and she was aware of Florrie coming in to draw the curtains. Amber trotted in behind her and came to rest her muzzle on Rose's knee. Rose blinked awake and fondled the dog's ears. Not to be outdone, Scraggles scampered across with his head on one side, one pointed ear flopped over comically, and Rose stroked his scruffy head with a faint smile. She hardly dared look at Henry, and when she did, his chest was rising and falling regularly but in shallow, wheezy breaths.

Florrie straightened up from poking the moribund fire into life. 'He seems peaceful enough,' she whispered.

Rose nodded her head, but a painful lump squeezed her gullet. 'What shall I do without him, Florrie?' she barely mouthed.

'What shall we all do without him?' Florrie's wet cheeks wobbled.

She drew up the other chair and sat by Rose's side. They exchanged not another word, both lost in a private world of sadness. The fire hissed in the grate, the clock ticked on the mantelpiece, and the dogs slept together on the hearth rug, Scraggles making squeaking sounds as he dreamt of chasing rabbits.

Charles came in with the promised lemonade. They all stirred, even Henry groaning in the bed, his eyes opening in a confused daze. Rose turned to him, eyes spangled with unshed tears.

'Father?'

'My dearest Rose.' The agitation flowed from his face as his vision focused on his beloved daughter, and in its place, a supreme calm seemed to smooth out the lines in his skin.

'We were just having some of Cook's lemonade. Would you like some?'

Rose thought she would break at the normality of the question, but Henry managed a weak smile. 'Won't be as good as Florrie's, but yes, I'd like some. If you can sit me up . . .'

At once Florrie went to assist him, and as Florrie's strong arms went about him, there was a look passed between them that Rose had never noticed before, and it filled her with a cruel joy. Had there been more between her father and their housekeeper than she'd ever realised? Some sort of understanding that had brought them happiness all those years? She hoped so, but it would mean parting would be so much the worse.

Rose poured some of the lemonade into the feeding jug and held the spout to Henry's lips. But he'd only taken a sip before he indicated he wanted no more, and Rose replaced the little jug on the bedside table.

'Would you like me to stay?' Charles whispered in her ear.

Rose could hardly bear to turn to him. She should want to lean on her husband, on the man she was supposed to love, but she couldn't. She didn't love him, and so it was better to face this alone. With Florrie, who knew her better than she knew herself.

'No. It's all right, thank you,' she smiled with forced sweetness.

'I'll just be in the drawing-room,' Charles breathed back, and slipped quietly out of the room, the dogs following him. It was as if they'd had enough of the tense atmosphere and the smell of death.

Henry took a deep breath and winced. Rose leapt to her feet. 'Do you want some laudanum?'

Henry's eyes misted. 'No. Not yet. I want to spend some time with my daughter. And my dear Florrie.'

He gave the older woman that special smile again, and this time it brought Rose a certain peace. They'd been so happy together, the three of them. For more than twenty-two years. Without Florrie, it wouldn't have been the same.

They spoke of the past. Of distant memories. A good life. But one that was to be curtailed by possibly twenty years, though no one said so, because of a granule of grit that had somehow found its way into the mixing trough. The room was stilled, their voices low and bitter-sweet. Trembling with a lifetime of deepest love. Henry was tiring, and though he tried to conceal it, Rose knew that the pain in his chest was worsening, but still he refused the laudanum.

Dr Power arrived at seven o'clock, his greeting when he entered the bedroom that of a friend, rubbing his cold hands as he held them out to the warmth of the fire. He spoke in his usual calm and reassuring manner, telling them of the bitter weather outside. But what did Rose care of what was happening beyond the four walls of the house?

Henry's eyes were clouded with pain, and the doctor frowned. 'I think you're ready for the morphine,' he said gently.

'Just give me . . . five more minutes.' Henry's voice was no more than a thin, feeble trail, and Dr Power nodded in understanding as he patted Henry's shoulder and withdrew to the far side of the room.

Rose held Henry's limp hand, not able to speak, not able to think of any words, relieved almost, and yet ashamed of it, as Henry turned his head to Florrie who held his other hand from the opposite side of the bed.

'Florrie, what a comfort you've always been to me,' he mumbled.

Florrie's chin quivered. 'And you, Henry,' she answered in a faltering whisper, 'you gave me a home like no other.'

Her tear-filled eyes met Rose's across the bed, and when Henry rested his gaze on his daughter, a look of such tenderness came over him that his face appeared lit with a transcendent glow. 'And you, my darling child, will never know . . . what joy you've given me.'

His eyes seemed to spark with life, the deep blueness of his youth flooding into them as he stared deep into her grieving soul. Misery closed her throat and made glittering tears spill down her cheeks. 'I love you, father,' she choked as she struggled against her wrenching sobs.

Henry smiled back. 'I know,' he rasped. 'But you must . . . let me go now. Just promise me one thing. Whatever happens in your life . . . always be . . . yourself. Be the headstrong, feckless Rose . . . I have known . . . and loved.'

'Yes, I promise.' But this time the words were merely mouthed as the agony strangled her.

Dr Power, silently, was beside her, syringe at the ready. When he moved away again, Henry was watching her. Peacefully.

'No life for me now, Rose.'

His eyes closed, and he slept. Dr Power checked his pulse and breathed in deeply.

'He's very weak,' he said with quiet compassion. 'I think it might be best if I stay a while.'

Rose's heart thumped in her chest. 'You mean . . . ?' She couldn't say it, but the doctor nodded soberly, and Rose's mouth contorted as she fought against her tears. 'Thank you,' she murmured. 'At least . . . I can be with him.'

Dr Power nodded again. 'And, I'm sorry to have to mention such a thing, but perhaps your groom could stable my horse? On such a sharp night . . .'

'Of course.' An understanding smile slipped across Rose's lips. 'Florrie, would you mind?'

'I'll see to it at once.'

'And I'll . . . wait in your drawing-room with your husband, unless you'd rather I were here?'

'No, no. That's . . . But Florrie, you'll come back?' she said, almost desperately.

'Of course, my lamb.'

And so they sat, one on either side of Henry's bed. The room was darkened, the heavy curtains drawn against the cold night, just the orange and gold brilliance from the fire, and the lamps turned low. Midnight ticked on into the new day. The doctor glided in and out like a shadow. At two o'clock, Florrie went to make a pot of tea, leaving Rose trembling and alone, and while she was gone, Henry took a few sudden, rattling gasps, opened his eyes to look at his daughter, and remained staring at her, unseeing, for ever.

For several minutes, Rose sat without moving, numbed, in a strange way glad, because the waiting was over and the dreadful time had come, and she would be forced to face reality instead of refusing to believe it. She leant forward to lay her lips on Henry's motionless forehead, and sank back down in the chair, for there was no need for her to do anything for her father ever again. When Florrie came back in with the small tray, Rose's head was resting on the hand that would never clasp hers again.

Florrie silently put down the tray and seconds later, Charles and Dr Power were in the room. Rose sat like a granite statue, her eyes in a sightless stare. Ten, twenty minutes, and she could not be stirred except to push Charles aside when he tried to take her away.

The doctor squatted down before her and took her icy hands. 'Mrs Chadwick . . . Death is an inevitable part of life. The only certain thing that comes to us all. I watch men die, prisoners, who've endured a living hell. Who've been pushed beyond what their bodies can take, albeit part of their punishment. Their last days are full of misery, and they die unloved. Probably haven't seen their families for years. And they are buried in Princetown churchyard, as you know, with not even a stone to mark their graves. But your father died peacefully and with dignity, with his loving family all about him. Please, I beg you, take comfort from that, and think of your own health now, as you know your father would have wished.'

A faint light seemed to come into Rose's eyes. She nodded, and rising to her feet, floated out of the room. Charles followed her, but instead of climbing the stairs, she made for the side doorway. Before Charles could stop her, she was out across the stableyard and into Gospel's loose box where her howls of misery lacerated the frosty night as she clung about the animal's neck.

* * *

The funeral took place three days later. Rose Maddiford — for no one could ever think of her by her married name — walked behind her father's coffin, her husband at her side, supporting her. She resembled a little ghost, dark smudges under her sunken eyes, her hair swaying down her back like the wings of a raven from beneath a small black hat. She was keeping her promise. Being herself as she laid her father to rest.

The hearse was drawn by a pair of shining ebony horses, and a rainbow of flowers adorned the mahogany coffin. Behind Mr and Mrs Chadwick shambled Mrs Florrie

Bennett on the arm of Mr George Frean, the humble house-keeper leaning on the wealthy businessman, proprietor of the Cherrybrook gunpowder mills. Behind them, Joe Tyler, who had virtually been a son to the dead man, and his betrothed, best friend of the deceased's grief-stricken daughter. At a respectful distance followed the entire workforce of the powdermills and their families. There were local quarrymen and miners, too, shopkeepers, the carrier and the telegraph officer, all wanting to pay their last respects.

And after the interment, when Rose staggered, half carried by Charles, through the churchyard, she remembered Dr Power's words and stopped for just a moment to glance back at the plot reserved for the unmarked graves of the prisoners. And her heart overflowed with sorrow.

CHAPTER FIFTEEN

'Really, Rose, you can't keep galloping over the moors like some deranged creature from an asylum!'

Rose glowered at Charles from the dressing-room door and strode across to the bottom of the bed where the cleverly designed riding overskirt lay at the ready.

'I'm not behaving like a mad woman, I'm simply going for a ride,' she said coldly.

'And that's all you ever do, charge about on that wretched nag! I might as well not exist! I've stayed here for weeks on end to talk to you, comfort you, when I should be in London seeing to our business affairs. But you're never *here*!'

'And why should I be? My father's been dead for little more than a month, and you expect me to be over it. But when I'm out on the moor, I feel some sort of peace. Surely you can understand that? And if you need to go back to London, then go. I shan't be the one to miss you. I shan't forget the way you treated me when we were there last.'

Charles lifted his chin. 'Yes, and I've apologised for that. But I really do need to go to London, just for a few days, anyway. And I suppose,' he paused to sigh, 'you wouldn't come with me? The change might do you good. Take your mind off of everything. After all, Mrs Bennett saw the wisdom of going away when she went to stay with her sister. And it must be doing her some good, seeing as she's decided not to come back yet. If you come to London with me, I know I should be out most of the day, but we could go to a concert or the opera every night. You enjoyed that, didn't you, the music?'

Rose's spine bristled. It was a thorn in her side, that Florrie had gone, abandoning her when she needed her most. But Rose understood. They each had to deal with their grief in their own way.

'You honestly believe that would stop me thinking about my father? No, you go to London. I have my friends here, even if you disapprove of them.'

'If you're referring to the Cartwrights or Joe Tyler, then yes, I do disapprove,' Charles answered tightly. 'You'd hardly associate like that with Ned, and they're no better than he is.'

'How dare you say that! Ned is . . . ' She bit her lip, her cheeks flaming. She didn't want Charles to know what had happened in the stable that day. Ned was right. Charles *was* the jealous type, and though he could dismiss Ned — or worse — God alone knew what he might do to *her*! 'Ned is just Ned,' she continued less vehemently. 'But Joe and Molly and her family are my friends, and just now I really need them.'

'More than you need me, apparently.'

'You said it.'

Charles stiffened and his face hardened to stone. 'All right. I'll go to London alone. But I'll give you something to remember while I'm gone. And it may help you to remember that you are *my* wife and no one else's.'

Before she had a chance to react, he grasped her arm and pushed her backwards onto the bed. In a trice, he sprang up and straddled her, and her heart began to hammer as she watched his grim expression alter into a smile.

'You know, you really do look very fetching in a shirt and breeches. I can see those lovely breasts—'

'You know perfectly well I'd be wearing the jacket over the top,' she retorted.

'Just as well, my lovely girl. We wouldn't want every man jack to desire you as I do, would we now?'

His fingers were at the buttons of her shirt, and she tried to pull them away, her eyes burning with defiance.

'For God's sake, Charles, can't you leave me alone for five minutes—'

'I shall have you whenever I please, my little tigress. You seem to forget you are my wife, and I get precious little else in return for the luxury I provide for you!'

'And I think you have me often enough.'

'You do, do you? Well, we'll see about that!'

He ripped open the carefully sewn buttons with one yank of his hands, and in her outrage, Rose's lashing fists pummelled at his chest. He laughed. And her fingers opened like claws, catching his neck and drawing blood. In an instant, his expression turned to a mask of iron, and he trapped both her flailing hands in one of his. She scowled up at him, incensed that she didn't have the physical strength to fight him off, no matter how she struggled. He merely grinned back as his other hand fumbled with the buttons of her breeches and she knew there'd be no stopping him. She turned her head away with a tearing sigh of infuriated resignation, biting hard on her lip and waiting for the moment when it was over. Charles writhed and jerked on top of her, and finally rolled away, his face flushed and damp with sweat. Rose lay for several seconds, her teeth gnawing at the knuckles of one of her released hands, before springing to her feet.

She tossed her head, and her hair whipped about her in a tumbled cascade of curls. 'Well, if you've had your fill,' she barked at him, 'I'd like to go on my ride now.'

He turned on her eyes still glazed with pleasure. 'You really are magnificent, you know,' he drawled languidly. 'And I'm sorry for what I said in the heat of the moment just now. I really do love you. And I really do wish you'd come to London with me. I'm sure it would be good for you.'

Rose flashed him a withering look. 'No.' And then, as an afterthought, she added with frosty sarcasm, 'Thank you.'

Charles released a sharp sigh through his nostrils. 'As you wish. But . . . you could buy some presents for Christmas.'

'Now that my father's dead, I have no one to buy Christmas presents for,' she rounded on him as she fastened the riding skirt about her waist.

'Not even me? And what about all these friends you're so fond of?'

She glared at him, smarting under his sardonic words. Too incensed to speak, she grabbed the hat and hatpin she'd left ready on the dressing-table — pausing for an instant to wonder if she shouldn't jab the hatpin into whatever part of Charles's anatomy she could get at — and then stormed out of the room.

'Ned!' she yelled imperiously as she hurtled across the stableyard, and when he emerged from Tansy's loose box, she ordered him to fetch Gospel's saddle and bridle from the tackroom. An instant later, she was pressed up against Gospel's comforting shoulder, her cheek resting on his warm, hairy coat to hide her stinging tears.

She felt used. Physically sick. Her body bruised and aching. She'd married Charles for her father's sake, had *made* herself believe she had loved him. She didn't regret it. Henry's last months at Fencott Place had been happy ones, and she would have had it no other way. But she'd been married in June and now it was the beginning of December, and she had to face the rest of her life tied to a man she could not love. If Henry had survived another few years, it would have seemed far more worthwhile, but just now it felt as if her sacrifice had been for nothing.

She pulled herself up short as Ned joined her in the box, and Gospel stamped with agitation at the unwelcome intruder. But within five minutes, they were out on the moor, crisp and white with a hoar frost.

Instinctively, Rose set Gospel's head in the direction of Princetown. As they approached, her eyes were inevitably drawn to the daunting buildings of the prison. Constantly battered by the worst of Dartmoor's wet and windy climate,

Rose knew from Jacob Cartwright that even the walls inside the newly extended cell block already ran with rainwater. Although Rose could imagine the inmates shivering through the bitter winter nights while she existed in the lap of luxury, she knew exactly how they felt, incarcerated in a living hell for years on end . . .

* * *

It was three days before Charles left for London, three days when the very sight of him brought on a bout of nausea. Henry's death had reduced Rose's appetite to that of a sparrow, but now she somehow felt sick and hungry at the same time, and eating something light and refreshing such as a raw carrot, seemed to settle her stomach. You be turning into a horse, like that animal o' yourn, she could just hear Florrie teasing her. But Florrie wasn't there, was she? Rose nearly gagged on her sadness. She felt so alone . . .

But not quite. She hadn't dared to sneak out while Charles was still there, though to be honest, he'd never physically prevented her from her lone rides. The truth was that, though she refused to admit it, since the day Charles had forced himself upon her and she'd stampeded across the moor in a maddened temper, she hadn't *felt* like going out. But his departure seemed to have given her a new lease of life, besides which there was one exciting event that she could now devote herself to whole-heartedly — and of which Charles, thank goodness, appeared ignorant.

On the fifteenth of December, Molly and Joe were to be married. Charles wasn't a churchgoer, so hadn't heard the banns being read, and as he refused to associate with the people of the lower echelons, there'd been no one to inform him of the news. In fact, his life at Fencott Place was fairly insular, and Rose supposed it was one reason for focusing his attentions on his wife with such zeal. To be fair, if she stopped to think about it, Charles had sacrificed much to be with her on Dartmoor, and she bit her lip in remorse. In her heart of hearts, she recognised that the problems with their marriage were not all one-sided.

No such qualms entered her mind now. She decided to walk into Princetown rather than take Gospel from his warm stable. The ground was frozen solid beneath her feet, the still, bitterly cold air so raw she could almost taste it. The sky was an iron grey, pressing down on her with low, ominous clouds, but she was determined that her visit would bring some respite from her depression.

She found the sitting-room in the new flat in happy chaos. Molly leapt to her feet and hugged her friend tightly.

'We'm so sorry 'bout your father,' she said quietly.

Rose nodded, and knotted her lips against the lump that swelled so readily in her gullet. 'Thank you,' she whispered, and then jerked her head towards two tea-chests in the middle of the floor. 'You look busy.'

'Yes.' Knelt next to them, Mrs Cartwright's eyes shone. 'We'm packing some things to go over to Molly and Joe's cottage at Cherrybrook.'

Rose smiled broadly, but somehow the usual vivid light was missing from her eyes. 'I'm so pleased for you. You must be so excited, Molly.'

The younger girl grinned. 'Well, you'm only just married yersel, Rosie, so you should know. And . . . you will come to the wedding, won't you? You and . . . Mr Chadwick? I couldn't bear it if you wasn't there!'

Rose felt her heart thud in her chest. There was no way Charles would even contemplate attending such a low-class affair as she knew he'd consider it. No doubt he'd do his best to prevent her from going, too. 'You just try and stop me!' she answered, tossing her head and praying Molly wouldn't see the doubt that flickered across her features. 'Now, are you going to let me see your wedding dress?'

'Oh, 'twill just be my Sunday best, but I doesn't mind.'

A thrill of enthusiasm spilled into Rose's troubled soul and she latched onto it gratefully. 'Oh, but you must have a new dress! Something you can wear afterwards as well, to be practical,' she added, for she knew Molly would need persuading to such extravagance. 'Just over a week, so there should be time if we choose some material today. So come along, Molly. Fetch your hat and coat. Oh, it'll be lovely to do some sewing. To feel useful again! It can be my wedding present to you. And anything else you need to start your new life with.'

'Oh, but, Rose—'

'No buts, Molly! What's the point of being rich if you can't spend some money on your best friend when she's getting married!'

A little voice inside her head grimaced that she earned her wealth in the marital bed. And that frittering away a few pounds of Charles's money on Molly when she knew it would anger him, was immensely satisfying. And so she spent the happiest day since Henry had died in the Cartwright's humble home, cutting out Molly's new dress from material bought in one of Princetown's few shops. And not just a dress, but an elegant, contrasting cape, for it was, after all, the middle of winter. When it was time to leave, Rose carefully folded all the material into a brown paper parcel to take home with her, as she had far more room to work in the dining-room of Fencott Place.

She kissed Molly goodbye, shivering on the doorstep as the arctic air licked about her slender form despite her warm coat. But there was one more thing she must do before she trod the path home. She crossed over the road and entered the churchyard.

The gloom at once closed about her aching heart again, dissipating the few hours of enjoyment she'd spent with Molly. She moved like a spectre to the slight mound in the grass with the simple wooden cross. No headstone as yet. You had to wait several months for the earth to settle, she'd been told. But the memorial she envisaged would be the finest ever made. Paid for from Charles's pocket, of course. Bitterness tugged at her lips, grief searing her throat until tears began to trickle down her cheeks. She knelt, still as a statue, as the misery tore at her chest. She wanted to howl her pain to the heavens so that somehow it might reach Henry and haul him back to the world of the living; so that the bottomless pit of her agony might make him appear to her and let her know that in some other way, he still existed, for no daughter could ever have loved a father more deeply than she had. But she knew it would do no good. There was nothing on earth that could free her from her despair. A good man, perhaps. One who understood, who saw her as a person with her own needs and feelings. But Charles was all she would ever have.

She tipped her head back, lifting her tear-ravaged face to the leaden sky, and the first snowflakes kissed her frozen cheeks.

CHAPTER SIXTEEN

Saturday week arrived and Charles had yet to return. Rose's heart lifted. The wedding was set for noon and there was nothing to stop her from going.

Molly looked radiant in the lovely dress Rose had laboured over into the small hours to have finished in time. The ceremony was perfect, and Rose managed to ignore the barbed pang in her side at the memory of both her own wedding back in the summer, and her father's funeral in the same church not so many weeks before. She shivered as a draught of air brushed her side. Was it Henry, for wild horses would not have kept him from the wedding of his semi-adopted son?

The celebration at The Plume of Feathers was a jolly affair. Joe made a short speech in which he thanked Rose for rescuing him from his miserable existence as a child, as without her, he would never have met his bride. And then, his eyes becoming solemn as he met Rose's gaze, he proposed a toast to Henry's memory. Rose was staggered. Every person, and there were many, stood to attention and a respectful silence settled over the merrymakers. Henry had touched all their lives, Joe said reverently, and would never be forgotten. And Rose shed a tear of pride.

The moment of sadness over, the festivities began in earnest. Two fiddlers struck up a jig, and the tables were cleared away to make room for dancing. At length, in the middle of the afternoon, when Rose knew she had to leave so that she'd arrive home before dark, her soul felt refreshed as she reluctantly said her farewells.

'The master be home,' Cook told her in a low, wary tone as she went into the kitchen to order a pot of tea. 'Wanted to know where you was, so I teld him. I hope that were all right, ma'am.'

Rose drew in a slow breath and then smiled boldly. She had been to Molly and Joe's wedding. Charles hadn't been there to stop her, and she cared little for what happened next. She'd left her slush-coated boots by the door, and now she hurried upstairs to slip into a pair of soft kid shoes. She changed her clothes, too, the hem of her skirts and petticoats being stained with damp. She chose what she knew was one of Charles's favourite dresses, with a scooping neckline to reveal quite enticingly the creamy skin below the well of her throat. Her hair was already entwined upon her head, and she simply tidied a wayward curl before tripping downstairs again.

She paused at the drawing-room door to square her shoulders before she breezed in with a brilliant smile lighting her face.

'Charles!'

She made herself run across the room, ready to give him a passionate embrace.

'Why didn't you come straight in here to greet me?' he demanded before she could do so. 'Cook's had time to bring you in some tea.'

Rose's weary heart sank. Were they to argue already?

'I hear you've been to Molly Cartwright's wedding,' Charles continued to bark at her. 'You deliberately kept it from me, didn't you, knowing I'd disapprove?'

Rose shrugged casually. 'You weren't here to tell. What time did you get back, anyway? Would you like some tea? I'll fetch another cup.'

She turned towards the door, but he caught her by the wrist and dragged her back. She yelped, though it was a squeal more of surprise than discomfort.

'If I wanted to go to my best friend's marriage to Joe who is virtually my brother, I didn't need your permission!' she hissed at her husband, her eyes flashing dangerously.

'Oh, yes, you did! My wife, hobnobbing with that rabble! I won't have it!'

It was all Rose could do to stop herself flying at him with hungry fingernails. Instead, she glared at him steadily, her cheeks colourless with strained composure.

'Nobody possesses me,' she grated levelly. 'If I wish to associate, as you put it, with good, honest, God-fearing folk, you won't stop me.'

'Oh, yes, I will. And may I remind you, madam, that in your wedding vows not so long ago, you promised to obey me.'

'And in all things reasonable I do. Which is more than can be said of *you* when it comes to honouring *me*! You treat me like some whore in bed.'

'Rose! I won't have such a filthy word coming from your mouth!'

He raised his hand, ready to strike her, and she instinctively sprang away from him. But his other hand still held fast onto her wrist, and her suddenly extended arm wrenched in its socket. He lost his grip, and with the force of her own movement, she twisted away from him, her feet going from under her. Her head narrowly missed the table as she fell, but her collarbone cracked against it instead. Pain stung across her shoulder, and her vision clouded with black spots as she crumpled onto the floor. Charles dropped onto his knees beside her, and she shuddered when she felt him take her in his arms.

'Oh, my darling, I'm so sorry!' his voice shook in her ear. 'I wouldn't have hit you, really I wouldn't!'

You did once before, she mumbled in her head, since her voice refused to work.

She felt him lift her up and carry her over to the chaise-longue. Her head swam giddily and when her eyes wandered into focus, Charles's face was looming over her, a mortified picture of concern.

'You don't think . . . It isn't broken, is it?' his lips trembled.

If she hadn't been in such agony, she would have launched a verbal attack on him, but as it was, she shot him an acid glance as she gingerly fingered her collarbone, exposed by the low neckline of her dress. It had already swollen into a tender lump the size of an egg, and she tentatively moved her shoulder in a small circle. It hurt, but overall, the pain was subsiding.

'No, I don't believe it's broken,' she found her voice at last, though it was small and shaking. 'So you won't have to explain to the doctor how it happened,' she added with caustic contempt.

Charles's eyes opened wide in his flushed face. 'It . . . it wasn't my fault,' he protested.

Rose glared at him, and suddenly all her resentment rose inside her like a bore tide. The contents of her stomach lifted to her throat, and with one hand clamped over her mouth, she fled the room and raced upstairs to the bathroom where she retched her heart into the pretty china washbowl.

* * *

Rose slowly blinked open her eyes. There'd still been a glimmer of light in the sky when, after a sumptuous Christmas dinner, she'd come over so tired that she felt she must have a lie-down. She hadn't drawn the curtains. Now, after a short sleep, it was dark outside, the only light coming from the glowing coals in the grate. Rose lay for a few minutes, her gaze meandering over the lovely room. Charles certainly provided well for her, and she *was* grateful, but . . . If only he'd continued to be the same man after their wedding as he'd been before, she perhaps could have loved him. But he wanted her entirely to himself, to *possess* her in every way, and it was ruining their marriage.

She stood up, wincing at her bruised collarbone, and still feeling really full from the meal. Goodness, she'd eaten too much, but Cook had excelled herself and Rose's appetite, which had been so poor since Henry's death, had seemed stimulated. Her dress was strained, and the ties around her waist which held the small bustle at the back, felt uncomfortably tight. It had been like that for a few weeks now, which was odd really considering how little she'd been eating of late. But then her monthly must be due, as her breasts were swollen and tender. She hadn't had the 'curse' as Molly called it since . . . since when?

She frowned. And a little flutter quivered through her body as she cast her mind back. Since her dearest father had passed away, her life had been one appalling black blur. The dark days since then had been lost in a mournful haze, all her strength expended in trying to claw her way out of her grief. She simply hadn't considered . . . But now the force of it hit her hard in the chest. She'd been 'on' when they'd arrived in London at the beginning of October. She only remembered because she'd been worried about the long journey and the frequency with which she might be able to find a public convenience. But she couldn't remember anything since. With everything that had happened, her bereaved mind had hardly taken note of . . .

She was pregnant. She must be. Everything pointed to it, the nausea, the thickening of her waist, the tiredness. She sat motionless in the silent room, trying to absorb what had just dawned on her. Charles would be thrilled. And her? Well . . . yes. A tiny kernel of joy was slowly unfurling inside her forlorn heart, driving away the wretched misery of the past weeks. Except that her father would never know the wonderment of being a grandparent.

Joy. And hope that the child would heal the deepening rift between herself and Charles. Because she *wanted* their marriage to be a happy one, *wanted* so much the loving relationship that was eluding her . . .

A smile crept across her lips. It must have still been there as she entered the drawing-room, for Charles glanced up from the book he was reading, and a quizzical expression creased his face.

'Ah, my dear, did you have a nap? You certainly look refreshed.'

'Charles.' She squatted down before him, her cheeks flushed with excitement. 'I have something to tell you,' she announced breathlessly. 'I believe . . . I think I may be with child.'

Charles's eyes almost popped out of their sockets. He cast his book aside and dropped onto his knees, wrapping her in his jubilant arms. Her heart took a little leap as her head lay against his shoulder. Perhaps, yes, this would bring them closer together.

'Oh, my darling, *clever* girl!' he murmured into her hair before pulling back and grinning almost idiotically at her before he asked, 'How?'

To witness the collected, dominant Charles Chadwick lost for words and quivering, was so comical that Rose laughed aloud. 'Surely I don't need to tell you that?'

Charles shook his head with a grunt of merriment. 'No, I meant . . . are you sure? I mean . . . when?'

Rose lowered her eyes, her face serious now. 'No. I'm not positive. But everything points to it. I hadn't really thought about it before, what with father . . . ' Her voice trailed off sadly for just a moment before she came back with a contented smile. 'But just now, I was thinking . . . and it dawned on me that . . . it could be—'

'Oh, I'm sure you're right! Oh, my lovely one! Come, now you must take care of yourself.' He helped her to her feet and sat her down in one of the armchairs like a piece of precious porcelain. Rose pushed the rueful doubt to the back of her mind. Would he treat her with kid gloves now that he had what he wanted from her? He'd certainly been the perfect, loving husband for the last ten days, ever since the incident on the evening of Joe and Molly's wedding, trying to make up for what he'd done to her, she grimaced bitterly. 'And you must take care of our son.'

He jerked his head towards her belly with a caressing smile, and Rose snatched in her breath. She was giving him a child, but was she giving him a son? She caught her lip, and forced a small nervous laugh. 'There's no need to cosset me. I'm not ill, just pregnant. It wasn't so long ago that women up north worked down the mines till they gave birth, and then carried on working the next day.'

'Women built like oxen, and they or the child were probably dead within the week.' Charles took her hand, stroking it adoringly. 'You're more like a fairy, and I won't have anything happen to you or our son. If it wasn't Christmas Day, I'd fetch the physician at once.'

'Oh, I don't think there's any hurry. Dr Power won't—'

'Dr Power! You don't think I'm going to let the *prison* doctor see to my wife during her pregnancy, do you?'

Rose's spine stiffened, the glory of the last half hour crumbling into dust. 'But he's an excellent physician—'

'And looks after the worst criminals in the country, for God's sake! He touches them and their filth, and then you expect me to let him put his contaminated hands on *my* wife!'

'Oh, I see! He's not good enough to oversee the birth of *your* child, but he were good enough for my father! Is that how you saw my father, then, as some being inferior to your high and mighty self? And am I merely the mare you wanted to service in order to get the son you wanted?'

Charles glared at her, his mouth a thin, tight line. 'You know that's not what I meant. But you will *not* have the prison doctor attend you. I'll go into Tavistock and make enquiries as to the best and most senior physician in the town.'

'Well, I'd leave it a while if I were you, till the bruising on my shoulder's gone! He might just ask how I came by it.'

She sprang across the room, tears pricking her eyes, unable to remain in his company a second longer. As she passed a side table, her arm caught the fine crystal vase displayed on it and sent it flying into the air. Just like her splintered heart, it crashed onto the floor and shattered into a million pieces.

CHAPTER SEVENTEEN

Rose stared out of the drawing-room window, not that she could see very much. It was mid-April, and though they'd been enjoying some kind spring weather, today felt as if they'd been plunged back into winter. A thick, grey, bone-chilling mist sat, heavy and motionless, on the moor like a life-extinguishing blanket. Moisture hung in the saturated air with not a breath of wind to blow it away, and since mid-day, visibility had been reduced to no more than twenty yards. It was the sort of day when the unwary traveller could easily lose his way on the moor and become treacherously lost. And the fog might possibly last for days.

Rose turned restlessly from the window. She thought she'd heard an explosion earlier, but what with the windows being shut against the muffling fog, and the walls of Fencott Place being so thick, she couldn't be certain. She forced to the back of her mind the explosion at the powdermills that had decimated her father's life. It was unlikely to be a repeat of the event, and was anyway far quieter. Besides, such sounds were not uncommon up on the moor, a guard firing a warning shot, or blasting either at the prison quarry, the new enterprise at Merrivale, or the massive quarries on Walkhampton Common, so Rose had taken little notice.

But that was some hours ago, and now she sat down in the armchair by the cheerful fire, and laid her hand on her swollen abdomen. To her delight, the baby kicked back, bringing a smile to Rose's lips. She was quite enjoying this stage of her pregnancy, the nausea long gone, and the final month which Mrs Cartwright had told her could be most uncomfortable, some time off as yet. Rose wondered how large she would become, for she already felt enormous.

Dr Seaton, whose services Charles had engaged as being the most senior physician in Tavistock, was very pleased with her progress. To her utter relief, he'd told Charles that from now on until at least six weeks after the birth — which was expected at the end of June — their marital relationship as he delicately put it, should cease.

Charles had evidently taken the doctor's warning to heart, and for the child's sake, had left her alone. Indeed, he'd treated her like a princess ever since she'd announced her condition to him. He'd insisted she shouldn't ride Gospel again, but drive everywhere she needed in the wagonette, and she'd agreed that this was a sensible precaution. He always wanted to know exactly where she was going — so that he would know both she and the baby were safe, being his excuse — and so she'd only seen Molly during the two trips Charles had made to London. The second time, a month ago now, Mrs Cartwright had been visiting her daughter, and Joe had managed to spend half an hour with them, so it had been a jolly company. But it seemed an eternity ago, and Rose was champing at the bit to see them again.

She clicked her tongue and stretched out her hand towards Amber and Scraggles who were toasting themselves in front of the fire. The scruffy mongrel at once trotted over to Rose's chair, wagging his unkempt tail nineteen to the dozen as she rubbed his ears. Amber was slower to heave herself to her feet, heavy with the unborn pups Scraggles had given her.

Charles had despaired when they'd realised what had happened. Was he to be landed with a houseful of mangy

169

curs under his feet at every minute? But Rose was delighted. The two dogs behaved like an old married couple, inseparable, Rose considered ruefully as she stroked Amber's golden snout that was resting now on her knee. The sort of relationship Rose herself craved, though Charles had been kindness itself since her announcement on Christmas Day. But that innate understanding, that unspoken intimacy of two fused souls, she knew could never be theirs. Charles still couldn't comprehend that sometimes she needed to be alone, out on the freedom of the moors where her heart and her spirit belonged. And his attempts to keep her all to himself were slowly asphyxiating her.

She glanced up carelessly as he came into the room.

'I've ordered some tea, my dearest,' he announced, smiling at her fondly. 'It will be served directly, and I'm sure you will . . . What the devil are those two creatures doing indoors?' he thundered, his expression hardening as he rounded the winged back of the chair that had hidden the two dogs from his view. 'Ned reckons she could whelp any day, and I won't have her making a mess all over the carpets! And as for that flee-ridden monstrosity—'

'Oh, Scraggles, what is he saying about you?' Rose crooned, ruffling the endearing animal's ears and raising a teasing eyebrow at her husband.

The annoyance around Charles's mouth slackened. 'I'm sorry, Rose, my love, but you know it makes sense. As soon as Amber's clean again afterwards, she can come back inside. But as for the pups, well, I don't know what I shall do with them!'

Rose screwed her lips into a knot. What *he* would do with them? Amber was *her* dog, and she considered Scraggles was, too, and so it followed that the puppies would also be hers. 'I've already promised one to Molly, and another to her brothers and sisters if they're allowed,' she said stiffly, 'so that'll be two less for you to worry about. Right, come along, you two. Back to the stables.'

'No, no, you rest yourself, my darling,' Charles said before she had even got to her feet. 'I'll take them.'

'Amber's basket is in Gospel's loose box. They all like being in together, but make sure you bolt the door properly, or Gospel will nudge it open!'

'Yes, yes, I do know that animal's desire to escape. A bit like his mistress,' Charles added wryly as he ushered the two dogs out of the door.

Rose sat back with a sigh. Poor Gospel. He must be so restless, so frustrated, far more than she was. At least she had the child to occupy her thoughts. Normally, the spirited beast would have been out in the paddock, but he was of thoroughbred stock, not a hardy Dartmoor pony, and with the penetrating damp of such a dense fog as this, it might not be wise.

Charles returned five minutes later, holding the door open for the young housemaid carrying the tea tray. Though servants were no more to Charles than that, he was not unkind towards them. He instructed the girl to ignite the remaining lamps. Although it was only mid afternoon, what light there was outside was already fading and Charles himself stoked up the fire to an even more comforting conflagration. He watched approvingly as the maid completed her duties and dipped her knee before backing out of the room.

'Shall I pour, my dear?' This was said with the gleaming silver teapot already in Charles's hand. Rose nodded absently, accepting both the bone china teacup and a matching plate upon which he'd placed a selection of Cook's delicacies. They took their tea in silence, since there was little they had to say to each other. Rose ate little. The thought of what Charles might want to do with any surplus puppies had robbed her of her appetite. Besides, the kindly Dr Seaton had reminded her that she should eat not for two, but for one small adult, meaning herself, and one baby.

Rose mulled over the elderly physician's visit the previous day. He wasn't one to beat about the bush, was Dr Seaton, no airs and graces and no being cowed by his wealthy patients. Rose had every confidence in him. Although Dr Power would have been equally as competent, she was happy enough to have the more senior physician oversee the birth of the child she prayed would seal her marriage into true love.

She glanced across at Charles now. They had so little in common, except perhaps that he was reading a book as he sipped his tea, and Rose, too, loved to read. The thought made her draw from the pocket in her skirt the letter she'd received from Florrie that morning, the postman having delivered it before the fog had closed in. The depressing weather had made Florrie's communication seem even more depressing itself, and Rose's eyes saddened as they scanned Florrie's childlike writing for the second time.

My dear Rose,

I hope you are well and that the baby is going on nicely. I never had no child of my own, as you knows. I had you instead, and that were enough for me. No one could be dearer to me than you, except perhaps your father. Though he loved me in return, we was never more than fondest friends. I misses him so much and I casn find it in me to come back to the house with him not there. I hopes that time will heal, and that it will for you, too. You was a wonderful daughter to him, but you has your husband and the baby to think of. 'Tis a great comfort to me staying with my sister and her children, and God willing, I will feel able to come home to you soon. I am well, and so is the family here.

Take care of yoursel, my little maid

All my love

Florrie

Rose moistened her lips pensively. Her heart had sunk when she'd first read the letter that morning, as she was hoping desperately that it would contain news of Florrie's return. But Rose understood. Florrie had loved Henry in the same way that Rose had believed she could have loved Charles, and the cruel separation of Henry's death after so many shared years must have been as devastating for Florrie as it had been for herself. She stared unseeing into the fire, her mind wandering over her past life at Cherrybrook, and the contentment which she'd believed would be eternal, but which had been brought to such an abrupt end. It shouldn't have been so terrible. Charles should have brought her comfort, but he never did. Rather she longed for when he was away in London.

She glanced across at him, engrossed in his book. Shut away in a different world. Somewhat as they seemed to live their lives.

'Charles?' her quiet voice shattered the silence.

He looked up casually. 'Yes, my dear?'

'I was just wondering, how is Mr Tilling and the gallery? Is he doing well?'

Charles shrugged his eyebrows. 'I've no idea.'

'Really? Oh, then I shall write to him and enquire.'

'You will do no such thing!'

The words were spoken in an angry snarl, and Rose sat up straight, her eyes startled. 'Why?' she stammered. 'I don't understand.'

The muscles around Charles's mouth were tight. 'I have nothing more to do with Mr Tilling now, since I withdrew my patronage.'

'What do you mean?'

'Well, what could he expect after his insult upon you? And then the blackguard made things worse by asking after you on several occasions.'

'Insult? He simply wanted—'

'Rose!' Charles slammed his open book onto his lap. 'I cannot have my wife posing for some lecherous young artist! I could see the look in his eye—'

'And you read something into it that wasn't there!' Rose fumed. 'He was polite and respectful and—'

'Oh, yes, my innocent, trusting girl, I'm sure he seemed so to you! But I have seen what can happen—'

'And you think *I* would allow it?'

'The matter is *closed*.'

'Oh, no, it isn't. I suppose that means you wouldn't trust *me* either? So *you* are the one who's insulting me, not Mr Tilling! I'm totally faithful to you, Charles, so why do you doubt me? Why do you want to *possess* me all the time?'

'I only want to protect you, my love, you and our son. You're so vulnerable, and I shouldn't want any harm to befall you.'

He picked up his book again and buried his nose in it, an indication that the conversation was concluded. Rose's mouth thinned to a fine line. What was the point in arguing? Though she was sorry for the young artist who'd been denied the promised opportunity to display his talents. Charles considered he *owned* her. And it could never be any different.

With a sigh of frustration, she reached her feet out to the fire and closed her eyes. She dozed a little, dreaming of a wild gallop across the moor. When she came to, Charles was still reading, apparently not having moved an inch. The tea tray had disappeared. The fire still crackled merrily, and Rose was grateful that she was warm and cosy when it was so raw outside. She knew she was lucky to be cocooned in such luxury, but just now she had nothing to *do*. She was bored. Cooped up like a hen. And she drummed her fingers fretfully on the arm of the chair.

'Oh, Rose, can't you find something to do?' Charles asked with mild irritation. 'Read a book, or . . . or do some sewing?'

'I would if you'd let me make something sensible, like baby clothes,' she answered tartly, though she had done just that in secret. 'Needle-point just seems such a waste of time.'

'I've told you before, making clothes is not a fit occupation for a lady. You can employ a seamstress for that.'

Rose ground her teeth in frustration. A heartfelt sigh exploded from her lungs, and before she knew it herself, she was on her feet. 'I simply must get out!' her lips declared, and she found herself glaring at Charles's startled disapprobation.

'Don't be so ridiculous!' he reproached her scornfully. 'You'd be lost in a minute in this fog.'

'No, I wouldn't,' she scowled. '*You* would, but I know the moor like the back of my hand. I'll go mad if I don't get some air!'

'But it's dark, Rose, and I absolutely forbid it. You're carrying our child, for God's sake! Think of him, if not yourself! And what behaviour are you proposing when he's born? You'll have to toe the line, then, my girl. No more gallivanting across the moor on that wild beast of yours. I might even sell him if you can't behave.'

Rose audibly gasped. 'W-what did you say?' she stuttered from between white, trembling lips.

'I think you heard me.' His voice was cold, unbending. 'I've been most lenient with you, knowing the freedom your father always allowed you, and your understandable grief over his death. But now it's time for you to become the respectable lady your position in society dictates.'

Rose stared at him, her eyes blind. Sell Gospel? It was unthinkable! She'd lost her father, she'd lost Florrie, and now if Charles was to sell Gospel, she'd lose everything she'd sacrificed herself for by marrying him! No! She couldn't let him do that!

'You wouldn't dare!' she challenged him, the words wrung from her throat.

'Wouldn't I? And if I say you shan't go out, then you shan't.'

'Oh, yes, I will!' Her eyes darkened to a sparking indigo as they bore fearlessly into his. And when he stood up to face her, his hand raised, she lifted her chin, blazing with defiance. 'That's right. Go on, hit me. You've done it before. But if you do, I'll show Dr Seaton the marks. And if you dare to sell Gospel, I swear to God, I'll disappear, and you'll never see me or your child again.'

Charles's face turned the colour of unfired clay as the shock of her scathing threat hit him below the belt. He knew her well enough to realise that it would be foolish to underestimate her; she possessed both the determination and the intelligence to outwit him in this wild region that she knew intimately and to which he was an outsider. Perhaps he should say that he wouldn't sell Gospel provided that she only rode him when he accompanied her on Tansy. But she didn't give him the chance. She spun on her heel and slipping beyond his reach, ran out into the hallway. He followed, flinging the door wide, but she was already down the passageway and into the small rear vestibule. Through the glass panel in the door, he saw her pulling on an outdoor coat hanging there, and though he ground his teeth, he thought better of it and stormed back into the drawing-room.

Equally as furious, Rose lit one of the storm lanterns kept on the side table in the porch. She shivered as she stepped across the stable yard. The dense moisture hung in the air in cold droplets that clung to her lashes and seemed to penetrate her very bones. It was just like winter again, the line of loose boxes veiled in a misty blur, and Rose hung the lamp on the special hook on the doorpost outside Gospel's stable.

The place was deserted, Ned having finished his duties for the day and taken himself off to his quarters above the tackroom at the far side of the yard. All he'd need to do was to check the horses before he went to bed, and lock the stable doors for the night. So Rose was able to slip into Gospel's loose box unseen, bolting the bottom half of the stable door, but leaving the top open to allow the uncertain glow from the lamp to enter the otherwise pitch darkness inside. The two dogs were hairy shadows in the gloom, Amber in her basket and Scraggles lying faithfully by her side. But Rose went straight to Gospel, burying her face against his sleek neck. The animal turned his head, whickering softly as he nudged his velvety muzzle against her arm.

'Oh, Gospel, what am I to do?' Rose whispered brokenly. 'I miss father so much, and that . . . that husband of mine is insufferable. You and the dogs are all I have, and now he's threatening to sell you!'

She rested her forehead against his shoulder and her body shook with wrenching sobs. Nothing else seemed to exist in the entire world but her agony. She didn't hear the rustle in the straw behind her, not until the strong hand closed over her mouth, and her desperate tears came to a sudden, shuddering halt . . .

CHAPTER EIGHTEEN

Rose's heart was pounding like a hammer, her terrified eyes staring blindly at Gospel's flank. For five long, agonising seconds, neither she nor the owner of the hand moved, and if it hadn't been for the pressure of the arm firmly about her, she might have thought she was dreaming.

'I'm sorry to startle you, miss, but as God is my witness, I mean you no harm.'

The whispered, agitated words might have been in a foreign language for all the sense her petrified, confused brain made of them. She remained motionless, battling against her taut nerves and trying to rationalise the desperate thoughts that tumbled in her head. The voice that had spoken was that of a man, polite, cultured, not local — more like Charles in accent, in fact — and it had *trembled* with fear as if its owner was as afraid as Rose was! Indeed, she was aware now that the hand over her mouth was shaking, and the man, whoever he was, was hesitant, uncertain of what to do next, and Rose waited, forcing her reeling mind to think clearly again.

'If I let you go,' the voice quavered again, 'do you promise not to scream?'

Rose stiffened, and then nodded, the small sound she made in her throat muffled by his hand. She felt his fingers slacken, and instantly tighten again, as if he'd thought better of it.

'You do promise?' he repeated. 'Please God, I *beg* you not to scream. Not until you've heard what I have to say.'

There was something in his tone, some desperation, that she recognised, for hadn't she been there, was *still* there, herself?

'I promise,' she managed to mumble through his fingers, and gradually, as the seconds ticked by, his hold reluctantly eased. Once she was free of his grasp, she had to steel herself to turn round, inch by inch.

She dared to look up into the intruder's face. The whites of his terror-stricken eyes glinted in the dim half-light, and she made out the pale shape of a bald head. No, not bald, as it fell into place with a sudden jolt, but cropped. Cropped to the scalp in a convict cut.

She hardly had time to gasp when he let out an astounded, 'Good Lord! You!'

Rose instinctively backed up against Gospel's side, and the felon went to step towards her, his hand outstretched. But as he transferred his weight onto his other leg, it seemed to give way beneath him and with a stifled cry, he plunged past her, landing in the thick layer of straw on the loose-box floor.

Rose stood, numbed by the last few minutes, blinking down at the figure by her feet. She could scream now, run into the house and raise the alarm. But she didn't. In that split second, she'd seen enough of the escaped prisoner to spark her memory. It was him, the same fellow who'd saved Jacob Cartwright's life, and had been unjustly beaten and kicked by the Civil Guards for his efforts. Who, she'd subsequently learnt through Jacob, had relentlessly protested that he was innocent of his alleged crime. No. Rose would not scream. Certainly not until she'd given him the chance to explain himself.

He groaned, and glancing down, even in the shadows, Rose began to distinguish what appeared as several dark, oozing patches on his yellow prison uniform. She knew at once what they were. She realised now it must have been a gunshot she'd heard some hours earlier. The Sniders carried by the Civil Guard were converted to lead shot rather than bullets, but if they hit in the right place, they could still maim or even kill, and this villain's shoulder was peppered with them.

'You're hurt,' Rose said mechanically, her voice frozen and expressionless.

Still lying half on his side in the straw, the man reached down with both hands to his ankle. 'I've done something to my ankle,' he grated as if in agony. 'The surprise of seeing you again . . . made me forget for a second.' He wriggled into a sitting position, and as he looked up at her, even in the dim light, she could see the contorted expression on his face. 'It is you, isn't it? The girl, by the quarry tunnel. All that time ago. You . . . do remember?'

Rose blinked at him. Yes, she had remembered, and her own stunned senses were at once unlocked. 'Yes,' she murmured. 'But I meant your shoulder. You're bleeding.'

He scarcely turned his head. 'I think I can put up with that. It's my ankle I'm really worried about. That's why I had to find somewhere to hide. Otherwise I'd have been half way across the moor by now. If it's broken, I'm done for. It could take weeks—'

'Let me see.' Rose dropped on her knees beside him, all fear dissipated but every nerve on edge, not for herself now, but unbelievably for *him*! She wished vehemently that the light was better, but there was enough to see that he wore no boots and that his coarse woollen socks were in tatters from his flight over the rough terrain.

He must have seen her frown. 'I got rid of the boots as soon as I could,' he explained.

Rose nodded. 'The nails in the soles, you mean? In the shape of an arrow?'

'Well,' he grunted wryly, 'they do leave a pretty distinctive footprint. But then my foot caught between two rocks as I was running. If I'd still been wearing the boots, it might have been all right, but . . . ' He paused, his eyes boring into hers with desperate intensity. 'You won't give me away, will you? Please, I beg you.'

His voice cracked, tugging at Rose's sympathy. But what did she know of him, a complete stranger? And a convicted criminal, to boot. 'And why should I trust you?' she demanded warily, though all the time, keeping her voice low.

'I can't answer that. Except that I *swear* I'm innocent, and might even be able to prove it, given the chance. I just couldn't stand another ten years locked up in that hell-hole for something I didn't do. Surely you can understand that? So, please, help me.' He paused, and in the gloom, she heard rather than saw him swallow hard. 'You . . . you know what will happen to me if I'm caught?'

Rose lowered her eyes as she nodded. The punishment cells, and then a flogging of up to thirty-six lashes with the cat o' nine tails. They said that the blood ran freely after the third stroke, and by the end of the punishment, a man's skin hung from his back in ribbons. Barbaric enough for the likes of the felon who'd attempted to split open Jacob Cartwright's head with a stone, but unthinkable for the man who'd saved him.

'I know I shouldn't ask it of you,' Rose realised he was speaking again. 'It isn't fair on you, especially with you being . . . ' He jabbed his head briefly towards her jutting stomach. 'God knows, I'm sorry for frightening you like that, but I had no choice. You *are* all right? I mean, I didn't realise . . . From the back, you don't look—'

'Yes, I'm fine,' she answered, taken aback by what appeared to be his genuine concern. 'A little shaken, that's all. And I'll not betray you.' For how could she live with herself if she was responsible for sending this man, who could well be telling the truth, to a certain flogging? 'But I don't know if I'll help you. I need time to consider it.'

'Of course. I understand.'

'You'll be safe here overnight. Hide yourself in the straw round the corner.' She pointed to the dog-leg of the loose box which was in complete darkness. 'Ned — our groom — he'll check on Gospel again later. But he'll only stick his head in. He and Gospel don't get on, you see. In fact, the only person who can manage Gospel apart from myself is Joe.'

'Joe?' he questioned in alarm.

'Oh, he doesn't work here. We only have Ned. But . . . I'm really surprised Gospel didn't try to kick the stable down when you came in. He always objects to strangers. Hasn't he bitten you yet?'

With her eyes accustomed to the mere glimmer of light that entered through the stable door, Rose saw the fellow smile. 'He's a magnificent animal. I could see he was spirited, so I just talked to him, and he let me in.'

Rose was about to express her astonishment, but the stranger — for somehow she couldn't think of him as the escaped convict — must have shifted slightly and released a gasp of agony. Without a second thought, Rose leaned forward and gently peeled off the remains of the sodden sock. The ankle was as swollen as a football and even in the shadows Rose could see it was turning a horrible shade of purple.

'You need a doctor,' she murmured at once, quite horrified.

'No. It's too risky.'

'My own physician, from Tavistock,' Rose insisted. 'He's a good man. He should be calling tomorrow. Perhaps I can persuade him—'

'Can you just check something for me now? It could be anything from a bad sprain to a break. If it's a Pott's fracture, I risk losing my leg. So would you mind seeing if you can feel a pulse? Look, just here. I can feel it myself, but that can be unreliable. I might just be feeling the pulse in my own fingers.'

Rose registered his medical knowledge as she did as he instructed. He was educated, then. And she was relieved when she felt the rhythmical vibration beneath her touch. 'Yes, I can definitely feel it,' she told him.

He released a heart-wrenching sigh. 'Thank God.' He dropped his head forward for a moment, then turned to look at her, his lip caught between his teeth. 'This doctor. Could he be trusted?'

Rose hesitated. 'I can't say for sure, but I should think so.'

She heard him breathe in, and then exhale heavily. 'Then I'll take the chance. I don't want to lose my leg, no matter what happens.'

'Should we try and strap it up for now?'

'It might help. If you can find something to do it with.'

'Yes. And I'll bring some dry clothes. Yours are wet through.'

'Oh, I'm used to that,' he snorted. 'But they are somewhat of a give-away. And do you think you could smuggle me out a glass of water?'

'I'll try. But I don't know how long I'll be. If my husband . . . he'd turn you over to the authorities at once.'

'I can't thank you enough.'

She barely acknowledged him since her wits were preoccupied, planning, scheming. In an instant, she was back across the yard, taking the lamp with her as everything must appear normal. She went inside and, though her heart was pounding, she made her way with what she hoped was a casual air to Henry's bedroom which hadn't been touched since his death. Rose needn't have worried. Cook and Patsy, the maid, were busy in the kitchen, and Charles was probably still in the drawing-room despairing of his wayward wife.

Rose went straight to the cupboard where Henry's bed-linen was kept. He'd preferred the worn sheets they'd brought with them from Cherrybrook, and one of those would be perfect for Rose's needs. A little nick on the edge with some scissors, and it tore easily into strips. A set of clothes, then. Her father had been quite tall so they should more or less fit the man hiding out in the stable. If anyone questioned her, she could say she was beginning to find the courage to sort Henry's effects and was going to offer them to Ned.

With the makeshift bandages — and, as an afterthought, the small bottle of laudanum that still sat on the bedside table

— stuffed into the pocket of her skirt, she carried the bundle of clothing to the table in the rear porch and placed it next to the storm lights. Then she went to the kitchen to fetch 'herself' a glass of water, unthinkable for the master to do so, but the young mistress would often come and help herself to whatever she wanted rather than ringing for the maid! So with the garments tucked under one arm, the lantern in one hand and the glass in the other, she was back out in Gospel's loose box within twenty minutes.

'Only me,' she whispered urgently.

In the inky obscurity of the dog-leg, there was no sign of the convict. But then the heaped straw moved and he slowly emerged from its shelter, propping his back against the wall with his injured leg stretched out before him.

'Thank you so much,' he croaked as Rose handed him the glass of water.

She couldn't help but wonder how a supposedly fiendish criminal could behave with such natural civility. 'I've brought some laudanum if you want it,' she told him.

'Laudanum? Oh, I'd love to take some, but I'll need all my wits about me if anyone else comes in. But thank you all the same.'

'I can virtually guarantee that no one will, and what could you do anyway? You can't exactly run off, can you?'

'No. I don't really know how I managed to get *here*.'

'Then take a few drops. It'll take the edge off the pain.'

'All right, I will. And thank you again.'

She unscrewed the bottle and with the pipette attached to the lid, released a few drops into the glass. He hesitated, then drank down the water in several thirsty gulps.

'And where exactly is here?'

'Less than two miles from Princetown.'

'Is that all? Christ, they're bound to come looking! Oh, I'm sorry,' he added sheepishly. 'I've forgotten what it is to be in the company of a lady.'

But Rose shook her head. Under the circumstances, she felt the oath was understandable. 'With your ankle and in the fog, I expect it seemed further. But just as well. If you'd wandered out onto the moor from here, you might've come upon Fox Tor Mire, and you mightn't have been the first to get stuck and die of exposure. You don't know the moor, I suppose?'

'Only the prison farmlands,' he scoffed bitterly. 'But it sounds as if God was on my side, for once, when He guided me to you.'

'I'm not promising to help you,' she reminded him tartly.

'You already are. And you'll never know how grateful I am.'

'Well, I'd best get on and bandage your ankle before I'm missed. Perhaps it'd be better if you changed first. I've brought you some of my father's clothes.'

'You truly are an angel from Heaven. You have no idea what it means to have someone *listen* to me after all this time.'

'You haven't actually told me your story yet,' she observed sharply.

He'd struggled to his feet and Rose averted her eyes as he began to strip off, hopping about on one leg.

'No. But I will. I must tell you everything.' He stifled a gasp as he was obliged to put his weight on his ankle for a moment, and Rose's caution was instantly washed away by her natural sympathies. He sat down again, wincing as he pulled off his upper garments.

'What about the pellets in your shoulder?' she murmured.

'They'll have to stay there. At least until morning. It'll need a good light. And some tweezers. That is . . . if you wouldn't mind?'

'I'll do my best. But let me see to your ankle first. If you can roll up the trouser leg.'

'Yes, of course. Oh, Lord, I'm feeling light-headed already.'

'But it has eased the pain?'

'A little, yes.'

Nevertheless, she felt him stiffen as she set to work. As for herself, having a task to concentrate on pushed the serious doubts to the back of her mind. She worked as quickly as possible, but was constantly aware that she must be hurting him. 'If I'm taking such a chance, helping you like this,' she whispered as her fingers wound the lengths of sheeting about the limb, 'don't you think I should at least know your name?'

'My name? Huh, I'd almost forgotten I had one. You just become a number once you're in there . . . ' His words ended in a thin, rueful trail, but then he went on as if with a start, 'Collingwood. Seth Collingwood.'

'Right, Mr Collingwood, that's done. And I really must go.'

'Call me Seth, if you wouldn't mind. Just to be treated like a human being again . . .'

She heard the catch in his voice as she rose to her feet. 'I'll try and bring you some food later, but I can't promise. Bury yourself in the straw again, and hide your uniform. Don't destroy it, though. If you're caught, you'll be punished for that, as well.'

'Well, thank you for that. And thank you for everything.'

He sounded exhausted, and as Rose hurried back across the yard, she wondered yet again at the foolhardiness of what she was doing. Nobody appeared to have realised where she'd been. When she returned the glass to the kitchen, Cook barely looked up from her labours except to assure her young mistress that dinner was on schedule.

Rose went upstairs to change for the evening meal, a ridiculous charade she'd grown used to. Her wardrobe was limited now to half a dozen new garments made to accommodate her growing stomach. But it always seemed to please Charles if she adhered to these society customs, and just now she wanted to keep him as sweet as possible.

'Ah, there you are, madam,' he declared abrasively as she entered the drawing-room. 'Recovered from your childish tantrum, I trust?'

He might have slapped her in the face, and she stopped in her tracks. In that instant, her mind was made up. Charles would be galled and horrified if he knew that she was protecting an escaped convict, and if she could do so under his very nose, oh, what joyful satisfaction that would bring her! Vengeance was sweet, didn't they say? Hopefully, Charles would never discover her deceit, and wouldn't be aware of how she'd defied him, but it didn't matter. Her triumph over him would be enough! What she was doing was illegal, but she didn't care. And if what Seth Collingwood claimed was true — though of course she had yet to hear his story — then the law was an ass, and what heed did Rose Maddiford ever pay to rules and regulations anyway?

She bounded across the room to her husband. On her face was the sweetest, most angelic smile she could muster, and which evidently won over Charles's displeasure at once.

'Oh, Charles, I'm so sorry. Please forgive me,' she begged, sliding onto her knees and resting her cheek against his thigh a little akin to an endearing kitten — though could he have seen her eyes at that moment, he would have been appalled to see them gleaming with the cunning of a tigress. 'It was just that I was so upset when you said you might sell Gospel. Please don't!' she cajoled, putting a sob into her voice. 'Only after our child is born and Dr Seaton says I'm fully recovered and we can safely leave the baby with a nanny, will I ride him. And only when you're able to accompany me on Tansy.' Though of course, when he was away on business, she would be streaking across the moor on Gospel's back before he reached Tavistock Station!

Complacency stirred in her breast as she felt Charles entwine his fingers in her hair. She'd deliberately left it to tumble about her shoulders, knowing Charles would find it irresistible. He'd fallen for it, and she lifted her pleading, velvet eyes to his face.

'I apologise, too, my dear,' he admitted warily, 'but sometimes you do make me so cross. But I won't sell Gospel, even though I feel I should like to sometimes, provided you keep to that promise.'

'Oh, thank you, Charles! And I will be a good mother, I know I will.'

She threw her arms about his neck as far as her bulge permitted, all the while laughing up her sleeve. He couldn't treat her so cruelly and expect to get away with it. He might think she was submitting to his will, but little did he know!

'I know you will, sweetheart. Now let us say no more about it, and enjoy the remainder of the evening.'

Rose flashed him her most dazzling smile, and Charles returned it as he drew her onto his lap. 'My only regret is that I have to keep away from you at night. It really is quite frustrating, but I'm sure this wouldn't hurt.' So saying, he slipped his hand inside her bodice and began to squeeze her swollen breasts. 'They really are quite delightful bigger like this, you know.'

Rose gritted her teeth against her revulsion. He couldn't leave her alone, could he? He was disgusting, and she was tied to him for life, though it was her own doing and she only had herself and her ignorance to blame. But surely, if he'd guided her body instead of using it entirely for his own gratification, she might have learned to love him. But it was too late now. The chasm between them was too wide, and as far as she was concerned, it would take nothing less than a miracle — the miracle of their child perhaps — to breach it.

When dinner was served, Rose feigned good humour, politely deploring the fog, when all the while she was engulfed in her contempt for the man who sat opposite her.

'I'm just going to feed the dogs,' she announced some time later, since no other ruse had sprung to mind all evening.

'Didn't Ned do that?' Charles glanced up in surprise.

'Probably. But I expect Amber could do with a little extra, and I want to say goodnight to her, anyway. What if she has the pups in the night? I think I'll take out an old blanket as well, just in case,' she added as an afterthought.

'Good idea. But change out of your gown first, and be careful out there in the dark.'

'I will.' And though it burned her lips to do so, she planted a fleeting kiss on his cheek.

Having hurried upstairs to change again, she took two blankets from the cupboard in Henry's room. Nobody would miss them. The loose box always struck warm from the body-heat of the animals, but lying down, sleeping, was a different matter.

Rose sauntered into the kitchen with a vivid smile on her face, though inside she was trembling. But, she told herself, she was mistress of the house and had every right to be there.

'Dinner was delicious, as ever!' she beamed, and Cook shivered with pride. 'Is there any left I could give to Amber?'

Cook's eyebrows shot upwards towards her snowy white cap. 'You spoil they animals, ma'am,' she observed with an amused smile. 'Let me put some in a bowl for you. How much would you like?'

'Well,' Rose hesitated, but the answer soon sprang to her devious mind. 'I expect Scraggles would like some, too.'

'Will that do?' Cook asked, ladling out the thick beef casserole. 'And you mind you tip it into the dogs' own bowls. Much as I love them, too, I don't want *my* bowl licked out by an animal.'

'Of course not,' Rose assured her. 'And is there any tea in the pot? I thought I'd take mine with me and spend a few minutes out there.'

'I've just made some for Patsy and me to have with our own supper. Milk but no sugar, ma'am?'

'Yes, please, but a mug will do nicely,' Rose said as Cook automatically reached for the bone china. 'I don't want to drop a best teacup out there!'

She grimaced ruefully to herself. Deception was beginning to come so easily. She even slipped a spoon — how else would the fugitive eat the stew? — and a couple of rolls into her pocket when the older woman was looking the other way. And so, armed with everything she thought Seth Collingwood needed, she made her way quite boldly out to the stables.

At her voice, he appeared cautiously from beneath the heaped up straw. He fell on the mug of hot tea with a grateful nod, warming his hands about it and sipping the scalding liquid while she draped the blankets over his shoulders. The casserole was only lukewarm, but he ate it appreciatively, washing it down with the remains of the tea and then leaning back gingerly against the stable wall.

'That was the best food I've tasted in years,' he muttered. 'It really is good of you. But you do realise what a risk you're taking?'

Rose felt her heart trip. Yes, she knew. But how could she betray this man who, just as he had by the quarry tunnel all that time ago, had once again thrown her innermost self into confused turmoil? And now he was hurt and must be in considerable pain. Yet he was suffering it in silence and was showing more concern for *her* than for himself.

'Let *me* worry about that,' she whispered back. 'Do you feel any better now?'

'Feel?' He gave an ironic grunt. 'It's such a long time since anyone's asked how I feel that I've forgotten how to ask myself. But, since you ask, I feel pretty rough, though the food and drink has helped. Thank you. But how did you . . . ?'

'I said it was for Amber, my dog. She's about to whelp.'

'Yes, I can see.'

Rose wondered for not the first time how he seemed so knowledgeable, as Amber's condition was far less noticeable than her own. But now didn't seem the time for explanation. 'I've got these as well,' she told him, producing the rolls from her pocket.

'Thank you. Again. I'll save them for the morning. Unless I'm discovered in the meantime. That fellow — Ned, I think you said — looked in. I was half asleep from the laudanum and it gave me one hell of a shock. But like you said, he didn't actually come in.'

'No. But he will padlock all the stables before he goes to bed. So you'll be locked in for the night. But you'll be safe, so try to get some sleep.'

'Yes, I will. Just now I'd like to go to sleep and wake up to find the last couple of years have just been a nightmare.'

'Yes, I'm sure. But there's nothing to be done overnight, so enjoy the peace while you can. And I suggest you take some more laudanum.'

'It can't hurt, I suppose. Huh! Perhaps I should take the whole bottle and my worries would be over for good.'

Rose snatched in her breath. 'No!' she gasped with a vehemence that astounded her. 'Even if you're caught and go back to prison, you'll be released in . . . how many years did you say?'

'Another ten,' he groaned in despair.

'But you'll still only be . . . what?'

'Forty. I've worked it out often enough'

'With a long life still in front of you, then.'

'Hardly. And who knows if I'd survive that long in that place. There's plenty who don't. But it's unfair of me to talk like that when you've been so good to me. But . . . perhaps I won't have another chance to know the name of my benefactress.'

'Rose Chadwick,' she replied without hesitation. 'But if I'm to call you Seth, you must call me Rose.'

'That seems . . . impolite.'

'Then impolite you must be. And I must return these things to the kitchen before Cook comes looking for them.' She clambered to her feet, gathering up the used crockery. 'Whatever happens, good luck.'

'Thank you. For everything.'

And with a pat to the horse and the two dogs, Rose let herself out of the loose box and bolted the door firmly behind her.

CHAPTER NINETEEN

They came for him first thing the next morning.

Rose woke to hear the dawn chorus of the moorland birds, and her thoughts instantly sprang to the injured man hiding in Gospel's stable. Charles lay beside her snoring. Rose glanced at him with a scornful eye and sighed. Charles should have made her an excellent husband. Indeed, he could have made the perfect husband for many a young woman, but not her. Not Rose Maddiford who had a will and a purpose of her own, and would not be down-trodden by any man!

How different he was from Seth Collingwood. How different he made her feel! With Charles, she felt she had to be constantly on her best behaviour, like a child being paraded before a visiting spinster aunt. Whenever she was herself, her *true* self, it always ended in a row. But, after the initial shock of encountering the escaped prisoner, she'd at once felt at ease with him. It was ludicrous, she knew. He was a criminal convicted of some heinous crime, and yet she had to admit it to herself, she *liked* him. He was hurt and in pain, but it was more than just an arousal of her sympathies. Helping him was not only reckless, it was illegal.

She bit down on her lip. *She should not be doing this.* But she *wanted* to. It was an adventure, exciting, and not just a supremely satisfying way of hitting back at Charles. If the fugitive had been a threatening, uncouth brute, it would have been a different matter, she recognised that. But Seth Collingwood was polite, refined, concerned for the risk she was taking for him. She couldn't believe he could have committed some dreadful offence that had warranted confinement in what everyone knew was the worst prison in the land. She knew from Molly's father that he'd been protesting his innocence, but last night he'd spoken of proving it, and Rose's instincts told her he was genuine.

She tried to go back to sleep, but the darkened interior of the stable kept creeping back into her mind. She hadn't been the least afraid, at least not after those first few minutes. And of course, when she realised who he was, that he was the very same prisoner who'd saved Jacob Cartwright's life, the panic had fled. He could have played on that, saying that she could trust him because she'd seen for herself that he was really a decent sort. But he'd barely mentioned it. It had been her by the tunnel, was all he'd said. No more. Of course, he didn't know that the warden in question was her best friend's father. That she'd discussed him with Molly, and that she knew about his claims of innocence. Nonetheless, if he'd been a cunning villain, he'd surely have used the incident to convince her. But he hadn't, and it all led her to believe him.

She realised her eyes were open again, the room fully light now and her mind wide awake. Had Seth managed to get some sleep, or had he been too afraid or in too much pain to rest? She wanted to bring him inside, put him in a proper bed, fetch the doctor to have injuries properly tended. But she'd just have to do what she could for him on the hard floor of the stable, and pray it was enough.

And that was another thing. Gospel. He behaved like a lamb towards herself, Joe and even Molly, though the poor girl was terrified of him. He disliked Ned and was distrustful of any stranger, and yet he had peacefully allowed Seth to enter the loose box when he would normally have created such havoc it would have had them all running! What was it

Seth had said? He'd *talked* to Gospel. Did he have a natural affinity with animals, as the dogs had accepted him in the same way? So he *must* be used to animals, and to horses in particular. And you only gained that kind of experience if you were a groom — and by the cultured way Seth spoke that hardly seemed likely — or if you came from a good class, *moneyed* family.

So why had he ended up serving a lengthy sentence in Dartmoor gaol?

It didn't add up. In Rose's mind, the only possible explanation was that he was indeed innocent of whatever crime it was he'd been convicted of. Mind you, she would insist on hearing his story at the very first opportunity. She was well aware that she was taking a tremendous risk, but she wanted to believe that Seth Collingwood was blameless.

Beside her, Charles stirred. She glanced across at the clock, but then pretended to be still asleep. Twenty past six. It was quite usual for Charles to wake at this time, tossing in the bed until it disturbed her sufficiently for him to demand his marital rights. Recently, of course, Dr Seaton had advised against it, and for the child's sake, at least, Charles had acquiesced, taking himself downstairs so that for a while, Rose enjoyed the luxury of lying in bed without Charles pawing at her. But this morning she felt differently. No sooner had her husband donned his dressing-gown and padded quietly out of the room in his slippers so as not to wake her — showing the consideration he was capable of at times and which mortified her — than she was out of bed and into the bathroom. There was only cold water in the jug, since Patsy was not expected to bring up the hot until later, but Rose hardly noticed as she quickly washed and then dressed herself. For her mind was occupied with the desire to see Seth Collingwood again at the earliest possible moment.

Charles raised his eyebrows in surprise as she entered the dining-room fully dressed. He sat at the table, leisurely sipping at a cup of coffee. The aroma of it mingled mouth-wateringly with the fragrance of the rolls and bread that were baking in Cook's oven ready for breakfast that would be served in half an hour. Rose poured herself some of the dark, steaming liquid and topped it up with thick cream before sitting down opposite her husband.

'You're up early, my dear. I hope you're getting enough sleep.'

'I was restless,' she answered, which was no lie. 'Baby was kicking and, I don't know, I just felt the need to get up. I can always put my feet up this afternoon.'

Charles smiled benevolently, making her feel somewhat guilty. 'Never mind. Only ten more weeks, and the little chap will be in your arms and it'll all have seemed worthwhile.'

She nodded, her face lit with a contented glow. Yes, in ten weeks' time, the child, be it boy or girl, would be putting in an appearance and changing their lives, healing, she prayed, the rift between them that for most of the time Charles appeared to ignore. And by then, in one way or another, Seth Collingwood would be gone, never to be seen again, and the idea strangely saddened her.

'It's a better morning,' she observed absently.

'Yes. The mist's lifting and I think the sun's trying to break through. Let's hope it'll warm up a little.'

And there the conversation ended. At that precise moment, there was a loud banging on the front door, so insistent that Charles was already in the hallway when the maid answered the impatient knocking. The hairs on the back of Rose's neck stood on end and she felt the slick of sweat break out over her entire body, for she knew who it would be. She sidled out into the hall. Patsy was still fumbling with the locks and bolts of the door which hadn't as yet been unsecured that morning, and Charles was striding up behind her, demanding who the devil was disturbing his privacy at that unholy hour. Rose slipped behind them both unseen and, borne on a tide of fear, let herself out through the rear porchway.

She hurried across to the stables, her shawl pulled tightly about her shoulders. The upper half of each stable-door was fixed open and Gospel's sleek black head was poking out of his loose box, eagerly awaiting his morning feed. Ned appeared from the store, buckets dangling from his arms.

'I'll take Gospel's.'

Rose hadn't thought what she was going to do, acting purely by instinct. Fortunately, the bucket wasn't heavy, containing only a small supplement of oats, and she emptied it easily into Gospel's feeding trough, and then, satisfied that Ned was occupied in the other stalls, she stepped round the corner of the loose box. In the light of day, though of course the dog-leg was in shadow, she could see clearly the mound of straw in which Seth lay hidden, but, her swirling mind demanded, would it be obvious to anyone searching for an escaped convict?

'Seth!' she hissed, burying her hands in the straw and shaking whatever part of him she'd got hold off. The mound stirred, and she pushed him back down. 'The Civil Guard are here!' she whispered frantically. 'Lie as still as a mouse!'

He did. And she heaped the straw over him in what she hoped was a more natural fashion.

When the guards came to the door of the loose box, what they saw was a young woman kneeling down by a pretty golden dog while another bedraggled specimen leapt playfully about her. When she rose gracefully to her feet and turned to them, revealing the obvious dome of her pregnancy, a soft and enquiring expression in her beautiful violet-blue eyes, they stepped back in humble deference.

'Yes, Officers?' she asked, not needing to put the alarm in her voice as it was already there! 'Is there something wrong?'

The most senior of the group, for there were several of them swarming over the yard, cleared his throat and put his hand up to the brim of his soldier's hat. 'An escaped prisoner, ma'am, I'm afraid.'

The gasp that came from her throat was genuine. 'Oh, dear!' she choked, and turned her eyes desperately on her husband who had come up behind the guard. 'Oh, Charles, how dreadful!'

'No need to be alarmed, ma'am. We'll catch the devil soon enough!' the sergeant assured her. 'Ran off from the prison farm yesterday. Crafty devil. Always pretended to be the model prisoner, and then when that fog came down yesterday, he was off! My men shot at him, though,' he smirked gleefully, 'and one of them got him. Unfortunately, only winged him in the shoulder as far as we know, but it'll slow him down. We've been searching all night, mind, and haven't found a trace of him.'

'Perhaps he were swallowed up in Fox Tor mire,' Rose suggested with a frown. 'Either that, or he's well away across the moor by now.'

'More like hiding somewhere and licking his wounds. Which is why we must search everywhere, ma'am, so if you wouldn't mind standing aside . . .'

For one horrible, sickening moment, Rose thought she was about to faint, but then Amber lumbered against her leg and pushed her snout into Rose's hand.

'I'd rather you didn't, Officer,' she heard herself say. 'You can see my dog,' and here she smiled sweetly down at Amber, 'is about to have her puppies, and I should rather she wasn't disturbed. I'm certain I'd know if there were someone in here.'

Dear God, her heart was positively bucking in her chest, and she was sure the fellow must be able to hear its thunderous beat. But he seemed to hesitate. 'Well, I really ought to . . .'

Right on cue, Gospel decided he'd had enough of the stranger who was molesting his beloved mistress as far as he was concerned. He stamped up behind her and stretching his long neck over her shoulder, ears laid back and eyes rolling, proceeded to bare his huge teeth and aim them at the guard's person. The man leapt back, a flush of terror and embarrassment colouring his face.

'Er, well, of course, ma'am,' he muttered, and Rose had the desire to laugh, though she knew she mustn't.

'Is this prisoner dangerous?' Charles was asking, his face a picture of consternation.

'Well, he's certainly a slippery customer. So be on your guard. And you, too, ma'am.'

He dipped his head at the young woman and the great horse beside her that shook its head irritably and looked as if it was just waiting for another opportunity to try and take a bite out of him! His dignity, though, was rescued in the nick of time by one of his men reporting that there was no one lurking about the house, its gardens or outhouses, and with another polite warning, the group of guards took their leave.

Rose felt her knees weaken as the bravado drained out of her, but it was far from over yet.

'You'd better come inside, Rose, if this felon's on the loose,' Charles was insisting, and Rose's desperate mind spun in a nauseating spiral.

'Yes, of course, Charles,' she answered, her voice anxious, though not for the reason Charles believed! 'I'm just going to move Amber's basket round the corner out of the way, so as Ned won't disturb her when he comes to muck out,' she told him loudly so that Seth would hear her. 'It's quite clean round there. So it doesn't need doing.'

'Let me do it, then. It's too heavy for you.'

Rose's heart nearly exploded as Charles stepped into the loose box, eyeing Gospel warily as the massive animal stomped his hooves in agitation. What if Charles . . . ?

'Don't be silly!' she laughed nervously, for indeed he did look somewhat comical. 'You're still in your dressing-gown, and you don't want to step in something nasty in your slippers! Look, I'll just drag it.'

And firmly grasping one end of the basket, she did just that, leaving it across the dog-leg, effectively barring the entrance to where Seth lay. It was still taking one hell of a chance, but what else could she do? Her face broke into its most enchanting smile as she came back to her husband, and she deliberately took his elbow, leaning her head against his shoulder. He responded at once, putting his arm defensively about her.

'Oh, Ned!' she called casually as he appeared from the tackroom. 'When you muck out Gospel's box, I'd be obliged if you wouldn't go round the corner. I've put Amber's basket there. She's behaving so oddly this morning, I think she must be about to have the puppies.'

'Knows her time's coming, I expect, Miss Rose . . . er, Mrs Chadwick,' he corrected himself under Charles's stern gaze.

'And will you turn Gospel out into the field later? It's a much better day than yesterday.'

'Yes, I were going to, ma'am, if he'll let me put his halter on.'

'Well, just call me if he gives you any trouble.'

'Will do, ma'am.'

They turned back to the house, Rose almost sagging with relief. The first hurdle was over, but it was only the first. The Civil Guard might return at any time over the next few days, few weeks even. Dear Lord, what had she got herself in to? Why was she putting herself at risk, trusting this stranger about whom she knew next to nothing?

And as they went into breakfast, she found she had very little appetite indeed.

CHAPTER TWENTY

'My dear, I really ought to go into Princetown and send some telegrams,' Charles frowned as he flicked over the correspondence in his hands. 'But I don't like leaving you, not with this felon still at large.'

'Oh, it's not as though I'm alone,' Rose shrugged, her mind leaping at his words, since she hadn't as yet found an opportunity to go out to the stables again. 'And there's always Ned. And Dr Seaton is due to call this morning. Besides, I don't imagine any escaped prisoner would stay around so close to Princetown. You wouldn't if you were in his shoes, would you? He'll be well away by now.'

'All the same . . .'

'Oh, I'm sure we'll all be perfectly safe. You can't neglect your business affairs on the off-chance that this fellow will turn up here when there's over three hundred square miles of Dartmoor to hide in! No, you go. How long do you think you'll be?'

'Yes, I suppose you're right. I'll take Tansy to be quicker, but I will need to await replies, so I could be little while. But promise me you'll stay in the house.'

'Absolutely,' she assured him, though she had no intention of doing so.

'I'll tell Ned to saddle Tansy, then.'

'Yes, dear.'

She caught his hand as he passed her, looking up at him with her dazzling smile. He smiled back, squeezing her shoulder before striding out of the room, and Rose leaned back in her chair. So far, so good. Ned must have mucked out the stables by now, and there had been no sudden cries of discovery. But it was a daily task, and how long would it take for Seth's ankle to mend? Weeks? Dear Lord, could he possibly remain there in secret for so long?

Rose watched from the window as Charles cantered off down the driveway, and before he had turned out of the gates, she was skating into the kitchen.

'Can I get you something, ma'am?' Cook asked.

'Is there any coffee left?'

'Yes, ma'am. I'll put the pot back on the heat. 'Twon't take a minute. Or I can make some fresh.'

'No, that'll do nicely, thank you. Oh, is that bacon left over? I'll take it out for the dogs.'

Cook shook her head. 'You should've called that stray cur Lucky instead of Scraggles, ma'am. And there's just a drop of cream left for your coffee. I could really do with some more, mind.'

Rose's face lit up. 'I'll send Ned.' And then, armed with the coffee and the bacon, she stepped out into the spring sunshine.

Ned was crossing the stableyard, his hands in his pockets, believing his morning's work was over.

'Ned!' Rose called, and he came over, ever hoping — though in vain — that his luck might be in with her. Still, this was a good job, and he was in no hurry to lose it! 'Did you have any trouble with Gospel?'

'No. Good as gold he were this morning. Romping round the field like a jack rabbit now.'

'Good! Now, be an angel and walk over to Tor Royal for some cream, would you, please, Ned? Ask the dairymaid to put it on our account.'

Ned went to scowl, but then remembered that the dairymaid was a pretty wench, a homely, buxom sort, who mightn't be averse to his advances. 'But what 'bout this yere convict? Maister said I'm to protect all yer women folk.'

'Oh, get away with you. He's hardly likely to come here, is he? And I promise I won't tell the master if you won't.'

Ned seemed to consider for a moment, a moment in which Rose felt her nerves jangle on a knife-edge, and then he was striding away with a noticeable skip in his jaunty gait.

Rose was in the loose box within seconds. The door had been left open so that the dogs could roam in and out, and clean straw had been shaken out over the floor. Scraggles was scampering about at Rose's feet, but as she came round the corner, Amber hardly lifted her head from the basket.

'Seth, it's all right,' Rose whispered as she stepped around the dog's bed. 'You can come out now.'

She waited as Seth cautiously pushed his head up through the straw and brushed it from his face. 'Are you sure?' he croaked.

'Yes. My husband's gone out and I've sent Ned on an errand, and Cook and the maid are busy in the house. And it's not one of the gardener's days, so we're quite safe. But we've no time to lose. Sit up and drink this, and I'll fetch the things to take the shot out of your shoulder. And here's some bacon. Cold, I'm afraid, but it was the best I could do.'

He glanced up at her, his forehead pleated as he shifted position. He winced as he leaned back against the wall, and Rose's heart squeezed with sympathy.

'Thank you, miss,' he said, but as he took the cup from her, she saw that his face was shadowed with agony and exhaustion. 'Oh, that tastes good,' he said, taking a sip of the coffee. 'God, I've never been so terrified in all my life as when those guards came in. I really thought they'd find me. You were wonderful! And then when your Ned was mucking out, well, he only needed to be a little more thorough. I hardly dared to breathe.'

'Well, you're safe for a while now. Get that down you, and I'll be back in a few minutes.'

'You know . . . you don't have to do this. I'd fully understand if—'

His voice faltered, and Rose felt her heart tear. 'But I want to,' she answered simply.

She brought the smaller of the bowls from the bathroom as it was easier to carry with just a little clean water in it, her heart tripping as she prayed she wouldn't meet Patsy on the way. She didn't, not that Patsy was likely to think anything of it. When Rose hurried back to the stables, the yard, as expected, was deserted, but she shut the lower section of the door so that if anyone should happen to cross the yard, they wouldn't be able to see in unless they deliberately peered into the loose box.

'Seth, you'll need to come round the corner into the light,' she told him as she set the bowl on the floor.

She heard him draw in a shaking breath, and then he was dragging himself across to her. As he emerged from the shadows, she saw that his face was strikingly handsome despite the convict crop and being ravaged with pain.

Rose frowned. 'Ankle not feeling any better?'

He shook his head, gazing up at her beseechingly. His eyes were a soft hazel, large and expressive. They seemed to reach inside her, touching something that burgeoned and blossomed in an instant. She turned away, driving the sensation from her mind, recognising the same intense feeling she'd experienced by the quarry tunnel, confused and bewildered . . .

'Turn your back to the light.'

Her voice was so small as she watched him struggle out of her father's clothes. When he got down to the shirt, it had stuck to the oozing wounds and she helped him ease it away, forgetting the strange, unwanted emotions that had gripped her as the overriding sense of sympathy engulfed her again. His shoulders were strongly muscled, but he was so thin, his ribs showed beneath his skin. Half- starved and expected to work like dogs, she'd heard Jacob Cartwright complain in the privacy of his own home. Now she could see for herself exactly what he meant.

'Hold very still,' she ordered as she took from her pocket the tweezers she had washed and wrapped in a clean handkerchief. 'I'll try not to hurt you.'

'Are you sure we're safe?'

'As sure as I can be.'

'If we're caught, I've frightened you into helping me. Understand?'

She paused, tweezers poised. Even now, he was thinking of her rather than himself. 'Yes,' she muttered, and then steeling herself against the sudden sweat that had broken out down her back, she laid the tweezers against the first small hole.

Her own mouth knotted as she worked them into his flesh, and he arched his back, choking back a stifled gasp. Rose bit down hard on her lip as fresh blood trickled down from the wound so that she couldn't see what she was doing and had to dig about until she found the small lead shot. She wet a piece of the bandaging left from the previous evening and twisted a corner of it into a probe to clean out the wound. She knew there was danger of infection from any dirt or fragments of material the shot had taken with it, infection that could kill the strongest man. So it had to be done, though even so, there was no guarantee.

One down and only five to go. Oh, dear Lord, she didn't know if she could do this! But she *had* to. There was no alternative. 'Thank goodness some of them missed you,' she murmured hoarsely.

Seth snatched in his breath as she began on the next one. 'Thirteen shots in a cartridge,' he muttered. 'I saw some of the others hit the ground. Thank God I was almost out of range, or the shot would've gone in deeper.'

'You know a lot about guns, then?' Rose asked, a twinge of caution tugging at her as she inserted the tweezers into the second hole. 'Are you sure you won't take some laudanum?' she pressed him as he stifled a cry of pain.

He gave a bitter grunt. 'I don't think laudanum would do much against this. And I want to keep my wits about me. Just get it done as quickly as you can, please. The sooner I can hide again, the happier I'll feel.'

'I'll do my best.'

She worked on, Seth holding himself as tense as a rock as the tweezers pierced into his injured flesh. It seemed to take an eternity, and by the time all six lead balls had been removed and the wounds cleaned, Rose was drained and exhausted. She was ready to go indoors and slump down on her bed, but there were still tracks to cover.

'I'll slip across and get you a clean shirt,' she told her patient.

She went with more confidence, but then checked herself. She must be on her guard at all times, and it wouldn't be long before Ned was back. But as yet there was no sign of him, and she could hear the busy goings-on in the kitchen. By the time she returned to the stables, Seth already had himself half hidden in the straw. She inspected his shoulder again. All the bleeding had stopped, so she used the last of the bandages to bind up his wounds, winding the strips of sheeting around his chest. It was better that sticking to the shirt which would pull every time he moved.

They were back in the darkened dog-leg of the loose box, and as Seth lay down again, she covered him with straw. She felt so angry. He should be in a proper bed, being carefully nursed and taking laudanum to ease his pain.

'I imagine it'll hurt worse now,' she mumbled as she cleared away the bloodied rags.

'Yes. But it should settle down soon. And thank you, Mrs Chadwick. That was very brave of you.'

'Call me Rose, please.'

The hint of a smile flickered over his generous mouth. '*A rose by any other name would smell as sweet.*' His eyes fleetingly met hers, and she was once again overwhelmed by the sensitivity in them that seemed to speak to her. And a convict who quoted Shakespeare with such feeling . . .

First, she returned the bowl to the bathroom and then she took the cup back to the kitchen. Cook was busy preparing soup for lunch, and looked up with a smile.

'How's the dog, ma'am?'

'Behaving strangely. I think we'll see the pups any day.'

'New life's always good, ma'am. Though 'tis that babby o' yourn I'm looking forward to.'

'So am I!' Rose grinned.

There. All quite natural. Nobody suspected a thing. And ten minutes later when she saw Ned turning the corner of the house carrying the canister of cream, Rose knew they were safe.

For now.

* * *

'Charles, I'm just taking Dr Seaton over to have a look at Amber,' Rose announced as she poked her head around the door to his study.

'Forgive me if I don't come with you,' Charles replied as the elderly physician's head appeared over his wife's shoulder. 'I went into Princetown earlier to send some telegrams, and now I have a deal of correspondence to deal with. But tell me, how is she, and the baby, of course?'

'Blooming!' Dr Seaton reassured him. 'Now let me see this dog of yours, Mrs Chadwick,' he smiled indulgently, for who could resist the charms of this vivacious young woman? He was semi-retired now, travelling by horse-drawn trap rather than on horseback as he once had. He sent his younger partner, Dr Ratcliffe, nowadays when medical attention was needed urgently. He wouldn't normally have agreed to take on a patient as far out as Princetown, but Mr Chadwick had been very persuasive and his young wife was a delight.

She skipped along beside him now as they crossed the yard, having insisted that he bring his medical bag in case the dog needed anything! But then her arresting, violet-blue eyes fixed him with their piercing clarity.

'Dr Seaton,' she began, her pulse accelerating. 'Isn't there some sort of promise that doctors make? That they'll treat a patient no matter who they are? And that they must keep all details about their patients confidential?'

The physician's grey eyebrows swooped into a frown. 'The Hippocratic Oath, you mean? Well, it's not as straightforward as that, but broadly speaking, yes.'

'And,' she went on, her heart doing its level best to escape from her ribcage as they stepped into Gospel's loose box, 'what would you say if . . . ' She hesitated, her dry throat closing up. Could she trust this kind, elderly man, or would everything she'd done for Seth have been in vain? But there was no doubt in her mind that Seth's ankle simply *must* be seen by a physician. 'What if the patient was an escaped convict?' she rasped in a whisper.

Dr Seaton stopped in his tracks. He glanced furtively about him, then studied the agonised expression on her face. 'I don't think I'm going to like what you're about to tell me, Mrs Chadwick.'

Rose drew him into the loose box, feeling more scared than at any other time in her life. 'Please, Dr Seaton,' she begged, her voice trembling. 'He escaped because he's innocent. And before you say that's what they all claim, I believe him. But his ankle might be broken, and he was shot.'

Dr Seaton paused, pursing his lips as he drew in a long breath. 'And you want me to help him?'

She nodded, and tears were glittering in her lovely eyes.

'And am I to assume that your husband knows nothing of this?'

She nodded again, perspiration oozing from every pore. The doctor hesitated, contemplating the compassion that creased her face.

'The Oath only goes so far, you know,' he finally answered, his voice low. 'I should turn him over the authorities at once. You do realise what you're asking of me?'

'Yes. But *please*! I beg you. If you talk to him, you'll see he's . . . *different* from most of the other prisoners.'

The doctor shook his head, and for one horrible, stomach-churning second she thought . . . 'All right. I'll take a quick look.'

'Oh, thank you,' she almost collapsed into his arms. 'He's just here. Behind us. Seth. Seth?'

The doctor's lined face jerked in surprise as the mound of straw moved. 'You've got him well hidden,' he confessed in amazement, and at once he was the professional physician, kneeling by his patient while Rose kept an anxious look-out, her heart in her mouth. 'Let's have a look at you, then. You have an injury to your ankle, I believe, and you were shot.'

Seth's eyes stretched wide. 'Thank you, Doctor, for not betraying me at once. Yes, the guards fired at me and I took some shot in my shoulder, but Mrs Chadwick got it out for me this morning.'

Dr Seaton raised an eyebrow. 'Did she, by Jove? But I thought they were supposed to aim for the legs. To stop you running.'

'They are. But Sniders aren't amazingly accurate. And I was almost out of range, so they'd lost their velocity.'

'Hmm. You speak like a man of the army yourself.'

'I am. Ex-army. And I'm not a deserter, if that's what you think. I resigned my commission.'

'Officer, then?'

'Yes. But perhaps if I'd stayed in the army, I wouldn't have got myself into this mess.'

Rose's ears pricked up. It was the first she really knew of Seth's background. But they were wasting precious time. 'What about his ankle?' she almost hissed in her apprehension.

'Yes, of course. Let me see.'

The pulse was thundering at Rose's temples as she stood guard, Amber gazing dolefully at her mistress, not understanding why she wasn't being patted and stroked when something very strange was going on in her belly. But Rose had other, more desperate matters on her mind.

'Looks like a fracture to me,' she heard the physician pronounce.

'Can you splint it?'

'I can do better than that. I'll use plaster of Paris.'

'Really? No disrespect, but I wouldn't have expected a provincial doctor—'

'Oh, I keep up to date, lad. And it *has* been in use for several years, you know. So let's get on with it, shall we? Fortunately, I can't feel any displacement so I won't need to reduce it. But I've only got one pair of hands and I'll need Mrs Chadwick's help.'

'Thank you so much, doctor. I can't tell you how much I appreciate it.' Seth's voice rang with gratitude. 'I'm just so sorry to have implicated you.'

'I'm fully aware of the consequences,' Dr Seaton said gravely. 'Certainly if you're caught, the plaster cast will be difficult to explain.'

'No. I'll say I stole the plaster from your medical bag,' Rose insisted. 'You thought you had some, but it wasn't there after your rounds. Anyone could have taken it. And you weren't sure, anyway.'

Dr Seaton inhaled deeply. 'All right. But I'll need a bucket of clean water, Mrs Chadwick.'

Rose reluctantly left her post, but there was nothing else for it. If they were caught now, they could make excuses, say they'd only just found him and were going to turn him in when his injuries had been treated. But Rose couldn't bear the thought of what would certainly happen to him.

Back in the loose box, she obeyed the doctor's every instruction, but with one ear constantly on the alert. Fortunately the process took surprisingly little time, and Dr Seaton was soon washing the residue of the white powder from his hands and rolling down his sleeves.

'That should feel more comfortable now,' he told his patient. 'Make sure you can wriggle your toes and if they start turning blue or cold, you must turn yourself in at once. The swelling should go down in a few days, but if the opposite happens, you *must* have medical attention. And I must warn you, it could take months before it's properly back to normal.'

'Months?' Rose's eyes stretched with horror.

'With the inevitable damage to ligaments and so on, yes. So, I really would strongly advise you to give yourself up,' he said, turning to Seth again. 'At least, you'd have the medical care you need.'

'And then I'll be flogged,' Seth muttered bitterly under his breath.

Dr Seaton's mouth twisted with compassion. 'As you said, you've got yourself into a mess. Though if you're innocent, you have my every sympathy. Anyway, I'll leave you this. It's phenol. A few drops in a bowl of water to bathe the shot wounds. A mild infection you can stand, but if you become feverish, well, you know my opinion.'

Rose's heart sank like a lead weight. Perhaps she should betray Seth for his own sake. But he'd put his trust in her, as she had in him. In the short time she'd known him — heavens above, was it less than twenty-four hours? — some invisible bond had developed between them. No. She must wait. But if he became seriously ill, she would do her utmost to persuade him to give himself up.

But they both knew what would happen when he was recovered.

* * *

In the event, she missed the birth of the pups altogether.

It was late afternoon before she had the chance to saunter casually over to the dogs carrying a glass of cool water and a biscuit. She was so hungry and thirsty, she told Cook. It must be the baby, she'd proclaimed, and the older woman had nodded in agreement.

Seth would be parched, she was sure, but as she entered the stable, her concern for the fugitive was interrupted. Snuggled up against Amber's golden flank were four tiny bundles of wet fur, eyes closed and pink button noses twitching as they instinctively searched for their mother's teats. The detritus of birth lay about them, and Amber ceased her tender licking of each of her pups to glance up proudly at her mistress, while Scraggles nudged his off-spring with bemused curiosity.

Rose held her breath, spellbound as she gazed down on the minuscule creatures, two of them the image of their beautiful mother, and the other pair black and white like their father, and all of them squeaking plaintively as they made their first attempts to gain sustenance. Rose hardly dared move in case she disturbed them, but stood in rapt amazement.

'This one's not doing so well.'

Seth's low voice destroyed her reverie, and a shiver ran through her as she remembered why she was there. She peered into the shadows around the corner. Though Seth was buried in straw from the waist downwards, he was sitting up, totally visible, his attention concentrated on some minute scrap that lay in the palm of his hand.

'Seth, you'll be seen!' Rose hissed at him in alarm.

'I couldn't let this one die,' he answered, and she saw that he was gently rubbing whatever it was with a hank of straw. 'The runt of the litter.'

He changed what he was doing then, and she was able to make out that he was holding a little damp bundle upside down, shaking it firmly until a string of mucus dribbled from what she realised now was a diminutive snout. Whipping the debris away with his free hand, Seth proceeded to blow softly into the tiny mouth which he held open between his thumb and little finger. After two or three attempts, he looked up at Rose with a grin that made him look so handsome, her heart jerked. Oh, good heavens, she felt so confused as she sank awkwardly onto her knees in the straw beside this supposedly heinous criminal.

'Oh, he's beautiful,' Rose whispered, watching the puppy breathing on its own now. It was a striking mixture of caramel and copper with a little white face and one black sock.

'He's a she, actually, and I suggest you put her with her mother. She'll take care of her now.'

Rose put down the glass with the biscuit balanced on top, and cupped her hands to receive the tiny creature. 'Oh, thank you so much for saving her.'

'Little ones are always wonderful.'

There was something about the way he said it, and Rose frowned as she carefully placed the little animal among its siblings. This enigmatic stranger had such a curious effect on her that she couldn't fathom it out. His past life was still a mystery and she was anxious to be enlightened, not just for his sake, but for her own. But first things first.

'How's your ankle now?' she whispered.

'It still hurts, but it's definitely more comfortable than it was. It was good of your doctor to take such a risk.'

Rose nodded. 'He's a good man. You know, Charles — my husband — insisted on finding another doctor for me. My father and I always had Dr Power—'

'The prison doctor, you mean?' Seth said in alarm.

'Yes. I was furious at the time. It was as if he were good enough for my father, but not for Charles. But I'm glad now. Dr Power's an excellent physician, but he'd have been obliged to turn you in to the authorities. It's ironic, really,' Rose snorted. 'Charles would hand you over without a thought, and yet because of him, you were able to see a doctor in safety.'

Her voice was laced with bitterness, and Seth raised his eyebrows at her. 'Forgive me for saying so,' he faltered, 'but I have the impression you're not too happy in your marriage.'

Rose caught her breath. Nobody — not even Molly who was so enraptured by her marriage to Joe that the hints Rose had dropped had never registered in her friend's mind — had ever gained the least idea that she regretted her marriage to Charles. Yet this stranger, this *convict*, had seen straight inside her. She wanted so much to unburden herself, but it hardly seemed right and she reared away from it.

'Drink the water,' she commanded instead.

The flicker of a frown creased Seth's forehead, but he said nothing as he sipped from the glass and ate the biscuit.

She noticed him wince slightly as he moved his shoulder, bringing her own thoughts back to reality.

'I'll bring out a bowl of water later if I can to bathe your shoulder, and you can have a wash. I can say it's to clean up the puppies.'

'That would be good. Thank you so much.'

'Rose! My dearest, where are you?'

Rose was convinced her heart missed a beat, then catapulted forward with the force of a sledge-hammer. She turned to look, wide-eyed with terror, over her shoulder.

'Quick!'

Seth's frantic whisper galvanised her brain into action and she was wildly heaping straw over him, tossing it over his head and then patting it down so that she hoped it didn't appear as what it was, a disguise for the human form hiding beneath it. She swept up the almost empty glass, standing solidly between the dog basket and the hump of straw. When Charles ambled into the loose box, though her heart was thudding savagely, she met him with an enraptured smile.

'Look, Charles! Amber's had her pups!' she cried. 'Aren't they gorgeous?'

'Indeed, they are, my dear.' Charles's words were stiff. 'How many are there? Good. Only five, I see. And that little runt probably won't survive, so that'll only be four to dispose of.'

Rose felt the barb cut into her side. Seth had risked his own safety to revive the fragment of life that was the ailing newborn pup, while Charles dismissed it as some vile, unwanted thing that he would prefer to be dead, as he would clearly have liked the others to be as well. Gall burned into Rose's throat, but she stepped forward with a fixed smile, taking Charles's arm and turning him away from both the animals and the obscured man.

'Come, Charles, I should like to take some tea now. To celebrate. This water has quenched my thirst, and now a cup of tea would go down very nicely.'

They were out in the spring sunshine again, and as Charles patted her hand, rancour stung deeper into her soul.

'You go and tell Cook or Patsy to make the tea,' she smiled sweetly. 'I just want a word with Ned about the puppies.'

'All right. But don't be long.'

She waited to make sure he'd gone back inside, and then went in search of Ned. She found him in the tackroom, lounging in the chair with his feet stretched out before him, scarcely bothering to move when she put her head around the door.

'Ah, Ned, there you are. Busy as ever, I see,' she observed scathingly. 'Well, I've a job for you. When you've time, of course. Amber's had her puppies, and I'm worried that Gospel might step on them, so I want you to put him in the spare box when you bring him in. So will you get the box ready for him, please. And I don't want anyone going in to Amber and the puppies until I say so. I'll put down some newspaper for them and see to all that sort of thing, so there's no need for you to do anything. I'll just put everything in a bucket by the door, and you can empty it into the incinerator with all the rubbish.'

'Right-ho, Miss Rose,' Ned grinned indolently. And as she turned away, she heard him mumble to himself that he didn't want to have anything to do with the bloody things anyway. And that suited Rose admirably! It had crossed her mind that she would have to think of something for Seth's personal needs, too, and this would kill the two birds with the one stone.

And feeling quite pleased with herself, she went indoors.

CHAPTER TWENTY-ONE

'Rose, my dear, I need to go to London, and I really would rather you came with me. The change would do you good, and they haven't caught this escaped convict yet.'

Rose's heart took an almighty bound, setting her pulse racing. It was with the greatest effort that she calmly swallowed the delicious morsel in her mouth, allowing her frantic brain time to think. The last few days hadn't been at all easy, and if it hadn't been for the excuse of checking on Amber and the puppies, she would hardly have been able to slip out to the stables at all. If she had to go to London, the game would be up. Without her help, Seth couldn't survive, and he would have no choice but to give himself up.

'Oh, Charles, that would be nice,' she replied with a pretty smile, 'but I really don't think I could face that long journey. A whole day on the train, I should find it too much. I'm beginning to get backache and I feel so uncomfortable, I really should prefer to stay here.'

'It would be your last chance for some time,' Charles argued. 'And once the baby's born—'

'Yes, I know.' She deliberately released a profound sigh and was quite pleased how natural it sounded. 'But then I'd have the whole journey to do in reverse, and I don't think it'd be a good idea.'

'You could stay in London. Have the baby there.'

'No!' She was genuinely horrified, her voice trembling at the very thought. 'I want it born here! Dr Seaton has been so kind and I have the greatest confidence in him. No, Charles. I'm sorry, but I will stay here.'

She met his gaze defiantly across the table, a look he knew only too well.

'But you will take care of yourself while I'm gone?' he conceded reluctantly. 'I really am concerned about this prisoner.'

'Didn't you say someone answering his description were seen over Ivybridge way?' she prompted.

'That's true. The Civil Guard are concentrating their search over there.'

'There you are then! And if it weren't him, then he'll have perished out on the moor by now. It's a treacherous place if you don't know it, and it's still cold enough at night to kill.'

'Yes, I suppose so.' Charles's twisted his lips. 'All the same—'

'I'll be fine! I've lived here all my life almost and there's never been any problems with the prisoners. It's more important you sort out your business affairs so as you can be here when the baby's born.'

'I won't be that long! About ten days should do it.'

'And when will you go?'

'The day after tomorrow, I should think.'

'Oh, so soon?' Heavens above, it was becoming so easy to play act, to lie and deceive, but what choice did she have? Besides, she was finding Charles more obnoxious by the day, just inconsequential, trivial matters, but ones that were growing into an increasingly tall pile. While out in the stable, the criminal she scarcely knew was drawing her curiosity and, dare she say it, gaining her trust, more surely with every day that passed.

* * *

She saw Charles off first thing in the morning, waving from the front door. The end of April might be approaching, but a few spring-like days had been driven out by lashing rain, violent gales and plummeting temperatures. Merry fires blazed in the grates in Fencott Place, but it would be a different matter for someone hiding out in the stables.

Rose hurried up the stairs and watched from the landing window until the wagonette was well out of sight. The train left Tavistock shortly before nine, and the round trip to the station and back would take Ned the best part of three hours. Three precious hours which she intended to spend with Seth Collingwood. She'd prepared a list of extra chores to keep Cook and Patsy busy, and if she wanted to sit out in Gospel's loose box watching the newborn puppies of her beloved dog, nobody was going to question it.

She'd breakfasted early with Charles, so having washed and dressed, it seemed quite acceptable to ask for a cup of chocolate to take out to the stables with her. Some extra scraps for the lactating bitch, well, it was the best she could do without arousing suspicion, and she'd rescued a jug of tepid water for she must take the opportunity to bathe the wounds on Seth's shoulder.

She could see he was stiff with cold as he dragged himself from his hiding place. He was shivering, and Rose tried to tuck the two blankets around him, but they, too, were damp to the touch.

'Thank you,' he murmured, falling on the steaming drink.

'You look dreadful,' she told him, biting on her bottom lip.

'I don't exactly feel on top of the world. But you get used to that,' he added with a rueful grimace.

Rose's mouth fined to a sympathetic line. 'How's the ankle?'

'Definitely easier, I'm pleased to say.'

'And your shoulder?'

'Worse. I can hardly move my arm it hurts so much.'

Rose felt her heart constrict. 'I'll take a look and bathe it with the phenol. I've brought some fresh bandages.'

Seth nodded as he began to struggle out of her father's clothes and she unwound the makeshift dressings from his shoulder. He winced as the stained material pulled away from wounds which looked angry and were starting to suppurate.

'I don't like the look of this, Seth.'

He instantly jerked up his head. 'But I'm not giving myself up. To be frank, I'd rather die than go back. If I was guilty, I'd serve my sentence like a man. But I'm not, and I might as well be dead as spend ten more years there.'

Rose didn't answer. What he said appalled her, though she could understand how he must feel. Life in the prison must be unimaginably harsh, and must seem so unjust for someone who was innocent. 'Let me see to your shoulder,' she said instead, 'and then you can tell me your story.'

She tried to be gentle as she could, but it wasn't easy. Seth held himself tense, not uttering a sound until she'd finished. She'd done her level best, but heaven alone knew if the cleansed wounds would now improve.

'Getting some air to them might help to dry them up. If I arrange the blankets around you . . .'

He shifted awkwardly into a suitable position, encumbered as he was by the plaster cast. Rose made herself comfortable on a bale near Amber, stroking the animal's silky head and looking down on the five pups nestled against her flank. They were tumbling over each other in a peaceful confusion of sparsely haired bodies and little round tummies that were becoming fatter by the day.

'Lovely, aren't they?' Seth followed her gaze, and when she turned to look at him, he was smiling through his strained expression. The breath quickened in Rose's throat. His even teeth were a white slash in the stubble of his unshaven jaw, his eyes shining softly. Beneath them were the dark smudges of a man who hardly slept, who passed every minute in fear, and Rose had deliberately to shy away from the emotion that stirred mysteriously inside her.

'Yes,' she gulped, and had to clear her throat. 'Now, whilst we have the chance, you'd better tell me your story.'

The smile faded from Seth's face and his eyebrows arched. 'It was the twenty-second of October 1874,' he began slowly, bowing his head to concentrate his thoughts. 'I think that date will be printed on my mind for ever. I'd been out of the army for about six months, just travelling about the country wherever I fancied, trying to decide what to do with the rest of my life. I worked as and when, casual labour, whatever was available. I didn't really mind. It was summer, and I slept in an inn, a barn, under a hedge. Just the freedom of the open road, not having to obey orders, to *give* orders to my men I didn't want to give. Everything I owned was slung over my back in a kitbag. I only had myself to please—'

'Do you not have any family?'

He jerked up his head. 'No. Not that I ever want anything to do with. That might sound dreadful, but I'm afraid it's true.'

'I'm sorry you feel that way. My father meant the world to me. Since he died, my life's not been the same.'

Her voice trailed off in passionate sadness, but the silence that followed didn't seem awkward.

'You have a husband. And a child to look forward to,' Seth finally said.

'Ah.' A wistful smile lifted the corners of Rose's mouth. 'But we're supposed to be talking about you.'

'Yes. Of course.' She was relieved when he didn't press her, but clasped his hands, staring down at his intertwined fingers. 'I'd spent a few weeks working as a drayman for a brewery in Exeter. I'll always jump at the chance to work with horses, you see. The chap had hurt his back, so I was just helping out, really. When he was better, I made my way to Plymouth. I still had some army pay left as well, so I was in no hurry to find work straight away. I'd had the idea that I might get on a ship. Work my passage to America, perhaps, and start a new life there. I'd been in Plymouth about a week, trying to decide what to do and making a few enquiries, but

I was so near to Dartmoor and I wanted to see it properly. Everyone said Tavistock was a good place to see it from, so I decided to walk there. I took two days over it, and arrived on the second evening. I called into a public house to ask about lodgings for a few nights. But I wish to God I'd never set foot in the place. If I'd chosen a different establishment, I wouldn't be in this mess now!'

His voice had risen with anguish, and Rose put out a hand to calm him. 'Sssh,' she warned. 'Ned won't be back for some time, but all the same.'

'Yes, of course.' Seth closed his eyes, sighing deeply. 'It was the Exeter Inn,' he went on, resuming his story. 'It's a coaching inn, and I didn't want to waste money staying there, so I asked the landlord if he could recommend somewhere cheaper. He told me of a lodging house in a back street around the corner. I bought a mug of ale and sat down on my own in a corner to drink it. Naturally, there were other customers, including one obnoxious fellow, drunk as a lord and annoying everyone else. He was obviously known to the landlord, and he warned him about his behaviour. He was boasting about how much money he had in his pocket. Even took it out and counted it for everyone to see. Said he'd won it gambling. Anyway, at one point he came over to me. Singled me out as a stranger, tried to taunt me, that sort of thing. It was all rather ugly, and I just let him get on with it. I went up to the bar to buy another drink, and he followed. I was getting fed up with him by then, and suggested to him that he'd had enough to drink. With that, he decided to give me a bloody nose for absolutely no reason. There were plenty of witnesses to the fact that I didn't retaliate. The landlord refused to serve him then and had him thrown out, but he was still shouting at me and saying it was my fault he couldn't have another drink. The landlord apologised profusely to me and gave me a glass of brandy on the house. I thought no more about it. I didn't stay long. I was a stranger and it was dark, and the sooner I found this place to stay, the better. I'd been directed into what I believe is the very old part of the town. I hadn't gone very far at all when it happened.'

He paused, as if summoning the courage to relive whatever it was had caused him to be detained at her majesty's pleasure. 'Go on,' Rose urged, aware that the time was ticking away.

She heard him take a deep breath. 'I saw two figures struggling in the shadows. And then I heard a cry. One of the figures collapsed onto the ground and the other pounced on him. It was dark, but there was enough light coming from the windows of the buildings for me to see that he was rifling through the other man's pockets. There was a couple walking down the street, elderly I think, but they just stood back and watched. Didn't want to get involved. God knows, I wish I'd done the same.'

'So, what did you do?'

'Well, I shouted out and started running towards the attacker. He ran off and disappeared into the darkness. It would've been pointless to give chase, and I was more concerned about the chap lying in the street. He'd been stabbed in the side and I was trying to stop the bleeding. I knew what to do because of the army, you see. I called out for help. But the couple hurried off round the next corner. Then, I vaguely remember seeing someone else come along and then he, too, disappeared. I'd stopped calling out by then. I was just concentrating on saving the fellow's life, he was bleeding so much. I was loosening his clothing, trying to make sure he was still breathing. The next thing I knew, I was being dragged away by two constables and was locked up in the police cells.'

Rose was horrified. 'You mean they thought it were you who'd attacked him?'

'Exactly. The other passer-by had evidently seen me loosening his clothes and assumed I was robbing him, and went off to the police station which I'm sure you know is just round the corner. I was covered in his blood, and they put two and two together.'

'B-but surely they couldn't convict you on that?' Rose stammered.

'Oh, it wasn't the only so-called evidence,' Seth snorted bitterly. 'It turned out the victim was the drunk from the inn. And . . . ' He paused, drawing in a long, slow breath. 'The bastard swore it was me.'

Rose's hand went over her open mouth. 'Oh, Seth, no. But surely it was his word against yours? I mean—'

But Seth shook his head. 'There were so many other factors as well. At the inn, there were plenty of witnesses to his punching me in the face, and it was reckoned I'd followed him out to have my revenge. If only I'd flattened him there and then in the inn, none of this would've happened. The money he'd been boasting about was gone, of course, and I had a similar amount in my pocket, when minutes before I'd been asking for a room somewhere cheap. I can't blame the landlord for testifying to that when he was questioned, as it was true. So they concluded that the money had gone from the drunkard's pocket into mine.'

'But couldn't you have explained how you got that money?'

'God knows, I tried! The trouble was, I'd often stopped at farms and other places, done a day or two's work, and then moved on. Most of the time, I didn't take any notice of the names of the places. The brewery was the only establishment I could definitely name, and I hadn't earned much there as they'd given me board instead. The police sergeant did contact a colleague in Exeter and confirmed it, but it didn't help at all. I needed a lawyer, but they confiscated all my money as evidence, so I had nothing to pay one with.'

'But I thought you said you still had some army pay? Couldn't you have got them to verify that?'

'I could've done, but there were reasons why I didn't want them digging up my past. Personal reasons. Nothing sinister, and anyway, as far as they were concerned, I was a stranger, a man travelling the road. Of no fixed abode. I fitted the bill, so I was convicted.'

'What about your family? Couldn't they have helped?'

'Oh, yes, my father would have loved that! He's a wealthy man, doing his level best to rub shoulders with the aristocracy. Our family home is a country house in Surrey with servants, land, dogs and horses. But I didn't fit into my parents' high society aspirations. Among other things, I was in love with a girl beneath my station, as they put it. I wanted to marry her, so my father hurriedly bought me a commission in the army. Often you can be on a waiting list for years, but he had a business associate who had a cousin who was a colonel — you can imagine the sort of thing. I was only eighteen, so I suppose I felt I had to obey him. But when I eventually came home on leave, the girl had disappeared and I never saw her again. I found out later that her parents had been handsomely paid to move away, taking her with them. Anyway, after a couple of years, I managed to transfer into the cavalry so that at least I was working with horses. My father had to pay extra for that, and he'd already had to purchase my promotion to lieutenant, as well. But it was worth it to him to keep me out of the way, especially as my regiment was posted to India soon afterwards. But by the time I got my captaincy, the Purchase System had been abolished so there was nothing to pay and there I was, thousands of miles away.' He paused for breath, sighing heavily. 'But I'd never been happy in the army. Not being aristocracy, I was an outsider in the Officers' Mess. And I'd never liked the idea of killing anyone. We'd been out there four years, just on patrols, so I never had to, thank heavens. But then I resigned my commission, made my way back to Bombay and found a ship I could work my passage home on. I never told my parents, although I expect it got back to them eventually. As far as they're concerned, I've disappeared off the face of the earth. That was why I couldn't tell the police about the army.' He bowed his head, lowering his eyes before looking up at her again. 'I'd been travelling under a false name to make extra sure I could never be traced. My real name's Warrington. Captain Seth Warrington of the Fifteenth Regiment The King's Hussars.'

'Good Lord.' Rose blinked her astonished eyes at him. 'It's a lot to take in.'

'Yes, I know. But for God's sake, please don't tell a soul. I can assure you, though, if you were to look up my army record, you'd find in it nothing but an exemplary career. My only fault,' and here he smiled wryly, 'was that I was known not to be as ruthless with my men as perhaps I should've been.'

Rose stroked Amber's head as she considered the thoughts that swirled in her mind. 'So the victim, the drunkard, I assume he survived?'

'Oh, yes. Mainly due to my own actions, the physician in question testified at my trial. If he'd died, I'd probably have found myself swinging at the end of a rope. Mind you, sometimes I wonder if that wouldn't have been the best thing.'

Rose was appalled. 'No. Don't say that.'

'But what future do I have?' He dropped his head back against the wall, eyes closed. 'I was an idiot to run off like that. I'd worked all through the winter in the quarry, and then nine months clearing the prison farmlands, soaking wet as we dug drainage ditches, or harnessed to chains dragging out boulders. So I'd done the worst part. If you work hard, you can earn marks towards your ticket of leave. My twelve years could've been reduced to a mere nine. The warder by the tunnel, he's in charge of me. I'm lucky in that, at least. He's a good sort. One of the few. I worked hard, and he awarded me maximum good marks. And because I'd behaved myself, I was considered trustworthy enough to be transferred to working with the animals. With the mist coming down, the land parties weren't allowed out. But the animals still have to be fed, and when the mist became so thick and the warder nearest me was busy taking a swig from his hip flask, well, I suddenly thought I might never have such a chance again. It was a split second decision. If I'd stopped to think, I wouldn't have been such a fool. So now, if I'm caught, I'll be flogged for my troubles and lose all my good marks. I could even have another five years added to my sentence.'

'But surely, if you can prove you're innocent—'

'If you can't prove it when you're on trial, you don't get another chance. I couldn't have a lawyer, but I was allowed to cross-examine the witnesses. But the victim, Jonas Chant, stuck to his story. Well, he would, wouldn't he? If I was convicted, he'd get his money back. Except that it was *my* money. The real culprit still had *his*. I pointed out that he couldn't possibly have known what his assailant looked like. It was dark, and he was four sheets to the wind. Christ, *I* didn't recognise *him* in the dark! But he swore blind it was me. And the chap who'd fetched the policeman, I asked him if he actually saw me attack him, and he admitted he hadn't. He just saw me going through the devil's clothes, as he thought, when I was actually trying to get to his wounds. But none of my arguments did any good. The jury was convinced, and that was it.'

Rose pressed her hands together as she mulled over what he'd told her. 'What if you could find the elderly couple? If they testified they saw the real attacker run off, and you coming to the rescue, surely that would prove your innocence? And maybe someone else at the inn saw someone behaving suspiciously. As if they were intent on following that devil out into the street. And what if you could retrace your steps, find some of the other places you worked and prove you'd earned that money?'

'No.' Seth turned his head towards her, a deep sadness glimmering in his eyes. 'It's too late. Once you're convicted, that's it. There's no way you can appeal, even if you come up with indisputable new evidence.'

'That's insane!'

'It's the law,' Seth murmured as he snapped a blade of straw and twined it tightly about his fingers.

'Then the law's an ass.' To her amazement, Rose heard Seth chuckle, but she didn't find anything amusing in it. She really couldn't believe the injustice of it. But the fact that Seth was being so open about everything that had happened, only served to increase her trust in him. 'Are you absolutely certain there's no other way?' she asked.

'Well, there's something called a royal pardon. Still makes it sound as if you're guilty, though, doesn't it, even though you have to prove yourself beyond a shadow of a doubt? But it's so rare as to be virtually impossible, and it takes a massive amount of power and influence, not to say money to pay high court lawyers and everything else that's involved. You're trying to overturn a jury's verdict and a circuit judge's sentence, after all. So I haven't a cat in hell's chance of that, have I?'

Rose sucked in her lips. Charles had money, and he knew people in high places. But she might as well try to jump the moon as ask his help. He'd always made his opinion of Dartmoor's convicts abundantly clear.

'The best I can hope for,' Seth went on, 'is that I'm not discovered here until I'm able to leave.'

'And what will you do then?' Rose questioned him, shying away from the sadness that gripped her heart at the thought of his leaving.

'I met someone while I was being held in the police cells in Tavistock. I shared a cell for a couple of days with a fellow who was waiting for a Coroner's Court hearing. I don't know for sure if he was released, but I never heard that he'd been hanged. Mind you, I was up before the magistrate and spirited away to Exeter to await the next Assizes. Anyway, I'd struck up quite a friendship with this chap, and I think he'd probably help me to get away. Maybe get on that ship to America. Ironic, really, that I ended up serving my sentence back here on Dartmoor. I served my initial period in Millwall, you see. They send you somewhere else for nine months' solitary to break you down first. It doesn't even count towards your sentence. And then I ended up back here when I could've been sent anywhere. But this other man was a local farmer. From a place called Peter Tavy. On the moor somewhere, he said. D'you know it?'

Rose nodded. 'Yes. Not far from Tavistock. I passed through there once with my father on the way to the huge mining agglomeration at Mary Tavy called Wheal Friendship.

My father were manager of the gunpowder mills just a few miles north of here, you see. It was on business, of course, but I often went with him.'

'I get the feeling you were very close to your father.' Seth's voice was so sensitive that with nobody to confide in for so long, Rose felt an overwhelming urge to let her grief escape in a raging torrent.

'Yes.' She scraped the simple word from her throat, surprised at how near she was to tears. But they'd been talking for some time, and she must have Seth hidden again before Ned returned. 'This farmer, what was his name?'

'Pencarrow. Richard Pencarrow. I can't be sure, but I reckon he'd help me.'

Rose frowned. He'd have to hide in the stable for at least another five weeks. They had to get through that first . . .

CHAPTER TWENTY-TWO

With Charles away, it was a case of dreaming up errands to keep Ned occupied elsewhere, too. She often dispatched him to Tor Royal for extra butter and cream, and never complained if he dallied an hour with the comely dairymaid there. One day, she'd declared a desperate craving for some bananas, if you please! If Ned couldn't find any in Tavistock, he was to take the train to Plymouth, where he surely would. Rose had told him it didn't matter if he took all day. But while he was out, Dr Seaton had come to see her, and she'd taken him out to the stables, where he was able to check on Seth in complete secrecy.

Rose felt as if Seth's presence had given her a purpose in life. She lived for the moment when it was safe to enter the loose box with whatever provisions she'd purloined for him. She couldn't wait to take up her position sitting on the bale near Amber and her pups, facing the door, the top half of which she left open to allow some light to enter. It meant she could also see anyone who approached and warn Seth to take cover in his hiding place around the corner. She bathed the shot wounds in his shoulder regularly, and there were at last signs of improvement.

'When's the baby due?' he asked one day when she'd finally sat down after cleaning up after the puppies and spreading clean newspaper over the loose box floor. At two weeks old, the little bundles of fur were finding their legs and beginning to stumble away from their mother. Amber watched over them indulgently, rising up to retrieve them in her soft mouth if they wandered too far. Rose felt she could be entertained all day by their antics.

She looked up at Seth as he hobbled around the confined space of the dog-leg in an attempt to take a little exercise while Rose was on guard. He'd paused for a moment and was laughing softly as the tiny runt of the litter had toppled onto her minute snout, but in an instant was valiantly heaving herself onto her wobbly legs once more. Seth's generous mouth was stretched with amusement in the thickening stubble on his jaw, and Rose's heart seemed to trip over itself for not the first time. Until then, she'd tossed the feeling away, but now she allowed it to lap innocently about her tangled emotions.

'Eight weeks.' She smiled a little ruefully. It seemed a long way off, and she didn't want to contemplate a time when Seth would no longer be a part of her life, and she'd have to endure her future as Charles's wife. Just now, she didn't want to think about it.

'And . . . are you looking forward to it?'

'Yes, of course!' She shook her head. It was a strange question, asked in an even stranger tone of voice.

'And your husband?'

'Oh, yes! He's always wanted a son. I'm hoping it'll bring us . . . ' She broke off, realising she'd said too much. But Seth was shrewd, and his eyes seemed to bore into hers.

'Bring you closer together,' he finished for her.

The seconds of silence that followed lasted an eternity and Rose wrung her hands in her lap.

'Every time you speak of him,' she heard Seth's quiet, intense voice, 'you seem to . . . I don't know . . . close up. To shy away from it. You're not happy in your marriage, are you, Rose?'

She lowered her eyes. She couldn't fathom why, but she somehow felt compelled to answer. As if it would ease the terrible ache inside. 'I thought I loved him,' she barely whispered. 'I *wanted* to love him. I still do. That's why the child's so important.'

She didn't see Seth flinch. 'I'm sorry. I shouldn't have asked. I hope it all works out well for you.'

She braced herself to glance up at him again. 'Thank you. I'm certain it will. We've been married less than a year, so there should be *some* hope for us.'

'You weren't married, then, when we first met?'

'By the tunnel, you mean? No. I thought back then that my charmed life would go on for ever. But it doesn't, does it?' she sighed sadly. And then she went on more positively, glad to change the subject, 'And what about you? You were new then, weren't you?'

Seth nodded briefly. 'I was, yes. The quarry was damned hard work, and dangerous with the explosives. But I survived my stint there, and then I was put to land clearance, yoked up like an ox to pull out boulders embedded in the ground. Or digging drainage trenches up to the waist in cold water all day. Your trousers chafe the skin off your legs, and your hands bleed so much that holding a spade or axe all day is hell. There's no way your uniform can dry out overnight in a cold, damp cell, so it's still wet when you put it back on in the morning.'

His eyes had narrowed and he was staring ahead at some unseen spot on the opposite wall, his face set. Rose reached out and squeezed his arm, her fingers tingling as she touched him. He brought his eyes to rest on her, and she saw the hurt in them.

'That's why I behaved myself,' he went on with an ironic shrug of his eyebrows. 'I knew the sooner I proved myself the perfect prisoner, the sooner I'd be put to something less gruelling. Working with the farm animals was ideal when my time came. And it gave me the chance to escape. Which I shall probably end up paying dearly for,' he finished with a wry grimace.

'But you might make it away. And if you are caught, they might be lenient. After all, you did save a warder's life.'

'If that's what I did. And I hardly think they'd take that into consideration. That warder, though, he might put in a good word for me.'

'He might well do that. He's my best friend's father, you see.'

'Really?'

'Yes. I know most people hereabouts. I've lived here, or at least over at Cherrybrook, for so many years. And I ride all over the place on Gospel, meeting people. At least . . . ' She faltered, pulling a wistful face. 'At least, I did until Charles stopped me. I don't mind while I'm carrying the baby, but he's forbidden me to ride out alone ever again.'

'I can see why you'd miss that. He's a magnificent animal, your Gospel. I'd love to ride him myself.' But the sudden excitement on his face died in an instant. 'But I'll never get to, will I?' he murmured.

And Rose turned away, choking on what she knew was the answer.

* * *

Her feet were leaden as she dragged herself across the yard a week later once she knew the coast was clear. The pain in her heart was tearing her to shreds, but there was nothing she could do but accept the inevitable.

'A telegram came earlier,' she told Seth, her voice broken and dejected. 'Charles is coming home. He'll be here tomorrow night.'

Their eyes met, recognising the appalled compassion of what it would mean to them. Seth lowered his gaze, his lips drawn into a tight knot. When he looked up at her again, he saw tears trickling down her cheeks.

He scrambled to his feet, taking her hands as she stepped towards him. 'You knew he'd be coming home soon. He *is* your husband.'

'Yes, I know.' She shook off his hands, flapping her arms helplessly in agonised frustration. She'd somehow sealed her mind to Charles's return. And it wasn't just because it would be far more dangerous to slip out with food and drink for Seth. 'But I don't want him to come back. Not ever. I wish to God I'd never married him.'

She flicked her head so that her hair, which she hadn't bothered to restrain in any way, whipped across her face. Seth smoothed it back. And then placed his hands firmly on her shoulders.

'You don't mean that, Rose.'

She raised her eyes to his face, but in her own anguish, didn't see the torment etched in his features. She drew in an enormous breath, trying desperately to calm herself. 'No, I suppose not. I married him to provide for my father. I wanted to love him. I honestly did. But it was a mistake and . . . Oh, Seth, I don't know what to do.'

All the regret, the bitterness and grief suddenly surged up and burst through the fragile dam of her self-control. So much sorrow. So much heartache, and she leaned against Seth as he hopped with her across to the bale and sat her down on it.

'There's nothing you *can* do. Make the very most of your life. Be a good wife and mother. Your husband can't be *so* bad.'

'But . . . he has no *soul*. He has no sympathy. No understanding. He always wants everything to be just the way *he* wants it.'

'Don't we all, in our own way?'

'Yes, of course, but he only wants . . . to possess me. He doesn't want the real me, just what he thinks I *should* be. You know, when my father died, he never allowed me to grieve. Never held me. Never let me cry in his arms. I just had to keep it all inside, because that was what *he* wanted.'

Her tears were flowing freely now, unchecked. It seemed that now the floodgate had opened, there was no way to stem the torrent of her misery, and all her suppressed emotions erupted in an unstoppable tide. It seemed so natural when Seth, perched on the bale next to her, drew her against his chest, tucking her head beneath his chin.

'I know it must be hard,' he whispered into her hair. 'Losing your father, especially when you were so close to him, must have been . . . well, I don't suppose there are words to describe it. But you must look to the future. Soon you'll be basking in the joys of motherhood. Just like Amber here. Look at her now!'

Rose turned her head, and through her tear-blurred vision, saw Amber giving the pups a wash with her strong, pink tongue. Rose couldn't help but smile, despite herself.

'Yes. You're right.' She looked back at Seth, quite accepting as he thumbed the drying tears from beneath her eyes. 'But he'll want more children. He . . . he never leaves me alone, if you . . . know what I mean.' She felt the flush in her cheeks, as it was hardly something to discuss with a stranger. But she felt as if she'd known Seth all her life. He'd touched something deep within her soul, and it gave her the confidence to say, 'He's the same in that as everything else. He treats me just like another possession. He never thinks that I might want something from it, too.'

'Perhaps you should try *giving* something yourself,' Seth said so quietly, it was almost a whisper. 'It might come more easily. And perhaps he'll respond.'

Yes. Perhaps Seth was right. Dear Lord, she was going to miss him so much when . . . 'It's going to be awful,' she said with a sigh. 'Tomorrow, when Ned goes to fetch him from the station, it'll be our last chance to talk. I won't be able to get Ned out of the way any more. And it'll be so much more dangerous for you.'

'Yes. If it wasn't for this wretched ankle . . . I wonder if I got away tonight. They're not looking for someone with his leg in plaster, after all.'

'No, but they are still looking. And you wouldn't get far. And even if you found this Richard Pencarrow's farm, Peter Tavy's probably ten miles by road. And that's going right past the prison gates. You'd need to make a detour of miles, and you'd be bound to get lost on the moor, especially at night. No. It's probably safer you stay here.'

'But if I'm found out, you're deeply implicated.'

'Oh, you let me take care of that,' she smiled reassuringly, though in truth, she had no idea how.

* * *

They made the most of those last few hours, talking as if there was no tomorrow. Which for them, there wasn't. Rose told Seth of her life at Cherrybrook, of how after Henry's accident, she'd tried in vain to secure a new home for herself, Henry and Florrie until the only answer had been to marry Charles, which she'd believed would bring them all happiness. She described the spectacular beauty of her beloved Dartmoor, only a small part of which Seth could experience from the prison. And Seth told her about his time in India, and described the harsh conditions in the army which, by comparison to the prison, seemed almost luxurious.

They talked on, relishing the ease which comes to two like-minded people, until they suddenly realised Ned would soon return with Charles. Seth must hide in the straw, and Rose should go into the house to ensure all was in order for Charles's welcome home dinner. It was like a final farewell, and yet not. It would be another two and a half weeks before Seth could limp out of her life. But those last days would be fraught with difficulty, and they would never again have the chance to open up their hearts to one another, trusting in the intimacy they'd discovered against all odds. Rose kept delaying the moment of departure, and when she finally lumbered to her feet and walked away, her heart was wrenching in strange, unwanted pain.

* * *

She heard him coughing as she crossed the yard and her stomach clenched with fear. The days since Charles had returned had been a torment to her. She'd hardly been able to come out to Seth at all, and yesterday, she'd been unable to bring him so much as a drink of water. This morning, though, she had a mug of hot, sweet tea. Seth would devour it, especially since there'd been no let-up in the cold, damp weather, though it was well into May now. But the sound of his cough froze Rose's heart. If she could hear him, so too could anyone else.

She hurried into Gospel's loose box. Seth wasn't even covered properly by the straw, but was lying on his front, half propped up on one elbow, his other arm clamped across his chest as he struggled against a violent spasm of uncontrollable coughing. Rose fell on her knees beside him, but dear God, what was she to do? When Seth finally managed to subdue the harrowing cough and drew the back of his hand over his mouth, to Rose's horror, it came away streaked with blood-stained spittle.

'Drink this,' she instructed, pushing the mug into his hands as he shifted into a sitting position.

He nodded and tried to take a breath to drink the tea, but only succeeded in spluttering into it and spilling some down his front. Rose steadied his hand, but as the hot liquid evidently soothed his throat, she placed her palm across his forehead. It was on fire.

Rose's heart flooded with the empty numbness of acceptance. Why now, when Seth was so near to being able to make his escape? It was as if the cruel hand of fate had been teasing them, only to hurl them back into the quagmire of despair at the last minute.

'You're ill, Seth,' she forced the words from her throat. 'You know what Dr Seaton said. You'll have to give yourself up.'

'No. I've got . . . to get to Richard's farm.'

'But, Seth, you could die.'

'I'll take that chance.' And he collapsed into another fit of coughing. 'I just can't face . . . another ten years, maybe more, in that hell-hole . . . for something I didn't do. If I give myself up, I'm no coward but . . . Oh, God, I'm so cold . . .'

Rose watched, her heart in savage pain, as he tried to slurp at the tea between rattling breaths. If only Dr Seaton were coming, but he wasn't due for several days, and Rose Maddiford, whose indomitable spirit would always fight back, had fallen into a yawning chasm of despair. All she could think of was to fetch a glass of water so that Seth could take a good dose of laudanum. With any luck, the drug-induced sleep might also suppress his racking cough. And give her time to think.

In her headlong anxiety, she hadn't seen Ned Cornish stand back from the tackroom door at the opposite end of the stableblock. His mind had been on one thing lately, seducing the dairymaid at Tor Royal. He'd managed to get his hand up her skirt, and was convinced his aching, throbbing member wouldn't be far behind. But the master's coming home had thrown a spanner in the works. Rose hadn't sent him on one of her fool's errands since her husband's return, and now Ned's free hours that he normally relished — as although he had nothing to do, he must remain on duty in case he was needed to tack up one of the horses at short notice — had become a frustrating burden to him as he dreamt of what he *might* have been doing.

Slowly, his half-witted brain became curious. It hadn't struck him as particularly odd the way Rose had been . . . yes, getting him out of the way, he was sure of it now. She'd even been neglecting that bloody nag of hers in favour of the two dogs and the litter of mongrels they'd produced, constantly crossing back and forth with a drink to sip as she watched the puppies, and extra food for the bitch. But, surely the dog couldn't eat so much. Surely there was something else going on?

And then he heard it. Someone trying desperately to muffle a vicious cough. And it sounded like a man.

Ned's eyes narrowed to cunning slits. That escaped convict a few weeks back had disappeared into thin air. Well, he hadn't disappeared at all, had he? He was in Gospel's bloody loose box, hiding around the corner in the dog-leg, no doubt. And Rose had been looking after him! Typical of her! She was known to have some sympathy for the bastards banged up in the prison, at least for those guilty of lesser crimes. How far had that sympathy gone? When Ned thought of the years he'd never had so much as a kiss out of Rose! But what had she given to that bugger out in the stable?

Ned's face twitched with seething rage. But for once, he checked himself. If he went charging into the stable, the criminal, well, he could be violent. And though Ned would enter into fisticuffs with anyone provided he knew it was a sure assumption he would easily win, he was bright enough to consider that the felon may well be stronger than he was!

No. He would make sure of his facts and then go quietly and politely to the backdoor of the house and ask to have a word with the master. Oh, yes, he'd get his own back on Rose Maddiford! Besides, the statutory five pounds reward for turning in an escapee — the equivalent of several months' pay — would be more than recompense.

* * *

Rose was lying on the bed, supposedly taking a rest but actually trying desperately to think up a solution. She must invent some excuse for Charles to send urgently for Dr Seaton. What should she say? What about that she was bleeding? Just a little. Yes, that would surely bring the doctor at once.

She was just getting up to put her plan into action, when she heard the commotion at the back of the house. Her heart froze into a painful block of ice as the sound of heavy boots on the gravel and men's raised voices sliced into her ears.

Her heart stopped beating. Guards. The Civil Guard from the prison. Armed. Marching towards the stableyard.

She started retching, but there was no time for that. She ran down the stairs, one hand clamped over her mouth to retain the bile that scorched into her gullet. She blundered out into the yard, heedless of the penetrating drizzle, and stopped dead as several pairs of eyes turned upon her, Ned's face in a leering snigger, the guard she recognised as the sergeant who'd led the manhunt, suffused with callous satisfaction, and then Charles . . . He gazed at her, his skin pale from anger and disbelief. Not a word passed anyone's lips, each figure a sculptured statue, until angry shouts, the sounds of a violent struggle, the barking of a dog, drew their attention to the loose box, and the two guards who had remained in the yard raised their Sniders and trained them on the door.

Rose felt she would faint, as if some huge hand had closed about her neck and was wringing the life from her. Her heart plummeted as two burly guards emerged from the stable, Seth held between them in a grip of iron. He was trying to keep up with them, half hopping on one leg as they marched him across the yard. But they were moving too fast and had to drag him over the cobbles before coming to attention in front of their sergeant. Seth's face was bloodless, his broad forehead bedewed with feverish sweat and embellished with a gash from the struggle. But when the sergeant spat at him with a taunting jibe, he drew himself up to his full height and stared straight ahead, his jaw lifted defiantly.

'You've led us a merry dance, you *scum*!' the sergeant snarled, driving his huge fist into Seth's stomach.

Rose turned away with an audible gasp, grabbing onto whatever was at hand, which happened to be Charles's arm. She heard even *him* wince and for a fleeting instant, their eyes met in horror before they both looked back. Seth had collapsed onto his knees, locked in a convulsion of coughing, and dangling between the unyielding grip the two guards retained on each arm. The sergeant sneered down at him, his face a pitiless mask of spite. Seth lifted his head, still fighting for breath, a streak of blood dribbling from the corner of his mouth.

'I-I had to get away,' he gasped, gazing beseechingly up at his tormentor. 'Don't you see. I'm innocent.'

The cough overtook him again, but the sergeant's lip curled implacably. 'Innocent, be damned! I suppose that's what you told Mrs Chadwick here, and her being of a kind nature and in a delicate condition, she fell for it, poor lady! Well, laddie, you'll be well flogged for it, mark my words!'

The sergeant's obvious relish plunged a crucifying pain into Rose's flesh. Her legs buckled beneath her and she clung onto her husband, burying her face in his shoulder and, miraculously, his arms came about her, buoying up her frail body.

'Oh, Charles, I've been so frightened!' she wept. 'I didn't know what to do!'

From the corner of her eye, she saw the sergeant glance in her direction with what she imagined was the nearest to sympathy he was capable of. In that instant, she knew that if she was to be of any help to Seth, she must establish her own blamelessness first.

'He scared me so much, I were too afraid not to do as he said,' she cried hysterically at the top of her voice.

'What I'd like to know, sergeant, is how the devil he got his leg plastered?' one of the guards demanded, and Rose trembled with cold sweat as she thought of the kindness elderly Dr Seaton had shown them.

'It was me.' She stepped forward on uncertain legs. 'I stole the plaster from Dr Seaton's bag when he came to visit me because of the baby.' And then — may God forgive her — she jabbed a finger at Seth. 'It were *his* idea. He told me to do it.'

The pulse was pounding at her temples as the sergeant frowned, but Seth raised his head, still half choking on the relentless cough.

'I said I'd kill the puppies if she didn't,' he rasped, putting an unfamiliar coldness into his voice.

Across the space that separated them, their eyes met in one last clinging, frantic gaze, and in the clear depths of his agony, Rose saw some calm and steadfast belief in the brief trust they'd come to share. And then she caught an almost imperceptible jerk of his eyebrows, a tiny gesture telling her to put herself first. And then the sergeant gave a barbaric grunt as he thrust his boot into his prisoner's side.

Seth had no breath to cry out, but sprawled forward again, coughing until blood from his lungs splattered onto the cobbles before him. This time, Rose screamed, her limbs flailing in frustration, and Charles had to hold her fast in his arms.

'For God's sake, do you have to treat him like that in front of my wife? Surely she's already been through enough without you—'

'No need to upset yourself, sir. Just needed to make certain he wouldn't try to escape again. If you'd like to take your wife inside, we'll take care of everything now. Right, get the cuffs on him, lads. And you, sir,' he said, turning to Ned who was preening himself proudly. 'If you'd like to accompany us, we can see about claiming your reward.'

Rose watched them all disappear round the corner of the yard, dragging Seth between them as he was unable to walk. It was only Charles's arms firmly about Rose that stopped her from running after them, but she knew she mustn't. She wanted to free herself from Charles's hold by sinking her teeth into his arm, but she had to stand, controlled and dignified as he turned her towards the back door of the house.

Faintness was already swimming in her head, and it only took the whipping hand that slammed across her face to tip her over the brink into unconsciousness.

CHAPTER TWENTY-THREE

Rose groaned achingly and her eyelids flickered before she finally forced them open. A sledge-hammer was pounding inside her skull, and as she moved the muscles of her face slightly and her cheek stung, the horrific events out in the stableyard crashed into her stricken mind. She became aware that she was lying on her bed, though how she'd got there, or indeed how long she'd been there, were a mystery. All she could think of was Seth, her thoughts a mangled torment of fury and sorrow. Dear God, he didn't deserve the cruelty the sergeant had meted out to him, and she knew exactly how he would be punished as soon as he was fit enough. If he ever was. Her throat closed up and moisture misted her eyes. Surely there must be something she could do to help him?

She hauled herself to her feet, ignoring the throbbing inside her head and squaring her shoulders determinedly. Charles! She wasn't really sure how he'd reacted to her part in Seth's concealment. Quite what he believed, she didn't know. But he'd slapped her so hard, it had been enough to send her reeling senses into the realms of oblivion. And she would never, *ever* forgive him!

She strode purposefully across the room and her hand closed on the door knob. Though the china sphere turned, she met with unyielding resistance. Charles had locked her in.

The *bastard*!

Hatred spewed into her gullet. Damn Charles! Damn and blast him to hell! If he thought he could treat her like that, he'd have to think again. She wouldn't give in without a fight. Her eyes narrowed dangerously, and she began to pummel relentlessly on the door.

It was a full five minutes before she heard him on the other side, and the string of profanities that tumbled from her mouth shocked even herself, but she didn't care! She stood back as Charles opened the door, her fingers ready to claw at his face.

'Shut your mouth, for God's sake, Rose!' Charles bawled at her. 'You sound like a fish wife!'

'And can you wonder at it, you treacherous sod! You—'

'Treacherous! My God, *you're* the one guilty of treachery, my girl, not me! Aiding and abetting an escaped convict, no less! I've already had a visit from the prison governor. While you've been reposing on your bed, I've had to do some pretty clever talking to get you and that stupid old doctor out of trouble! Blaming it on your condition and your frail nerves, though God knows if he could see you now . . . I've been lying through my back teeth to save your hide! And if you think for one moment I believe your story about stealing the plaster from the doctor's bag, well, it's lucky for the old fool I managed to convince the governor of it!'

He clamped his jaw shut, his cheeks flushed puce with rage. Rose burned to make some scathing retort, but though she was poised to fly at him, her sharp mind managed some restraint. To challenge him would be fruitless. What she needed was to *outwit* him. Besides, she recognised that she'd put him in a difficult position, and she was sorry for that.

She lowered her eyes, and allowed the tears of anguish that were blurring her vision again to meander down her cheeks. She sank down on the edge of the bed, head bowed over her jutting stomach, and wrung her hands.

'It really was true, even if you don't believe me. I *did* steal from Dr Seaton. He wasn't involved at all. To be honest, I was so frightened, I didn't know what I was doing. They said the convict was dangerous, so I really thought he might kill the pups if I didn't do what he said! And then you went away and . . . then he told me how he was innocent, and I was so confused . . .'

Her shoulders sagged and she allowed her hair to fall forward about her taut face. For a moment, she looked so vulnerable, her tear-ravaged beauty so touching, that Charles's heart softened.

'All right,' he said stiffly. 'I'm prepared to forgive you. But I really don't trust you, Rose. I'm sure that when the child is born, you'll come to your senses and have other new priorities to govern your life. But until then, you will keep to this room. And you'd better behave yourself. I'll not be prepared to protect you from any other act of perjury.'

Keep to the bedroom! Rose's mind rose up in protest, but she checked herself at once. Play his game, but be as devious as hell. Though at present, she had no idea in what way.

'Yes, Charles,' she sighed ponderously. 'It'll be such a relief, not to have to face that villain again. I were truly terrified.'

'Well, now you'll never have to see him again, and he'll be rightly punished. He didn't actually *hurt* you in any way, did he?'

'He didn't slap me across the face so hard that I passed out, if that's what you mean.' Her eyes sparked, and she saw the colour flood back into Charles's cheeks.

'You just watch your step, madam,' he hissed. 'If it wasn't for the child, I'd have given you a good hiding, so don't push your luck! I'll send Patsy up with a tray later, and in the meantime you can contemplate your crime alone.'

He went out, shutting the door behind him and turning the key. Rose fell forward onto the bed, weeping freely with tears of exasperation and defeat. But her self-pity didn't last for long. The image of Seth on his knees as he coughed blood onto the cobbles, slashed into her mind. And there would be worse to come. Unless she did something about it.

Thoughts began to chase each other round inside her head. The baby was due in a little over six weeks now, and Florrie had promised to be back in time for the birth. But Rose needed her now.

When Patsy came in with the tray, she was ready. Charles waited outside to unlock and then lock the door again. Patsy, already too traumatised by events earlier in the day, and too young and timid to do anything beyond obeying the master in silence, simply gazed at her lovely mistress as a letter was slipped surreptitiously into the pocket of her apron. The poor girl merely bobbed a shaky curtsy before she fled the room, and Rose was left alone once more.

Her tears were all spent now, and in their place, a squall of rage choked her rebellious heart. Rage at Charles, yes, but more so at the circumstances that had placed Seth in the position he was now. Was the sergeant right? Had Seth told her a pack of lies to gain her sympathy? No! She was convinced of his innocence, and nothing would shake her faith in him.

* * *

It took a week before Florrie burst in upon their lives again, a week during which Rose was only allowed out of the bedroom for Dr Seaton's visit. Florrie was like an unstoppable whirlwind, marching into the hall and demanding to speak to the master. Charles was so astonished both at her sudden reappearance and at her bellicose attitude when she had always shown him such cool deference before, that he stepped out of his study in bewilderment. It had never crossed his mind that she looked upon Rose as her daughter, and that if the situation demanded it — which it evidently did just now — she would be willing to fight tooth and nail for her!

'They've just tell me in the kitchen that you'm keeping my Rose locked up in her room!' she exploded, remembering the exact words Rose had instructed her to say, since

Charles mustn't know of the letter and how little Patsy had secretly posted it. 'I comes back here to help her prepare for the babby, and find you'm treating her like a criminal! You should be ashamed o' yoursel'!'

She stood, hands on hips and glowering at Charles while he regained his usual composure. 'May I remind you, Mrs Bennett,' he said coldly, 'that you are only here under my sufferance.'

'Don't you play Mr High and Mighty with me! Your wife had already engaged me as nanny to her child, as I were to her virtually all her life!'

'And you can just as easily be dismissed by me.'

'And I could easily reveal the truth about you to Mr Frean. 'Twouldn't do your precious reputation much good, would it, especially with Mr Frean being of such influence hereabouts?' she demanded, crossing her arms firmly over her bosom. 'Now I'm going up to my Rose, and from now on, that door is to remain unlocked or I shall want to know the reason why! She won't want to far, being due soon now. But she's to have the run of the house and the garden whenever she wants!'

And leaving Charles dumbfounded by the study door, Florrie flounced up the stairs.

* * *

Dr Power crumpled the letter into a ball and launched it into the fire, watching its edges scorch until it finally fell victim to the hungry flames.

Rose Maddiford. Her maiden name suited her well. She truly must be mad. The letter was a full confession of how she'd willingly helped Seth Collingwood, that she believed unequivocally in his innocence, and that the story that he'd terrified her and threatened to kill Amber's puppies was a complete and utter lie of Collingwood's fabrication in order to protect her. She knew that he would almost certainly be flogged for his escape, but he was sick and could the doctor do anything to prevent it, especially as the poor man had been wrongly convicted in the first place and didn't deserve his incarceration, let alone the terrible punishment. Dr Power had been so good to her in the past especially with her father, and she trusted him to do what was morally right.

The doctor slumped back in his chair. Ah, Rose . . . That very first time he'd clapped eyes on her crept into his brain. Six years ago, when he'd taken up the position of prison surgeon. The position provided a roof over the heads of his growing family, and also offered him the opportunity to help the working classes of the area who couldn't afford the usual charges of a private doctor. He was given a house of almost equal standard to that of the governor, and was paid a reasonable wage. So that when the local community needed him, he could charge but a nominal fee.

Among his patients were the workers at the gunpowder mills. The first time he'd been summoned there, it had been at the behest of a mettlesome young girl resembling a picture from one of his children's fairytale books as she sat atop a prancing steed whose coat matched the shining ebony of her hair. She could have been no more than sixteen then, and at more than twenty years her senior, he was old enough to be her father. But shamefully he couldn't deny that, had he been younger and not already long and happily married, his heart would have been strongly drawn to her. As it was, there was nothing more than admiration for her in his breast, not only for her beauty, but for her strength of character. She had such compassion for the men and their families who had worked for her father. The father whose death, he'd witnessed for himself, had broken the poor girl's heart.

And now this plea for help.

Did she realise what she was asking? And yet he understood entirely. His own position at the prison was humbling and irresolute, his allegiances torn asunder. He was supposed to be a man of mercy, healer of the sick, and yet he had to uphold the cruel regime of the harshest punishment imaginable. The prison infirmary was full of convicts sent to Dartmoor not because they were particularly heinous, but because they were suffering from consumption, and the clean air was thought to be good for them. There were other inmates who feigned illness to escape the back-breaking hard labour, some who even put their own lives at risk by swallowing anything to hand — such as soap, ground glass or even pins — that would incapacitate them. Dr Power had to be equal to all their tricks. And then, ironically, perfectly fit and healthy men had their constitutions decimated by the starvation diet and the gruelling tasks they were put to daily, enduring conditions to which no farmer would subject his animals.

Men like Seth Collingwood.

A while back, Dr Power had heard how he had without doubt saved the life of warder Cartwright as the work party returned from its day's toil at the quarry. Cartwright had confessed to the physician a liking for his saviour, and even an inclination to believe his protestations of innocence, saying he'd proved himself the model prisoner.

And then, ten days ago, Dr Power had discovered the poor devil chained in a punishment cell, awaiting sentence from the Director of Prisons for his attempted escape. He'd taken some lead shot in his shoulder from one of the guards' Sniders, but the wounds were healing well. How well his broken ankle inside its plaster-cast was mending would only be known when it was removed. It was the doctor's considered opinion that the cast had been professionally applied and was not Rose's own remarkably successful attempt, as she claimed in the letter. He would, however, keep that view to himself, not wanting to get either Rose or his respected colleague into trouble. What had horrified him, though, was that the prisoner was running a fever and coughing up blood, yet was chained in a sitting position and made to pick oakum, in a cold, damp cell, with nothing but bare boards for a bed and existing on the so-called jockey diet of bread and water.

Dr Power didn't even wait for the result of his immediate report to the governor, but had the convict removed to the infirmary at once. Apparently, it had been less than forty-eight hours since his recapture, but had it been much longer, it may well have been a death certificate rather than a medical report he needed to complete. The governor had been furious with the vindictive sergeant who'd lied about the escapee's state of health, but that was it. For who cared about the fate of just another convict?

And now the authorisation for Collingwood's punishment had arrived. The maximum of thirty-six lashes with the cat o' nine tails, not just for his escape, but also for his terrorising of the heavily pregnant young woman.

Dr Power ran his hand over his jaw. A couple of days previously, Florrie Bennett had come to his door with the letter from her little mistress which, once he'd read it, he'd secreted where no one could ever find it, and now he'd committed it to ashes. What could he do? Collingwood — though of course he was referred to by his prison number only — had improved somewhat. After lying for days and nights on end on a stable floor which had probably caused the illness in the first place, ten days of being propped upright in bed had vastly helped his chest infection. Together with the superior invalid diet, the felon's condition was much better. But he was nowhere near sufficiently recovered to endure the barbaric torture to which he had been sentenced.

And yet . . .

Dr Power dropped his head into his hands. It was a huge risk, but it was the only way to save Collingwood from the entire punishment. Though a leather hide was placed as protection over the vital organs, within a few lashes, the swelling flesh would open and run with blood until the cat ripped through to the bone. The agony of it must be indescribable. The physician shuddered. He'd seen it many times, and now, Dear Sweet Jesus, he was to witness it again. He shook his head. What in the name of God was he doing in this job?

He stood up, his eyes screwed tightly at what he knew he must do.

* * *

The prisoner's face was inscrutable as he was spread-eagled on the flogging frame, waiting patiently while the problem of how to secure the plaster-cast was solved, as the prison surgeon would not have it removed. When he offered the felon a gag for his mouth, he refused with a shake of his head, but the doctor leant forward to hiss in his ear.

'Take it, you fool. I don't want to have to stitch your tongue or your lip as well. For God's sake, do as I say. Mrs Chadwick won't want to have risked herself for nothing.'

He drew back hastily, not wanting to arouse the suspicions of the governor and the burly warder who'd been chosen to deliver the punishment. But he caught the flash of amazed comprehension in the convict's eyes as he took up his spectator's position. And then he shuddered as he saw the governor give the nod to begin.

He'd known great, swarthy bullies holler like babies from the very first stroke, but this unfortunate lad scarcely flinched, his narrowed eyes locked onto some point of focus on the far wall and merely twitching as the whipped ends of the cat raked like barbs into his exposed back. Dr Power's own sickened heart pounded inside his chest, sweat prickling beneath his shirt. By the count of five, nothing had escaped the victim's lips but a whimper, and the physician balled his fists. Dear God, give me something, lad! And then with the next stroke, the warder seemed to add extra force to the sweep of his arm as he slammed the cat through the air. The shock of the redoubled agony was so powerful, the convict couldn't cry out. Instead, his chest rasped with a sharp and massive intake of breath that made his enflamed lungs react with a spluttering cough.

Dr Power almost rejoiced. It was what he'd prayed for. At a repeat of the warder's action, the bound man almost choked on the prolonged coughing it drew from his strained insides. Another two strokes and the cough exploded into one continuous, violent spasm. The surgeon observed carefully the tortured criminal. With his arms spread above his head, his concave stomach was so taut with suffering, there seemed little between it and his spine. His head had drooped forward and his shoulders were hanging from his stretched arms.

Dr Power held up his hand. 'That's it. He's had enough,' he pronounced. 'If he coughs like that any more, he'll rupture his diaphragm. Sir?' he questioned, addressing the governor who, to his utter relief, nodded his agreement. 'Now take him down carefully,' Dr Power instructed at once, 'or we'll have a corpse on our hands.'

The warder gave a shrug. What would one more dead convict matter? As he released the felon from his restraints, the fellow collapsed, senseless, into the doctor's arms.

Raymond Power ground his teeth. He'd instructed his surprised medical assistant to have a morphine injection at the ready. He'd treat this poor wretch's mutilated back with the greatest care, binding down the swollen flesh and mending it where possible with the neatest stitches and the finest thread. He'd be scarred, yes, but the doctor would make sure it was kept to the minimum, and nowhere near as badly as if he'd taken the full thirty-six. And if Dr Power's recommendations were heeded as they most likely would be, he never would. For the doctor felt he was fully justified in writing in Collingwood's medical notes that, due to his weak chest, he should never be flogged again.

The physician knew he'd done what he had, not only for the sake of the wronged man, but for the lovely young woman who'd begged for his help. And the guilt of it would go with him to the grave.

CHAPTER TWENTY-FOUR

Florrie Bennett's shrewd eyes observed the young girl as she yet again pushed the food around her plate. The older woman had been back at Fencott Place for five days, and in all that time she was convinced hardly a morsel had passed Rose's lips. Though the colossal bulge of her stomach appeared to be growing before their eyes, the rest of her had withered to nothing more than skin-covered bone. And what made Florrie heave with anger was that, at the opposite end of the table, Charles Chadwick hardly seemed to notice as he tucked into his own meal with relish.

'And what have you two ladies been up to today?' he enquired as he speared his fork into the succulent slice of roast beef, his casual attitude demonstrating that he didn't really care as long as he approved of their activities.

Rose looked up, her sunken eyes enormous in her pale face. She fixed her empty stare on her husband, evidently without the will to utter a word.

'Making a quilt for the babby's cradle,' Florrie answered for her, though in fact, despite Rose's skills with a needle, it had been Florrie who'd been engaged on the fine embroidery while Rose had gazed out of the window — in the direction of the prison.

'Ah, good.' Charles nodded his approbation. 'I'm glad you're making preparations for the arrival of our son. By the way, I've told Cook to interview for a second housemaid, as I believe the child will create extra work, particularly in the laundry department. And as he was leaving the other day, I instructed Dr Seaton . . . ' Charles paused for an instant to clear the hint of disdain from his voice. 'I instructed Dr Seaton,' he began afresh, 'to be mindful of engaging a wet-nurse.'

'What!'

Rose's eyes sparked with resentment, the first sign of life in them, Florrie noticed, for days. 'I'll be feeding our child myself! And I don't care if it's not the done thing in your mind! It's not as if I've any high society engagements to attend, nor should I wish to if I had!'

She stood up abruptly, flinging her napkin on the table, and shambled out of the room with as much dignity as her swollen abdomen allowed, leaving both Charles and Florrie staring after her open-mouthed.

* * *

She was peering into sepulchral darkness, her eyes dimmed with terror. Moans, disembodied voices, wailing. Spectres with faces stretched and distorted. She saw him then, stretched out on the torture rack. Heard the whine of the lash as it cracked through the air. The unearthly cry from a voice she recognised, and her heart tore. There was blood. Blood everywhere. And when she turned towards the source of the diabolical laugh, the face of Satan dissolved into other features she knew so well.

Rose blinked her eyes, and was overcome with relief as she realised she was sitting bolt upright in bed looking down on Charles as he lay on his back beside her, breathing heavily in an undisturbed sleep. The raging pulse in Rose's skull slowed, and she snuggled down under the blankets, for the cold sweat that slicked her skin was making her shiver.

Just a nightmare. But it wasn't, was it? Seth either had been, or was about to be, flogged. Seth, who'd resigned his army commission because he was never the fighting sort; who wanted a quiet life, a good night's sleep after an honest day's work; who knew and cared for God's creatures, and had saved the stunted puppy's life. Had done the same for the wretch in the dark Tavistock backstreet, and had ended up in hell because of it.

Rose tossed her head from side to side in frustration. How could she sleep when Seth would be suffering such agony? Her sense of helplessness was so powerful that it was beyond tears, and she ground her teeth in fury.

Dawn was breaking. In the faint light, she gazed on her husband's slumbering face. In that, her dream had been wrong. It wasn't Charles's fault. He'd been appalled at what she'd done. It was against the law to help an escapee, and the Charles Chadwicks of this world never broke the law. It was no wonder she'd incurred his wrath. He'd lost his temper and struck her, but she'd pushed him too far. She didn't love him, and he could be blamed for that no more than he could for Seth's punishment. And she knew he'd been genuinely shocked at the sergeant's brutality.

But it didn't help. Oh, Seth. Seth . . .

She couldn't lie there a minute longer. She heaved the bulk of the unborn child upwards, and wrapping her dressing-gown about her, silently let herself out of the room. Perhaps she should go down to the kitchen, bring the banked-up range into life and make herself a soothing hot drink. But what she really needed was to talk, and there was only one person . . .

'Florrie!' she whispered up in the servant's room on the top floor, wanting to wake Florrie but without too much of a start.

The older woman's eyes flickered and then stretched wide with surprise. But at barely fifty years old, Florrie Bennett could easily cope with being woken at the crack of dawn.

'What is it, cheel?' she answered, her mind at once alert.

'Oh, Florrie,' Rose groaned, 'I just can't get him out of my mind. What they'll do to him. It's so unfair. So unjust.'

Her face crumpled, her lovely eyes spangling with tears. She managed to gasp one shuddering breath before the first howl of despair strained from her lungs. Florrie was out of bed in an instant, her arms about the girl who, in Florrie's heart, was her own daughter. Rose buried her head in Florrie's shoulder, trembling against her as closely as her bulge allowed.

'If only father were still alive,' the girl muttered desolately, weeping against Florrie until the anxious woman thought the child's heart would break. 'He'd have done something about it, I know he would. Oh, I miss him so much . . .'

She was lost again in the swirl of her misery, and Florrie calmly patted her shoulder. She wasn't the only one who missed her dear Henry. Yes. If only he were still alive and running the Cherrybrook gunpowder mills. Then Rose would never have married Charles. Florrie was not such a fool that she hadn't always known. But the marriage must work. For the sake of Rose's sanity, it had to. But Florrie was terrified for her. The story of the wrongly convicted man was one thing. The way Rose had told it to her was another. Anger over the injustice of it was fair enough, but when Rose had spoken of the fellow himself, her eyes had shone, her face lit with something the girl herself didn't recognise. But Florrie did.

A sudden intake of breath pulled them apart.

'What? 'Tis not the babby?' Florrie demanded in a fluster.

'Oh, no.' Rose smiled at Florrie's worried face. 'It's not due for five weeks. But Dr Seaton said I'd start getting practice contractions about now. So it's quite normal. I've had one or two the last few days.'

'Oh, right then,' Florrie sighed with relief. 'Now you need to get back to your husband before he misses you and get a little more sleep, my young maid.'

'Yes, you're right.'

Rose turned swiftly, forgetting the burden of the child. A sharp pain stabbed through her as her belly hardened, taking her breath away and stopping her in her tracks. She felt something snap inside her, and then her eyes met Florrie's in horror as warm liquid flooded down her legs and settled in a puddle on the rug.

* * *

'Well?' Charles demanded.

Dr Seaton glared at him as he entered the drawing-room, but didn't reply until he'd finished rolling down his shirt sleeves. 'Your wife, Mr Chadwick,' he began guardedly, 'has been through a most difficult labour, as I'm sure you'll have realised by my sending for Dr Ratcliffe to assist. Forty-eight hours isn't unusual in a first child, but the contractions were strong and close together from the start, and there's always a risk when the waters break first. Mrs Chadwick became weak and exhausted, and I had to administer chloroform. And it was a forceps delivery.'

Charles leapt to his feet, his cheeks flushed a bitter puce. 'This is all that bastard's fault, isn't it?' he snarled. 'She's been pining for him . . . Yes, *pining*,' he repeated acidly as the doctor raised one bushy grey eyebrow, 'ever since he was re-arrested. That's what brought the baby on before its time, isn't it? And you're as much to blame! Helping them like that! I had to perjure myself to get you out of trouble!' Charles barked, poking his head forward so that his nose was only inches away from Dr Seaton's.

The brittle air crackled between them, but the doctor regarded his patient's husband with a steady eye. 'I was, of course, interviewed by the authorities myself,' he said levelly, 'and perhaps I should remind you that I have a sworn duty to heal the sick no matter who they are. As for bringing on your wife's labour prematurely, I can say quite categorically that it had nothing to do with it. She is a most passionate young woman, but emotions cannot induce labour. So please, Mr Chadwick, do not make a fool of yourself by blaming things that are physically impossible.'

Charles appeared to struggle to regain his composure, but one thing his pride could never allow him was to stand down from a situation. 'And what about my son, then?' he pressed menacingly.

'Your *daughter*,' Dr Seaton answered pointedly, 'is very small, as is to be expected. That in itself is not so much of a problem, but her early arrival has meant that her lungs are not quite as stable as I should have liked. And, I'm afraid, her heart is not strong.'

Charles stared at him, the colour draining from his skin. But his next words dumbfounded the doctor. 'A daughter, you say?' he mumbled. 'But . . . Rose will be able to give me a son? In the future? Next year, perhaps?'

It was Dr Seaton's turn to feel a flood of anger. 'Your wife, sir, is very ill,' he stated through tight lips. 'She's utterly exhausted, and I've given her a sleeping draught to ensure she has a proper rest. She's lost a lot of blood, and has many stitches which will be most uncomfortable for her. We've done everything in our power to save her and avoid infection, but you never can tell. Dr Ratcliffe will stay with her for the next twenty-four hours. I will return to Tavistock and arrange a wet-nurse. I know Mrs Chadwick wished to suckle the child herself, but I doubt she'll have either the strength or enough milk to do so. She'll need careful nursing, but I believe Mrs Bennett is capable of that. I can see you're disappointed that you don't have a son,' he observed bluntly, 'but I beg you to keep that to yourself. For your wife's sake. Let us have her fully recovered before we start talking of other children.'

But he could see from the vexed expression on Charles's face that it would be a tall order.

* * *

255

'Oh, Florrie, isn't she beautiful!'

Rose gazed with rapt eyes on the tiny scrap of humanity that lay peacefully in the crook of her arm. She lay, propped up on a bank of pillows, her face as white as their snowy covers, and her hair tangled about her in untidy confusion. She'd slept for several hours, a deep, drugged unconsciousness that had nevertheless been punctuated with anguished moans that folded Florrie's brow.

'She certainly is!' Florrie's homely face split with an enchanted grin. 'Just like you when you was a babby.'

'Really?' Rose's sunken eyes lit with stars.

'Oh, yes,' Florrie smiled again. 'And you just like your mother, too.'

'Then . . . I shall call her Alice,' Rose stated fiercely. 'After my mother.'

Dr Ratcliffe's eyebrows shot up as he came across the room to them. It had been an incredibly difficult birth, the young mother struggling to bring her child into the world. It had left her in a frail and exhausted condition, and yet her voice just now had rung with defiance.

He cleared his throat. 'It's time we got the baby to feed again,' he instructed. 'Dr Seaton should be returning with the wet-nurse later this afternoon. He has someone in mind and I think she'll take little persuasion. But in the meantime, we believe the mother's milk in the first few days has some particular quality . . . Now then.'

The younger physician had the same balance of confidence and understanding as his senior partner, and with his help, little Alice was persuaded to take another small feed. She was weak and reluctant, preferring to sleep and slip quietly from life, but Dr Ratcliffe was having none of it. He showed Rose little techniques in how to stimulate the infant's instinct to suckle properly, and how to hold the downy head firmly against the breast so that she wouldn't slip off again. For the inexperienced mother, it seemed so much more complicated than she'd imagined, but soon Dr Ratcliffe was smiling with satisfaction as Rose experienced the gratifying sensation of giving nourishment to her own child.

'The waxy substance on her skin,' he explained as he watched the contentment on his patient's face, 'that's because she was so early. It'll rub off on its own, and that fine down will come with it. And the tiny spots on her face, they're quite normal to any baby. But,' and a cloud passed over his brow, 'she will need the greatest care. Early babies lose their body heat even more quickly than full-term ones. And we must build up her strength, protect her from infection. But she's really lucky in that she's in the best sort of home to survive.'

Rose raised her eyes to him, and he saw that they had darkened with doubt.

'Yes,' she croaked. 'Dr Seaton explained.' And noticing that Alice was slackening off from her feed, Rose used her newly learnt skills to rouse her enough so that she continued sucking.

'There you are! You're doing well!' Dr Ratcliffe encouraged her. 'Now when we've finished, I expect you'll be ready for a cup of tea. I want you taking a full glass of water or lemonade or a couple of cups of tea every hour. It'll make your urine less concentrated, and Mrs Bennett, I want you ready with a jug of tepid water to rinse over Mrs Chadwick's lower parts every time she relieves herself. That is *essential* to minimise the chance of infection.'

'Oh, Florrie, I didn't realise it would all be so complicated,' Rose sighed some ten minutes later when she was back in bed after using the commode. 'Amber didn't have all this trouble with her puppies, did she? And . . . Oh!' She sat up with a start, her eyes wide. 'Are they all right? Who's looking after them?'

'Oh, they'm fine. And 'tis Ned who feeds the dogs, just as normal. And Gospel's in fine fettle, too.'

But Rose's face had hardened with bitterness. 'He didn't decide to hand in his notice, then, now he's got his reward in his pocket? Oh, I could murder him!' she cried with such vehemence that Florrie caught her breath. 'Just another couple of weeks, and Seth would've been away. Oh, Florrie! You must go to Dr Power for me. Find out . . . what happened.'

She fell back on the pillows, her head tossing frantically in a flurry of agitation. Florrie pursed her lips, for this really would not do!

'I'm not leaving your side till you and the babby are settled,' she announced determinedly. 'But don't you fret none. I promise I'll find out for you in a few days. You did all you could, and 'tis no point in worrying your head about it no more. 'Tis the babby and yourself you've to look to now.'

Rose drew in a long breath. 'Oh, Florrie, why has everything gone so wrong?' she groaned. 'All this, and . . . Did you notice when Charles deigned to put in an appearance, he didn't even look at Alice? He doesn't care, because he wanted a son. And don't try telling me otherwise, Florrie, for I know it's true.'

She turned away, biting on her knuckles as her stomach cramped with an after-pain. Her beloved father was dead, she was married to a man she didn't love and who only wanted one thing, her tiny daughter was scarcely clinging to life, and the one person who had brought her solace was locked away in that horrendous place, suffering the most gruesome punishment. That was . . . if he was still alive . . .

CHAPTER TWENTY-FIVE

'The child, sir, is doing as well as can be expected given the circumstances,' Dr Seaton reported a few days later. 'The wet-nurse is brimming with milk, which is ideal. The woman's own infant may bawl his head off at any time of the day or night, as I believe you have complained, but it's surely a small price to pay.'

Charles glanced up with a scowl. He'd employed Dr Seaton as the most senior and highly respected physician in Tavistock, but the elderly fellow was inclined to be blunt, and Charles resented his tone. 'And my wife?' he questioned, choosing to ignore Dr Seaton's inference.

'Ah.' The older man's face fell. 'I'm not at all happy about Mrs Chadwick's condition. Though I can assure you every precaution has been taken against infection, she is a little feverish. But what worries me most is her state of mind,' he went on unhesitating, never one to beat about the bush. 'And I believe your own ignoring the child does not help. Your wife cannot be blamed for the gender of her baby, you know.'

Charles lifted his chin stubbornly. 'I make no secret of my disappointment,' he admitted. 'I want a son who can build on the success I have worked hard for all my life. A daughter would be no more able to cope with the business affairs I will one day leave than Rose herself would. But I love my wife dearly for all her light-headed ways, and what you say grieves me deeply.'

'I believe you underestimate your wife's capabilities, sir, but that is none of my business. Her health *is*, and in my opinion, a little more show of support from yourself could well be beneficial.'

Charles studied the expression on the doctor's face, and nodded slowly. 'So be it. I couldn't bear to lose my wife,' he muttered as he got to his feet and going out into the hall, made for the stairs.

* * *

'Oh, Rose, Rose, my darling,' Charles pleaded in a broken whisper, wiping her sweat-bedewed face yet again. Her sunken eyes were closed, the long, dark lashes fanned out on her cheeks which were no longer pale, but flushed with fever. She looked more like a child than did the tiny infant up in the nursery that Charles hadn't visited since his wife had sunk into the consuming delirium three days previously.

There were no symptoms of infection or puerperal fever, both physicians had confirmed. It went deeper than that, something Dr Seaton couldn't explain but had witnessed before, though usually in someone lost in grief. It was as if Rose couldn't face reality, and had willed herself into some unconscious state where it was peaceful and safe.

'Why don't you get some rest, Mr Chadwick?' Florrie suggested, for though she'd never liked Charles, he'd been sitting at Rose's side for two days without a break. 'I can take over for a while.'

'No, Mrs Bennett,' he answered wearily. 'I can't leave her.'

He lifted Rose's hand to his lips, kissing each thin finger in turn. He wanted to pump his own strong will into her frail body, to fill her again with that maddening resolve he'd striven, he realised now, to smother.

'Rose?'

His heart soared as her eyes half opened, but he saw at once that they were unfocused, lost in some dim fever-stare. What was it that lurked in the dark shadows of her tortured mind? She began to whimper, as she had on several occasions in the last few days, her lips muttering in incomprehensible anguish.

'Oh, my poor lamb,' Florrie breathed in a desperate sigh as she hurried over to the bed. 'What is it, my sweet?'

As if in reply, a gasp caught in Rose's throat. 'No!' she wailed quite distinctly now. 'Seth! Oh, Seth!'

She suddenly sat bolt upright and reached out to one side of the bed which happened to be Florrie's, her eyes wild and yet blank at the same time. Florrie embraced her wasting form, rocking her like a child until she appeared to calm, and then settled her back in the bed where her sobs slowly faded and her mind was lost in sleep once more.

Florrie glanced up in despair to see Charles rise to his feet, his face rigid, and walk silently from the room.

* * *

Rose's heavy eyelids lifted, her dulled eyes wandering uncontrolled until they finally began to focus. It was some moments before her disorientated mind placed itself back into reality, her gaze settling on the familiar room. June sunshine slanted through the large open window, filling Rose's head with peace and tranquillity. Over by the table stood a figure she recognised but somehow couldn't place, yet she knew it was someone who was close to her. She sighed softly, too weak to move. Tugging at her memory was a horrific, half-remembered dream, but it was far, far away and mingled with a tender sweetness that had once soothed her troubled soul.

'Florrie?'

The name seemed to speak itself, and the figure turned, slow and unbelieving, before stepping over to the bed. Colour flooded into the older woman's cheeks as she grinned with joy.

'Rose? Oh, my dearest! You'm back with us!'

A frown flickered over Rose's forehead. 'Florrie, I-I don't remember,' she croaked. 'What . . . what's happened?'

Two fat tears trickled down Florrie's cheeks. ''Tis proper poorly you've been, cheel. A fever of some sort.'

'A fever?' Rose's frown deepened. She tried to sit up but had no strength and fell back with a groan.

'You'm not to worry. Little Alice is soldiering on upstairs in the nursery,' Florrie said with a proud smile. 'Pretty as a picture, and putting on weight. Which is what you must do. Thin as a stick you be.'

The corners of Rose's mouth twitched. 'How . . . how long has it been?'

Florrie lowered her eyes. 'Nearly two weeks. Oh, little maid! You've no idea how worried we've been. But here's me wittering on, when you must be gasping for a drink. I've some nice cool water here. I bring it fresh twice a day and somehow you've managed to take a little.'

She didn't add that in Dr Seaton's opinion it was what had just about kept her alive. Florrie flustered about her charge, propping her up on extra pillows so that she could sip at the refreshing liquid. Rose felt so strange, weak as a kitten and yet relaxed and serene. Something deep and troublesome was taunting her mind, but for now she was happy to ignore it.

'Will you bring Alice to me, please, Florrie?' she asked eagerly.

'If the doctor says 'tis safe. He'll be here after lunch, as he is every day.'

'Oh, dear, poor man. It's such a long way. And . . . what about Charles?'

The shadow flitted across Florrie's face so quickly that Rose was not aware of it. 'Been at your side constantly. Just taking a well-deserved rest right now,' she added. For how could she tell Rose that since her tortured mind had called out Seth's name, Charles had not set foot in the room?

* * *

262

He finally put in an appearance later that afternoon. Earlier, a delighted Dr Seaton had pronounced the fever gone. In his opinion, the protracted and exhausting labour, and the dread that the infant might not survive, had simply tipped Rose over into a state of limbo. Her mind and body needed time to heal, and so both had closed down while nature cured her. Now she was awake and refreshed, though she would have to be careful not to overtire herself for some time, she should be up and about in a week or so. In the meantime, little Alice was holding her own, though neither her heart nor her lungs were strong, and she would probably always have to be mindful of her health.

Rose was sitting up in bed now, bright and alert after a short nap, her minuscule daughter in her arms. It was a warm and sunny afternoon, and she had unwrapped the shawl to examine the tiny arms and legs. The child moved very little, and when she did, it was with the characteristic, uncontrolled jerks of a young infant. But when Rose placed her little finger across the miniature palm, Alice's hand closed about it, filling her mother's heart with unutterable joy. The grip wasn't strong, and there was still a faint blueness about the child's heart-shaped jaw, but when she opened her eyes wide, they bore with such intensity into Rose's face that they almost spoke to her.

'Rose, my dear.' Charles greeted her with as much emotion as if she'd merely been out to the shops. But, entranced by the magical spell of her daughter, Rose didn't notice.

'Charles!' Rose glanced up at him with a beguiling smile. 'Isn't she lovely? Florrie says I looked like that when I were a baby.'

'You've had us worried,' Charles answered flatly.

'Yes, I know. And I'm so sorry. But I feel so much better now. And isn't Alice adorable? Why don't you sit here on the bed and have a hold of her? Only just for a few minutes, mind, because I missed the first two weeks of her life and I want to make up for it.'

She'd spoken quickly, hardly drawing breath between her words and beaming up at Charles before returning her mesmerised gaze to the precious bundle cradled in her arms. Charles's nose twitched and he took a step backwards.

'No. You hold her while you can. I'm really far too busy.'

Rose tipped her head. 'Can't you spare just one minute?' And then her lips pouted in that mutinous way he'd come to know so well. 'I'm sorry it's a girl,' Rose went on tersely. 'I know you wanted a boy, and I promise I'll give you a son one day. But please, don't love Alice any the less because of it. It's not her fault.'

'Really, Rose, I don't have time for babies no matter what their gender,' Charles snapped irritably. 'You know how time consuming it is running my affairs from two hundred miles away. Besides, children are a woman's domain. I'm just looking forward to when I can sleep in my own bed again. And how long will that woman and her howling brat have to stay here? It might be up in the nursery, but I can hear it all night long!'

Rose flashed her eyes at him, ready to retort that the wet-nurse was keeping their own child alive, but it was true that he did look tired and a little gaunt, so she bit her lip instead. 'Some time yet, I'm afraid. So, please, Charles, try to be patient. And . . . I know you don't approve, but I should love Molly to visit. I can't wait to introduce her to little Alice.'

Charles's face stiffened. 'If you must. But only when Dr Seaton confirms that both you and the child are well enough.'

'Oh, thank you, Charles,' Rose said passionately, but when she lifted her head, it was to see his back as he left the room, and she pulled a derisory grimace at it. She had the impression he'd only agreed because she'd promised to produce a son. One day. But perhaps it was a promise she couldn't keep. And, of course . . . Her mind reared up at the thought of what had to happen to produce another child. But just now, that seemed a lifetime away as she turned her attention back to the infant who had fallen asleep in her arms.

* * *

The days passed in a blissful haze, gradually establishing a routine of rest, a little exercise within the confines of the room, and bonding with her daughter. She insisted, much to Charles's disgust, that the wet-nurse came down from the nursery to feed Alice, chatting to the woman who was a good, homely sort. It was only at night and during Rose's daytime rest periods that Alice was taken back up to the nursery by a doting Florrie, who considered herself the child's grandmother. Rose grew stronger by the day, waiting impatiently for Dr Seaton to give his permission for visitors. Her days were filled with euphoric rapture over her baby, and when the occasional uneasy shadow passed over her, she shook her head with a scornful snort, since Alice, so far, was doing well and becoming more active as she gained a little strength.

It was Daisy who broke the spell. Daisy, the new maid, was as effervescent and garrulous as Patsy was quiet and reserved, nattering away nineteen to the dozen as she cleaned the room or saw to the fire. That summer, the sun had only rarely appeared from behind iron-grey clouds, and today was no exception as Daisy coaxed the coal into a dancing conflagration.

'They say a prisoner fell to 'is death yesterday,' she announced cheerfully. 'You knows how they'm building they prison blocks up to the sky wi' convict labour. Well, him must've felled off. Still, there be plenty more to take 'is place.'

A cold, black dread slashed at Rose's heart, and somewhere deep inside, the horror was re-awakened. Her mind had somehow succeeded in shutting itself down to some hidden fear, and now the monster reared its ugly head. Yes, that was it, the nameless torture that had been gnawing away inside her.

Seth.

Anguish washed over her in a drowning wave. 'Poor man,' she sighed almost inaudibly, and then was staring blindly at the foot of the bed.

'Oh, well, there's me done,' the young maid announced with her usual merry grin, undaunted by Mrs Chadwick's sudden silence. 'Be there ort else I can get 'ee, ma'am?'

'Er . . . no thank you,' came the muttered reply, and Daisy waltzed contentedly out of the room.

Oh, no. The words wrung themselves helplessly from Rose's shocked mind. It mustn't be him. It mustn't. There were upwards of eight hundred men in the gaol, so why should . . . But she didn't even know if he was still alive. He'd been so ill when they'd dragged him from the stables, treating him with such brutality. Seth, who'd spoken, for want of a better word, to Gospel and instantly won over the difficult animal's trust, who'd shared Rose's enchantment of the newborn puppies, who'd laughed softly with her — and who'd been subjected to the most cruel injustice. How could she possibly have forgotten? She felt shot through with fury, anger at what had happened to him, but also with a deep, crippling guilt because she'd let it slip from her mind.

She'd been sitting up, cross-legged, in the bed, and now she rocked herself back and forth, teeth gritted as she battled to stop herself from howling aloud. It was just like when her father had died. Rose Maddiford, who would always fight back with the ferocity of a tigress, had finally been defeated.

Florrie knew there was something wrong the instant she came back into the room. There was Rose, *her* Rose, looking almost demented, her eyes haunted as she tossed her head from side to side.

'Rose, my—'

'Oh, Florrie!' she cried, reaching out to grasp the older woman's arms as she came towards her. 'Florrie, you must find out for me!'

'Find out?' Florrie frowned, but in her heart, she already knew.

'Seth,' Rose answered, her face taut with anguish. 'Go to Dr Power. *Now!*'

Florrie's expression closed down. She had the greatest sympathy with the lad's story, even though she'd been miles away at her sister's at the time and hadn't met him. But part of her blamed him for Rose's illness, and she'd prayed that Rose's apparent loss of memory over the events would continue. But now it seemed they had returned to wreak havoc with her little maid's mind yet again.

'Of course,' she soothed. 'But not now. Dr Power will be at work in the prison, and I wouldn't be able to speak with him. But this evening, I'll go while the master's having his dinner.'

'Oh, Florrie.' Rose's face crumpled, and as Florrie held her in her comforting arms, she wept inconsolably while Florrie's heart blackened with worry.

For where would it end?

CHAPTER TWENTY-SIX

'He were flogged,' Florrie said gently, and she watched anxiously as Rose twisted her head torturedly. 'But 'tweren't as bad as 'twas supposed to be. Dr Power, he . . . he said he had to be cruel to be kind, whatever that do mean. He only got nine, when 'twas meant to be the full thirty-six.'

A groan came from deep in Rose's throat and her hands literally tore at the tangled mass of her hair that tumbled about her in disarray. 'But they'll give him the rest some time,' she squealed. 'Oh, Florrie, I can't bear—'

'No, they won't,' she told Rose firmly. 'Or at least, 'tis highly unlikely. Dr Power has strongly recommended against it cuz of his chest.'

'He's still ill, then?'

'No. He were a fortnight in the infirmary afterwards, but since then, he's been back at work. Breaking stones within the prison, cuz he'll not be allowed on an outside work-party again, not since he bolted. So he weren't the one as fell to his death, so you can stop worrying and forget all about him now.'

'Forget! How can I forget? Just being in that place is bad enough! The conditions they have to suffer, and then made to work like slaves—'

'Which is no more than most of them deserve—'

'But not Seth! Not when you're innocent!'

'Well, that's as may be, but right now, young maid, you've a tiny babby and your own health to think about!'

Rose glared at her, her mouth screwed into a rebellious pout. But then she let herself fall back on the bed with a distraught groan. 'Oh, Florrie, I feel so helpless! I just don't know what to do!'

'Get yoursel and babby Alice well, 'tis what! And then maybe some time in the future, *then* you can see if there's ort to be done. From what you've teld me, he's a strong young man and he'll come to no harm.'

'*Was* a strong man,' Rose protested. 'His health's been broken, and no one cares at the gaol if you live or die. There's not many warders like Molly's father who tries to get to know each prisoner and treats them accordingly.'

'There you are, then! Mr Cartwright'll look out for him.'

Rose's shoulders jolted. 'Yes, of course! Oh, you're wonderful, Florrie! What would I do without you? When's Dr Seaton coming again?' she asked, her mind working furiously.

'Monday, as I believe.'

'Monday,' Rose repeated, unconsciously chewing on her thumbnail. 'Three days. And if he says Alice and I can have visitors, I can send for Molly. And I can write Seth a letter for her father to give him. Officially, they're only allowed a letter every three months, aren't they? And that's only supposed to be from a relative, and they'd hardly allow a letter from *me*, would they, the person who helped him when he escaped! But . . . just a note to tell him I've not forgotten. Oh, I can't wait for next week. To show Alice to Molly, I mean. Fetch her over to me, would you?'

Florrie's expression was humourless as she took the sleeping child from her cot, but Rose's enchanted smile as she took the tiny bundle into the protective cradle of her arms drove the doubt from the older woman's heart. For though Florrie disapproved of Rose's association with the convict, she had accepted long ago that Rose did everything with passion. And that included being a mother.

* * *

'I be that sorry,' Molly said almost shame-facedly as she held out the crumpled letter. 'Father said 'twere more than his job were worth. But he said he'd have a word with him on the quiet. Tell him you'm still thinking of him.'

It was late July, and the weather was being kind. Rose was sitting outside under the shade of a canopy the gardener and his boy had rigged up for her. She was propped on one elbow, gazing down quite entranced on the infant, a perfect miniature of herself, who lay on the blanket beside her, tiny legs free to kick in the warm air in jerky, uncontrolled movements, and her little starfish hands grasping at nothing. Her eyes, the exact lavender blue of her mother's, stared up at Rose as if some invisible thread were linked between them, and only Molly's arrival could distract Rose from doting over her daughter.

'Oh, I do understand,' she answered, forcing a disappointed smile to her lips. 'It was good of you to take it all the way over to him. But could you possibly take it home with you and destroy it for me. If Charles found it—'

'Of course. You'm my best friend, Rose, and I'll do anything to help, you knows that. I just wish . . . well, that things were better between you and your husband.'

'Oh, it's not really Charles's fault,' Rose sighed. 'I'm just not a very good wife. But I *am* a good mother,' she brightened. 'Now I'm recovered, I do everything except feed her, which you know I can't.'

'Can I hold her?'

'Of course! But do be careful. You have to support her head. Look, like this. Oh, but how silly of me! Of course you know, with all your brothers and sisters!'

They sat for some minutes in relaxed companionship, cherishing little Alice's curved chin, her rosebud mouth, her button nose. Molly instinctively rocked the infant against her shoulder until her little head drooped and she drifted asleep. Then, with the practised skill that came from being the eldest of a large family, Molly laid the slumbering child back on the blanket.

'Will you and Joe have children, d'you think?' Rose asked dreamily.

Molly's pretty face scarcely coloured. 'Oh, yes, I's sure of it. Only . . . we does try to resist . . . but not too well. A babby would stretch what Joe earns—'

'Don't let that stop you! One thing I can't complain about in Charles is his generosity. I have a personal allowance I really don't need, and . . . Well, you're like a sister to me, so it wouldn't be charity if I were to share some of it with you. I'd be like an aunt to any child of yours, just as I consider you to be Alice's aunt.'

Molly lowered her eyes awkwardly. ''Twould be more than kind of—'

'Nonsense. How could I not help you to know the same joy as I have with Alice? And Joe, too. It must . . . it must be so good to . . . lie with someone you really love.'

Her words had ended in a bitter trail, and Molly cocked one sympathetic eyebrow. 'Rather than have to suffer it with someone you doesn't, you mean.'

Rose's chin quivered. 'I just don't . . . feel anything for him. And though he's not a bad man, I'm sure he thinks of me as a possession rather than a person. Not like . . . ' She stopped abruptly, rearing away from the thought that had hit her like a thunderbolt.

'Not like your convict, you mean?' Molly said softly.

Rose felt the blood rush from her head. 'Oh, Good Lord, nothing like that! We just seemed to share a lot in common, that's all.' She swivelled her eyes to glance sideways at her friend. 'Did your father say anything about him? Is he well again? Florrie found out he'd been put to breaking stones, but that were nearly two weeks ago now.'

Molly's mouth twisted. It was a question she'd hoped not to be asked. 'Father found he'd been put to work in the boneshed.'

'The boneshed! Rose cried, for most local people knew of the most dreaded building in the prison. It was where gone-off meat bones were crushed and mixed with the contents of the cesspit to make fertiliser for the fields. The smell and the dust were said to be unimaginable. 'Oh, dear Lord!'

''Twas because he has to wear the parti-coloured uniform of an escapee. Some other warder decided breaking stones were too easy on him—'

'Oh, Molly, with his chest, it'll kill him!'

'Now don't you fret none. Father's senior to the other warder, and had your chap moved. He's been on the building works for the last few days. 'Tis the best father can do for him for the moment. You can't expect to work in tailoring or bootmaking if you've only recently escaped. But if he behaves himself over the next few weeks, father should be able to get him into one of the workshops then.'

'Oh, Molly.' Rose exhaled her breath in a long, weary stream. 'Do thank your father for me, won't you? And ask him, if he has the chance, to tell Seth that I said to take care. A prisoner fell to his death on the building works not so long ago.'

Their eyes met, but not a word more was exchanged as Alice chose that moment to wake up, her little face wrinkling as her feeble cry demanded a feed.

* * *

The frantic knocking on their bedroom door in the middle of the night woke them both with a start. Florrie burst in without waiting for an answer, light flickering from the candle she held in her shaking hand.

''Tis the babby, Rose!' she cried, her normal reluctant deference to Charles completely forgotten in her frenetic distress. 'She's a fever and—'

She had no time to finish before Rose fled past her, careering blindly along the landing and up the stairs to the nursery. Alice. So tiny. So helpless. It wasn't possible. She'd been doing so well. But Dr Seaton had warned them . . .

Rose snatched Alice from the wet-nurse's arms. The child was on fire, her cry no more than a feeble whimper. Oh, Alice. Darling little Alice. With a mother's instinct, she laid the infant in her cot and tore the clothes from the bundled form. Her daughter's temperature must be lowered. But before she could start bathing the minute body with tepid water, the thin limbs went rigid, the spine arched, and the scrap of life jerked in a violent paroxysm. Rose stood back, feeling as though she might crumple to the floor. Oh, good God. And there was nothing she could do as Alice's tiny form shook until she suddenly turned as limp as a rag doll.

Rose stared, transfixed with horror as she gazed on her beloved daughter. No! But there was still life . . . Breath was crackling uncertainly in and out of Alice's lungs, and Rose grasped her in her arms again as she heard Charles enter the room behind her, bleary-eyed with sleep.

'She's had a fit,' Rose screamed at him. 'Go and tell Ned to ride for the doctor! Tell him . . .'

Her eyes rolled savagely. She was about to say to take Gospel, for surely no other horse could fly over the moor in the dark at such speed. But he wouldn't allow Ned on his back. Perhaps *she* should go. But she couldn't leave Alice . . .

'I'll tell him to fetch Dr Ratcliffe. He'll be quicker than the old man.'

'No. Dr Power. It'll take half the time.'

Rose met Charles's gaze challengingly. She knew how he felt about the prison surgeon. But Charles nodded and then turned and she heard him hurry back down the stairs. She looked down again on Alice, holding the child gently against her, and keeping her upright to assist her laboured breathing. She paced up and down, hushing her though Alice was unconscious, trying to staunch the flow of life from the failing fragment of existence.

Charles didn't reappear, but the gall barely stung Rose's throat as Alice faded in her arms. The rattle quietened to a wheeze, the wheeze to a whisper, and Rose herself hardly breathed as the room fell silent but for Florrie's muted sobs.

Little Alice had gone.

Rose slumped forward. Numbed. Empty. With no one to lean on. No one to hold her. Charles . . . Oh, how she longed for those other arms. Seth, she knew, would have understood her pain. Seth who . . .

She jolted, her shoulders suddenly braced. The runt of the litter, apparently dead, but Seth had breathed life into it. Literally. So could she possibly . . . ? She could never forgive herself if she didn't try.

She blew softly into the still, blue lips. And her heart soared as Alice's chest lifted. Yes! If she could just keep her alive until the doctor arrived. He shouldn't be long. Twenty minutes or so for Ned to ride to Dr Power's house, the same for Dr Power to arrive at Fencott Place. The intense darkness of the cruel night was already lessening, and dawn would soon be breaking. If only Rose could keep going . . .

Her ears pricked as she caught the sound of horse's hooves scattering gravel on the drive. Thank God! She was exhausted, her neck aching from bending over Alice's motionless frame. But she mustn't stop. She must give of her own life. She didn't care what became of herself. But Alice *must* live.

She barely glanced up as Dr Power strode urgently across the room.

'Mrs Chadwick, Rose, let me see her.'

Rose raised her head, and bent again to transfer her own life to her daughter. The doctor felt for a pulse at the tiny wrist, took the stethoscope from his bag and listened intently to the infant's chest.

'A light, please, Mrs Bennett,' he called over his shoulder.

Florrie obeyed at once, her face taut with distress. Dr Power took the lamp from her, held open each of Alice's eyes in turn, and waved the source of brightness in front of them.

The doctor sighed regretfully as he replaced the stethoscope in his bag, then his eyebrows swooped as he contemplated the new mother as she breathed tirelessly into her baby's mouth. He shook his head, putting out his hand to touch her arm.

'Mrs Chadwick, I'm so sorry, but your daughter is dead.'

Rose blinked at him, a blank look in her haunted eyes. 'N-no, look!' she stammered. 'She's breathing—'

'No. I'm afraid *you* are breathing for her. There's no pulse, no heartbeat. No eye movement. I would say she's been gone a little while.'

Rose stared at him, her brow corrugated with incomprehension. Slowly, very slowly, she lowered her gaze to Alice's motionless face as the horrible, crucifying truth slithered into her rebellious mind, and her lips rested on the tiny, marble forehead.

'I understand from your husband she was born quite early,' the doctor whispered reverently, 'and Dr Seaton was concerned that her heart and lungs were not strong. So this sudden illness was just too much for her. Nobody's fault. No medicine we have could have saved her.'

Whether young Mrs Chadwick heard or not was debatable. She began to rock back and forth, crooning to the child in her arms as if she were soothing her to sleep. She scarcely flinched when her husband came and sat beside her on the bed, not until he put his hands about the diminutive corpse.

'She's dead, Rose,' he said without expression. 'Let the doctor take her now.'

She flicked up her head, eyes flashing as she hugged Alice tightly against her. 'No!' she wailed, and when Charles tried to take the child by force, she began to howl a deep, unearthly lament that made his blood run cold.

'For God's sake, man, isn't there something you can give her?' he demanded.

Dr Power considered the broken, grief-stricken woman before him. She needed time to say goodbye to her child. Time her husband was unlikely to grant her.

Dr Power reached sadly into his bag.

CHAPTER TWENTY-SEVEN

Charles watched as Rose bent to lay a delicate posy of flowers on the tiny coffin as it was lowered into the ground. So graceful, so dignified, so *glorious* in her sorrow. A gust of wind lifted the mourning cape about her shoulders, revealing the slenderness of her pliant, narrow waist. She straightened up, her neck as long and elegant as a swan's, and beneath the veil of her black hat, her lovely face was as white as alabaster.

Oh, how Charles yearned to have her in his bed again. Of course, he'd been back *sleeping* in their marital bed for weeks. What a torture that had been, not being able to touch her. Penetrate her. At long last, Dr Seaton had examined her and pronounced her fit to resume her duties as a wife provided Charles was gentle with her. He'd planned to take her the very next morning, but the child had died that same night, and even he could not be cruel enough to impose himself upon her.

Did he care so much about his daughter? It was difficult to say when he'd hardly got to know her. He'd never even held her. But what he *did* care about was the gnawing misery that had enshrouded his wife ever since. Even the two dogs sensed it, laying their heads on her knee and looking up at her with doleful eyes while their off-spring romped and rolled beside them. She didn't even notice.

What Charles found curious was that she hadn't even turned to her blessed horse for comfort, though the creature whinnied to her every time she appeared, so loudly that it alerted Charles to the fact that his wife had wandered off into the pouring rain yet again. He would run out after her with a coat to shield her from the unseasonable weather, as despite the odd day of brilliant sunshine, it was turning into one of the wettest summers for years. She would let him lead her home, not uttering a word, nor swallowing a morsel of the tempting food Florrie and Cook between them produced on her plate, and only drinking when Florrie forced her.

Charles put his arm about her now, for without it, he feared she might fall. It was time to leave, to allow the little soul to lie in eternal peace beside the grandfather she'd never known. Rose came on faltering steps, not seeing the tear-filled eyes of Florrie Bennett, George Frean, Molly and Joe, and all those who'd come to share in her grief.

They made their silent way through the graveyard to the iron gates, the hem of Rose's gown soaking up the rainwater from the puddles. She seemed oblivious to everything around her until they came out to the road. Just at that moment, a group of six or seven people, dressed more suitably for the fashionable streets of London, hurried gaily along on the opposite side of the street in the direction of the prison.

'Oh, what a frightfully grim place!' one of the ladies tittered gleefully.

'What do you expect, my dear?' a gentleman replied with equal delight. 'This *is* the worst prison in the country. You have to be a pretty dastardly criminal to be sent here, you know!'

'Of course!' another fellow declared with enthusiasm. 'I wonder who they'll show us? Thieves and murderers, I expect!'

'Not murderers! They hang *them*!'

And with a chorus of laughter, they marched on up the road.

Rose halted, hatred in her breast. It was despicable, this custom of showing people over the gaol as if it were some sort of attraction, pointing out to them the worst criminals, the gruelling labour they were put to and the horrendous conditions in which they existed — when many of them had only been caught up in a life of crime in the first place through poverty and starvation.

Rose's mouth thinned into a fine line. On the opposite side of the road, stood the tall, quite attractive building of the warders' new flats where the remaining Cartwright family now lived in relative comfort. Beyond them, Rose could just glimpse the forbidding walls of the first prison block to reach five storeys, completed a few years earlier. Next to it, other blocks were building sites as they were being raised to match, all by the human sweat and toil of convict labour.

Rose frowned. Teasing her brain was an emotion triggered by the sight of the gaol, a tenderness, a faint memory of something that had once soothed her aching soul. And then her heart tripped and began to beat faster as a vision of that lean, strong face formed itself in her mind.

A long, sighing breath fluttered from her lungs, and her husband caught her as she slithered to the ground.

* * *

Charles padded across the thick bedroom carpet and came up behind her as she sat at the dressing table in her nightgown, mechanically brushing her hair. In the mirror, he met her dulled eyes that stared sightlessly at him from her pale face, her skin taut as ivory. Dear God, she was so beautiful, and he already felt the uncomfortable rising in his loins.

He smiled benevolently, and felt his heart expand as her eyes widened a little and her lips curved upwards in a strained response. His hands came to rest on her shoulders. She tilted her head, but the hope expired inside him, since she didn't turn to brush her cheek on the back his hand, nor lean against him to take the comfort he was attempting to offer her.

He cleared his throat. 'I'm so sorry, Rose. I know the child meant more to you than to me. I suppose a man doesn't become close to his children until they're older. But a mother . . . Well, I *am* sorry.'

She remained motionless, as if his words could not penetrate her grief, and he was about to turn away when she mumbled something under her breath.

'Pardon, my dear?' he prompted at once, seeing as it was the first word she had spoken that day.

'I said, her name was Alice. Our daughter's name was Alice.' Her voice was empty, as if coming from some other, ethereal being, and Charles felt not the least reprimanded.

'Of course it was,' he replied tentatively, anxious to seize any shred of communication. 'And we will always remember her. But there will be others. This time next year, there will be another little Chadwick, I promise you. And over the years, we will fill the nursery with our children. So the sooner we start, the better.'

He just caught the thin sound that gurgled at the back of her throat, but chose to ignore it. Instead, he bent to kiss the bare milky skin at her neck, and his hand found its way beneath the yoke of her nightdress to the warm, soft mound of her breast.

She flinched. Her shoulders instantly stiffened and she jerked up her head. 'Charles, I really don't think—' she croaked hoarsely.

'And why not, my dear?' he purred, his voice oily. 'Dr Seaton pronounced you fit and well a week ago. And the sooner we conceive another child, the better.'

'But not when we've only just laid Alice in her grave.'

Her tone was stronger now, a blend of sadness and resentment that was beginning to try Charles's patience. But anger wasn't the way to get what he wanted, and he was determined that he would.

He withdrew his hand and instead began to stroke her hair. 'I understand how you feel, my darling,' he said persuasively. 'But surely you must see it would be for the best? Another child would give you something else to think about. Help you to get over Alice more quickly.'

He saw in the mirror that she lowered her eyes, and a glow of satisfaction warmed his blood. He was winning her over, and turning her about on the stool, he knelt down before her and with one hand on the back of her head, placed his lips forcefully on hers and used his tongue to probe into her mouth.

She pulled away. 'Charles, please,' she moaned. 'Not now.'

'Oh, but you know I'm right,' he murmured into her ear now as his hands began to fumble between her thighs. 'Another child . . .'

The sensation of disgust shot up to her stomach, and her muscles cramped. She instinctively pushed him away, and the words were out of her mouth before she had time to think what she was saying.

'But I'm not certain I *want* another . . .'

They both froze, two statues glaring at each other in conflict. Rose wanted to swallow, but it seemed a stone had lodged in her gullet. The buried truth had wormed its own way to the surface without her having consciously considered it.

'Don't want any more children!' Charles spat. 'But it's your duty as my wife to give me as many children as you can. *Sons*, to carry on my work! I know you dislike the act of love-making—'

'*Love*-making!' Rose reared up her head. 'There's nothing *loving* in it, the way *you* do it.'

Charles jerked as if he'd been shot by a bullet. 'And how would you know any different, madam? It was that bloody convict, wasn't it? You made love to him, but you refuse to make love to your own husband!'

'No! How dare you! There was nothing like that—'

'You expect me to believe you -?'

'Yes, I do. Because I swear on Alice's grave that it's the truth.'

Charles locked his eyes on hers. Contemplating, his thoughts racing. Whatever sort of wife Rose was to him, he knew in his heart she wouldn't jeopardise her daughter's soul by lying. He was sure the escaped convict had touched her sensibilities, but anything physical, well, he couldn't really imagine it if he thought about it rationally.

'All right,' he conceded, tight-lipped. 'Come to bed, and perhaps you'll feel more like it in the morning. And no matter what you think of me, I do love you, you know. But we *will* have more children, I assure you.'

Rose remained silent, turning her back on him as they climbed into bed. He was right, of course. She was his wife, and it was her duty. And in time, she probably would want more children. Thousands of mothers lost their infants each year, and went on to find solace in further off-spring. But it didn't help her just now.

At last, Charles's heavy, even breathing told her he was asleep, and she let her tears come then, quiet tears of despair. There was nothing to be done. She was Charles's wife and would be so until one or the other of them died which could be twenty, thirty years. She couldn't bring Alice back. Perhaps other children, the son that Charles craved, would bring her contentment in the future. But that time seemed a long way off, in some distant haze that her present pain couldn't begin to envisage.

Her own soul was eternally lost. But there was something she could perhaps do to save someone else's. At least she could try.

There was just a faint glimmer of dawn when she rose. She slipped quietly into the dressing room and fumbled for her riding habit at the back of her wardrobe. It fitted her regained figure perfectly. She crept silently down the stairs, pulled on her riding boots that waited in the rear porch, and let herself silently out of the back door.

A dank drizzle hung in the warm, moist air. The house still slept, but not so the horses in the field. Gospel kicked up his heels with joy at the sight of his beloved mistress. She fetched him just a handful of oats and while he munched happily, she stole into the tackroom. She must be careful as

Ned — whom she now hated — slept directly overhead. She could hear him snoring soundly, and as she took Gospel's bridle and heaved the saddle from its bracket, the rhythmical droning above her was not interrupted.

When she finally mounted Gospel's back, she could feel him quivering with excitement. They went off at a trot, keeping to the grass beside the gravelled driveway to deaden the sound of his hooves, and evaporating into the swirling mist like some mythical spectre. They were gone. Free. As if Fencott Place no longer existed, and they belonged to some other mystical world, horse and rider fused as one.

Even so, Rose was cautious. She knew that the shadowy gloom of mist as morning broke could confuse and disorientate, so she kept Gospel reined in tightly in order not to lose the track in the half light. When they came into Princetown, the village was still deserted. What time was it? Half past five? Cook and Patsy and Daisy would be up, preparing for the day ahead. Florrie wouldn't be far behind, wondering what she would do now little Alice was dead and buried. Ned would doubtless still be snoring his head off, and though it wouldn't be long before Charles awoke, he'd remain in blissful ignorance of his wife's disappearance.

Nobody saw them slide through the vapour-enshrouded prison village. Lights flickered at the row upon row of small, high-up, barred windows in the massive buildings of the gaol. After a long night locked away in their damp, lonely cells, sleeping on wooden beds, with a thin straw mattress if they'd behaved themselves, the inmates would be slopping out, eating their dry bread and watery porridge, going to morning prayers to ask God's blessing on the gruelling day of punishment ahead.

Rose paused for an instant near the gates. Somewhere in there, Seth Warrington would be preparing for another day of back-breaking labour when not even a word of companionship was permitted to ease one's misery. The Silent Rule. Just another cross to bear.

Rose gritted her teeth as she urged Gospel onwards. She wanted to rebel, to hit out. At Charles, for his possessiveness, his lack of understanding. But mostly at whatever force it was had taken her darling, innocent Alice. Doing whatever she could to help Seth was a way of cleansing her soul of its black anger. Of allowing herself to find some peace.

They trotted on past the prison, then turned left along the old toll road across the moor. Rose knew it like the back of her hand, but was nevertheless grateful for the daylight that was beginning to penetrate the mantle of fog. They passed on their left the track that led off to Foggintor, King's Tor and Swell Tor quarries, reminding Rose of happier times when she'd accompanied her father on many a visit to the hard-working community there.

Soon afterwards, the bank of mist suddenly rolled away as they descended the hill to Merrivale and the new Tor Quarry just beyond the inn. The world seemed to explode into life as men were arriving for work, doffing their caps in astonishment at the young woman of obvious class out so early on the lonely moor, and *alone*.

Now that they could see clearly, Rose gave Gospel his head. He catapulted forward, neck arched, fine legs stretched as they ate up the ground, joyous to be reunited with his mistress and ridden again after so many months. Rose's heart lifted in unison with his, leaving her sorrow and grief behind for a short while. When they reached the top of Pork Hill, though, the steep incline meant she had to slow Gospel's headlong speed back to a trot. And then, at long last, they turned right down the lane that would eventually lead to Peter Tavy.

CHAPTER TWENTY-EIGHT

The village was just as Rose remembered it from her visit several years ago with her father. A couple of farms were within the village itself which once again struck her as unusual. A group of men were heading down towards a lane beside the inn. They looked like miners, and she recalled driving down the lane with Henry in the dog-cart. It led down to the River Tavy, on the far side of which lay Wheal Friendship, once the most extensive copper mine on the moor, but now surviving on arsenic production.

While she'd stopped to remember her trip to the mine with Henry, the men she'd assumed were miners had disappeared down the lane, but Rose was sure she'd soon find someone else to ask. She needed to find the man Seth had befriended in the police cells in Tavistock nearly three years previously. Wandering around the village, she spied a middle-aged couple crossing a grassy square in front of the church.

'Excuse me, sir, ma'am,' she said politely, bringing Gospel to a standstill. 'I'm looking for a Mr Richard Pencarrow. I believe he has a farm somewhere near.'

'Up at the Hall, miss,' the man said, touching his cap. 'He be the maister.'

The master? In her headlong haste, Rose hadn't considered that she knew nothing about the stranger she was seeking. Seth himself had known precious little. From what the man before her had said, Richard Pencarrow must indeed have been released, but what if he really was a violent criminal — a murderer as it had involved the Coroner's Court — and she would be putting herself in danger? Though to be honest, at that particular moment, she didn't really care.

'But p'raps 'tis 'is wife you wants,' the woman put in with a reassuring smile. 'Our village wise-woman?'

'Ah,' Rose answered somewhat relieved. Richard Pencarrow was considered 'the maister', the charges against him had evidently been dropped, and the husband of a caring and respected member of the community was unlikely to be a vicious brute. Rose felt encouraged. 'Perhaps you'd be so kind as to direct me to the Hall?' she prompted.

'Yes. Rosebank Hall,' the man answered, proceeding to give her directions. ''Tis a fair step, but thee cas'n miss it.'

'And mind you goes in the back door. 'Tis always open.'

'Oh, right,' Rose replied with surprise. 'Thank you kindly.'

She flashed her lovely, natural smile and turned Gospel along the way as directed. As they gradually climbed out of the valley, Rose relaxed and admired the view as a watery sun began to break over the higher ground. She felt she was in a different world, one in which the pain in her heart ceased to exist. And when Rosebank Hall — a building not nearly so imposing as Fencott Place — came into view, Rose began to wonder about the said Mr and Mrs Pencarrow. A wise-woman would surely be of a certain age, and she prayed they'd both be sympathetic to her cause.

Mrs Pencarrow was nothing like she'd imagined. Crossing what was clearly a farmyard, Rose found somewhere to tether Gospel and then rapped gently on the back door of the house. She started when a voice at once called out to her to enter.

She found herself in a farmhouse kitchen, but rather than the aroma of cooking, an overwhelming fragrance she recognised but couldn't immediately name permeated the air. Then she noticed bunches of herbs hung in rows from drying racks. Jars lined the walls, filled with powders from green to brown, or liquids of all manner of colours. Not just a wise-woman, but a herbalist. Rose was amazed.

'Morning, miss. Can I help you?'

Rose's eyes widened. Mrs Pencarrow wasn't many years older than herself. A petite young woman, she was dressed in a simple blouse and skirt with a riot of golden hair secured only with a ribbon. The pretty face was smiling in welcome, the eyes the most striking, translucent amber Rose had ever seen.

'Mrs Pencarrow?' she mumbled.

'Yes. But call me Beth. So what can I do for you? Not from round here, are you?'

Before Rose could reply, a further door opened, and a girl of about twelve years old bounded into the kitchen, an infant in her arms. Rose might've been punched in the chest, and the room spun around her.

'*Elle s'est réveillée*,' the girl said casually as she handed the child to Elizabeth Pencarrow. '*Tu veux que je fasse la vaisselle?*'

'*Oui, s'il te plaît*. Oh, I'm sorry. This is my daughter, Chantal.'

'Pleased to meet you, madame.' And bobbing a curtsy, the girl went over to the deep stone sink.

Rose made a conscious effort to take a grip on herself. A baby. Much older than Alice. But a baby. Its presence slashed at her heart, throwing her bereaved soul into turmoil. Elizabeth Pencarrow and the older girl might have been speaking in a foreign language, and then, as her mind cleared, Rose realised that they *had*.

She blinked hard as she battled to put her thoughts straight. 'I'm sorry,' she muttered. 'It's Mr Pencarrow I need to see. I have a message for him from . . . someone he met in the Tavistock police cells.'

The colour drained from Mrs Pencarrow's cheeks. She fumbled for one of the kitchen chairs and lowered herself into it, dandling the infant subconsciously on her knee. ''Tis an episode we thought were behind us,' she croaked.

'No, it's nothing for you to worry about,' Rose said quickly. 'It's just that . . . this other man, he was convicted and now he's serving his sentence at Dartmoor Prison. And he needs Mr Pencarrow's help.'

'Yes. I remember . . . Richard did speak of someone,' Elizabeth mumbled. 'Someone he said didn't seem at all like a criminal. But he never knew what happened to him. Is he . . . your husband?'

Rose frowned. Seth her husband? The question unnerved her.

'Er, no. I'm married to . . . someone else,' she faltered. 'But Seth . . . ' and she saw Elizabeth raise a surprised eyebrow at the use of a Christian name, 'he escaped. He's innocent, you see, and in a moment of folly, he just . . . But he broke his ankle and took refuge in our stables. We live two miles the other side of Princetown, you see. I helped him, and we became friends. He told me everything that happened. He was convicted on what I think they call circumstantial evidence. But I believe he's innocent. But he were caught and taken back to prison. Which is where he'll stay if someone doesn't help him. But I really don't know what to do, and Seth mentioned your husband . . . '

She gazed beseechingly into the woman's eyes. Elizabeth slowly set the child on its feet and watched as the infant tottered across the floor. It seemed an eternity to Rose before she spoke again.

'And what about your own husband?'

Rose drew in her bottom lip. 'My own husband believes that if you're convicted, then you must be guilty. He doesn't know I'm here. But I *beg* you, Mrs Pencarrow—'

'Beth, please,' the other woman corrected. 'And of course you must speak to Richard, though I'm not sure when he'll be back. He went out at the crack of dawn to check on the sheep up on the moor. But you're more than welcome to wait if you have time. How did you get here? 'Tis a good way.'

'Oh, I rode,' Rose replied, filled with relief that Elizabeth was willing to listen to her.

'Then put your horse in the stables and I'll make us a cup of tea.'

'Thank you so much. It's most kind of you.'

Rose hurried outside, already feeling happier. She found the stables easily enough, putting Gospel in a stall beside a dozing cart-horse, and finding a bucket of water for him. When she returned inside, Elizabeth was pouring a cup of tea for each of them. The girl, Rose noticed, wasn't remotely like Elizabeth, and surely she was too old to be her daughter.

'Chantal's my step-daughter,' Elizabeth explained as she saw Rose looking at her. 'Richard was widowed in France long afore we met.'

'Ah.' Rose's curiosity was drawing her mind from her grief over Alice. 'So it was French you were speaking?'

'Yes. When we first met, neither of us spoke the other's language. But we've learnt from each other. Oh, do sit down, Mrs . . . ?'

'Chadwick. Rose Chadwick.'

Just as she sat down, the infant toddled across the room on wobbly legs, saving itself by leaning on Rose's thigh. The child smiled up at the stranger, revealing a set of little front teeth.

The knife twisted in Rose's side. 'How old?' she managed to gulp.

'Hannah? Thirteen months.'

The child gurgled contentedly, her cap of coppery curls bobbing around her inquisitive face, and all at once Rose felt two fat tears stroll down her cheeks.

'Mrs Chadwick?'

Elizabeth's brow furrowed as she put out a hand, and Rose felt herself tumbling into her pain again.

'I . . . buried my own daughter yesterday,' she croaked. 'She was . . . just eight weeks old.'

It was too much, and Rose sank willingly into the savage agony of her grief. She shook with tears and instantly found herself comforted not only by the arms of Peter Tavy's wise-woman, but also by her French step-daughter. It was a moment of release, and when it began to subside, Rose felt freer than at any time since her father's death. Elizabeth gave her some herbal drink before she sipped at her tea. But in this lonely farmhouse, amongst these total strangers, Rose began to feel some peace as she explained how she'd come to marry Charles and how her life had deteriorated since.

Elizabeth was a good listener. 'Our first child was still-born,' she murmured in a torn whisper when Rose had finished. 'So I know how you feel. But now we have Hannah. So there's always hope.'

Rose thumbed away her own tears. Elizabeth seemed so . . . complete, and Rose could scarcely absorb what she'd just said. 'Oh, I'm so sorry. But I don't think I want any more children. Not with Charles, anyway.'

Elizabeth breathed out slowly. 'That I'm afraid I can't help you with. I love Richard so much, so I can't imagine being in your situation. But we will try and help with your convict. Though to be honest, I'm not sure there's anything we can do.'

Rose felt her heart drop like a stone. 'Yes, I know,' she mumbled. 'But I can't bear to think . . .'

Just then the door opened, and in walked a tall man, broad-shouldered but slim of waist. For a few seconds, he was taken up with greeting his wife and children, while a pair of black and white sheep-dogs trotted at his heels. When he at last looked across at the unknown visitor, his face broke into a friendly smile.

'Who have we here?' he asked amiably. 'Do you own that black horse in the stable? What a wonderful animal! I've given him a haynet, by the way.'

Rose's thanks were lost in the confusion of introductions and explanations. The kitchen suddenly overflowed with the four adults, the unsteady baby and the two dogs. But as the chaos settled, Richard Pencarrow gratefully took from his wife the mug of tea she offered him, and lounged back against the wall next to the range, one foot raised on the fender, to drink it.

'I've often wondered what happened to Seth,' he said thoughtfully. 'But it was hard enough picking up the pieces of my own life, let alone someone else's I'd only known for a few days. But I feel guilty about it now. Serving twelve years at Princetown, you say? Poor devil.' He spoke the words with passion, and stared silently at the stone-flagged floor for some seconds before lifting his head again. 'So, how do you come to know him?'

'He escaped,' Rose answered at once, eager to grasp Richard's support while he seemed so sympathetic. 'He hid in our stables because his ankle was broken. I helped him. But he was caught.'

Richard's mouth closed into an angry line. Pushing himself away from the wall, he crossed the room and pulled out a chair to sit down opposite Rose at the table. 'You do . . . ' he began hesitantly, 'you do realise what will have happened to him?'

Rose had to turn away. Despite the comforting way she felt Richard take her hands, she couldn't speak and instead gave a small nod of her head.

'Rose, tell Richard everything you told me,' Elizabeth encouraged her.

It wasn't easy, for her heart was hammering nervously. She *had* to convince this man of Seth's plight. He listened intently, balancing his baby daughter who'd clambered onto his knee. He nodded occasionally, interrupting Rose only to clarify a detail here and there. When she'd finished, she held her breath, not daring to hope . . .

Richard's face was totally still for what seemed to Rose an age before little Hannah started wriggling about on his lap, and he passed the child to his elder daughter. Rose watched him chew his lip for some moments, and then he sat back in his chair and ran a hand through his dark wavy hair. He sighed weightily and slowly rubbed his jaw.

'I don't know that I can help you,' he pronounced with a fierce swoop of his eyebrows. 'I'm a farmer, with only such legal knowledge as that entails. But I do know that once you're convicted, that's it. There's no appeal.'

Ice trickled through Rose's veins. Helping Seth was her only reason for staying alive just now, and she couldn't have her hopes dashed. 'That's what Seth said,' she mumbled. 'But he mentioned something called a royal pardon—'

'A royal pardon? But they're virtually impossible.'

'I know.' Rose lifted her chin stubbornly. 'But I don't believe Queen Victoria would approve of an innocent man suffering twelve years penal servitude for a crime he didn't commit.' And then a flash of inspiration darted into her desperate mind. 'If it's money you need . . .'

But Richard solemnly shook his head. 'It's not that. It's just that I wouldn't have a clue . . . But we know someone who might. I can't promise anything, of course, but there's no harm in asking. A good friend of ours, Captain Adam Bradley. A man of strong principles who decries injustice of any sort. He inherited a large estate in Herefordshire which is his main home now, but he's originally from London and still has his house there. He has lots of connections in the capital and is far more influential than I could ever be. I'm sure he'd have a much better understanding of the situation than I do. He deals with lawyers all the time. Only to do with the legalities of his business. Nothing to do with criminal law, but he might have connections. He's a very busy man, but I'm sure—'

'So where can I contact him?' Rose demanded.

Richard gave a serious smile. 'Well, I think it would be better if you spoke to him in person. As it happens, Adam and his wife, Rebecca, are coming down this way at the end of the month to visit her family. And they'll be staying with us for a few days. We'll send you word when we know exactly when.'

'Not to me. To my friend, that's Molly Tyler. At Cherrybrook gunpowder mills.'

Richard shot a glance at his wife, but Elizabeth nodded. 'I'll explain later.'

Rose smiled at her thankfully as she stood up. 'I'd best be off. I can't tell you how grateful I am. And if Seth were here, I know he'd be thanking you, too.'

'I know Adam will do whatever he can. But, please, don't get your hopes up.'

'Yes, I understand. And thank you again. So much.'

'It's the least we can do.'

'You're welcome to stay—'

'No, thank you, Beth,' Rose answered resolutely, making for the door. She would have loved to remain a little longer, but it was only putting off her return . . .

CHAPTER TWENTY-NINE

'Where the blazes have you been?' Charles bawled at her from his desk.

But Rose didn't falter as she marched boldly into the study. The long ride home had given her time to reflect, and though her muscles ached from such a lengthy period in the saddle when she hadn't ridden for so many months, it had only served to strengthen her resolve. The comfort she'd received from total strangers that day had been more than anything Charles had offered her since little Alice had died. For now, all her emotions were channelled into what she knew would be a detestable confrontation with Charles.

She stood squarely in the centre of the plush rug. 'Out,' she said simply.

'I know that! But where? For God's sake, Rose, it's three in the afternoon, and you've been missing since dawn. I've been worried sick.'

'Yes, I'm sorry. But I've told you before not to worry if I'm out on Gospel. He'll not let me come to any harm.'

'It's because of him that I worry, the great brute!'

'Well, don't.' She stepped forward and placed her palms firmly on the edge of the desk. 'You must understand that I had to do something. Because of Alice. You know I feel at peace out on the moor. It has . . . helped me. I know the moor like the back of my hand, and I'm not fool enough to put myself at risk.'

'But you're my wife, dammit, and you should give that some consideration.'

'Oh, I do, Charles, believe me I do!' she answered, her voice laced with irony. 'And you and I must have a frank discussion on that subject.'

'What do you mean?' He shot round to her side of the desk, his cheeks puce. His wrath robbed him of his good looks, and Rose wondered how on earth she'd once thought him handsome. It was her instinct to shrink away, but she forced herself to face him.

'I do believe you love me,' she began frostily. 'In your own mean and possessive way. And I truly believed I loved you, too. But once we were married, I found you were not the man I thought you to be.'

Charles's eyes bulged from their sockets and he viciously gripped her wrist. But Rose merely cast her eyes towards his hand with caustic distain.

'There you are, you see. The man I thought I was marrying would never have done *that*!' She glared at him, her eyes darkened with rancour, and he slowly released his grip. 'Thank you,' she bristled. 'As you say, I am your wife. And I shall remain so. A good housekeeper, and loyal to you. I'll even warm your bed at night and bear your children, though I should appreciate a little more gentleness in that department. But in return, you will allow me to come and go as I please, visit Molly or anyone else I choose, ride out over the moor, whatever I fancy.'

She stopped then, her mouth firmed to a defiant line. Charles's face was suffused with fury, fists working at his sides. Rose might have recoiled, but there was no room for fear in her heart. Just bottomless grief, and the tiny grain of strength her visit to the Pencarrows had planted in her.

'You little vixen!' Charles spat at her. 'After all I've done for you! But I won't have you cavorting all over the place—'

'Rest assured, I'll do nothing to disgrace you, Charles,' she answered without flinching. 'I'll tell you where I'm going so that you needn't worry. And I apologise for today. It were wrong of me, but I just felt I had to get away, or I'd go mad. But, if you ever try to stop me, I'll disappear from your life for good, and you'll never see me again, and that wouldn't do your precious reputation or your ego any good, would it?'

With that, she spun on her heel and flounced out of the room, leaving Charles spitting feathers as he stared after her.

* * *

He didn't force his attentions on her that night, or the following morning, and everyone else in the household put the silence between the master and the mistress down to their bereavement. Dressed in mourning, Rose ordered Ned to drive herself and Florrie to the church in the wagonette to visit Alice's grave. She and Florrie cried in each other's arms, and since she spent the following two days quietly indoors avoiding the rain, Charles almost began to think he'd imagined the ugly scene in his study.

He was mistaken. The hollow pit in Rose's stomach was being filled with plans of vengeance. Or, at least, of deceit, since she was noble enough to recognise that the situation wasn't entirely Charles's fault. He, too, had thought he'd found the perfect marriage partner, lively, entertaining, yet the ideal hostess. But it was that very vivacity that had come between them, infuriating his possessiveness and his desire to dominate. They simply weren't right for each other, and Rose mourned also for the happiness she and Charles had failed to find together.

It was three days before he demanded his marital rights, and he did show her a little consideration which made it more tolerable, so their bitter exchange had achieved some good. She still felt soiled, but the next morning, Charles was in a better mood.

'I'm going to the powdermills this morning,' he announced. 'The new manager's facing prosecution over various regulations the government inspector found weren't being properly adhered to. As one of the major shareholders, I find that quite worrying.'

Rose looked up sharply. 'My father would never have allowed that to happen. He was always praised by the inspectors.'

'Yes, I know. My confidence in him was one of the reasons I bought even more shares when trade was lessening. But I was wondering if you'd care to accompany me? You could visit Molly while I carry out a tour of inspection of my own.'

The corners of Rose's mouth curved upwards. 'Yes, I should like that.'

Charles returned her smile with some satisfaction. It was a gesture of reconciliation on his part, and she'd accepted. There was hope yet. Little did he realise he was playing right into her hands!

She was able to tell Molly everything of her visit to Rosebank Hall, and also explained that she'd cleared the way for Molly to visit Fencott Place at any time. But she must come regularly so that when she had a message from the Pencarrows, Charles wouldn't suspect anything.

They'd decided upon Wednesdays to visit each other, Rose informed him as they drove home. One week at Fencott Place, the alternate one at Molly's humble cottage at the powdermills. Charles conceded with a grimace. He didn't exactly approve, but at least one day a week, he'd know where Rose was.

On her first projected visit to Molly, he secretly followed on an hour later. When he spied Gospel in the powdermills stable, he was satisfied. For her part, each time she went out, Rose gave him her route or destination, returning at the estimated time. Once or twice, she rode into Tavistock, spent some while shopping, and returned with her purchases to show him. It meant she was out most of the day, so when on her next visit, Molly brought the dates of Captain and

Mrs Bradley's stay at Rosebank Hall, Rose set out on the appointed day in the same direction, confident that Charles wouldn't follow. She also took a couple of trinkets she'd previously bought at Tavistock market and had secreted from Charles, but would reveal to him upon her return as evidence of her claimed visit to the town.

She heard laughter as she rode up the track to Rosebank Hall, and discovered the happy party on the lawn at the front of the farmhouse. It was the very end of August, and for once the sun was shining. Chantal Pencarrow was racing about the grass with two younger children and a toddler, whom Rose imagined must be the Bradleys' off-spring. Though Richard was nowhere to be seen, another man was running and dodging about, carrying in his arms a delighted baby Hannah Pencarrow. Two kitchen chairs stood empty by a small table set with drinks, but two others were occupied by Elizabeth and another woman of about thirty years old, both laughing uproariously at the antics of the man and the children in front of them.

Rose's heart contracted, for wasn't this the scene of domestic bliss she'd once imagined for herself and Charles? Alas, it could never be.

Gospel shied at the shrieks of hilarity from the lively group, and Rose slid from his back and patted his neck reassuringly as he shook his head with a snort. When she turned round, Elizabeth was coming up to her, arms open to welcome her like a long-lost friend, with the man close on her heels.

'Richard's having to make use of the good weather today, I'm afraid, Rose,' Elizabeth apologised. 'But this is Adam.'

The captain's face was still flushed with merriment and he had to catch his breath as he approached. The lines about his eyes put him at about forty, and there was something about him that instantly inspired an awesome respect which anyone but Rose might have found daunting.

'Mrs Chadwick. Rose, if I may be so bold,' he said with quiet confidence, passing the child in his arms to her mother,

Rose noticed, in quite an awkward fashion. 'Would you mind if I remove my coat? Running about with the children . . .'

'But of course,' she smiled, taking an instinctive liking to him.

'Thank you.'

He was slipping with just a little difficulty out of his coat, when the woman Rose assumed was his wife, came up behind him and greeted her with such friendliness that she might have known Rose all her life. Then she turned to help her husband, and as she slid off the left coat-sleeve, Rose saw with amazement that his hand was made not of flesh and blood, but of metal.

Captain Bradley caught her eye with the hint of a wry smile. 'Ah, you've discovered my little secret. An accident at sea that nearly cost me my life *and* my sanity. And would have done so, had it not been for my wife here.'

His arm went about Rebecca's waist and she leaned against him, the love that they shared seeming to flutter in the air about them. Rose felt a lump swell in her throat. Of envy, perhaps, but also of relief, since it was this well-balanced, mature man, who'd clearly known his own share of tragedy, who would hopefully be taking up Seth's cause.

'Do come and have some lemonade,' Elizabeth invited her, jiggling Hannah in her arms. 'You must be thirsty after that long ride.'

'Could I put Gospel in the stable first, please?'

'Of course. You know where it is.'

Rose settled Gospel in the stable and then returned to the others on the lawn at the front of the house.

'Beth has told us all about you,' Rebecca Bradley announced. 'And we're so sorry about your situation, my dear.'

The woman spoke with such compassion that Rose indeed took heart. They sat, sipping the cool lemonade for some time before retiring to the farmhouse kitchen for a simple lunch. With so many young children, it was hardly a quiet affair, and Rose wondered ruefully if Charles would ever have allowed Alice to dine with them before she reached the sensible age of sixteen. But she'd never know. Alice was dead . . .

After the meal, Adam took Rose's elbow. 'We must have that talk now. Richard wouldn't mind us using his office, would he, Beth?'

'No, of course not. We'll take the children for a walk, shall we, Becky?'

'This way, Rose,' Adam invited her, leading the way across a hall not as grand as Fencott Place, but impressive, nevertheless. The house, though, had an air of having seen better days, and Richard's office was no different.

Adam indicated that Rose should be seated. Then sitting down at the desk himself, he put on his spectacles, took a fountain pen from the ink stand and drew towards him Richard's writing pad. He looked up, staring deep into Rose's eyes. 'Begin at the beginning. Take your time. Tell me everything you know.'

Adam was so calm and unhurried that Rose found herself remembering all sorts of details as she related Seth's story. Adam made notes as she talked, stopping her occasionally to clarify a fact here and there. It must have been an hour before he sat back in his chair and removed his spectacles.

Rose knew he was about to give her his opinion, and her heart missed a beat. Adam Bradley was a good man, but he also seemed a realist. She felt the sweat oozing from her palms as he drew in a breath to speak.

'I understand from Richard you've mentioned a royal pardon?'

Rose's throat had dried like parchment, and she nodded in reply.

'Well, it's certainly the only possible way,' Adam began hesitantly. 'There are some new laws regarding appeals in the civil courts, but it's quite right that there's no such thing in the criminal justice system. A conviction's a conviction. And unless you can produce absolutely irrefutable new evidence of Mr Collingwood's innocence, you haven't a chance. And even then, it would be one hell of a business.'

Rose felt sick. Was that it, then? She'd wanted so much to have faith in the captain, and now it seemed he was turning her down.

'However,' he went on, rubbing his thumb across his pursed lips, 'this is an appalling story, so I'll tell you what I'm going to do. We'll be returning to Rebecca's parents in a few days and she'll be perfectly content there without me. I'll go up to London by train and discuss this with my lawyer up there. Find out all I can about what a pardon would entail. I'll do all I can, but I have to say that I don't hold much hope. But just tell me one thing. Do you believe Seth Collingwood is telling the truth?'

He was staring at her unflinching, his gaze unnerving. He was testing her, and she met the challenge. 'Without a doubt. I've been over everything he said a thousand times, and it all makes sense. So, yes, I do believe him.'

'Well, if we can gather sufficient evidence in his favour — which won't be easy — and I can find my way through what I'm sure will be a legal nightmare, then I expect I and whatever legal representative will be required will need to visit him in prison. But I really must warn you that as far as I know, a royal pardon is a rare thing indeed. It'll take time and influence, not to say money—'

'Oh, I can get you money!' she told him, relieved that there was at least something she could do.

Adam spread his right hand. 'There was a time when I would've had to take you up on that. But now I can safely say that my pockets are deep. And nothing would give me greater pleasure than to see such a grave injustice rectified.'

'Well, I can only thank you from the bottom of my heart.'

'Don't thank me yet. Nothing at all may come of it. But I promise you, I'll try my damnedest. You must be patient. But in the meantime, I suggest you examine your own involvement in this. You're a married woman, but not happily so, I gather. If you have . . . any feelings for Collingwood, you'll need to confront them.'

Rose lowered her eyes. Adam Bradley had seen right through her. Seen something she'd been refusing to admit to herself. But even if by some miracle, a royal pardon was obtained, that would be the end of it. She was married to Charles, and that was that. But if she could help Seth, she would be content.

* * *

As Adam had said, it was taking time. Weeks passed, what remained of the dismal summer turning into an even more dismal autumn. If it weren't for her visits to Rosebank Hall and the news she received there of Adam's progress, Rose felt she'd have gone mad.

Adam's London lawyer himself had no experience of such things, but he had a friend and colleague who was a circuit judge. When he heard the facts, he was shocked that in his summing up, the judge at Seth's trial hadn't tried to sway the jury away from a conviction. He was willing to take up Seth's cause when sufficient evidence was available, and Adam had also enlisted the support of the local Member of Parliament. The latest news was that Adam had hired a private investigator to track down the witnesses in the case.

It was this knowledge and the faith she had placed in Adam that enabled Rose to survive her numbing grief over Alice. She attended the little grave at least twice a week. Charles never accompanied her.

It became easier to deceive him, the remorse she'd felt at first soon slipping away. She did her duty as a wife, bearing it with acid resentment, and pleased each time she discovered she wasn't pregnant. She didn't want to replace Alice. Not yet, at least.

She accompanied Charles to London, held a dinner-party at Fencott Place for Mr and Mrs Frean and the Duchy's agent from Prince Hall. Did all Charles asked of her. He clearly felt convinced that Rose was being a proper wife, as in return, he tolerated her lone rides across the moor, though she made no objection if he decided to accompany her.

But it was all a ruse so that she could spend time in the healing ambience at Rosebank Hall. Elizabeth always welcomed her with open arms, and Chantal, even baby Hannah, came to look upon her as an aunt. And of course, there was always news from Adam.

The witness who'd seen Seth with the victim and assumed he was robbing him, had been easy to find. He'd agreed to repeat what he said before, that he'd not witnessed the actual attack, and that he may have jumped to the wrong conclusion. Tracking down the elderly couple who *had* seen the real assailant commit the crime and then make his escape, had taken a deal longer, but they, too, were willing to testify in Seth's favour. All the legal contacts Adam had been consulting in London, however, weren't entirely convinced it was sufficient, and so Adam's enquiries continued.

Despite her promise to Seth, Rose revealed to Adam that Seth had been using a false name, and the reasons for the deception. To her relief, Adam was of the opinion that, although unhelpful, it wouldn't hinder the investigation, and he'd keep the knowledge to himself unless it became vital to prove where Seth had obtained his money. In the meantime, without revealing why, he'd managed to verify the army record of Captain Seth Warrington, and everything was exactly as Seth had said.

Rose's visits to Rosebank Hall maintained her sanity, but as the days shortened, there wasn't sufficient time for the journey there and back in the daylight, so she had to curtail her excursions to Peter Tavy for the winter. She thought she might suffocate, and as her resentment of Charles grew to breaking point, she wondered quite how she would survive through to the spring. She received letters via Molly from Elizabeth, but it wasn't the same. And, for some time, there had been silence from Adam.

CHAPTER THIRTY

'Oh, God.'

Rose's vision blurred at Adam's neat handwriting on the envelope. There'd been no word from him for so long, and she was convinced the letter that Molly had just handed her must contain bad news.

'Go on, then, open it,' Molly encouraged her.

Rose's heart was pounding as she tore open the envelope and extracted the sheet of paper. For a few moments, the fear of what it might contain made the letters dance on the page, but slowly its meaning took root in her brain.

'Oh, Molly,' she managed to force from her tight throat. 'It's Jonas Chant.'

'Who?' Molly's freckled brow frowned.

'The man Seth is supposed to have robbed. Who swore it was Seth who attacked him. Adam's been searching all over for him, and now suddenly he's turned up in the workhouse. It were William Greenwood as found him, Richard and Elizabeth's doctor friend. He's the medical officer, and he had to examine this new inmate. He recognised the name at once. And . . . he's dying. Drunk himself to death, William says. Won't last longer than a week, two at most. And would you believe, he's catholic and he's asked for the priest? And

William says the priest has agreed that if Chant confesses to lying about Seth, he'll try to persuade him to sign a written confession.'

'So . . . it could be what you've been waiting for?'

'Well, yes.' Rose's bloodless lips quivered. 'But . . . what if he won't confess? What if he dies, and it all goes wrong? Oh, Molly, I couldn't bear it!'

'But this doctor,' Molly quickly put in, 'you've met him, and you trust him to do what Captain Bradley says in the letter?'

'Oh, yes. He's been Elizabeth's friend since she were a child.'

'There you are, then. I'm sure 'twill be all right. Do the letter say ort else?'

Rose took a deep breath and quickly scanned the remaining lines of writing. 'They've had another stroke of luck, too,' she told Molly. 'A man who was drinking at the inn that night and remembers the way Chant was behaving, and the scene he caused with Seth. He also remembers someone else who appeared to follow Chant out into the street. Someone he actually *knows* and can identify. And this chap always wore the same old clothes and never had much money, but after that evening, he was always smartly dressed and was never short of cash.'

'So, you means, he could be the real culprit? And maybies he destroyed his clothes cuz they was stained with blood?'

'And if the elderly couple could also identify him . . . Oh, dear Lord, I daren't even think about it! But Adam says if all this evidence can be established, then after Christmas, he'll go up to London and he'll push and push . . . But he says not to get my hopes up. That a royal pardon would still be incredibly difficult, and it's such a complicated process . . . Oh, I just don't know what to think.'

And as she rode home from Molly's, Rose's stomach was clenched so tightly, she felt sick. When they arrived back at Fencott Place, for once, Rose left the untacking to Ned, and she hurried indoors. She must tell Florrie, as she couldn't face the suspense alone.

Charles took her more forcefully that night. He said it was about time she became pregnant again. He was damned well going to make sure of it and this time it would be a boy. Rose suffered his attentions that night, and all the following nights, in silence. She tried to refuse him once, but he slapped her face so hard, her ears rang.

January passed, and February. As the weeks dragged by, Rose began to despair that, despite all of Adam's efforts, the pardon was going to prove impossible, even with the confession Chant had made on his deathbed. And all the while, Seth was subjected to the horrors of imprisonment.

Rose had received news of his welfare through Molly's father. He had toiled in the workshops during the harshest months of winter, allowing his health to recover, but now, because of his escape attempt, he'd been put back to the most gruelling labour within the prison walls. Jacob had tried to look out for him as had Dr Power, but working on the extensions to the cell blocks, exposed to the worst of the Dartmoor weather, his chest was beginning to suffer again. Adam, accompanied by the criminal barrister from London, had been allowed one short visit, and had reluctantly reported that Seth was suffering from an alarming cough. No wonder, working in the same rain-sodden uniform day after day with no hope of it drying out overnight. No matter that there was clear evidence he was innocent; he had once tried to escape, and that was enough. Unless his pardon was signed and sealed, he was considered amongst the scum of the convicts.

The one consolation the coming of spring provided was that Rose was able to resume her visits to Rosebank Hall. Life there was dominated by lambing, and Rose's heart was reborn with every tiny woolly creature that struggled into the world. There was no word from Adam, only that he remained in London, and had abandoned everything else as he pursued justice for one man.

When Molly unexpectedly arrived at Fencott Place one warm afternoon in May, the room started spinning before Rose's eyes. Molly pulled a crumpled envelope from her pocket, a telegraph message, and Rose felt faint.

'The maid said as your husband's out,' Molly whispered urgently.

Rose nodded, her throat knotted into silence. Molly held the envelope out to her, but her muscles were locked in paralysis. Dear God . . .

'I can't,' her lips mouthed, her eyes glittering with fear.

'But, if 'twere bad news, Captain Bradley wouldn't have sent a telegram. Surely he'd have waited to see you in person.'

Rose took it then, in shaking fingers. Was Molly right? Would Adam have foreseen her dread? There was only one way to find out, and her heart thudded for several cruel, agonising seconds.

The first few words gave her the answer. Molly watched as she cried out and broke into a wailing sob. Oh, no. Oh, poor, poor Rose. Molly sucked in her lips as her friend continued to weep, and she gently prised the paper from her hands.

Molly began to read, and then read it again, distrusting her own skills of literacy. But . . .

'Rose!' she gasped. 'He's . . . he's—'

'I know.' A tiny squeal uttered from Rose's mouth as she lifted her tear-ravaged face. 'I just can't . . . Oh, Molly! He's . . . he's free!'

* * *

Oh, why was Peter Tavy so far? Rose had wanted to go there the day after Molly had brought her Adam's telegram, but she must wait for a suitable opportunity so as not to arouse Charles's suspicions. He'd commented that she was looking happier, and she'd replied it was merely the thought that summer was on the way. His own sap was rising, Charles admitted, and to prove it, he took her twice that night. She wanted to lash out, but she mustn't anger him. And she supposed she should give him another child. But not yet. Not until she'd seen for herself that Seth was safe and well. Safe, he was. At Rosebank Hall. But Adam had warned her of Seth's deteriorating health. Though if anyone could nurse him back to his former strength, it was Elizabeth.

The next day dawned fresh and clear, and Rose was away early, leaving a drooling Charles announcing that he'd enjoyed the previous night so much he couldn't wait for the day to be over so that he could repeat the experience. Rose shuddered. But the day was long.

A strange mix of joy and anxiety choking her as she entered the farmhouse kitchen. Elizabeth was drying her hands on a towel and gave her a calm, reassuring smile, her eyes soft with understanding.

'He's upstairs,' she said, knowing that was all Rose wanted to know. 'I'll show you the way. And I can understand why you believed in Seth. He's a lovely chap.'

'H-how is he?' Rose dared to ask as she followed Elizabeth upstairs.

She heard Elizabeth's deep breath. 'Well, he's been half-starved for so long, he can't keep any decent food down, so I'm building up his diet gradually. And he has a dreadful cough. He's up and about, but William advised he keeps to his room in case he passed anything on to Hannah.' She stopped and turned to Rose, her face a picture of mortification. 'Oh, my dear Rose, I'm sorry. I didn't mean—'

But Rose shook her head. 'Oh, Beth, you can't worry about everything you say, just because . . . I'm just so grateful for everything you've all done. And you don't know what your friendship has meant to me.'

Elizabeth smiled appreciatively, and then knocked gently on the door she'd stopped by. Rose held her breath as she followed Elizabeth into the room, her heart pounding. Next to the slightly open window, a human form was huddled in an old easychair and wrapped in a worn blanket. Rose approached on tiptoe, every fibre of her being on tenterhooks, and then stood staring at the sleeping figure. She'd tried so often to conjure up a vision of him in her mind, and now here he was. Except that he was so thin, his face so gaunt. He sported the virtually scalped convict crop, of course, but he looked so *old*, his skin ashen and dark smudges beneath his eyes. Tears from the strain of all those months of waiting and praying, of lying and deceit, trickled unheeded down Rose's cheeks.

'D'you think he'll get better?' she whispered to Elizabeth. 'I mean, *really* better?'

'I reckon as he'll be as strong as ever in time. He sleeps a great deal, but sleep is the best healer, and he's utterly exhausted. How they expect them to do such hard work in such a state, I really don't know.'

But Rose was hardly listening as Seth coughed in his sleep. She saw his Adam's apple rise and fall as he swallowed, and then his eyelids flickered open, his glazed eyes wandering for a second until they focused on Rose's face.

His mouth stretched into that winsome smile. 'Rose,' he croaked.

There was no need for him to say any more. As Elizabeth slid out of the room behind her, Rose battled to think of some words, but none would come. She felt Seth take her hand and she looked back into the clear depths of his hazel eyes which were suddenly bright and gleaming. They both laughed awkwardly, hesitating, and then restraint was thrown to the four winds as they were in each other's arms, all the pain and suffering of her marriage to Charles, the loss of her father and baby Alice, her yearning — oh, yes, she knew it now — to be with this man she knew she never could, erupting in a torrent.

How long was it before they dragged themselves apart? Rose's gaze was locked on Seth's face, and she could see his eyes were glistening with moisture, unaware of her own fresh tears until he thumbed them away.

'Rose,' he repeated, his voice rasping. 'I can't thank you enough.'

'Me?' she squeaked her throat was so tight. 'No, it's Adam you must thank.'

'Believe me I have.'

'And I must, too. Is he here?'

'He's gone back to Herefordshire.'

'Oh, then I must write to thank him.'

'And so must I.' Seth's face was aglow as he glanced down at their hands which still clung to each other. 'Of course, I thanked him a million times the other day when he arrived at the prison to meet me when I was released. You know, he came straight back from London the minute the pardon was granted so that he could do so. I was only told myself the night before. I just couldn't believe it. I still can't.'

'He's a good man is Adam.'

'And his wife, too, for allowing him such time away from her, to help me, a total stranger. And Richard and Elizabeth, too, letting me stay here.'

He looked across the room as a knock came on the door and Elizabeth entered the room carrying a glass of deep green liquid. Seth pulled a grimace and then chuckled as he took the remedy from her hand.

'Beth's making me drink the most disgusting concoctions you can imagine, but I have to say I'm feeling a little better after only three days.'

'Well, I'll leave you two to talk,' Elizabeth said knowingly as she left the room, 'but don't tire him out.'

'I won't. I'm just happy to sit here and hold his hand.'

Which is what she did as Seth dozed in the chair, his mouth in a soft curve. A little later, Richard returned and came up to see them. It was clear that he and Seth had struck up a good friendship in the short time they'd known each other. Observing both men, Rose's heart lurched. Radiating with good health, Richard appeared the younger man, although Rose knew he was seven years Seth's senior. Rose caught her lip. Seth should regain a more youthful appearance as he recovered and his shorn hair grew back, but she mustn't think like that! She was a married woman, and one day, in the not too distant future, Seth would be well enough to leave Rosebank Hall, resume his travels and no doubt find a wife of his own.

The thought sobered her, shattering her euphoria. Through Adam, she'd rescued Seth from his grim prison sentence and possibly saved his life. But there could never be any more to it than that, and she must resign herself to being Charles's wife for life. She lowered her eyes, knowing she went quiet. Did Seth know her heart was breaking?

'I was so sorry to hear about the baby,' Seth said quietly when Richard had gone and they were alone again. 'It must've been dreadful.'

Rose managed a wan smile. 'Yes. It was. Eight weeks old, poor little soul. Charles didn't care much for her. She was a girl, and she was sickly. So perhaps it was for the best she died before she were old enough to understand that.'

'You . . . you don't really think that, do you?'

She grunted. Seth understood, while Charles . . . 'No, not really. But I think if I keep telling myself that, I'll come to believe it and it'll help me. I still feel so raw. As if the grief is trapped inside. It's all very well to cry with Florrie, or Molly or Beth here. But I need to cry with Charles. With her father. But he'll have none of it.'

Her voice had cracked, and as she looked at Seth, her eyes misted. He spread his arms and she had no strength to resist, laying her face against his chest as she sobbed inconsolably until slowly, very slowly, the torture eased. But in its place was a barb just as cruel.

'That husband of yours is a fool,' Seth choked. 'He doesn't know how lucky he is to have you, while I . . . I thought of nothing else but you. The risks you took to help me. All those months, everything they put me through, I just kept imagining your face. Otherwise, I just couldn't have taken it.'

Rose stiffened and drew back. Surely he'd suffered far worse than she. She'd emptied her weary soul on him, but he . . . His face clamped down in a fierce frown.

'Isn't it time you were getting back to your husband?' he said abruptly.

A tremor shuddered through Rose's fragile body. 'Oh, God, yes. I'm supposed to have gone shopping in Tavistock.' She froze as she buttoned herself into the coat of her riding habit that she'd left on the bed. 'Oh, Seth, I don't want to go.'

'But you know you must.'

She gulped. 'Yes. You will take care, won't you?'

He gave a wry shrug. 'I've no intention of doing otherwise. But . . . you will come again?'

'Of course.'

'Well, goodbye then, Rose.'

He held out his hand. Deliberately. For what else was there? Rose shook it, and fled the room without looking back. It was the only way.

CHAPTER THIRTY-ONE

'Where've you been?'

'To Tavistock. Like I said.'

'All this time?' Charles grabbed her wrist with such force that she let out a squeal of pain. 'And what have you bought then, eh,' he spat, 'that it took you so long?'

'Nothing!' she snarled back.

Her heart had been lost in sadness as she'd ridden back from Peter Tavy like the wind, and she'd had to put a curb on her own devastated emotions. She would be with Seth as much as she possibly could until it was time for him to move on. And then those memories would have to last her for the rest of her days. Her despair had turned to anger, and if she had to fight Charles tooth and nail to acquire those precious, bitter-sweet moments with Seth, then so be it. For after that, there would be nothing left, and she really wouldn't care what became of her.

'Well, you've been a bloody long time buying nothing!' Charles's hot breath was like fire against her cheek.

'Exactly. I couldn't find anything I liked, so I went on looking.'

'I don't believe you, you lying little slut! You've been with someone, haven't you?' he bawled deafeningly into her ear, wrenching her forward so that he could then bang her head backwards on the wall. 'Well, I'll teach you to be unfaithful to me!'

Rose glared at him as she regained her senses. 'Oh, yes! You would, wouldn't you?' she hissed back. 'Some gentleman *you* turned out to be! Well, if I *had* been with someone else — which I haven't — it would've been with a far better man than you!'

The challenge that glinted in her fearless eyes scorched into his pride. His face seemed about to explode, his cheeks puffed out like footballs. But after seconds that to Rose seemed like hours when she thought her heart had ceased to beat, he slowly lowered his raised fist.

'Well, I'll damned well make sure you're not cuckolding me! I'm going to London tomorrow, and you're bloody well coming with me!'

'If that's what it takes to prove I'm not lying!' she railed at him, her tongue burning with contempt as he stomped out of the room, slamming the door so hard behind him that the whole house shook.

Rose gazed at the closed door for some minutes. Oh, why had she given in so easily? She hadn't, though, really, had she? She'd forced Charles to stand down, not the other way around. But, London. For how long? Would Seth still be there when she returned? Were his feelings for her as strong as hers were for him? But what did it matter? It was hopeless. And perhaps it would be better if he left, disappeared from her life, without saying goodbye.

She slid down the wall to the floor and buried her head in her hands.

* * *

A whole month. A month in which she played the dutiful wife, behaved with perfect etiquette in the society circles Charles frequented. But inside, her soul was slowly bleeding to death. She thought of nothing but Seth, his spirit filling her every waking minute with ecstatic joy and tearing grief, and her restless nights with dreams and nightmares. When Charles made love to her, which was almost every night, he took her passiveness for compliance, not knowing that as she lay there, behind her closed eyes was the vision of a man with light hair and hazel eyes and a tender, gentle smile that lit up the sky.

She managed, just twice, to post a short letter to Seth, knowing that he couldn't reply. She didn't write of love. How could she, when she knew — they both knew — that destiny had sealed their fates long ago? On the day she'd married Charles. The letters seemed ridiculous, since she could merely say she hoped he was recovering and feeling stronger. That she thought of him every day, and hoped he would still be there on her return. Whenever that might be.

The moor was enshrouded in dense mist the day they returned. As Ned drove the wagonette up the steep hill from Tavistock to Princetown, however, Rose picked out the turn-off to Peter Tavy. Her heart contracted, bringing a slick of sweat to her skin. She forced herself not to turn her head, but gazed straight ahead at Ned's back. Oh, Seth. Are you still there? How I long to be with you.

It was good to be home. To be with Florrie, who hadn't known what to do with herself in Rose's absence. Charles only kept her on, he'd said curtly, because she had proved herself a good nanny to Alice and would be so again to the son he intended Rose should bear him. And the sooner the better, he growled, as he took Rose again that night.

'I need to take Gospel for some exercise,' she announced the following morning. 'He's so bad-tempered at not having been ridden for so long, he bit Ned again last night.'

'And where will you go, madam?'

'Oh, Charles, when will you learn to trust me?' she sighed wearily. 'Haven't I done everything you've required of me? But since you ask, I think I'll ride out to Vixen Tor, and then down along the Walkham to make a circle. It's so pretty down in the valley.' And then a flash of inspiration — said

314

with her fingers crossed behind her back. 'Won't you come with me? It's such a lovely day after yesterday.'

Charles looked up in surprise, and Rose's heart thudded painfully while he seemed to consider. 'No. I think that's too far for either me or Tansy. I thought, actually, I might visit the powdermills. You could come with me. See Molly.'

'Hmm.' Rose tilted her head, pretending to be making a decision. 'I'm tempted. But I think Gospel needs to kick up his heels somewhat further than that. But if you see Molly or Joe, you might tell them I'll be over on Wednesday as usual.'

With that, she gave him a deliberately affectionate kiss, though her lips stung with bitterness. He caught her hand, whispering in her ear something about what he would do with her that night. She smiled. And felt sick.

She was away, her spirit flying between excitement, despair and fear as Gospel's strong legs ate up the ground. When they clattered into the yard at Rosebank Hall, Rose felt she might faint. She hurried inside, not even stopping to knock.

A figure sat in the battered chair by the range, a petite young woman who looked dreadful.

'Rose!' Elizabeth nevertheless greeted her brightly.

Rose was numbed. Something must have happened. Oh, not Seth. Please God, no. 'W-what's the matter?' she stammered.

Elizabeth smiled. 'Nort. Just the opposite in fact. 'Tis just that I'm with child and I feel awful. Even my own remedies aren't helping with the sickness.'

'Oh, what wonderful news! I'm so happy for you! And Richard must be pleased. I . . . ' Rose paused, shying away from her own thoughts. But she gritted her teeth and went on, 'I expect he's hoping for a boy.'

'Probably, yes. He's never said as much. I mean, he's always joking about being surrounded by women. 'Tis why Seth being here is so good for him. But a farmer needs a son. Chantal's a great help. But you need a man's strength. Talking of which, you'll be wanting to see Seth.'

Rose gulped. 'He's still here then?'

'Of course. He's much better, though he still needs to build up his strength. He's been helping Richard on the farm. They're down in one of the fields near the village, planting flatpoles. Richard's asked him to stay on. We can't afford to pay him, but we've an old farmworker's cottage just on up the track. Used to be old George's, but both he and his widow have passed on now. We've said Seth can live there if he wants. He's still thinking about it.'

'Oh.' Rose's thoughts spun at this unexpected news. So Seth might stay on at Rosebank Hall. And she could continue to steal away to see him for . . . how long? Until Charles found out? And his jealous rage led him to the wrong conclusions? For it wouldn't be an affair, not in the carnal sense. It would be a deep and intimate friendship, no more than that. And one day, Seth would find a wife. It would break Rose's heart. But to know Seth was happy and safe, and to see him on occasion, would perhaps get her through the bleak and barren years ahead with Charles.

Elizabeth gave her directions to the field and it wasn't difficult to find. One of the farm horses was pulling a cart loaded with seedlings that the two men were planting individually in the pre-dug furrows. It was laborious work, and both men straightened up, arching their backs, when they saw Rose approach. She slipped from Gospel's back, tethering him to the gate, and hurried towards them.

'Congratulations, Richard!' she called as she neared them. 'I hear you're to be father again!'

A proud grin spread over Richard's weather-browned face. 'Thank you, Rose! Good to see you!' He was still smiling as his eyes swivelled across at Seth. 'But it's not me you've come to see, I'll be bound. Go on, Seth. Take a rest. Beth wouldn't be very pleased with me if I made you work too hard!'

He went back to the arduous task, and Rose's heart gave a little squeal as Seth came towards her. A wide smile lit his face, and she couldn't believe how much better he looked. His gentle, hazel eyes shone, the dark hollows beneath them vanished.

His ashen skin was now a healthy amber and his hair, a deep, golden blond, was an inch-long cap on his head that already curled around the nape of his neck. His bones were fleshing out, and the hand he held out to her was strong and firm.

'I'm sorry,' he said sheepishly. 'I'm covered in earth.' But then his handsome mouth stretched into a broad grin. 'I'm so glad to see you again. How was London?'

Rose couldn't answer for a moment. Seeing him so recovered and more attractive even than the vision of him she'd conjured up in her mind, had quite taken her senses away. And yet it was a spear in her side.

'London was . . . London,' she laughed, shaking her head. 'Busy. Tedious. I hated every minute of it. Apart from the two concerts Charles took me to. I loved those.' She broke off. It seemed incongruous, telling him this here, nearly three hundred miles from the capital, when her soul was empty of everything but her love for him. When he could be never be hers. 'And you, Seth. How are you?'

Seth glanced down at himself, his palms spread. 'As you see, much improved. I can't work nearly as hard as Richard does. Not yet, anyway. But did Beth tell you, they've offered me a cottage in exchange for work, if I want to stay on?'

'Yes,' Rose murmured as her stomach flipped over. 'And will you?' she hardly dared to ask.

His voice was serious, cautious. 'If *you* want me to.'

She gulped, her heart racing. 'Yes. I do. But . . . you know there can never be anything between us. No matter how much . . .'

'Yes, I know. I understand. But we can still be friends.'

She turned to him, her mouth twisted in a wistful smile, so grateful to him. 'Of course. But my husband must never know. He's . . . a very jealous man. Which is why I should be getting back. But I'm so glad you're so much better. And you will take care?'

He answered her with an anxious smile. 'I think you're the one who needs to be careful. Come again soon, Rose. But only when it's safe.'

They stood, facing each other, for just a few seconds. And then once again, they did the only thing they could. They shook hands.

* * *

'Did you have a good ride, my dear? You didn't say.'

Rose prayed her voice wouldn't betray her uneasiness as she turned down the sheets that night. 'Yes, thank you, Charles. You know how I begin to feel stifled in London after so long, even though you try to make it interesting for me. So it was good for me as well as Gospel.'

'You're not a very good liar, you know, Rose.'

His voice was suddenly ice-cold and she threw up her head. 'Pardon?'

'We weren't back twenty-four hours before you were off to see your lover.'

'My lover?' Her eyebrows arched in derision, her mouth open in a contemptuous laugh. 'A chance would be a fine thing with the way you keep a check on me!'

'Well, I shouldn't have to, but first it was that convict, and now it's . . . Well, God knows who! Joe, perhaps—'

Fury spiralled up within her, grasping her by the throat. 'Joe?' she rounded on him, her eyes flaring. 'How dare you! Joe's like a brother to me, and he's Molly's husband! My God, your mind's even filthier than I thought!'

'Well, you're the one having the affair, not me.'

She watched as his eyes hardened to steel, his mouth in a cruel line, and her heart turned to stone. 'An affair? Good God! And suffer what *you* put me through every night at the hands of another man as well? You must be joking!'

Before the bitter words had even left her lips, he'd gripped her by the arms and with a violence that terrified her, shook her like a rag-doll.

'So, it's all my fault, is it?' he roared. 'You're only doing your duty as my wife!'

'I know that!' she yelled back as they glared at each other like two rutting stags. 'But at least I'm *trying* to do something to make our marriage work. I want another child as much as you do,' she lied. 'But I wish you'd be gentler with me. Show me that you love me as much as you say you do. And I swear on Alice's grave that I'm not lying with another man.'

His forehead dipped in a wary frown as studied her, his cheeks sucked in distrustingly. 'Show me, then,' he rasped.

Outrage, disgust, the triumph of deceit, pain, grief and an unfathomable despair all tangled about her soul as she stripped off her nightdress and stood naked before him.

Her spirit died as his hungry hands reached out.

CHAPTER THIRTY-TWO

'Rose?'

She couldn't hold the tender concern in those clear hazel eyes, and slowly averted her gaze. She wanted to lean against him, let him soothe and comfort her wounded heart, but she must hide it from him, for there was nothing to be done. It was the same every time she managed to escape from Charles's jealous vigilance, meeting Seth at some pre-appointed hour and a nearer venue, since she couldn't rely on Charles's absence for long enough for her to ride to Peter Tavy and back.

She'd discovered, too, that Ned was relaying her movements to Charles, and it tested her ingenuity to keep him out of the way. She communicated with Seth through Molly, but it wasn't always safe for her to go. The last time she'd succeeded, Charles had suspected something and she'd paid dearly for it.

Now she knew Seth wouldn't be satisfied with a denial. She'd winced when he'd held her at arms' length as they found each other in the woods along the Walkham valley. The summer was drawing to a close, the stolen moments they snatched together the only flickering candle in the darkness of her life. Half an hour at most they'd sit and talk, no gesture of love passing between them. For it was impossible.

But this time, the fight had gone out of her, her spirit exhausted. The memory of Charles's attack on her the previous night was too much. She'd told him she had her monthly, and he'd lost his temper, cursing her for not being pregnant. And now she stood still as Seth unbuttoned her riding jacket and the shirt beneath just enough to slip them over her shoulders.

'The bastard,' he muttered as he took in the livid fingermarks on her arms and even around her neck. 'Not again, Rose. This can't go on. I can't just sit back and let . . . ' He rolled his head with an agonised sense of helplessness, balling his fists angrily at his sides. 'I just want to give that bloody husband of yours a taste of his own medicine. And how often has this happened, eh?' He shied away, his jaw clenched in maddened frustration. 'I feel such a coward, doing nothing to protect you.'

He tipped his head skywards, his eyes wildly searching the trees for an answer that simply wasn't there. Rose stepped up to him, leaning her cheek against his shoulder.

'There's nothing to be done,' she whispered. 'It's not your fault. It'll be better once I'm with child again.'

'And what then? I'll never see you once you have a family to care for. I just couldn't live, thinking of you under the thumb of that . . . ' His voice faltered, and he gulped hard before he croaked, 'You know I love you, Rose.'

'Yes.' The word was hardly breathed. Lodging in her throat like a stone.

'Then leave him.'

Rose blinked at him, and he watched her pupils widen. 'What?' she mumbled.

'Leave him. And come away with me.'

Her fine brow puckered, her eyebrows arched as she shook her head. 'He'd find us,' she moaned piteously.

'No, I mean *really* come away. America, South Africa. Anywhere.'

His eyes were piercing earnestly into hers, and she felt herself shiver. 'But . . .'

'I know I'm a pretty poor catch. I've nothing to offer you but my love, but we could start a new life together. I'd work hard for you. We could travel under my real name. As Mr and Mrs Warrington. No one would know any different. We could sail on one of Adam's ships to France or Spain, so there'd be no passenger list for your husband to find us on, even if he knew what name to look for. Then we could take a ship from there. He'd never find us.'

He was speaking urgently, his expression sharp and alert as she stared at him. Escape. Freedom. Her heart began to crash against her ribs, as she tried to take in the enormity of it.

'But . . . leave Dartmoor?' she stammered.

'I know.' His voice was low, deep with understanding. 'You'd have to leave the place you love. All your friends. Without saying goodbye. It'd be best that way. Adam would know, of course, and Richard and Beth. And I'm sure Richard would give Gospel a good home. He could always say he bought him from some beautiful young woman in Tavistock if it ever came to it.'

'Oh.' The world seemed to drop away as Rose felt herself swooning. But Seth caught her, and she could hear his heartbeat, strong and steady, as her head drooped against his chest. Leave Gospel? Even with Richard? And Florrie? Joe and Molly, everyone she knew and loved? The dogs even?

But Seth was right. It was the only way, though it would break her. And what did she *really* know of Seth? But *love* had touched her. And it was nothing like the uncertainty that had made her hesitate over Charles. This was so strong. With Seth beside her, there would be no more fear.

She lifted her head, and his dear, beloved face was there. Ready, waiting. Trusting.

'Yes,' she croaked.

And when his lips brushed against hers, she knew her heart was lost for ever.

* * *

Charles sauntered into his study with a large brandy in his hand. He had to look over some papers his agent had sent him that morning, but he could barely concentrate as he drooled over what he had in mind to do with Rose when he went up to join her in bed a little later. She was back 'in working order', and he would make up for what he'd missed. He'd have a son out of her, and he'd bloody well enjoy the making of it!

Oh, drat it! The fire was nearly out. He went to ring the bell, but the thought of Rose's body exposed to his greedy hands had put him in a good mood, and he supposed he was quite capable of rekindling the moribund embers. Some old newspapers were stacked in the corner, and he began to crumple the sheets of the top one into balls.

He stopped dead as his eyes focused on a minor headline. *Royal Pardon for Escaped Prisoner at Dartmoor*. The tiny print blurred as he forced his brain to read the short article below, and his heart jerked in his chest. He couldn't believe it. That damned convict Rose had hidden in his own stable under his very nose, had proved his innocence and had been released over four months ago. So . . . where was he? And *who* had helped him? Someone on the outside, since a royal pardon was a bloody difficult thing to achieve.

There could only be one answer.

The strangling anger, the *hate*, grappled in Charles's throat. Good God! That lying, whoring little harlot! He'd kill her! Could feel his fingers closing around her neck, throttling the life from her.

But that would be too good. He'd make her suffer first. Make her tell him who had helped her, since there was no way she could have done it alone! He'd deal with whoever it was later, but first of all, he'd deal with *her*! And he'd make her wish she'd never been born!

* * *

'I'm going into Exeter tomorrow,' he told her casually when he'd taken his fill of her tender flesh. 'A new business my agent has got wind of. I'll ride Tansy there. It's too far to go and come back in one day, so I'll stay overnight. I've told Ned he can take the day off. He can spend some time with that tart of his.'

Rose didn't reply. She was stinging from Charles's onslaught, since the mild consideration he'd shown her just that once had long since been forgotten. How many more times would she have to suffer his attentions? Not too many, she prayed. All she could think about was the plan to escape. Would they succeed? Was it the right decision? All she knew was that she couldn't possibly go on living the way she was.

So Charles and Ned wouldn't be there tomorrow. She waited half an hour after they'd both departed, and then brought Gospel in from the field, saddled him, and set off for Rosebank Hall.

She went a different way now. Richard had pointed out a more direct route following an old track that led to the new quarry at Merrivale. Gospel cantered along at a steady pace, and Rose sat astride him, her heart saddened. How many more times would she ride this beloved animal whose spirit and mettle matched her own? Never to see him, or the rugged, spectacular moorland that was part of her soul, ever again.

Was it worth the sacrifice? Her vision misted with tears that spangled on her lashes in the early autumn sunshine, but she would be free from Charles. She *had* to do it, but she would do it in great pain. And she would be with Seth. Good, kind, gentle Seth, who wanted nothing from her, but whose love had flowed into her with that one fleeting kiss.

She hadn't wanted it to be this way. She'd expected her marriage to Charles to be whole and fulfilling. If Charles had been the man she'd once thought he was, a man like Adam or Richard, he would have *helped* Seth as they had done, and there simply wouldn't have been room in her heart to love someone else. But now she knew her salvation lay only in Seth's embrace.

There he was now, with Richard and the two dogs, driving some sheep down from the moor. The two men saw her, exchanged a brief word, and then Seth came towards her, leaving Richard to carry on down to the farm.

She slid from Gospel's back into Seth's arms. And the doubt fled as they turned towards the tiny cottage.

* * *

It wasn't easy following her along the road through open moorland, as much of the time you could see for miles and she only had to look back . . . Charles had to use the contours of the land, keeping well behind her, sometimes losing sight of her for five or ten minutes, before reaching the crest that would bring her into view in the far distance.

She was easy to spot, a horse and rider moving at speed. At one point, she seemed to have vanished into thin air. He'd reached the brow of the hill a little past Merrivale Quarry, and the road ahead was deserted. He drew Tansy to a halt, and turning round in the saddle, spotted Rose skirting the quarry. She'd left the road and was heading steeply uphill over the moor. There was nowhere for Charles to hide and if Rose glanced around and saw him, his ruse would have failed.

But she didn't. As soon as she disappeared, he urged Tansy up the hill, cutting off a corner, towards an outbreak of rock, what the locals called a tor. He dismounted, leaving Tansy to graze. Scaling the boulders, he used them as cover to spy on his unfaithful, adulterous wife.

She was heading across a long dip in the land between two further tors, higher than the one where he was hiding now. A natural pool somewhere between them had attracted a small herd of cattle to drink, but Rose didn't deviate. Where was she heading? It was an area Charles was unfamiliar with, but it appeared an empty wilderness. Could it be that he was mistaken? That she really was doing nothing more than enjoying a long ride out on the moor?

He climbed back down to where Tansy was patiently waiting, and swung himself into the saddle. Should he ride out and find somewhere to spend the night in order to disguise his own trick, satisfied that Rose was telling the truth? She'd told him she didn't love him. But she insisted upon her fidelity, and heaven knew he wanted it to be true. He loved her. Worshipped her. Wanted to possess her as he had the right to do. Just grant him the son he wanted, and it would bind her to him.

But the thought of her in another man's arms. Another man's bed! The curve of her tiny waist, the roundness of her breasts . . . The image brought the saliva to his mouth. She was his. HIS! The law said so.

She'd suddenly dropped out of sight and he set Tansy at a gallop to catch up with her. He *must* be sure!

There were enclosures, fields, a brook in a narrow gully. Charles slid from Tansy's back again, using the stone walls and tall boulders for cover. He peered out. And his heart froze into a lump of ice. Two men, two dogs and some bloody sheep. One of the men came towards Rose. She dismounted and — damn and hell — she melted into his arms.

Charles leaned back against the wall, choking and spluttering and tearing at his collar as he battled to draw in some air. The bloody lying, deceitful bitch! Jesus Christ, he'd so nearly believed her! And after all he'd done for her, buying the house on this God-forsaken moor and abandoning his luxurious life in London! He was gasping, struggling to stay conscious as realisation seeped into his brain. Surely he was mistaken. He turned back, even now hoping . . . But there she was, arm in arm with the blackguard, heading — dear God above — to a small, isolated cottage and disappearing round the back.

His instinct was to fly down the hill, barge his way inside, and drag the hussy all the way home where, by God, he'd flay her until she begged for mercy. But she had the bastard to protect her. They hadn't been so far away that he couldn't recognise him. It was that bloody convict! He'd kill him! He'd take a meat-knife as he stormed through the kitchen and ram it into the cur's belly as he lay in bed with Rose, and she could watch her lover die in agony. Charles wouldn't care about the consequences, he wouldn't bloody care! He wouldn't be made a cuckold of! But there was the other chap, too. Tall, broad-shouldered, one of those strong farming types. He'd likely come to the rescue. And if Charles didn't manage to disable the — oh, he couldn't believe it — the *convict* with his initial blow, he certainly wouldn't want to grapple with *two* strong men!

Charles's face was puce as doubt wormed into his deranged fury. Think. Wait. But half an hour later, they were still inside. Satisfying their lust. No doubt she didn't lie like a wet fish in *his* bed. Well, when he got the trollop home, he'd make sure he took his fill of her! Take her by force every night.

The thought set him panting harder, his lips drawn back in an ugly snarl. And as the idea came to him, the irony struck him clean between the eyes, and he threw back his head in a mindless, diabolic laugh.

* * *

Charles was going to London.

This was her chance to escape. To slip from Charles's bed and the ever more brutal way he was treating her in it. She should be light-headed with joy, tingling with anticipation. But how could she when it meant she would be leaving Dartmoor and everything she held dear, never to return? The magnificent, craggy landscape that was at the very core of her being, her friends and everyone she loved? But the days of contentment were vanished, destroyed by her husband's vicious jealousy.

Everything was in place. She and Seth had sat in the tiny cottage that day, making their plans. Richard and Elizabeth, and Adam and Rebecca shared their secret, of course, but not a word was to be whispered to another soul. A glistening teardrop had slipped down Rose's cheek at what felt like betrayal of her lifelong friends, but there was nothing else for it, and Seth had squeezed her hand with infinite compassion.

No more than that. Just a gentle, trusting kiss when they'd parted.

She'd visited Molly on the usual day. Saying goodbye, promising to see her again the next week, when she knew it was a lie, fragmented her nerves. Yet she mustn't give herself away.

As she left, she saw Joe at a distance and he waved cheerily. Rose's vision blurred with moisture as Gospel trotted away along the familiar track, and she drew him to a halt. She turned in the saddle to take one last look back at the powdermills. Grief clawed at her throat like barbed wire, and she felt if she stared at the place an instant longer, she'd drown in her misery. She dug her heels into Gospel's flank and they shot forward, turning their backs on Cherrybrook for ever.

She watched Charles turn out of the driveway, sitting up on the wagonette next to Ned, unknown to him, heading out of her life. But there was no relief in her heart, just the regret that he was driving her away from the place that gave her life. She'd be with Seth, of course, and he would be the cornerstone of her existence from now on. Kind, thoughtful Seth, who understood her pain. He'd asked nothing of her but to accept his help. If the physical aspect of their love ever blossomed, she would welcome it without fear, since she knew that he'd treat her with gentleness and respect, but as yet a fleeting touch of their lips was all that had passed between them.

She took nothing with her but her personal allowance from Charles of which she'd spent very little since Alice's death, so that it amounted to a substantial sum. To take anything else might arouse Florrie's suspicions, dear Florrie who'd been like a mother to her. She'd be sick with worry when Rose didn't return that evening, and would send Ned out to look for her. But he'd never think of going as far as Peter Tavy. They'd planned to leave on foot under cover of darkness, arriving at the river port of Morwellham at dawn. From there, they'd cadge a lift on the first vessel heading downstream to Plymouth and there they'd await one of

Adam's sailing ships to take them to wherever it was headed, and hence on to a new life on some distant shore.

'I'm just going out for a ride,' she told Florrie with a forced smile. 'I think I'll head out towards Dartmeet for a change. So I won't be back till later this afternoon.'

She saw Florrie's face move into its usual comforting lines, and pain seared into her throat. She swept across the room and enveloped the older woman in her arms. For a split second, she was lost, her resolve dissipated, and her heart dragging. 'I do love you, you know, Florrie,' she mumbled into Florrie's grey hair, and had to grit her teeth to tamp down the torment.

'Get away with you, cheel! And take care. 'Tis coming on for a mist, I reckon.'

Rose battled to disguise her deep swallow. 'Possibly. But I'll keep to the road, so I'll not get lost.'

'That's my little maid.'

Rose nodded, and steeled herself to walk calmly out of the room, pausing for a moment as she closed the door behind her, before heading for the stables. She moved mechanically, fetching Gospel's tack and saddling him up. For the very last time.

She opened the loose-box door, and her eyes gave a final sweep of the dark corner where Seth had lain hidden for all those weeks. And now she was going to him. But she felt nothing, not even relief or fear of discovery. Just a pall of sorrow.

Eager to be off, Gospel nudged her in the back, but no smile of amusement tugged at her lips as she led him out into the yard. The dogs had pattered outside, Amber and Scraggles and the runt — the one puppy Charles had grudgingly allowed her to keep. Rose tried to catch it, but it pranced away, so with a heart-wrenching sigh, she ruffled Scraggles's head instead, and then squatting on her haunches, buried her face in Amber's golden coat. The tears came then, a deluge of misery, and she knew the only path open to her was to swing herself onto Gospel's back and set him at a blind gallop across the moor in the opposite direction from the one she'd indicated to Florrie. She'd still have the magnificent animal beneath her. At least, for just a few hours more.

The barren uplands of Walkhampton Common were cloaked in low, swirling cloud, but Rose knew it like the back of her hand. She slowed Gospel to a walk, staring directly ahead, focusing on a particular blade of grass, and making straight for it, thus following a line as rigid as a mine-rod through the disorientating vapour. She crossed the main highway leading down to Yelverton, and sure enough, shortly came across the horse-drawn tramway. She glanced to her right, knowing that, a mile or two away, her father and her daughter lay together beneath the cold, damp earth.

The tramway now showed her the direction to follow, and she was able to set Gospel at a canter, glad that the fog was providing a shield of invisibility. They met no one, not even as they passed the sidings that led off to the quarries at Foggintor. At last, the tramway swung to the left, but Rose must head straight on, crossing the River Walkham at Merrivale, and gaining higher ground on the far side of the road. The banks of grey mist began to roll away as they finally began to descend towards the Tavy valley, as if they were emerging from the depths of hell to the pale light of a new world beyond.

* * *

Seth had to use all his strength to prise Rose's arms from about Gospel's neck. The faithful creature turned his sleek head and whinnied softly to her as Seth finally managed to drag her to the stable door. The will drained out of her in a hopeless torrent, and she leaned against him, sobbing helplessly as her heart broke, so blinded by her tears that she scarcely noticed as Seth began to walk her up the track towards his cottage. Elizabeth had given her a set of working clothes to change into there, far less remarkable than the smart riding habit she was wearing. There was also a small carpet bag to collect, then they would pass Rosebank Hall again and say their farewells to Richard and Elizabeth before they went on their way.

Even before they reached the cottage, Rose couldn't help but stop to glance back towards the stables. Seth tenderly smoothed the wild hair back from her face and dropped a kiss onto her forehead.

'Gospel's in safe hands,' he soothed, trying to comfort her. 'No one could give him a better home than Richard. When we've got a permanent address, we can write and find out how he is. But he'll be fine. They're good people, Richard and Elizabeth.'

Rose nodded, unable to speak, and they set off again, her head resting on Seth's shoulder, and thankful for his arm tightly about her. The night was dry, though heavy clouds hung low above their heads and they prayed it wouldn't rain for their long walk to Morwellham Quay. They would walk quietly through the silence of the sleeping world, meeting only the nocturnal animals that would scurry from their presence.

But Rose's head would be swirling with sadness at what she was leaving behind. Every tie with her former life must be broken. Elizabeth and Richard would remain their only contact, and Rose's shoulders drooped with shame and guilt at the devastating anxiety her disappearance would cause her dear Florrie. She knew that, when after months she still couldn't be traced, Florrie would return to living with her sister, and perhaps in a year or so, Rose would feel safe to write to her there. The thought gave her some purpose as they began to progress more swiftly along the track.

Seth suddenly stopped dead, pulling her up short, and she glanced sharply at his tense profile. A horrible sinking feeling gripped her stomach, twisting it viciously.

'Oh, God, we're not being followed already?' she whispered in terror.

'No,' Seth murmured back, his keen eyes searching into the darkness ahead. 'But did you see that? I'm sure I saw a light. A candle, perhaps, or a match. Moving about in the cottage. Yes, look! There it is again! There's someone downstairs.'

Rose felt herself shrink with dread, cowering against Seth as she turned her gaze towards the cottage. A flicker of light shimmered through the window of the downstairs room, then disappeared again. She went cold. An intruder? Hardly likely. Such a humble dwelling would hardly house anything worth stealing. No. There was only one explanation. It had to be Charles.

A tiny squeal died in her throat. Charles must have tricked her, just as she had believed she'd duped him; followed her instead of catching the train. Or maybe he'd followed her before and knew where to come. And now he was lying in wait, ready to drag her back home and do God alone knew what to Seth. And if Ned was with him to help . . .

'Run!' she croaked frantically into Seth's ear. 'Get away before he sees us!'

She shook his arm with a violent force, torn with agony as he stood rigid, staring ahead at the cottage. And then, somehow, she sensed it, too, that appalling instant of clairvoyance, when the earth stands still for one horrific moment. Her gaze joined Seth's in time to see the flash, and then that ominous silence, the hiatus of terror when time stops and the heart explodes . . .

'Get down!'

She heard Seth scream at her, and as the crashing blast reverberated in her skull, she found herself thrown to the ground with Seth lying protectively on top of her. The boom rolled away and she lifted her head, but Seth pushed her face back into the grass as stones, broken slates and splintered timbers landed all about them. She lay still until Seth's weight lifted from her, and they crouched together, stunned, staring at the burning building as scarlet tongues of flame flicked out of the windows.

They staggered to their feet, watching as fire ripped through the half demolished cottage. Most of the roof had gone, the remaining shattered trusses standing like broken bones in the lurid blaze of dancing light. As they stood, mesmerised in fascinated horror, another jarring crack, perhaps a beam giving way, thundered above the spit and rattle of the conflagration, and another shower of sparks shot into the shroud of smoke that was gathering in the dank air.

It was Seth who recovered from the shock first.

'He could still be alive!' he yelled at her above the din, and Rose was crippled with terror as she realised what he was about.

'*NO!*'

She put out her hand, her fingers clawing towards his arm, but he was already out of her reach.

'I'll try the back!'

Her whole body was locked in paralysis as she watched Seth run forward, vault the low stone wall that enclosed the little garden, and disappear around the side of the cottage. She tried to cry out, to screech at him to come back, but no sound came from her strangled throat, and she could only stand and offer up a silent prayer to a God who'd never listened to her before. Her limbs shook convulsively, her teeth chattering as she slithered to her knees. No. Oh, sweet Jesus Christ, no . . .

She didn't turn her head as Richard stampeded up the track and joined her in silent contemplation of the burning ruin, his face set like stone, before he, too, raced forward. Rose's heart shrieked in agony. Richard not only had a wife, but two children and another on the way. She could never forgive herself if anything . . . And then her senses all but slipped away. Was her tormented mind hallucinating, making her see only what she wanted to see?

The tall figure of Richard Pencarrow met the stumbling silhouette of another man sagging under the weight of what looked like a sack of coal, and together they carried the lifeless form towards her. They laid the body on the grass, and she bowed her head, too frightened to look. Her terrified glance shot across at Seth as he coughed harshly from the smoke, but he waved a dismissive hand, and then horror pulsed through her as she dragged her gaze to the man stretched out on the ground. In the flaring inferno, she could see his clothes were charred, his face blackened, red raw and grotesquely blistered in places, half his hair gone and one ear lost in a distorted, bubbling mass. Then his eyes opened, two glowing orbs in the satanic, burnt mask.

'I should have learnt properly,' the cracked, ghoulish hiss scraped in his throat, and his scorched mouth twisted. 'I was going . . . to set a charge. I thought you . . . were upstairs . . . in bed . . . with him.'

Rose's chin quivered. She took his hand, burned beyond pain, in hers, and stroked it against her cheek.

'No, Charles,' she breathed in a savage, tortured murmur. 'I told you. I've never been unfaithful. I *was* leaving you, though. I just couldn't live as we were. It wasn't how it were meant to be. I *wanted* us to be happy. Truly I did. And . . . I'm so sorry.'

Her throat closed, aching, agonising, as she cradled his mutilated head in her lap.

* * *

He died the next morning, the pain of his horrendously burned body eased by the administrations of Dr William Greenwood. Richard sent for the constable from Mary Tavy to take Charles's confession, and the fellow went off to make enquiries at Cherrybrook, where he learned that the dying man had quite openly bought some gunpowder 'for his own purposes'. As a known and respected shareholder, the manager hadn't questioned it. Poor chap must have been demented, the constable thought wryly. But then if you had such a beautiful wife as that, and she was being unfaithful, it would be enough to drive you insane, wouldn't it? Nevertheless, to try and *kill* her . . .

The silent widow sat, staring sightlessly out of the bedroom of Rosebank Hall. Another young woman came and carefully washed her grimy hands and face. She appeared not to notice, her eyes blank, swallowing obediently the odd-tasting concoction in the glass that was put into her hands. But she wouldn't move when begged to take to the bed. A young man, his own clothes still smudged with smoke-smuts, was summoned, but she merely shrugged off the compassionate hand he lay on her shoulder and didn't heed his anxious words.

They left her alone, then, moving quietly around the house. But while they sat about the kitchen table, eating a meal none of them wanted, they looked up in unison when they heard the clatter in the farmyard. The young man sprang to the back door, just in time to see the great black horse streak out of the yard, the slight, fragile rider glued to its back.

CHAPTER THIRTY-THREE

She buried him in London.

She was gone three weeks, accompanied by the ever-faithful Florrie. Passengers on the train to the capital turned their heads and sighed at the young woman in black velvet mourning weeds. They judged the kindly-looking older woman with her to be her mother, but it seemed the girl was encased in some impenetrable trance as she watched the miles race past the window. But despite the state of hypnosis in which she appeared suspended, there was an air of purpose, even determination, about her when the train finally drew into Paddington. Undertakers were waiting on the platform to receive the coffin, male passengers and railway staff respectfully removing their hats, and ladies bowing their heads. The widow spoke a few words to the funeral director, and then she and her mother swiftly made for the row of waiting cabs.

Rose had instructed Charles's solicitor, his agent and the butler to compose a list of his acquaintances to inform of the funeral arrangements. To everyone's amazement, she didn't hold a wake, since she scarcely knew any of them, and her face was a mask of stone as Charles's earthly remains were laid to rest. Did they consider her a gold-digger, an adulterous hussy, for the story of Charles's demise must surely have filtered through to them? Only the inhabitants of Rosebank Hall together with Captain and Mrs Bradley knew of what she'd suffered at Charles's hands. And now Florrie, who'd hidden her face in her apron when Rose had finally revealed to her the truth about her marriage.

She closed up the house, entrusting its sale and that of its contents to the solicitor, and dismissing the servants, though not without providing each one of them with an excellent character reference, a month's wages and some item of value from the house to keep or sell as they chose. She held a meeting with the bank manager, the lawyer and the agent, and when everything was in order, she returned to Fencott Place.

Florrie watched her keenly from the opposite seat of the compartment. Would the sight of the moors bring some animation to her set face? Apparently not. She hadn't telegraphed ahead to tell Ned to meet them. Dusk was gathering, and she decided to spend the October night at the Bedford Hotel, overwhelming Florrie, who'd never slept at a common inn, let alone such a renowned establishment. Then first thing next morning, Rose hired a carriage to take them home, the driver wilting under her brusque words.

'Oh, ma'am, Florrie,' Patsy greeted them in surprise. 'We didn't know you was coming. I'll tell Cook.'

'Tell her not to worry about preparing any fancy dishes.' The first hint of a smile twitched at Rose's mouth. 'We'll eat whatever's available.'

'Oh, right, ma'am. And there's been a gentleman calling for you. Several times. Leastways, I *think* 'er's a gentleman.'

'Mr Collingwood?'

'No, ma'am. I think 'is name were Warrington.'

'Ah.' Rose lifted her chin. 'If he comes again, tell him I'm still in London.'

'As you wish, ma'am. Shall I serve some tea, ma'am?'

But Rose had no time to reply as Amber came bounding in through the kitchen door with a bark of delight, while Scraggles and young Lucky skittered about in an array of confusion, tails wagging nineteen to the dozen. Rose dropped onto her knees, hugging them all. The shield of indifference she'd drawn about herself against the horror of Charles's death finally cracked as Scraggles pushed his snout into her face, his tongue rough and rasping against her cheek.

She stood up, her shoulders stiff with resolution once more. 'Just give me five minutes, Patsy, and then tea would be lovely.'

Rose flicked her skirt and strode purposefully towards the back door, the dogs scampering about her knees as she disappeared out into the dismal autumn air. She was caught somewhere between euphoria and a tearing desire to burst into tears as she entered Gospel's loose box. She was with him again, the creature who shared her spirit, not separated for ever as so nearly happened, but never to be parted. She wept then, her tears streaking his ebony coat, her emotions twisted into a confused knot.

When she heard Ned whistling, her brittle nerves fractured. Her tears instantly dried and she marched across to him, thrusting an envelope into his hands.

'There you are,' she said with utter control. 'I've written you a good character, though you don't deserve it. To help you find a new position. But I want you out of here by dinnertime, and then I never want to see you *ever* again!'

* * *

She thought she saw him as she climbed the stairs to bed, and she shivered. It wasn't possible, of course. His bones and mutilated, decaying flesh were lying deep underground nearly three hundred miles away. But it was as if he stood there, waiting for her, a thing of torment to haunt and unnerve her. She knew it wasn't real, just a figment of her tortured imagination, as she hurried into the bedroom. Was he there, too? But her heart sagged with relief. A welcoming fire blazed cheerily in the grate, and the room was pleasantly warm.

She changed quickly into one of the new nightdresses she'd bought. Lovely though they were, she could never again

338

bear against her flesh the nightgowns that had witnessed Charles's abuse, and she'd had them burnt. Now she stared at the bed where it had all happened, but when she forced herself to slide between the crisp, snowy sheets, the corners of her mouth flickered upwards at the comforting stone hot-water bottles dear Florrie had placed there. Tomorrow Rose would have Florrie move down from her servant's room in the attic and occupy instead one of the bedrooms on the same floor as herself. They were five women now — Rose, Florrie, Cook, Patsy and Daisy — living alone in the isolated house, but with the three dogs now sleeping inside to guard them at night. Rose planned to take on some male servants in due course, but just now she was deathly tired, and her exhausted mind slipped easily into slumber.

But Charles crept into her sleep like some serpent from the depths of hell, his blackened, scorched face leering at her, his burned disembodied hands reaching out to drag her down into the inferno that raged about him. She sat up, the haunted scream strangling in her throat, and her eyes blank with terror as the ghoulish spectre faded into the darkness.

Oh, God. Though she knew it had been but a nightmare, it had speared into her heart. Oh, Charles, I'm so sorry. I really didn't want it to be like that. I wanted us to be happy. But I just couldn't go on as we were. It was my fault. I was the wrong wife for you. And now you can never forgive me.

She slid out of bed and crossed to the window. The glass was cold against her cheek, the night so dark that she could hardly distinguish the garden let alone the moor beyond. But that was what her bleeding soul hungered, the solid eternity of the land that no man could ever tame. Constant, powerful, the very bedrock upon which her life was founded.

It flashed beneath Gospel's hooves early next morning, the purple heather, the tufty grass, the pale shafts of sunlight filtering through the scudding clouds. She stood atop Sharpitor, gazing out across the southern moor and the winding Tamar in the west, Gospel languidly cropping the grass. Then away they raced down to the Walkham valley, to what she'd always called the fairy wood at Eggworthy, where moss clung to boulders forged in the realms of time in the watery glen, and where she had met with . . .

No! She forced him from her mind. She didn't deserve him. She'd been the cause of her husband's horrific death, and the guilt sliced into her. She dug her heels into Gospel's flank and they bounded up the steep incline towards the tiny hamlet of Sampford Spiney. Out onto the moor again past the familiar crags of Pew Tor and Heckwood Tor, and the piled rocks of Vixen Tor. She paused when they came to the road. She could quite easily turn left . . . towards . . .

She set Gospel's head for home, her soul ripped to shreds. But there was one visit she must make as she rode through Princetown. The churchyard. There were fresh flowers on the two graves, chrysanthemums she recognised from the garden at Fencott Place. Florrie had been there before her. She bowed her head. In her fragmented mind, she was holding Alice in her arms, and she felt her father touch her hand.

It was the same, day after day, once she'd seen to the needs of the three horses, since she'd not yet employed any new staff. She ate, almost in a trance, whatever Cook put in front of her, hardly speaking at the table or as she sat with Florrie by the evening firelight as a miserable autumn deepened and the first snow of winter peppered the heights of the moor. She seemed impervious to the lacerating wind and penetrating damp as she spent her days traversing the moor on Gospel's back. She visited Molly once, but she barely heard what her dear friend said, and was soon wandering desolately again in search of her lost self, scouring the exposed ridges, the tumbling river valleys, never able to find the peace she craved . . .

* * *

'You cas'n keep turning that poor lad away,' Florrie berated her. 'Twice a week he comes, and all that way! Now that I've met him, I can see why you made such an attachment to him, and you never even opens the letters he leaves, nor those he brings from those good people he lives with. You should be ashamed on yoursel! No matter what the weather, he's on the doorstep, and you'm either not here, or you refuses to see him.'

'I just can't, Florrie.' Rose's voice was flat and expressionless, as if she'd gone beyond despair, locked in a world where nothing seemed to matter anymore. Florrie shook her head. Where had the tempestuous, spirited child gone?

* * *

The bundle of papers arrived from London during the second week of December, and Rose opened the package with a ponderous sigh. Both lawyer and agent had sent letters, begging her to come to the capital, and since she'd ignored them, they'd got together and sent the papers to her instead. The London house and its contents had fetched a sum Rose could scarcely believe, but the small fortune must now be invested. The sheaf of papers made various suggestions of stocks and shares with what risk or return each might carry, plus the most recent reports on the investments Charles had held, and which had made him rich but might now need reviewing.

Rose's heart sank. It was all very well to be monied, but it meant you had responsibilities. Charles had been brought up to it, but she . . . Domestic economies she understood, and those of the moor. For instance, there was talk of Sir Thomas Tyrwhitt's horse-drawn tramway being replaced by a steam railway that would not only serve the quarries far better, but also the needs of the prison and the civilian population of Princetown. But what did Rose know of national companies, or of those Charles held all over the world, of which there were more than a few?

She'd been about to saddle Gospel and set off over the moor when the package arrived. She cast an eye over the accompanying letter and put it disparagingly to one side.

But it was nagging at the back of her mind, and she cut her ride short.

It was during the third day of sitting at the desk in the study, trying to make sense of it all, that Rose was disturbed by a commotion in the hall. The dogs were barking and voices were raised, and Rose wondered what on earth had broken the peace of the female household. Not Ned come back to cause trouble? Good God . . .

'Sir, you really cas'n—' she heard Daisy's offended voice just seconds before the door flew open.

Rose's heart vaulted in her breast. Seth stood on the threshold, snow dusting his shoulders. Rose had risen to her feet, and as her eyes locked with his across the room, her pulse almost faded away.

'I'm so sorry, ma'am, but I couldn't stop 'en. Came bursting in through the kitchen, bold as brass—'

'It's all right, Daisy,' Rose said, though her white lips hardly moved. 'You can leave us now.'

'Yes, ma'am.' Daisy retreated with a confused curtsy, though not without a glance at the good-looking fellow who had been trying to see the mistress for weeks.

They stared at each other, and Rose was aware of her heartbeat thudding painfully. The clock ticked, the fire crackled in the grate, and still neither of them moved.

It was Seth who broke the silence. 'I just wanted to be sure you were all right,' he said quietly.

Rose was paralysed. To see him again was just too much, and she knew why her tortured soul had wanted to blank him from her life. Her brain was still too tired to unravel the tangled threads of her life.

'I am well, as you see,' she answered, her voice indifferent.

'Yes. I do indeed.' His words were crisp, and she saw the spasm of hurt flinch across his face. 'And you're obviously busy with your new life, so I shall intrude no more.'

His shoulders stiffened and he turned on his heel. Rose gazed at his retreating back, and her knees buckled as panic flooded into her limbs.

'Seth, please, don't go!' She sprang around the desk and grasped his arm. 'I'm so sorry. I was . . . just so engrossed in all these papers.' She let go of him, waving her hand at the chaos on the desk, wanting to apologise though without making a fool of herself. 'It seems I'm a wealthy widow, but I don't understand the half of it. I really don't know where to begin.'

Seth's troubled eyes moved across to the desk, and then back to her anxious, tentatively smiling face. 'Can I help?' he asked gravely.

Her shoulders sagged. 'I don't know. Can you?'

'Well, I can't tell unless I have a chance to study them. My family were a little like your . . . late husband. Made most of their money out of speculating on the stock exchange. I was quite young, but I was brought up with it, so I should have a reasonable idea. Even when I was in the army — before I went to India, of course — there were always business matters to discuss when I was on leave.'

'Oh, would you take a look, then, please? I'd be so grateful. It'd be such a weight off my mind.' She frowned up at him, and relief swept through her as his mouth broke into a wide grin.

'I think I'm going to have my work cut out, mind.'

Rose almost danced about him. 'Let me take your coat. Warm yourself by the fire. I'll fetch you some tea. And we'll be having lunch soon. Nothing special, but you will stay, won't you?'

'By the looks of things, I'll need to.'

'Oh, thank you, Seth!'

She skipped out of the room, colour flaming into her face. She'd been caught in a mesh of despondency for so long that she couldn't grasp the enormity of her renewed happiness. As she sat by Seth's side all afternoon, she found it hard to concentrate as she fought against the curious draw of his masculinity. He was still too thin, but there was a healthy colour to his cheeks and he'd lost that gaunt, haggard look. She couldn't help keep glancing sideways at him as he explained so much to her. He made reams of notes and sorted the papers into neat piles, instilling Rose with confidence.

'I really should go now. I don't know the moor as well as you do, so I need to be home by dark.'

Rose felt a dart in her side. 'Do you have to? I mean, it'll take days to sort this out.'

'At least,' he agreed. 'Let me talk with Richard. I can't let him down after all they've done for me, but perhaps I can come and stay for a while to get everything straight. There's less to do on the farm this time of year.'

'Oh, yes! That'd be so good of you. And take Tansy. That'll be quicker than walking. And how's Beth? Can't be so long till the baby now. Do give her my love.'

'Of course.'

His voice was perfectly polite, but a little too cautious for Rose's liking. Nonetheless, for the first time since her return from London, Charles's ghost didn't come to haunt her that night.

* * *

Christmas was only days away. Seth had been staying at Fencott Place, occupying one of the guest rooms along the landing. He'd remained distant as they worked together, but Rose didn't mind. It was enough that he was there. She barely noticed the quiet contentment creeping into her heart. Now she could retire to bed safe in the knowledge that the cruel, charred spectre would no longer come to haunt her.

Seth was mucking out the stables, and Rose had retired with Florrie to the drawing-room fireside to discuss their plans for Christmas which she wanted to be extra special. For the first time since Henry's accident, she was actually looking forward to it. Anticipation pervaded the house, and that afternoon, they were to start making paper-chains and other decorations.

When they'd finished, Rose stayed for several minutes, gazing into the flames. It was good to feel like this after so much fear and abuse. She would always have affairs to deal with, since Charles's legacy had turned her into a woman of enterprise and business. But, hopefully, help would always be at hand.

But she couldn't sit there all day. She must put out clean towels in the bedrooms, Daisy's job normally, but she was busy with Christmas preparations in the kitchen. Rose saw to her own first, and Florrie's, then sauntered into Seth's room, her vision half obscured behind the pile of thick fluffy towels in her arms.

Bright winter sunshine was streaming through the windows, its brilliance dazzling her so that at first she'd been unaware of the tall figure by the wash stand pouring steaming water into the bowl. He was stripped to the waist and Rose gulped hard. But the best way to avoid any embarrassment was to act casually.

'Oh, I'm sorry. I thought you were seeing to the horses.'

'I've finished. It's hot work and I needed a wash.'

Rose nodded as she placed the towels on the bed but as she turned round, she stifled a gasp. Seth had his back to her, and the sunlight was falling directly across his bare torso. He clearly realised she'd seen, and he stiffened, the muscles tense beneath his scarred skin. A wave of horror, of anger and sorrow washed down to the pit of Rose's stomach. The agony he must have suffered, the cruelty of his unjust punishment, seared into her heart. She knew he'd be marked for life, but to see it in reality was a sickening shock.

But it had to be faced. She padded up behind him, her heart vibrating hard in her chest. 'Oh, Seth,' she murmured, her voice no more than a whisper as her trembling finger traced one of the lines that latticed his back. Some were faint scratches healed to a healthy white, while others were deep and purple, the flesh seamed where Dr Power had done his best to stitch it back together.

Seth flinched at her touch. 'Not a pretty sight, is it?' he croaked.

Rose waited for the grief of it to sink into her heart. 'Does it . . . still hurt?' she whispered.

'No. Not hurt exactly. Sometimes it feels tight. Beth's been rubbing something onto it that does help it feel more comfortable. She says it'll help it fade over the years. But the scars will never . . . completely . . .'

His voice cracked, and his chin drooped onto his chest. Rose felt his pain tear into her. It was instinctive as she leaned forward, her lips brushing the disfiguring scars.

'Rose, *don't*. Please.' He turned round abruptly, his hazel eyes scowling. 'I must go back to Rosebank Hall. This afternoon.'

Rose took a staggering step backwards. 'Go back?' her tiny voice faltered.

'Yes. I must. Richard needs my help. He can't afford to employ anyone properly, but I'm happy just to have a roof over my head. I've one of their attic rooms now, but a farm labourer would need a tied cottage and since, well . . .'

Rose's chest clenched with panic, the peace that had been seeping into her soul instantly turning to desperation. 'I'll pay for the cottage to be rebuilt. It's only fair as it was my fault. But . . . please don't go, Seth! I need you!'

Her voice was a howl of anguish, but Seth threw up his head with a bitter laugh. 'No, you don't. You're a woman of substance now. You can pick and choose who you want.'

'But I only want you!'

'Then why did you refuse to see me for so long? Going to London to bury your husband where he belonged, that I can understand. But turning me away for two whole months . . .'

'B-but we were running away together. I was giving up everything for you—'

'No, Rose.' Seth took her hands, his steady gaze boring earnestly into her tear-streaked face. 'Everything's changed. We were equal then. I was a penniless wretch and you needed to escape from a brute of a husband. But *now* . . . You're a rich widow with a respected position in local society. And I'm an ex-convict with the scars on my back to prove it.'

Rose's white lips were trembling. He was hurting more than she'd ever imagined. Not just the physical pain he'd suffered, but a mental torture that had gone deep inside. But no one understood that better than her. And since when did Rose Maddiford give up so easily?

'D'you think that matters to me? To someone who knows the shame of being abused by her husband like I was? I'm sorry I turned you away. But Charles, he . . . It took some getting over. But I feel free of him now. With you here. What they did to you in the prison will be with you forever, and you *must* accept that. Just as I must accept that I were once married to a man who . . . ' She straightened her shoulders, lifting her chin. 'I love you, Seth Warrington, and a few scars can never change that!'

She could see his haunted eyes were glistening with moisture and he opened his mouth as if to speak. But Rose reached up on tiptoe and brought her lips against his, smothering any words in a kiss so deft and reverent, it sent a shiver down his spine. It took but that one second of overwhelming love, of intense harmony of two broken spirits, for his taut nerves to snap, and a moment later, his hand reached into her hair. Their lips clung hungrily, and when Seth's hand moved tentatively down her throat to her breast, she welcomed it with a deep, heaving sigh, lost in something so powerful it would not be denied, everything falling away from her but her love for this sorely tried man.

He laid her on the bed, slowly undressing her, stroking, kissing every inch of her flesh as it was revealed. When his mouth closed over her breast, gentle and caressing, she gasped with a desire that astounded her. Just for a split second did the vision of Charles, clawing at her, hurting her, spear into her memory. Then the pain and fear was cast aside forever by this man who truly loved her, who was driving out her demons until she moaned with pleasure and he let out a joyful cry as their love exploded in unison and their flesh became as one.

She gazed up at him, breathless, drowning in his glorious, smiling eyes that roamed tenderly over her face.

'God, I love you,' he muttered as he kissed her again. He drew her against him so that she lay, wrapped in his arms, her naked body, unashamed and unafraid, pressed against his. A supreme and exquisite peace washed through her, and she wanted the moment to last for ever.

Seth reached out to gather the counterpane about them, reluctant to let her go. She snuggled against him, breathing in his masculine scent, intoxicated by his closeness and the wonder of what had just passed between them.

'That's what kept me going, you know. Thinking of you,' he murmured, and all at once, the hairs bristled down the back of Rose's neck. 'When I was . . . being flogged, I just concentrated on thinking of you. Creating a picture of you in my mind. It was . . . the only way I could take the pain.'

His voice was thick. Ragged. Rose drew his head against her breast and he wept wretchedly like a child. Oh, yes. She had wept for her own lost soul, but she had found herself again because of this good, worthy man. And now she must be strong for him.

'We can get through this, Seth,' she whispered into his tousled hair. 'We have each other now.'

She paused, and waited as Seth drew back, wiping away his tears. 'I'm sorry,' he sniffed awkwardly. 'You must think me . . .'

'Don't say another word, Seth Warrington. I love you. And to my mind, a man who can't cry isn't worth his salt. However, I suggest we get dressed before someone walks in on us. And then we'll go over to Rosebank Hall and sort things with Richard. I want you living back here with me as soon as you can.'

Seth raised his eyebrows. 'Are you sure? I mean, that'll set tongues wagging.'

'And since when do you think I ever cared about that? Besides, it wouldn't be so bad if we were married.'

'What!'

Rose turned to him, the look of incredulity on his face so comical that she gave a bellow of laughter. 'Surely you don't expect me to live in sin, now?'

But Seth's expression was grave. 'Think about it, Rose. You've been widowed barely three months. And when people find out who I am, which they're bound to in time, they'll say I was after your money—'

'But we'll know differently. So come on. Hurry up. I want our future settled as soon as possible!'

Twenty minutes later, they were galloping across the frost-encrusted moor, the crisp air blushing their cheeks with the joy of a deep and trusting love. His face flushed, Seth glanced across at the young woman he knew had saved his life and enslaved his soul. And as she grinned back, Rose's heart soared. For, at long last, she'd found the man with whom she wanted to spend the rest of her life.

* * *

Raymond Power signed the letter, then leaned back in the chair with a wistful sigh. He would hand it to the governor in the morning. The position of prison surgeon had provided him with a decent wage and reasonable accommodation for his wife and family, allowing him to attend the poorer inhabitants of the area at nominal fees. But it was time to move on, and now he'd secured a partnership with an elderly physician in a fashionable quarter of Exeter, and with luck, he'd acquire the entire practice in time.

His wife had hated Princetown. The dismal settlement cut off from the rest of humanity, the appalling, damp climate. But it wasn't because of his wife that he was leaving.

He was a man of medicine. Of healing. And he simply couldn't reconcile his vocation with the position he held. When an already half-starved convict caught pneumonia digging drainage ditches on the open moor, had a limb blown off or was blinded by explosives at the quarry, or fell from the high prison blocks they were building, *he*, Raymond Power, was the one who had to patch him up so that he could return to some other gruelling task. But the worst part was having to pronounce a man fit for punishment, to be birched or flogged.

Raymond had reached the stage where he could stand it no longer, but the turning point had been the begging, passionate letter from the young woman he'd admired so deeply and who'd implored him to help the recaptured escapee. Poor beggar had turned out to be totally innocent and now, it seemed, he was to marry his saviour. Well, good luck to them both. They deserved some happiness after what they'd both been through.

Raymond had never liked that husband of hers. He didn't like him being wed to the vivacious young girl who'd captured his own heart so many years previously. He'd reared away from his feelings, shot through with guilt, but it was a secret he'd thankfully managed to keep safely locked away. He was already married with a wife and family whom he loved dearly; was old enough to be her father, and yet . . . She wasn't just beautiful. She was captivating. With a generosity of heart, a fervent compassion, a wild, free spirit. He would miss her terribly, an ethereal figure charging over the moor on that enormous, elegant horse of hers, as reckless and headstrong as she was. But it was better that way, though he would never forget her. Rose Maddiford from the gunpowder mills at Cherrybrook.

Cherrybrook Rose. The gunpowder girl.

THE END

ALSO BY TANIA CROSSE

THE DEVONSHIRE SERIES
THE GUNPOWDER GIRL
THE RAILWAY GIRL
THE QUARRY GIRL
THE WHEELWRIGHT GIRL
THE AMBULANCE GIRL

Don't miss the latest Tania Crosse release,
join our mailing list:
www.joffebooks.com

FREE KINDLE BOOKS

Please join our mailing list for free Kindle books and new releases, including crime thrillers, mysteries, romance and more, as well as news on the next book by Tania Crosse!

www.joffebooks.com

Follow us on Facebook, Twitter and Instagram @joffebooks

DO YOU LOVE FREE AND BARGAIN BOOKS?

Thank you for reading this book. If you enjoyed it please leave feedback on Amazon, and if there is anything we missed or you have a question about then please get in touch. The author and publishing team appreciate your feedback and time reading this book.

www.joffebooks.com/contact

We hate typos too but sometimes they slip through.
Please send any errors you find to
corrections@joffebooks.com.
We'll get them fixed ASAP. We're very grateful to
eagle-eyed readers who take the time to contact us.

CPSIA information can be obtained
at www.ICGtesting.com
Printed in the USA
LVHW111115060622
720584LV00015B/54